CIRCLE
OF FIVE

CIRCLE
OF FIVE

DOLORES STEWART
RICCIO

KENSINGTON BOOKS

KENSINGTON BOOKS are published by

Kensington Publishing Corp.
850 Third Avenue
New York, NY 10022

ISBN 0-7394-5102-2

Printed in the United States of America

For Rick
whose love and encouragement
make everything possible

ACKNOWLEDGMENTS

My warmest gratitude to all those whose enthusiasm and valuable insights helped me with this book, especially Nancy Brady Cunningham and Joan Bingham, who read the early manuscript; the circle of friends in our writing workshop, who cheered me on week after week; and Ann LaFarge, my wonderful editor at Kensington.

Prologue

The truck driver, a big ruddy-faced man with a cheerful demeanor, was whistling a tune from *Gypsy* as he applied a mask of clown makeup. He felt snug and private in his "roomette," a space just in back of the driver's seat. He'd stocked these quarters with all the necessities and a few of the comforts for a life on the road. The man had owned the rig for several years and enjoyed the freedom trucking gave him to follow other pursuits. There was a downside, however—having to bear the ever-increasing expenses of gasoline, tires, and taxes and to hustle up small jobs he could handle. Those considerations and the uneasy feeling that he'd traveled on his luck a little too far had caused him to decide to get out of trucking. Because this would be his farewell trip north, he'd resolved to combine pleasure with business.

There weren't many independents left; they were a disappearing breed of loners, just like cowboys. But whoever drove this rig after he'd sold it would be getting a first-class deal with a lot of extras he'd built in himself. With his passion for neatness, he'd combined efficient storage with a cozy nest for relaxation or even a nap at the end of a long drive. Now he was not tired at all—he was excited.

He'd parked in a rest area that he knew to be deserted just outside Portland, Maine. It was the end of October, 4:30 in the evening, but already getting dark, with brooding, overcast skies that promised a chill, gray rain before morning. The man peered intently into the makeup mirror and was satisfied that nothing about his face could be recognized. Snapping the latch on the metal lunchbox that held his makeup and mirror, he stowed it away in one of his clever cubbyholes. From his duffel bag, he removed a new lightweight, bright blue jumpsuit from Wal-Mart, cutting off the price tag with a hunter's skinning knife, which he returned to its sheath in his belt. Then he eased himself into this garment carefully, so he wouldn't upset any of his storage arrangements, a big man working in a small space. Rummaging around under the driver's seat, he came up with a roll of duct tape and a plastic rubbish bag, which he put into the jumpsuit's pockets. A cheap pair of imitation leather gloves covering supple surgeon's gloves completed his outfit. Finally, he took out a plastic party hat and carried that in his gloved hand as he jumped out of the truck tractor and locked it securely.

This was always a dangerous part of the operation, open to the risk of someone driving into the rest area just at that moment and later connecting the clown to the truck. If that happened, he would leave Maine immediately, simply chalking up the whole wasted evening to unavoidable loss. After moving swiftly around to the rear of the rig, he slid open a door and removed a bicycle, stolen earlier that day in a Bangor parking lot. The load of Canadian boneless dried cod he was transporting to Boston exuded a strong odor right through the containers of compact wooden boxes. He was glad to slam the door and take off, gliding down the highway on the bicycle, veering off at the nearest exit onto a secondary road heading into Portland.

He knew this place well. There was a small shopping mall with a video arcade about three miles from the rest area where he'd parked the truck, if one traveled by the roads, as he was doing now. But it was less than a mile away if someone were to walk straight through the woods.

Pedaling down the road, he passed a Chevy full of teenagers who honked and waved. He waved back, and noticing that the bike had a bell, rang it madly.

Luck was with him. His merry, red-painted lips smiled in satisfaction. He wouldn't have to take his chances at the arcade, after all. A thin, dark boy, about eleven years old, was walking along the road with a golden retriever running circles beside him. The man in the clown mask rode past the boy, then stopped. Before he got off the bike, he took the plastic bowler hat out of the bicycle basket and perched it on top of his head. This made the boy laugh and the dog bark. The man patted the dog and began to talk with the boy.

The boy said he was on his way to a party, showing off a ghoulish mask he had stuffed in his pocket. The man gave the boy the plastic hat to wear, and they chatted amiably for a few minutes before the man took his chance, asking the boy to come with him. Reluctantly, the boy put his hand on the dog's collar and hung back on the road's shoulder where the tall grass of summer had dried and stiffened. The man explained that he'd bicycled past a suitcase, and they ought to go back and see what was in it. The suitcase must have fallen off a car and slipped off the road into a gully. The boy said he didn't want to be late for the party, but the man promised it wouldn't take long to retrieve the suitcase. It might be something the boy could use, or at least there might be a reward for returning it to its owner. When the boy still hesitated, the man offered to pay the boy five dollars to help him secure the suitcase.

Later, when they got out of sight in the woods, the man had to slit the dog's throat before he could attend to the boy. There was very little noise to be heard once he got the tape around the boy's mouth—just a little mewing sound, like a stifled small animal.

This was one of the most satisfying episodes he'd had—ecstatic paroxysms that were nearly uncontrollable. There was so much blood, he had to remove his rubber boots as well as the jumpsuit and gloves. He stuffed them all into the plastic rubbish bag he would dump elsewhere on the road. Although the thick wool socks gave some protection to his feet, he was limping by the time he got through the underbrush to the rest area.

The big truck was slumbering in the shadows, unattended and unremarked. The man was not surprised that no one else had chosen to park there. He knew that truckers favored the well-lit, conveniently furnished rest area only a few miles farther south.

After he'd cleaned the makeup off his face with cold cream and water he kept in gallon jugs in the roomette, he drank an icy Coke he took out of the cooler. Then he started up and headed for Boston. He would have preferred a beer but made it a rule never to drink when driving. As he lit an unfiltered Camel and drew in the smoke gratefully, the tune he'd been whistling earlier came back into his head and stayed with him, bringing back images of the boy and what he had done to him. The man let the radio stay silent rather than have it disturb this satisfying reverie.

That same weekend, in Plymouth, Massachusetts, in a saltbox house by the sea, five women were celebrating Samhain, the Wiccan festival of Halloween. This was their first Samhain, and the ceremony was not without some awkwardness. It was necessary to consult various texts at each stage. Only when they went outdoors to draw down the moon—which was nearly full that evening, showing itself fitfully between gray, puffy clouds tinged with rosy light from the town—did they begin to feel a tingle of energy in their upraised hands. The energy grew in power, surging through their arms, down their bodies, down, down until their feet danced without thought, moving with the rhythm of the incoming tide, the primitive music of waves roughly embracing the shore. In the joy and freedom of the dance, they felt they had become part of the Great Mother.

Afterward they drank white wine, ate the traditional seed

cakes, and laughed together. The force of the ritual had been an exhilarating discovery. Talking about it long past the moon's setting, the five women became quietly resolved. This circle would continue, they agreed. It would work, it would do good, it would be their secret.

As the changing seasons passed, the circle celebrated the ancient high holidays of the year. They met for Sabbats and Full Moon Esbats, learning traditional Wiccan arts and strengthening their skills. When Samhain drew near again, the lives of these five women intersected with the life of the man who had worn a clown's face.

Esbat of the Harvest Moon

Having a vision is a weird experience. It may last only a few moments, but it feels endless, a suspension of ordinary time. I had just glanced at my watch—5:15 P.M.—and was heading at full tilt for the express checkout of Angelo's Supermarket. My thoughts were on an unopened bottle of merlot at home and the crisscross stack of wood in the kitchen fireplace needing just the touch of a match. No doubt I negotiated that blind curve around an end-of-aisle display too wildly. My cart sideswiped a portly, pleasant-faced man in a green cap as he pushed his cart in the opposite direction. Phrasing my apology, I looked into his eyes. In that one heartbeat, I had a horrifying vision.

This had happened to me before, a kind of waking dream. The air around me took on a misty radiance with blurred edges. Everything that had been solid and real a moment before simply disappeared from view. The song wafting over the loudspeaker, which I had been humming to myself, although I dislike it intensely—another whine for love—faded out as if a gentle hand were turning the knob down to silence. Instead, I heard the faint, agonizing cry of a child.

Gone was the throng of scowling shoppers. Within this vision's dimension, I was standing at the edge of a small, clear space in what was otherwise a densely overgrown patch of woods. It was night, the air heavy with the promise of a chilly rain. A momentary break in the overcast skies suffused the scene with moonlight that brightened, then went dark as a screen of clouds passed over the moon's face. In the distance, I could hear cars and trucks rumbling by on an unseen highway. Tall arms of pine trees loomed over me, and I could smell their oozing sap. A child shrieked. I saw the child's thin, bare arm flail desperately, the way a drowning person, grabbing for any handhold, clutches at empty air. A shadowy man, his back turned to me, was struggling with the child against a tree. I was shouting, but no sound came. I tried to run toward them, but, helpless as a dreamer, I couldn't move. The man stepped between the boy and me, doing something I couldn't see. When he moved away, the child had stopped trying to wrench free. Dead, I was certain. I felt or heard something like a camera shutter blink open and closed.

Abruptly, I woke from my trance, finding myself exactly where I had been only a moment ago. The details of the vision began to fade at once. But the big, cheery stranger was still there, leaning over me where I'd staggered into some sort of display. I shrank away from his hand. The cookie packages behind me crunched, giving off the reassuring scent of artificial vanilla.

"You all right?" Beaming at me, his eyes merry. If he'd had a white beard and a red hat, he could have been Santa Claus. But to me, the good humor seemed forced; that slanted line beside his mouth looked mean.

Did that really happen? Is this the man? Why do these seizures happen to me?

I felt light-headed and queasy. I'd had unwelcome visions before, some of them actual clairvoyant episodes that had proved accurate enough later. Yet none was quite as shocking as this. When I'd hurried into the supermarket, my thoughts had been clear and centered. I was sure no distracted anxiety of mine could have been projected into this lurid mental picture.

"No problem." The man in the green cap continued to speak

to me reassuringly despite my appalled silence. He righted some six-packs of Diet Coke that had tipped over in his cart onto a jumbo bag of generic dog biscuits. "Guess we're all in a hurry at this time of night, aren't we? Have a nice evening, dear." His smile radiated kindliness as he moved off, whistling a show tune from *Gypsy*. I couldn't quite recall the words.

At the express checkout, I came to my senses sufficiently to ask the cashier if he knew the big man in the green cap. His gaze never turning away from the bagger, with whom he was enjoying a lively discussion of some recent soccer game, the cashier shook his head negatively without missing a single kick.

Pulling up the hood of my poncho, I rushed out and stashed my groceries in the back of the Wagoneer, where my dog Scruffy stuck his nose into each bag in turn, sniffing deeply. Between inhalations, he looked at me reproachfully under his bushy eyebrows. I, too, felt as if hours had passed since I'd entered the store, although the clock on the dashboard showed only 5:35 P.M.

Should I find out who he is, or should I just forget it, I wondered. I may have spoken aloud, which I don't happen to think is crazy at all. At least Scruffy was listening. Questions nagged, like the swish, swish of the windshield wipers sluicing away the chill October rain.

Chalk up the whole experience to fatigue and a touch of paranoia? No, that would be cowardly, I decided. Think how I'll feel if I pick up a newspaper someday and read about a nasty murder I could have prevented. But how will I find out who he is? Hey, what about his license plate? And if I do identify him, what then?

This was supposed to have been an emergency in-and-out sort of shopping trip. I'd definitely not been planning to bump into an ominous stranger who would obsess my thoughts for months to come. Just bread, milk, fruit, and some ground turkey to make burgers for Scruffy and me. The dog was used to sharing my meals since I had no one else around the house to indulge.

Although I waited in the car for the man in the green cap to emerge from Angelo's, somehow, in the dark, wet shadows of the parking lot, with a horde of other last-minute shoppers milling around, I missed him. Maybe if I'd jumped out of the car, I would have caught Green Cap's plate number before he drove off. To tell the truth, I was not eager to look into his eyes again. After all, the entire incident might have been a delusion brought on by inhaling too many herbs—perhaps from the dream pillows I'd been scenting with lavender, anise, myrrh, and other essential oils that very afternoon.

Otherwise, it had been a radiant and peaceful October. A time of seeking to attune myself with the natural rhythms of life, to release past pain and live as much as possible in simple awareness of the present moment as it was happening. Learning to let go as easily as nature lets go. Soon it would be Samhain, final harvest of the Wheel of the Year. The veil between the physical world and the world of spirit would be thinner than at any other time. We would celebrate death and the return to life, the old passing into the new. We were a circle of five seekers—beginners, really—but never dabblers. All we had learned from ancient texts or discovered in our own rites persuaded us to work magic cautiously, and never on the dark side.

Occasionally, however, the dark side could be accidentally invoked, even from a relatively minor annoyance. One day, just as I was coming out of the trees with a basket of bayberries harvested from where they grew low and thick in old Lucien Jenkins's woods, I'd seen my neighbor, Reverend Peacedale, kicking my dog Scruffy off the church lawn—for good reason. Nonetheless, I was enraged and began to struggle with some black thoughts that stayed with me when I returned to my kitchen with Scruffy whimpering at my heels.

"Ugly scenes like that wouldn't happen if you'd stick to your own yard," I told Scruffy, rubbing the dog's sore place with my menthol decoction, a kind of topical herbal aspirin made with wintergreen. "You have perfectly adequate facilities right here, better than most dogs enjoy along the shore."

I like to keep my own territory clean, Scruffy defended himself. Oh, not aloud, of course, but I always hear what he's thinking.

Seven herbs and various decoctions and tinctures, along with a bottle of 100-proof vodka, were spread out across the kitchen counter. I'd been experimenting with a universal antidote, the elixir all herbalists sought, before setting out to steal bayberries. I poured some of the pale green liquid into an old Nyquil cup I keep in my herbal chest and drank it down to steady my nerves. This version tasted amazingly like Chartreuse liqueur, an herbal formula still guarded from the world by French monks. It certainly had an immediate effect. A blissful, floating feeling of warmth and vigor suffused my limbs. Suddenly, the room seemed stifling and steamy. I flung open the kitchen window. Still in a dreamy mood, I began to reconstruct the scene on the Garden of Gethsemane Church lawn. Picturing Peacedale's black-clad leg lashing out, I imagined this time it missed its mark and twisted at an odd angle to swing harmlessly over Scruffy's rump. The minister's plump body was thrown off balance, falling, falling . . .

"Serves him right," I said to Scruffy.

"Are you talking to yourself again, Cass?" asked Phillipa, her dark head appearing suddenly over the bird feeder as she came up the back stairs to the porch. The house had a front door, but so strong was the New England prohibition against using it that the stone walk simply bypassed the front of the house and led directly to the back door on the ocean side. In defiance of the rules of restoration, my grandmother had arranged for a pleasant porch to be built outside the old keeping room, now the kitchen.

My friend Phillipa Gold is a cookbook author and sometime poet, supporting her literary leanings with goat cheese-arugula risotto and grilled squab salad, or whatever is trendy at the moment. She wears uncompromisingly straight black hair, and her eyes are such a dark brown they hide her thoughts like opaque sunglasses. We'd met while researching at the Plymouth Library, herbs being adjacent to cookbooks in the Dewey decimal system.

"Of course not. I'm talking to Scruffy," I said. "Come in and try this stuff. I'm wondering if I have a hint too much verbena."

"No, thanks," Phillipa said, "but I'd like a cup of ordinary caffeine-laden tea made from a tea bag." She handed me a basket of biscuits, muffins, and preserves—the usual recipe-testing overflow—and settled herself into the kitchen rocker with her feet on the log carrier. She looked discouraged and exhausted. Scruffy dropped the orange ball in her lap expectantly.

"How about ginseng? That ought to pep you up. Or raspberry leaf. Is it menstrual? What's the matter, anyway? You look as if you've just lost your last friend. Which you haven't."

"Don't you have something ordinary like Red Rose or Earl Grey, Cass? Listen, I can't get these blue-corn muffins right. There's a dry, powdery aftertaste. And my poetry manuscript thumped back into the mailbox for the thirteenth time . . ."

"Thirteen is a lucky number for us," I advised her.

". . . And Jess left a message on my answering machine that he's not sure he's ready to commit himself to the kind of long-term relationship that I deserve. I never should have cooked that pot roast for him. It brought on the most frightful anxiety."

"He wants you to throw it."

"Throw what?"

"Scruffy is waiting for you to throw that ball."

"Cassandra, have you been listening to me?" Phillipa picked up the saliva-coated ball with two fingers and, with an expression of distaste, dropped it onto the floor.

She may be your friend, but she's no fun. Scruffy looked at her in disgust, but Phillipa was too distraught to notice him. Letting the ball roll back under the log carrier and taking a nervous stance at the kitchen door, the dog pressed his nose against the knob. *Now! Now! I have to go out right now!*

"Cut it out, you faker. You just went," I reminded him. "Which of these crises will you be bringing to the Esbat?" I asked Phillipa as I hotted the pot. "What about the poetry manuscript? Getting that published would be a real challenge—no offense. What's this jelly—rose hip?"

Scenting the muffins I was putting out on a plate, Scruffy leaned against my leg and looked up at me.

"No, something new—jalapeño beach plum," Phillipa said. "I'm working up an article for *Modern Maturity*. 'Wake Up and Smell the Coffee—Lifting Breakfast Out of the Doldrums.'"

"This should do it," I agreed, tasting a smidge of the deceptively rosy stuff.

"It must be true that people get to look like their pets," Phillipa commented. "Do you realize that you two have the same color bangs?"

I studied the shaggy, sandy fringe that half-covered Scruffy's eyes while I fed him a piece of blue-corn muffin. I have it on good authority that Scruffy's mother was a purebred French Briard, but his father was probably some kind of terrier of a tawny color and an enterprising nature. "Is that some roundabout way of telling me I need a haircut?" I asked, resisting the impulse to push my own hair back off my forehead.

Ack! said Scruffy, spitting a half-chewed morsel of muffin onto the braided rug.

"No, dear, there's strength in that thick, long mop of hair. But maybe a trim wouldn't hurt." Phillipa's own hair was as neat and shining as a crow's wing, a tribute to the rosemary-sage rinse I'd concocted for her. "First things first, I guess. Getting a slim volume of my poems into print may be closer to my heart than Jess, especially this week."

"Didn't you sense that Jess was getting ready to sprint? Wasn't it in the cards?"

"A reader can't read for herself. It doesn't work that way, as I've told you before. It's like a doctor self-diagnosing. No, I just went ahead and presented Jess with that magnificent prime beef round and unwittingly convinced him that I was setting the scene for some kind of permanent domestic arrangement. He was out the door before the flames on the Cherries Jubilee died. So . . . when are we working this month?"

"Couldn't be more auspicious." I lit one of my gray-green bay-berry candles. Such a clean, bracing scent—it quite cleared the cobwebs out of the brain. "Full moon on Friday the thirteenth. And I have something urgent to put on the docket."

"You mean besides your usual 'death to the Pilgrim Nuclear Plant'? Which I do wish you wouldn't phrase that way. The exact wording is important if you don't want a spell to backfire."

"Very well, then. A solution for the good of all, and harming none, to the problem of Pilgrim, such as its removal to another site, preferably a distant planet."

"I shouldn't worry," Phillipa said, waving away the muffins and taking a gingersnap out of my cookie jar. "Pilgrim is a some-what ambitious undertaking, after all. But I have another project to propose—besides my manuscript, that is—one that ought to be within the realm of possibility."

"So do I," I said, thinking of Green Cap. "I may have bumped into a murderer at Angelo's. The trouble is, I don't know his name."

Phillipa sighed. "So just how did you discover his little secret? Suppose you start at the beginning, and if this was another clair-voyant inspiration, I am going to take a lot of convincing."

I described the incident, the vision of the boy's killing, which still chilled me to the bone. Phillipa was silent and serious for several moments. "I don't think we ought to get into this," she said finally. "Bad, bad vibes. Besides, we don't have any missing boys that I know of."

"What about that boy from Pembroke last year? Summer peo-ple . . . I forget his name."

"Didn't they find him? I thought he turned up at a friend's house in Braintree. Or maybe that was another one, from the Boy Scout jamboree."

"I'm going to bring the matter up at the Esbat, Phil. Let's see what the others have to say." Rummaging in the coat closet, I took my grandmother's shawl off the shelf and wrapped it around me. It was creamy wool and warm, an immediate source of comfort. "So tell me about your project, then."

"Jenkins's woods is up for sale. Did you know that? The old man's decided to sign over his soul to the Serenity Golf Retirement Community in High Brewster. And guess who's sniffing around! Sam Tucker."

"Tucker! But he can't build there. What about the zoning?" A sickening image flashed through my mind of bulldozers razing that lush stand of pines, flushing out rabbits and pheasants, squashing my bayberry bushes into oblivion.

"What about the zoning for every other condominium he's built? North River Farm. Willow Walk." I knew that Phillipa, who lived on the other side of the Jenkins property, cherished its wildness as much as I did. "He fiddles with the zoning board somehow," she said. "Magic, I guess."

"We'll show him magic," I muttered darkly, then caught myself.

"Suppose our woods turned out to be the habitat of some critically endangered species . . ." she murmured speculatively.

"To my way of thinking, they're all endangered, but I can't think of any creature I've seen there that's rarer than a possum or a raccoon."

"Then we'll do a summoning ritual and call something here."

"Like what, for instance?"

"Oh, I don't know. What does it matter? Some cute little wild thing with a declining population rate."

I thought we ought to be more specific than that, so before the October Esbat, I researched endangered species at the library and found only one that was native to our region: the Plymouth red-bellied turtle. But surely the red-bellied turtle would much prefer some fresh or salt water to Jenkins's overgrown hilly acreage. Walking through the old paths with my dog yielded no brainstorms for keeping off developers. Scruffy and I tramped home with a handful of forked witch hazel twigs, used for divining underground water, and a basket of spice bush roots.

Scruffy tugged one of the twigs out of my hand—*Catch me! Catch me!* He cavorted wildly through my herb garden where rosemary, thyme, and parsley had withstood the frosty nights and still sprouted fragrant green leaves.

"Forget it. I'm not in the mood to play Fetch for you," I warned him. Setting down my small harvest, I rested on the wrought-iron bench, gazing past the garden to dark blue waves shimmering through a clump of leafless white birches. "Isn't this a splendid place we have here, Scruffy!" Again I felt a warm rush of gratitude to my bustling little grandmother who'd left me her gray-shingled cottage, along with her lilac and forsythia bushes, her scrub pines and peeling birch trees, beach roses and eroding bluff, her rotting wooden stairway leading to the rocky beach and icy waters of Cape Cod Bay. A precious lot of shoreline only the rich could afford these days.

With Scruffy racing ahead up the porch stairs, I brought my woodland gleanings into the kitchen. As I cleaned and sliced the spice roots for drying, I thought about the handsome offers that had been made for this property each spring when realtors descended like locusts. My family was split on the matter. Becky, my oldest, advised me to reap an immediate profit, not for her own gain but to keep me from becoming a burden in my golden years. Adam and Cathy disagreed with this program, possibly considering the benefits of allowing this choice parcel of waterfront to appreciate in value. My talent for clairvoyance never seemed to help me decide on the wisest course for my own life. Yet somehow, in this serene cottage by the sea, I felt I'd come home at last.

There hadn't been much energy for prescience left in me when I'd moved here from Salem three years ago, wearing dark glasses to hide the marks of sleeplessness and depression. But the flip slide of depression is that it forces you to take action or die. With my children now young adults, working and living elsewhere, in Salem I'd felt completely alone and deep in a rut, still living in the same place where I'd grown up, and still working in the family business—Shipton's Perennial Pleasures. Whether it was midlife crisis, empty-nest blues, hormonal roulette, or all of the above, I'd come to a dead end.

The children were still in middle school when both my parents died in an accident. I'd already filed for a separation. Taking over the garden shop, I was able to divorce Gary Hauser without leaving myself financially dependent on him. I'd made a good life in Salem for the children and me. But now, desperate for a fresh start, I'd sold the business and moved to Plymouth with enough money to begin again—just barely.

The tough, cold Atlantic, refusing to pamper or to sympathize, had stiffened my spine and restored that prized New England virtue of *self-reliance*—shades of Emerson. Week by week, I'd taken in more of the ocean's strength by a kind of watery osmosis, while the spirit of Grandma, still warm in the house, had set about healing me with the small, seasonal tasks she'd loved that I'd inherited along with the snug New England saltbox.

Now, in October, I'd already harvested and dried many annual herbs from her extensive gardens. It was time to put the gardens to bed for the year: final weeding, cutting back the aggressive plants, mulching the tender ones. In the evenings, I continued to study Grandma's notebooks of handwritten recipes. Herbal lore had been passed down in my father's family for many generations. In earlier times, Shipton women had been famous for their medicines, cosmetics, and even potions. And I was a Shipton, too. I had determined to turn that heritage into a successful business venture.

Right after my divorce, I'd resumed the family name. What a feeling of freedom! Well worth the bother of having to change credit cards and license. I'd also changed my given name from Sandra to Cassandra. Because to me the very sound of *Cassandra* has a mythic ring to it. It's Sandra taking on the power of the earth mother. It's a name that resonates with the mysterious myths and ancient enchantments of the traditional seer. And it's a long way from the woman I was, the poor wimp who put up with an alcoholic husband—all the deceptions, disappearances, ruined family life, and occasional brutality that went with that existence. A woman with the legendary authority of Cassandra might have stood up to the threats and false promises, packed up the children, and left the drunk for good. With fears of not being able to make it on her own, of scarring the children, of their blaming her for the breakup, it had taken Sandra too many years.

My new checks and new business cards bore the legend: *Cassandra Shipton, Earthlore Herbal Preparations and Cruelty-Free Cosmetics*. It's not Mary Kay, but it's a living.

Choosing a true name is magic in itself. My canine companion had been called Scruffy, and scruffy he'd looked—shaggy and bedraggled, with tangled bushy eyebrows—when I adopted him from the Animal Lovers Shelter. Wanting to perk him up with a noble name, I dubbed him Lancelot du Lac, in honor of his mother's pedigree. The dog had his own ideas, however, and refused to answer to Lancelot or Lance or any version thereof, and stubbornly held out for "Scruffy." It had a certain vagabond cachet that suited him.

"Should I have a cat, for better control?" I wondered aloud a few days later, as I stirred and tasted yet another formula for the universal antidote. "Scruffy, how would you feel about adding a cat to our household?"

Scruffy snarled and shook his eyeless mop rabbit with a neck-breaking snap. *Anything a cat can do, I can do better.*

We'd just finished lunch, during which I'd read a small item about Peacedale in the biweekly *Pilgrim Times*. So that afternoon—marvelously warm for mid-October—I'd been giving some thought to mastering impulsive magic. It wouldn't do to allow negative energy to get away from me, a loose cannon on the deck. That is, assuming that my musings had indeed influenced Peacedale's mishap. More likely, it was a robust wind off the water that had tilted him off balance. What had he been thinking of, clambering about on the windowsill? Word went around the neighborhood that a gull had blessed his windowpane, and the chalky gray splash on the glass had put him off a sermon he was writing on Francis of Assisi. Nothing would do but he must get out there and squeegee it clean.

Usually I tried to wish no one ill—"Thoughts are things," Grandma had always said—but what about Green Cap in the supermarket? If he were the man of my vision, and the vision true, there must be a way to combat such evil without repercussions. After all, we weren't Quakers. We were Wiccans. Just pointing a little finger toward someone ought to dispatch a spell, so we have read. Rather the opposite of a green thumb. The Borgia finger.

Our circle had come together two years ago, in a women's study group sponsored by the local library. The history of women's issues had led us inevitably to goddess myths and legends. As we delved into ancient matriarchal religions, some of the group lost interest, but five of us had discovered this modern equivalent to the old earth religions—Wicca, meaning "the wise ones." We liked the way Wiccans revered nature and recognized female spirituality. And Wiccans believed life energies could be used to control events—*the power of magic.* A little scary, perhaps, but so appealing to us!

"But we can't just go blundering around psychically," I continued my thesis to the dog's pricked-up ears. "You never know what troubles might recoil upon ourselves. We'll need to handle this matter of Green Cap with caution and finesse."

Scruffy gazed at me speculatively. *What are you so wound up about, Toots?*

"I mean, look what happened with Peacedale's leg," I pointed out. "Was that my doing? And if it was, shouldn't I be saving myself for more important objectives?"

Turning his gaze toward the window, Scruffy assumed a bored expression. A blue jay lighted on the kitchen window bird feeder and pecked at the sunflower seeds. Immediately the dog charged the window I'd left open to air out some of the strong herbal aromas. A big show of barking amid a flurry of blue wings. I pulled him away before he could leap through the screen.

"So personally you'd prefer less introspection and more action—is that the idea?" I asked.

Diving under the log carrier, Scruffy produced his best ball, a spongy orange thing with bites missing. *How about materializing a guy to play ball with?* He pranced and wiggled his rear end.

"Oh, I don't know about that, Scruffy. Am I too old, too set in my ways for a live-in relationship? For getting used to a new man?" As a single mother in Salem, I'd had my share of affairs, none of them lasting. Three children, old enough to view any guy dating their mother with suspicion and derision—what a bucket of cold water to douse any hot romance! But "that was then . . ." I'd finished with the Parents Without Partners phase of my life. "Maybe it would be different now, Scruffy. Maybe it's time."

When you want to discuss your innermost feelings, the ideal listener is a dog. Steadfast, loyal, and loving, they're never in a hurry to judge or advise. Unless you say some disruptive word such as "ride" or "cookie," they will comfort you with unconditional attention as long as you wish.

On October 13th, the moon rose out of the Atlantic in its full bronze majesty. Then, as it climbed through the vaguely pink horizon into the darkest part of the sky, it turned magnificently, coldly silver, its expression severe. What did that presage? Ever since Fiona had put forth the theory that the full moon's features subtly alter from month to month and what you read there forebodes the days to follow, I'd realized that the moon's face was, indeed, softly variable, possibly predictive.

Fiona Ritchie, our Black Hill branch librarian—the branch itself so small as to be no more than a cottage—and the oldest member of our circle, is a genius at serendipity, always able to lay her hands on the very bit of obscure information that is most needed. Never parted from a greenish carryall that could only be called a reticule—filled with ancient pamphlets on the Cabala or Egyptology, snippets of poetry, yellowing recipes, thin volumes of delicious magical theory, and a bag of butterscotch candies— she doles out goodies from its depths continually. She often wears a nebulous coat sweater, a faded rainbow with bulging pockets. With her queenly crown of carroty-gray braids, she looks like everyone's fairy godmother. Ever since her husband was swept off the deck of his commercial fishing boat, the *Fiona Fancy*, she's lived alone except for Omar Khayyám, her Persian cat. She confessed to me once that she felt guilty sometimes about how much she enjoyed her solitariness and hoped she hadn't inadvertently whistled up the sixty-foot wave that had made her a widow.

What a talent, I thought, while reassuring her that she didn't have it and brooding over the weekend drunk I'd lived with for fourteen years. At least Gary had managed to keep his chemical engineering job at a Boston firm that managed hazardous waste—and that had paid for the children's college tuitions. But how I would have enjoyed whirling him into the depths of the sea!

Fiona's picturesque Cape Cod cottage, located near Plymouth Center, was hung with nets and buoys, while inside every conceivable nook and cranny was crammed with stacks of books, and the books themselves stuffed with a motley array of bookmarks. Since it was Fiona's turn to host our circle, some halfhearted attempt at tidying up had resulted in a broom leaning in the corner of the living room over a forgotten pile of trash. Glinting with amusement, Phillipa's ebony eyes took in the tableau. "A perfect witch," she murmured.

When the others, Deidre and Heather, arrived, we greeted each other with a formal kiss. "Merry meet, merry meet," Deidre sang out in her little-girl voice. Our Esbat was complete on an evening chilly but fine enough for working outdoors. In Fiona's tree-screened backyard, we huddled in sweaters and jackets we would soon be flinging away when we danced our circle.

The fire roared in Fiona's outdoor fieldstone fireplace. From time to time, I cast into the flames dried sprigs of sage and mullein, herbs of protection. After the ritual, we toasted the moon and all of her myths, raising our glasses so that its round luminescence showed through the delicate, flowery white wine Phillipa had brought. As we drank, we swallowed that image like a communion wafer, making our several wishes, which included the summoning of an endangered animal to protect Jenkins's woods.

When we finally went indoors, we were in such an ebullient mood that at first I found myself reluctant to dispel our natural high with the story of Green Cap. But I knew that I must. Reliving the vision in my mind's eye, I found it had lost none of its ability to fill me with dread.

"This is better than consciousness raising," Deidre was saying with a pleased glance from pale blue eyes as she stirred extra honey into her peppermint tea. "I wonder if this energy we're feeling could be made to deflect that new Vita-Life place that's competing with Nature's Bounty." Along with mothering her three young children, lively Deidre managed a natural vitamins franchise in the high-overhead, cutthroat environment of Massasoit Mall. Devoted to handcrafting, Deidre focused her intentions with needle and thread, stitching her wishes into everything from poppets to embroidered prayers.

"Isn't that restraint of trade or something?" Heather Morgan wanted to know. Long-legged, chestnut-haired Heather donated most of her time and trust income to Animal Lovers, Plymouth County's shelter for abandoned pets. She drove a Mercedes whose windows were never quite clean of dog drool and was responsible for my adopting the redoubtable Scruffy.

Herbs, books, food, animals, children—it wasn't surprising that we had found a common thread in all this, a connection that survived even the running argument about the plight of crated calves versus the pleasure of eating veal between Heather, the animal rights activist, and Phillipa, the cook.

While we were warm and cheerful, having wine and tea and cakes in Fiona's cluttered living room, with Omar striding back and forth over the laden coffee table, I finally related the horrifying vision I'd had when I looked into Green Cap's eyes. The immediate consensus was that my experience could have been a true incidence of clairvoyance and therefore called upon all of us to investigate. Deidre, her motherly instincts up in arms, especially wanted instant action—no "innocent until proven guilty" blunted her resolve.

"If this green-capped person is a child killer, why don't I just make a poppet and stab it through?" asked Deidre. Her busy fingers at that moment were delving into her craft basket for the current embroidery. So much for working on the white side. "Or cut off its . . ."

"Stop this minute, Deidre," ordered Heather, her voice suddenly resonant and commanding, a voice that could quell a mastiff at full gallop. *"Take that out of the law,"* she charged the unseen moon, risen pure and far above Fiona's dusty window.

"We can't simply hack up the fellow," Fiona explained in her reasonable, teacherly way. "Let me remind you that we must work within the law . . . because we're not psychic vigilantes, after all. You wouldn't want those chickens to come home to roost, would you, dear?"

"What Fiona means in her mixed-metaphoric way," Phillipa explained dryly, "is that maleficent spells are believed to rebound. So we must put our thinking caps on—not those delightfully pointed *chapeaux* in which Fiona's neighbors expect to see us fly off on our brooms. Then, if we discover we have truly identified an evil-doer, we must bring him to justice in some good white way."

We agreed that it was late and we were too drained of emotion to decide how we would proceed. Perhaps, if no emergency arose, we would table the matter until we met together again on Samhain. As we hugged each other, saying "merry part and merry meet again" and "blessed be!" on Fiona's doorstep, was it my imagination, or were drapes and window curtains twitching in nearby houses? The high, full moon slipped behind a dark wall of clouds, and fat drops of rain began to fall.

Samhain—All Hallows, Feast of the Dead

It continued to rain off and on through the rest of October, alternating between drenching downpours and fine, wet mists. A few bright days that relieved the dank, dismal ones were made all the more brilliant by the sun's reflection in vast shallow pools of standing water collected in the low places of roads and fields. I don't suppose we should credit our magic work with influencing the weather, but the constant deluge did turn out to be inspiring in the matter of Jenkins's woods.

The first brainstorm came about a week before Samhain, on a day when sheets of rain were being so strongly whipped by a northeast wind that Scruffy had to be coerced into going outdoors to relieve himself. *Why can't I have indoor accommodations?*

"Because you're a dog," I explained reasonably, "and dogs customarily prefer trees and bushes around a fair stretch of well-kept lawn."

He hunkered down, but I pushed him out the door anyway. Watching through the kitchen window, I saw him stand on the back porch looking mournfully at the foaming waves. He lifted his leg against one of the white columns. A moment later he was scratching at the kitchen door that was already raked down to the bare wood.

I let him in with one hand while answering the phone with the other, wondering how he managed to get drenched without putting a paw off the porch. He gave me a dirty look, then shook himself off in a leisurely manner.

"Wetlands," Heather Morgan crooned in my ear.

"You must be looking into my kitchen." Sadly, I surveyed the droplets of mud on the dishwasher, refrigerator, and my last pair of clean jeans.

"No, I was looking into some old issues of the *Pilgrim Times* and I found this small news item, two years ago last August, about an accident that occurred between a sand truck and a station wagon up near Phil's place."

"I don't understand how that could be meaningful to us," I said, stretching to swipe at the refrigerator with a soapy sponge.

"The sand truck was coming out of Jenkins's woods. According to this article, Jenkins had sold some fill to a builder who was having it trucked away when the mishap with the station wagon occurred." Heather sounded really excited. As a counterpoint, a chorus of the canine crew inhabiting her Federalist mansion was barking in the background. "And that means holes."

"Holes?"

"When you take out fill, it leaves holes. If enough earth is removed, the area may get swampy. When you've been foraging in those woods, have you ever seen the place I'm talking about? Could it by any remote chance be classified as wetlands?"

I smiled at the rain hitting my window like someone throwing a bucket of water. "I think you have something there, Heather. When this mess lets up, I'll do some exploring and let you know." I was, after all, the most affected by the threatened rape of the woods, except for Phillipa, who couldn't be drafted for this detail while she was busy completing her *Modern Maturity* article by its deadline.

The rain continued into the next day, but during a short letup in the late afternoon, when it was merely foggy and deeply overcast, I put on my poncho and boots. Scruffy pretended to be asleep in front of the kitchen fireplace where heat from glowing embers toasted his backside. When he saw I was really going out, he stirred. *Am I missing some fun here?*

"I'm going for a good, long tramp in the woods. And you'll be stuck in the house, if you don't get a move on right now," I said.

He was up off his fake sheepskin cushion in an instant, pushing ahead of me as always. *I am alpha dog, leader of the pack.*

"Oh, yeah?" I clipped the leash firmly to his collar. During the following hour, we zigzagged through the underbrush in a hit-or-miss fashion. The wooded area was nearly a half mile where it fronted on the main road, Route 3A, within view of the ocean if cleared of trees, close enough to the shore for a developer to reap a fortune from his investment. Searching for a promising swamp, we found nothing more exciting than a few trees that merited Scruffy's marking. His little bladder seemed a miraculous reservoir when he was staking out new territory.

From time to time on our wanderings, I thought I heard a flute playing but put that down to my imagination, which is notably vivid. Then, as we came to a small, clear brook that runs through Jenkins's woods, I saw a figure sitting on a flat rock some way along that tumble of water in a place where there was a slight embankment on both sides. His back was toward me. Quite a small person, yet not a childlike silhouette with that large-brimmed hat and shapeless coat. His feet dangled over the edge of the rounded earth while his arms moved back and forth. A strange, sweet tune rose into the sodden trees.

I pulled Scruffy's leash taut, thinking he would spring toward this gnomic intruder. In his view, any place we frequented became our personal property to be guarded. But Scruffy stood stock still, his head cocked, listening—then pulled me in the opposite direction. *I'm not afraid, you understand,* my companion explained, *but this is the kind of bizarre encounter that my species, with our keener senses and superior instincts, naturally avoids. Can't you walk any faster?*

I shared Scruffy's respect for the occasional weirdness that runs through ordinary life, like a streak of mold through cheese, so I didn't really mind being tugged away. I felt as if I'd come across some New England version of Pan, the Greek woodland god, piping a magical melody. Drifting along on lines of poetry that emerged from the dim cavern of my high school memories— "What was he doing, the Great God Pan, Down by the reeds of the river"—I hardly realized where Scruffy was hauling me until the difficulty of lifting one foot after another finally penetrated my consciousness. A meadow of mud seemed, with every step, to be sucking my boots down to China.

"Say, Scruff, I think we've stumbled onto something here. It's swampy, all right. Can this be the true wetlands of Heather's dreams?"

What do you mean "stumbled onto"? A dog's canine pretension is that he always knows where he's been, where he is, and where he's going. *Just let go my leash, and I'll lead the way* . . . And with that, he lunged forward, pulling me to my knees in the chilly ooze while he flushed a brace of squawking wood ducks out of the tall grass, heavy and bent with rain at the edge of the clearing.

"Oooooh!" I screamed, which raised the remaining ducks out of their secret places with a raucous clamor and an annoyed beating of wings. Along with the wood ducks, a pair of black-bellied tree ducks and a snowy egret sailed up into the air. "There *is* a wetlands habitat here! Now we can slap a restraining order on building anything in these woods."

In the midst of my rejoicing, which included a few splashing dance steps that Scruffy observed with marked concern, the rain began again, making up for the hour's respite with a new ferocity. As the woods darkened, I felt a small pang of worry, not being sure exactly where I was, considering all the twists and turns we had taken. "I'm sure you know your way home through the woods," I said to the dog, whose befuddled expression was not encouraging, "but I think we ought to follow this old truck track to the main road and walk back along 3A."

Rain was running off his ears, and his bangs appeared to be plastered over his eyes, as were my own. Obviously insulted by my lack of faith in his tracking prowess, he trotted away as briskly as he was able with me floundering at the other end of the leash. *Just try to keep up this time. I hope I can expect a good dinner after this workout.*

"How about that turkey stew you like so much?" I suggested.

Scruffy quickened the pace. I was surprised to see how near the main route we were. Just as we arrived at the shoulder of the road, the dog stopped abruptly and began to paw the earth. Eager to get home, I tugged briskly on the leash, but he persisted in digging until he had unearthed his prize from the mud and rotting leaves. *Hey, Toots! Look at this swell thing I got you.* He tossed it up gleefully so that the object, which looked like a small dead animal, touched my hand. With a grimace, I let it drop straight back down to the ground, but after leaning over for a closer observation, I picked it up again. A rabbit's foot on a beaded chain with two keys attached; a house key and a smaller, padlock-type key. And a metal identification tag: Gerry Kirschmann. A youngster's keys, I decided. Although the name sounded familiar, I couldn't remember why. I put the set in my pocket, thinking I might find the right Kirschmann in the phone book and return the key.

From where we came out on Route 3A, it was no more than a ten-minute walk through the face-numbing cold rain. I could hardly wait to brew a hot cup of juniper tea—an anti-inflammatory precaution—and call Heather, in that order.

The first Kirschmann I called reminded me of why that name seemed familiar. Gerry Kirschmann was the ten-year-old who had disappeared from a rented cottage in Pembroke last August. Because his fishing pole was also missing, everyone except his parents believed he'd drowned in one of the many ponds and lakes in that area.

The rabbit's foot key ring was the first trace of Gerry that had been found. Two Plymouth County detectives immediately took charge of the keys. Apparently the drowning theory had been set aside in favor of foul play, because police officers began investigating the area where Scruffy had dug up the rabbit's foot. On the morning of the thirty-first, squad cars parked all along the Route 3A border of Jenkins's woods. One of the detectives, Stone Stern, a tall, scholarly man wearing oval, metal-rimmed glasses, looking like a *Gentleman's Quarterly* model, knocked on my kitchen door to ask if I'd bring my dog over to the woods where the keys had been found.

"We have our own K-9s, of course, but since the little fellow found the keys, maybe he's the one to follow the scent to whatever else may be buried in that area." He smiled reassuringly, but I couldn't help shuddering at the thought of what might turn up next—the curse of my colorful imagination.

Glancing back, I saw that Scruffy had shaken off his mid-morning nap on the battered sheepskin cushion and was standing in an alert posture, growling just slightly. *Who's he calling "little fellow"?* I decided to have the detective wait on the porch.

"All right. We'll be there in a few minutes." I closed the door on Detective Stern and turned to the dog. "Fancy a bit of detecting, Sherlock?"

Those K-9s are all show and no nose. Scruffy took tooth-hold of the extra-long leather leash hanging on the peg by the kitchen door. *Let's get tracking, Toots.*

A few minutes later, the chosen leash attached to his collar and wearing a sporty blue bandanna with the legend *Animal Angel*, a gift from Heather, Scruffy was sniffing the rabbit's foot key ring. Finally the dog appeared satisfied, and I handed the keys back to Detective Stern. Scruffy began by scenting the ground where he'd dug before—with a slight excess of showmanship, I thought. I hung around at the other end of his leash, feeling useless and wishing I could have told the detectives what—or who—I suspected, but I didn't even know Green Cap's name. Besides, I felt certain my vision would not be considered evidence, except of craziness.

What followed then was a dog-led amble through the woods, where most of the time I had to duck-walk to avoid low-growing branches. This went on for a half-hour or more, in ever-widening circles, until my thigh muscles threatened to collapse. Finally, Scruffy halted in his tracks and began to paw the ground industriously. *Hey, guys . . . there's something here.* One of the officers pushed him aside and stuck a pointed shovel into the earth that Scruffy had laid bare of rotting leaves. In a minute, the man had turned up a mucky sneaker.

With my stomach already turning, I didn't wait for more. "Let me know what else you find," I called back to Detective Stern as I fled back to the house, dragging a reluctant Scruffy. *But I haven't finished solving the case.*

"Don't go getting any fancy ideas, Scruffy. Let's just leave any further detecting to the detectives." Making a cup of stomach-soothing ginger tea with one hand, with the other I called Phillipa, then Heather, leaving it to them to pass on the news.

Later, when Stone Stern came by to thank me, he said they'd decided to call in K-9s after all. The German shepherds had the officers digging all afternoon, but they hadn't found a body. All there was to show for their work was that one sneaker. He hoped it would reveal some blood evidence when turned over to Forensics.

It was raining again when I arrived at Deidre's to celebrate Samhain. After hanging my dripping poncho in Deidre's mudroom, I kissed my hostess's cheek and presented her with dried dittany from Crete, traditionally burned to share with the dead on Samhain, and, of course, sage for the ritual cup. From listening to the hilarity in progress in the living room, one would never guess the significance of this holiday. It seemed a shame to douse their high spirits with my continuing tale of woe and possible murder.

"My dears, I've seen something in Jenkins's woods this week that tops even my wildest dreams. I just hope that Cassandra's detectives haven't spoiled things," Heather was saying. "I could hardly wait to tell you!" Her long legs were crossed yoga-fashion—without any apparent agony, I noted—as we formed a circle on the hand-hooked rug in Deidre's living room.

The brick-fronted garrison colonial glowed throughout with Deidre's excess energy. Needlepoint cushions depicted cherubs, bunnies, and poodles. Pine pieces rescued from the town dump were refinished to gleaming usefulness. Framed embroideries declared *Friend Forever* and *Two Hearts, One Love.*

"How does she find the time to create all this crap?" Heather whispered, shaking her long chestnut mane, worn tonight in a single burnished braid swinging down her back.

"Energy burns high in Deidre," I commented in an answering whisper. "I only hope some of it rubs off on me. Not the artsy stuff, though. Just the sheer dynamism."

"Well, here we are, then." Our hostess came in from the kitchen to fill glass cups with steaming cider. The cheering scent of hot spices tingled my nose. "Tell us what miracle we've wrought with our summoning spell, because I personally am prepared to take full credit if it's good news." She plumped down beside us on the rug and swirled the cinnamon stick in her cider, intoning, *"Boil and bubble, toil and trouble . . ."*

"Eagles!" Heather announced with a triumphant glance around the circle. "A beautiful pair of bald eagles."

"Impossible," Phillipa declared, dark eyebrows rising in disbelief. Nevertheless, she smiled the quick, broad smile that always lit up her severe features with surprising warmth. "They're all in Alaska or someplace like that, aren't they? Are you sure? Where exactly did you see them?"

"Day before last. My second trip out to the wetlands Cass discovered. I'm preparing a report for the Department of Environmental Protection. And there they were, oh-so-gorgeous, devouring a duck carcass! In winter, eagles often follow the track of waterfowl like ours—I've already counted five different species, including mallards—to sheltered wetlands where they know they will dine well on the weakest members of the duck flock through the cold weather." Heather educated us from her inexhaustible fund of nature lore.

"Will they stay, do you think, once spring comes?" Fiona asked, passing a plate of Phillipa's cheddar crisps.

"Not unless the DEP makes that part of Jenkins's woods off limits. Eagles are *very* intolerant of human intrusion into their nesting sites." Heather worried deeply about the sensitivities of all earth's creatures, providing they weren't people, who, she felt, ought to be able to look out for themselves.

"We couldn't have actually called them here?" I said, crunching into another savory crisp. "They must have been here already."

"Of course we called them," Deidre affirmed. "Especially Heather. You know what a way she has with animals." She glanced jealously at Heather, who was at that very moment being courted by Deidre's own two toy poodles, Salty and Peppy.

"Eagles, of all things. I was expecting maybe a Delmarva Fox Squirrel or the Pennsylvania rattlesnake—something more local, you know. What a lucky break," I rejoiced. "It will be the saving of those woods."

We fell silent then, savoring the power of magic and the glory of eagles. Picturing those majestic new residents of Jenkins's woods, I was drawn back again to the dark, wild tangle of trees, the chilling things Scruffy had found there, and the fate of that missing boy.

"Since our magic seems to be working, let's devote some of that power to finding out the name of the man in the green cap," I suggested. "I feel that the disappearance of Gerry Kirschmann is related to him." I told them again about the police search in Jenkins's woods and how Scruffy found a sneaker that might have belonged to the missing boy. Just talking about it gave me an intuitive chill down the back of my spine. I *knew* I was on the right track with Green Cap—and I was beginning to feel obsessed with foreboding.

Fiona looked distressed. "How can we be certain you're right about this man and the Kirschmann kid? You said yourself, Green Cap looked perfectly harmless, even cheerful."

"What if Cass *is* right, and he's after *our* youngsters right here on the South Shore?" Deidre said. "I thought we all agreed last time that this is a bona fide clairvoyant incident. So shouldn't we do what we can to apprehend Green Cap before he strikes again?" With three youngsters—four, if you counted her husband, whom she treated as one of the brood—Deidre was in the throes of being a total mother. Will Ryan *was* a rather simple soul, a fireman whose Cherokee bore the flaming bumper sticker: *Firemen Are Hot Stuff.*

Fiona's expression grew even more fearful and her round chins shivered. "You are *all* certain, then?"

"Dead certain," I answered for everyone. "I've never had a more compelling vision"

"I could read the Tarot," Phillipa offered.

"I think I have a better idea," Fiona said, her eyes shining with misty enthusiasm. "Tonight of all nights—when the dead may come to us—perhaps we should hold a seance to call on Green Cap's victims to identify their attacker—that is, if there are victims. No offense, Cass." She pulled a small, dark volume, heavily bookmarked, from her reticule. *Seances Made Simple,* in gold-leaf cuneiform letters. Sticking out behind it was a glossy paperback titled *Toward a Postmodern Paganism.*

"I might have made a perfectly effective poppet to settle the matter in the time you're taking to find out this guy's name," Deidre complained. She passed store-bought arrowroot biscuits on a hand-painted plate bearing the legend *Sweets to the Sweet.* Despite Phillipa's scornful gaze, we all took one.

Later, after Deidre had cast the circle, the sacred space in which we would work, each of us lit Samhain candles for our beloved dead to celebrate the eternal life of the spirit. Since the rain had forced us indoors, we began in a quiet way to raise our cone of power—a visual image that we would send soaring into the universe of infinite possibility—simply passing the energy from person to person, hand to hand. We hummed as the power flowed through us, a rising resonance. Phil's strong, cool fingers squeezed mine. I passed the clasp on to Deidre's soft, moist hand. The energy moved slowly at first, then faster and faster between us. The humming grew louder to match its speed. Soon the power could no longer be contained. At a signal from Deidre, all arms flew up at once, letting the power fly straight up to the invisible world, bearing our hopes and intentions.

"Ooooh! I'm exhausted," moaned Fiona, struggling to uncross her plump legs without falling flat on her face. To close the ritual, Deidre earthed any remaining swirls of energy with a sprinkle of salt and broke the circle with her athame, a ritual knife.

Personally, I felt exhilarated and nearly danced my way into Deidre's cheerful yellow kitchen where I brewed sage tea to dispel any mists of negative gloom. Perhaps we'd had enough of the dead for one Samhain evening.

But not enough for Heather, apparently hot on the trail of my green-capped demon. "Is there time, do you think, for a seance?" she queried, looking at Deidre as the sage tea was passed around.

"Oh, don't worry about *him*," Deidre reassured us. "He'll be playing cards all night at the firehouse. A lot of the guys pull extra duty on Halloween, in case of pranks gone wrong and so forth. My little one's fast asleep upstairs, and the other two are sleeping at their cousin's. We can raise hell or the dead, just as we wish, my dears. There couldn't be a more appropriate night for it."

It was our first seance and pretty much of a fumbled affair. I felt a little silly and stagy as I exhorted the spirits, if any, connected to the man in the green cap to come forth and speak to us. Fiona's reading aloud step by step from her instructive manual—in a tone suitable for story hour at the library—rather took away from the spooky atmosphere. We sat on the floor again, this time around the truncated oak dining table that served as Deidre's coffee table. The lights were extinguished except for three candles, our slow, deep breathing eddying the flames. Our hands were spread out on the smooth golden wood, little fingers touching.

"Maybe we should have used a Ouija board," Heather hissed on my left as Fiona finished her recitation. Deidre's poodles were curled up against Heather's back. I envied her their support, however slight, as the minutes continued to tick by silently now, except for the occasional spitting of the fire onto the hearth. Fiona, across from me, seemed to be nodding off in the warmth and stillness, her gold-rimmed half-tracks slipping down her nose, her chin falling on her chest. Heather nudged my knee with her elbow and gestured toward our friend sinking into her frazzled coat sweater.

Fiona began to sing a wordless tune.

The rest of us suddenly sat up straight as though someone had put ice cubes down our backs. The candles flared, then guttered out, leaving the room completely dark except for the shifting glow of firelight.

Fiona's voice, usually low and raspy, grew higher and more tremulous, repeating the same two lines continually: "Starting here, starting now, Everything's coming up roses."

"Who are you, spirit?" Phillipa asked, leaning down to peer into Fiona's face, probably to see if she were faking this outburst—but we all knew that she wasn't. It seemed as if some entity with a young boy's soprano—and not a very good soprano at that—had taken over our friend's consciousness for the moment.

We held our collective breath, waiting for an answer to Phillipa's question, but the voice merely continued to sing the same phrases.

"Are you connected to Cassandra's man with the green cap?" persisted Phillipa when Fiona paused. I didn't much like his being called "Cassandra's."

A thin, high-pitched scream seemed to issue from Fiona's

throat, and she threw back her head with an agonized expression. "Stop it! Help! You're hurting me . . . Help . . . Help . . ."

I could hear Salty and Peppy's little toenails clicking rapidly as they skedaddled out of the room, slipping and sliding on the polished pine floor between rugs.

"Hey, that's about enough of that," said Deidre. She stood up and leaned over Fiona, shaking her awake. "Fiona! Fiona! Snap on those lamps, will you, Heather?"

I think we were all relieved when light returned the room to its normal dimensions.

Fiona looked around her with a befuddled expression. "What happened?" she asked. All talking at the same time, we began explaining.

"You conked out, you crazy lady," said Deidre.

"It looked as if you'd fallen asleep," Heather said, "but then you began to sing like a child."

"Clearly, we went into a trance, my dear." Phillipa rubbed Fiona's wrists briskly.

"I think you stopped her too soon," I complained. "That tune Fiona was singing—I seem to remember Green Cap humming it the night I bumped into him."

"Don't be an ass, Cass," Phillipa snapped. "Quite enough for our first foray, *I'd* say. Especially for poor Fiona. Besides, as far as I'm concerned, you've made your case."

"Right," said Deidre. "The man in the green cap did something disgusting to this little kid with the squeaky voice. And we're going to get him for it. Now, for heaven's sake, let's have some wine. I don't know about you, but I'm completely shook."

Having ensconced Fiona on the sofa, Phillipa continued to explain quietly what had happened until the dazed look gave way to a smile of success.

"My, it really worked!" Fiona exclaimed with satisfaction, patting her copy of *Seances Made Simple*. "But you know, I don't think I'm going to want to do it again in any hurry. It's given me the most ghastly emotional hangover, like a bad acid trip." We must have looked at her with some surprise, because she added, "You forget, ladies, that I'm Berkeley, Class of '65."

Even with her untidy braids and unraveling coat sweater, I could look in Fiona's round, gray eyes and see the pouches and wrinkles melt away into the red-haired war protester and free spirit she must have been. I bet she'd never in her life worn a bra, not even to a job interview. Didn't she realize that her insistence on untrammeled freedom—which went far beyond underwear or the lack of it—while delightful at nineteen, eventually had diverted her into the worst assignments in the library system?

To dispel such a critical thought, I immediately went over to hug Fiona. "You're a real medium, just like it says in the book," I praised her.

"Yes, well, I resign from that assignment, Cassie. You think there was something to the song I sang?"

"It's a tune from *Gypsy*," Deidre said.

"Could the assaulter have been a gypsy?" Fiona ruminated.

"Roving gypsies who make off with a child for nefarious purposes is the stuff of paranoid fiction," Phillipa declared. "Like white slavers."

"Well, Cass thinks it's important," Fiona insisted. "Now how are we going to find this murderous Green Cap of yours?"

"The problem is, I'm the only one who knows what he looks like," I said. "Let me think about this." A plan was already forming in my mind—I did not wish to be warned away from it by the others. Perhaps if I carried a camera constantly and haunted the supermarket where I'd first encountered Green Cap, I could snap a picture of him and pass it around the circle, like a private "wanted" poster. Yes, then I could involve all of us in the search.

Scruffy seemed to enjoy the extra rides to Angelo's during the following week. He bounded into the Wagoneer with undiminished enthusiasm each time. I'd drop into the market at different times during the day as well as at the exact hour I'd first seen Green Cap, a camera hung casually around my neck. At least, I hoped it was casual, since I noted that no one else in the market seemed to be sporting one.

I was deep in a comparative study of turkey cutlets when he finally appeared. Out of the corner of my eye, I saw Green Cap stroll past the beef roasts, carrying one of Angelo's plastic baskets over one arm. With dismay, I felt the camera bumping against the refrigerated meat counter. How would I dare use it? I dropped the cutlets I'd been considering—which were instantly scooped up by the woman standing behind me—and straightened up to face my target. Again I was assaulted by an overwhelming impression of evil.

What the hell, I thought, and aimed the camera directly toward Green Cap, who was in the act of picking out a package of pork ribs. His profile would be better than nothing. But even as I pressed the button and heard the camera click, he turned toward me with a surprised expression

"Comparison shopping," I said aloud to all and sundry, the first wild explanation that came to me. Quickly I took another few shots of end-of-aisle displays at random—a pyramid of tinned soups, a fortress of cracker boxes, a logjam of paper towels—then let the camera drop against my shirt.

Green Cap's genial smile was strained. "Comparison of what, miss? For what?"

I dashed past him for the front of the store, then remembered my cart and had to run back and grab it. Counting items as I ran—*good, less than twelve*—I found the express check-out line blessedly short. Only one of the two people ahead of me had clearly crossed the line into weekly shopping, quite unconcerned about the twenty-*plus* items she was unloading onto the counter.

I felt rather than saw Green Cap join the line, heard him breathing behind me, a smoker's wheeze. The teenager at the cash register looked up from my order and smiled past me.

"Hi, there, Mr. Q. How's it going?"

Mr. Q! It wasn't a whole name, but it was a start. I wanted to dash for the car, but I lingered, repacking my two plastic bags, pulling out a loaf of bread from underneath the apples.

"Can't complain, Joey. And yourself?"

"Okay, as soon as I get out of here. Working some extra hours today."

"Very enterprising," Q said in a hearty tone. "Saving up for the senior class trip?"

"Yep. That'll be $12.67," said Joey.

I paid up, grabbed my bags, and sprinted for the Jeep.

"Hey, wait a minute," Q called after me.

Pretending I didn't hear him, I opened the driver's side door, hurled my packages onto the passenger's side, and jumped in, fumbling with my keys. Scruffy leaped into the front seat on top of the groceries, growling.

"Oh great, you horse," I muttered as I snapped the locks shut and turned the key in the ignition, relieved to hear the motor roar into life.

"Just a minute, miss," Q said, putting his hand through the four inches of open window I'd left for Scruffy when I went into the market. Q was waving what looked like one of my brown leather gloves. Scruffy grabbed the glove between his teeth, dropped it, then took hold of Q's cuff just as we drove off.

"Thanks," I hollered back without looking out the window. I didn't want to see Q's expression. A thrill of terror coursed through my body as I drove away. Despite the fact that my knees were knocking—literally—I did manage to step on the gas pedal hard and urge the slow-and-steady Wagoneer to a getaway spurt of speed.

Wow! That was exciting. Scruffy spat out the ribbing of Q's cuff. *I like guarding our car from characters like that one. Am I a good boy, or what?*

"You're a very good boy," I agreed. As I drove, I used one hand to grasp one of the jerky beef treats I keep in the glove compartment as a reward. "I wonder what Q stands for. Quentin? Quiller? Quackenbush?"

Regrettably, investigating Q took a backseat during the following week because of a furor that arose over our eagles. During their earlier homesteading, before becoming a *cause célèbre* in Plymouth and environs, Mr. and Mrs. Majestic National Symbol had built themselves a nest in the substantial crook of one of Jenkins's loftiest pines. A stick construction about ten feet high and at least six across, it looked like a large thornbush stuck up there. No doubt the inside was lined with softer dried grasses. Our feathered predators had lived there in quiet anonymity, dining on wood duck, bluefish, and the occasional confused small rabbit, until Heather informed the zoning board that Jenkins's woods would have to be considered an eagle sanctuary safeguarded by the Bald Eagle Protection Act.

All was going well until one of Phillipa's neighbors claimed an eagle had threatened her baby as she was wheeling him in a carriage near Jenkins's woods on her way to a friend's house. According to this young woman, the huge bird had circled two or three times, then dive-bombed the carriage, obviously intent upon carrying off the baby to its nest. The mother had grabbed the six-month-old child out of its carriage and run down Route 3A, screaming.

Some of the locals who heard about this incident came out with rifles, hoping for a legally sanctioned eagle shoot. This was the same bunch whose usual civic duty, as they saw it, was polishing off rats at the town dump. The cops who arrived to check on these hotshots kept nervous hands on the butts of their own revolvers and constantly scanned the treetops. The situation was beginning to look rather ugly.

"Do you think it was something we did?" Fiona whispered. "I mean, calling all endangered species without any thought of how we would protect them once they got here. We should know bet-

ter. Half a spell is *not* better than none. We could have surrounded the eagles with a white light or some other spiritual
armor. I have a book on psychic protection here somewhere."
She searched through her reticule in a distracted fashion.

I made us each a calming cup of camomile tea, which we
sipped as we sat on my front parlor's window seat to watch the
gathering throng across the road. Besides the rat-boys and the
cops, an assortment of neighbors with folded arms and pursed
lips had settled in to monitor the developing drama, shifting and
lowing like a herd of cows. When the guys with the rifles got
tired of milling about, they began cooking up a scheme to flush
out the eagles. A group of "beaters" would thrash their way through
the eagles' territory, making a racket while the others positioned
themselves to shoot. The only thing that prevented the hunters
from putting this plan into action was not the presence of the police but their own inability to agree on who would do what. No
one opted to beat the bushes; everyone wanted to shoot.

Fiona kept her doubts *sotto voce* so as not to annoy Heather,
who considered the effort to preserve Jenkins's woods to be our
finest hour and who was at that very moment camped out in my
kitchen summoning help from every possible quarter. She had
found my place to be the ideal command post for her campaign.

"Now, Cass, I want you just to hand over this phone bill to me
when it comes," Heather had said as she preempted my telephone for lengthy calls not only to the local EPA but also to the
headquarters of the Sierra Club, Greenpeace, the Audubon
Society, plus our congressmen, local and national, and the White
House.

As luck would have it, the *Greenpeace*, a 218-foot tug put into
operation after the *Rainbow Warrior* was blown up by French secret agents, happened to be docked in Plymouth Harbor. The
crew was resting up for a few days following their recent protest
against the discharging of uranium into the Irish Sea from a nuclear waste disposal plant in northwest England. Greenpeace
headquarters agreed to send a team from the tug to look into the

matter of our eagles. It didn't take the office long to get the message to the crew. Golden shafts of sunlight slanting through the pines had just begun to signal later afternoon when a Jeep skidded into my driveway and bounced to a halt. Heather flew around the side of the house, her long chestnut braid swinging as she hurried to greet her rescuers.

"My, they're a bonny bunch," Fiona breathed, echoing my own inner response precisely. "Let's get out there and join the welcoming party."

Four men and a young woman had piled out of the Jeep and were introducing themselves to Heather—and then to Fiona and me as we appeared at her side. They all seemed to be muscular and tanned that tawny shade that can only be achieved at sea. Their smiles were dazzling and their steps lithe. The woman's sweatshirt bore the legend *You Can't Sink a Rainbow*. Three of the men were in their late twenties or early thirties, casually attired in Banana Republic's best world-traveler togs.

The fourth man was different from the others, somehow more real—fortyish, compact in build, his chest and arms brawny, his tightly curled black hair shot through with gray, and his eyes as dark blue as an Aegean horizon. With features that were cast in a Mediterranean mold, a short, neat beard did not hide the strength of his square chin. Unlike the younger men, his gray sweatshirt offered no information, his salt-weathered jeans were frayed—but the Greek cap was new and jaunty. No jewelry visible, no tattoos, no hints. I noticed all of this in one instant's alert—the sort of alarm you feel when your car skids on ice and for one second you don't know if you're losing control of the wheel. I couldn't remember the last time I'd been introduced to a man whose smile literally made my knees weak. Not to mention my breath quick, my mouth dry, and my cheeks flushed. Good Goddess! Did it show? After one heart-shaking look into those sea-dark eyes, I moved back into the crowd, cautiously avoiding eye contact, certain that this uprush of long-buried feelings was somehow written on my face. This wouldn't do. I was in no mood for it.

Joe Ulysses. I repeated the name to myself silently, wondering when I'd last combed my hair. This morning? Last night? I looked down at my old green sweater and baggy pants of many pockets. Scruffy, indignant at being leashed in the presence of the law, was tugging me toward a neighbor's retriever running free through the crowd of onlookers.

Why are we standing here? Come on, Toots—let's go, let's go.

"Be quiet or I'll lock you in the house," I said. Fiona looked at me sharply. "It's Scruffy. He was whining for a run after that golden bitch," I explained. She raised an eyebrow expressively.

"What does Heather think a mere five people can do?" I asked.

"Eight, counting us. Ten, when Phil and Dee get here." Pulling her faded coat sweater more closely around her, Fiona took a resolute stance as if daring someone to push her around. "Then there's Heather's crew from Animal Lovers. They're bringing a *Save the Eagles* banner. And a host of people from the Unitarian Church have promised a prayer vigil. I believe I heard Heather call the Boy Scout headquarters, too. It'll be like a mini-jamboree for the Plymouth troop and a leg up on some environmental badge. Wait, you'll see."

The brilliant afternoon was coming to a close by the time the Greenpeace team had organized us into a hand-holding human barrier to Jenkins's woods—at least on my side of it. Anyone could still have walked in somewhere along Route 3A. Holding our *Save the Eagles* banner breast-high, Heather and the Greenpeace woman, Kelly, blocked the most obvious entrance to the woods, a natural footpath created by a generation of woods walkers. The hunters bristled and shifted their weapons impatiently from one hand to the other. They consulted one another in angry huddles, and one of them always seemed to be sighting his rifle to the top of a pine tree as if an eagle might appear there at any moment. At one point I thought I saw a green cap moving among the rifle toting terrorists, but when I looked again, the apparition had disappeared among the trees.

Just a natural case of jitters, I told myself, unable to repress a shudder. Besides, there are lots of green caps in the world, not all of them on the heads of depraved killers.

A woman's shrill voice, emerging from between parked cars, provided a distraction from my feverish speculations. "Never mind the damned eagles—save our babies!"

"They're just a bunch of bleeding-heart, birdbrained liberals," an armed man muttered.

A television crew arrived from Channel 6 News to interview Heather and the Greenpeace team leader, whose name was Saul. The reporter, looking like a high schooler on holiday, asked what we had planned, obviously hoping for a spirited fracas and a few split heads. But Chief of Police Hurley promised there would be no vigilante action against the eagles until the matter of the baby attack had been thoroughly investigated. His interview was partially drowned out when some volunteers from Animal Lovers took turns reading aloud the text of the Bald Eagle Protection Act. Scruffy relieved himself on the police chief's squad car.

The only words I exchanged with Joe Ulysses, while the eagle-savers were still milling about, were brief and banal. "Cute dog," he'd said, turning on that devastating smile. I wondered if the heat I felt was late-blooming desire or an early hot flash. "He talks to me," I'd foolishly replied. He must have thought me balmy. Living alone too long. "He looks smart enough," he'd said. "I had a cat like that once." I was going to ask him what had happened to the cat, another dumb remark, but just then Kelly had pulled him away to confer with the rest of the crew.

Sandwiched between Phil and Fiona, I did not get to hold Joe Ulysses's hand in the human barrier, but I saw him look for me, and when he found my face, he smiled and held my gaze with his before he shook free to drive off in the Greenpeace Jeep. It wasn't my imagination. His eyes *did* reveal the same searching and surprised expression that must have been in mine.

"Where's Joe going?" I asked Saul.

"We're setting up a patrol around the perimeter of the eagle sanctuary—to discourage anyone from sneaking in there for a little dawn shoot spree."

"You mean Joe is going to drive around the borders of Jenkins's woods all night long?"

"Jonathan and Kelly will spell him sometime between one and two in the morning. Heather and I are going to camp out near the habitat itself. A little extra insurance."

"Won't all this commotion frighten off the eagles?"

"Trust us. We know what we're doing here." Up close, Saul's sincere, pale eyes had flecks of undecided hazel, but his smile was reassuringly superior. I stopped worrying about the eagles and started thinking about Joe driving around the dark woods for hours and hours.

I glanced at my watch. Only six-thirty. Suppose I hailed Joe with a thermos of coffee about nine o'clock? Would that be considered a thoughtful gesture or a come-on? Or would he simply mistake me for an eagle hunter and run me over? How did I know what sort of defensive training they received at Greenpeace?

How about some dinner, Toots? Scruffy planted himself squarely in front of me. Then he wiggled his rear end engagingly while fixing me with his best alpha dog stare.

"Good idea," I agreed.

"What's that?" Fiona asked.

"Dinner," I said in an absent fashion, my thoughts rifling through the contents of my closet. All my good shirts were in the ironing basket.

"Oh, don't fuss about us. Saul says the Vegetarian Pantry is opening its doors to us workers of the inner circle."

"Fine. I think I'll skip the vegetable party, though. After all this excitement, I need a quiet evening to myself."

"Oh, yeah?" Fiona said skeptically.

After the sun had set and most of the troops departed, I fed Scruffy and myself, then stole away to a nice hot bath scented with jasmine oil. Jasmine is a stimulant, and I meant to stay alert. My body didn't look its forty-four years, I thought—no scars on the torso or cellulite on the thighs yet.

"What the hell's the matter with me!" I said, springing up out of the lulling warmth. *Am I going to be crazy enough to let someone in that close again . . . close enough to really hurt me?* Toweling off with self-punishing agitation, I soon found myself rummaging through bureau drawers for some decent underwear.

It was around 8:30 when I decided to make coffee and three kinds of sandwiches. Ham, because real men are supposed to love ham. Chicken on the off-chance that Joe was Jewish and kept kosher, although with a name like Ulysses, it seemed doubtful. Egg salad for the possibly vegetarian Joe. But surely those brawny, tanned, untattooed arms must have been nourished by something with a little sinew to it. Should I have made roast beef? I poured the coffee into a thermos. Black? Cream? Sugar? Should I bring tea? Beer, of course, if I'd had it, which I didn't.

"This is a good example of why new relationships are so stressful," I said to Scruffy. "I know absolutely nothing about this man. What are his tastes? Is he kind? Is he literate? Is he married? Is he in the habit of practicing safe sex, because I'm not in the habit of practicing any sex so I have no proper supplies."

How about a ham-on-milkbone, Toots. Hold the mustard. Scruffy's nose seemed to be glued to the edge of the kitchen counter. Absently, I piled small slivers of ham on three dog biscuits and laid them on his sheepskin cushion.

"This is ridiculous," I said while he crunched contentedly. I wasn't going to brazenly chase Joe down the road waving a thermos, and my own nerves were jangled enough without a shot of caffeine. I poured the coffee down the sink and refrigerated the sandwiches.

At 9:00 I made another pot of coffee and filled the thermos a second time. At 9:30 I poured it all down the sink again and rinsed out the last traces with vicious thoroughness. Forgetting that I wasn't wearing my usual old sweats, I dried my hands on my best raw silk slacks—beige, to complement my pink-and-beige paisley shirt, which I thought must be stylish since it was a gift from Phil.

It was raining again, a raw east wind slapping droplets against the kitchen windows. I thought about poor Heather out with Saul in Jenkins's woods—and hoped they were guarding the eagles from the comfort of a warm, chummy tent. The thought of being outdoors made me desire a hot drink myself. When I'd made a hot lemonade with a good slug of brandy in it, I sat in the kitchen rocker to drink it, rocking double-time and feeling sorry for myself. Scruffy hightailed it out of the way. Licking the last trace of ham fat from muzzle and paws, he settled down for a snooze on the belly-cooling tile in front of the refrigerator, which now could not be opened without alerting him. I reached out and turned on the radio to WCRB "all classical, all night." Mendelssohn's Violin Concerto in E Minor. Big tears welled up in my eyes. "Ridiculous," I repeated.

At 10:00 there was a low tap at the kitchen door. Scruffy bolted upright instantly, barking and snarling, obviously embarrassed to have been caught napping when a stranger approached. My heart fluttered wildly in the sudden fear that the man Q had found the phantom photographer of the supermarket and had come to demand that his photos be destroyed. But seeing a dark, compact shape with a jaunty Greek cap through the glass panel, I snapped on the light to an appealing smile that warmed the cold November night—not a stranger at all, but someone whose eyes I remembered from another lifetime. Pausing only to quiet Scruffy with such a low, fierce, threatening tone that he backed up to the living room doorway and crouched down, eyeing me warily, I opened the door to the rain and Joe Ulysses.

"Hi," he said. Was his voice absolutely thrilling, or was it just me? "Is it too late to beg a cup of coffee?"

Gusts of rain blew into the kitchen, whipping several notes off the refrigerator door. As I stood there grinning stupidly, he must have felt the need to keep talking. "I feel silly driving around and around the woods while all the shooters have certainly gone home to get out of the foul weather. I thought the troops might still have been here making merry, but I see now that you're alone. Perhaps you're too tired to entertain. That's okay . . ." He turned slightly as if meaning to leave again, so I took hold of his sleeve and pulled him into the steamy kitchen, shutting the door on the whining, wet wind.

"Please sit down. I'm really glad you came by. Coffee will only take a few minutes. Are you hungry? How about a sandwich— ham, chicken, egg salad?" Now that I'd found my voice, I wondered if I was going to be able to stop chattering. But in the next minute—when he asked, did I know how wonderful my smile was, like a welcome home after a long voyage—I was struck dumb again.

Sitting sternly on the living room threshold, Scruffy studied this strange person. Joe leaned over to hold his hand out to the dog, who gave it a cautious sniff before allowing himself to be scratched between the ears. *He doesn't smell dangerous, but watch your step, Toots,* Scruffy cautioned.

We had our coffee in the living room, lacing the last half-cup with brandy. Joe had made a small but efficient blaze in the fireplace with just the few dry logs I happened to have stashed indoors. He ate a ham sandwich and a slice of Phil's Divine Decadence Chocolate Gâteau. I asked about his work with Greenpeace, wondering just how committed he was to saving whales and exposing toxic waste dumps.

"There are two kinds of people on Greenpeace ships," he said. "The youngish, idealistic, politically committed activists and a few seasoned characters who are paid to get a stalled engine up and running when trouble is brewing, the ones with merchant marine background, like me. Sure, I believe in what I'm doing—it's certainly more gratifying than, say, shipping Toyotas to the States, and it has its moments of high excitement. But it's still a job. How about yourself?"

As we downed the last of the brandy and coffee and burned the last dry log, I told him about the herbal products and the surprising success of my fledgling catalog. "You should see what I have stocked in the cellar. Those pine shelves that once stored jars of preserves and pickles when my grandma was alive are now filled with jars of dried herbs and essential oils, and with the salves, cosmetics, teas, and fragrant pillows I've made from them. And I love messing about with the herbs—growing and harvesting them, creating new products. It's really soul-satisfying."

"You're so beautiful," he said. He touched my cheek with one finger, just tracing lightly from eye to mouth. The skin burned where he'd stroked me.

I couldn't help myself. "Are you married, Joe?" I asked.

"I was once, but it's over. How about you?"

"The same. I thought I got clear away from him, but then he transferred to the Pilgrim Nuclear Plant. Children?"

I thought there was a slight bitter twist to Joe's mouth when he said "no." And he didn't ask me, so I volunteered nothing more about my own family. Suppose he wanted to know how old the little shavers were, and I had to admit they were all in their twenties?

The whole time we were talking, Scruffy sat beside me in a vigilant posture. *So far, so good—but you can never tell about the ones with furry faces.*

"He's cautious of my beard," Joe said, reaching over to rub Scruffy's shaggy head. His body in the neat, plain gray shirt gave off the aroma of cinnamon basil on a sunny hillside. An icy wall around my heart gave way when he turned and took me into his arms. Still, I wondered, in some small part of my brain, if that whole maneuver were not rather carefully and gracefully choreo-graphed. A girl in every environmentally threatened site?

"There's something extraordinary going on between us," he said. His lips touched mine in gentle exploration. "I think I'm bewitched."

I put my arms around his neck and drew him into my heart. "I know, I know." It had been a long time. I was hungrier for love-making than I'd ever guessed, and the feel of his beard on my bare skin nearly drove me wild. My first-floor bedroom was close by, but somehow we never got there until much later that night. I did, however, firmly shut Scruffy into the kitchen, causing him to sulk all the next morning. The sofa was deep and soft, sensu-ously scented with the herbal pillows I'd made with anise, purslane, and rose petals. We were hasty and awkward at first, but so mesmerized with each other that it didn't really matter.

Joe knew me intuitively . . . knew how to please me vividly and splendidly, and how to take for himself all that he wanted. Later, after we'd made love in a more leisurely way the second time, there was nothing strange about the feel of him beside me. Having our bodies wound together seemed entirely familiar and inevitable.

But there was one tiny pinprick of worry—the small gold cross that had been hiding under Joe's shirt. I managed to refrain from asking him if he was Catholic, if he was well and truly divorced, and did he think a difference in religion was all that important? *That* discussion might be somewhat premature. Besides, he had drifted off to sleep.

This is crazy, I scolded myself. Last I heard, you never wanted to live with a man again. So can't you have a simple one-night stand without starting to work out the wedding guest list and flower arrangements?

Not unless you pass into Summerland and come back to life as a man, I answered myself. Finally I followed Joe into sleep, but not before wondering what he was dreaming about.

When morning came, a short time later, we looked tired. We

looked our age in the surprising sunlight. And Joe looked embarrassed to be saying good-bye so soon—the *Greenpeace* was leaving that day for New York, then bound for some secret adventure he could not reveal. It occurred to me that Joe was an engineer, the same as Gary, my ex. What a scary thought!

Yet, holding him, kissing him at the door, it was all magic again. "I'll be back as soon as ever I can," he murmured. "And I'll call you. Or write. Wait for me, my beautiful, green-eyed siren."

Thinking about this later—and believe me, I did little else—I realized that my eyes are actually hazel, not green. Well, maybe green when I'm standing under a sunlit leafy tree in July. And wouldn't it be better to be likened to Penelope than to some fly-by-night siren?

Everyone in the circle knew, of course. Having driven home at eleven last night and back to the eagles at six this morning, Heather had noted that the Greenpeace Jeep was still parked in my driveway. Word of my indiscretion flew around from witch to witch while I was still buttering Joe's toast. Later, little hints were strewn in my path, but I didn't feel the need to confide in a soul. Especially not when the knowing looks turned sympathetic as the days passed and I still hadn't heard from Joe.

"Did that fantastic night really happen? Or was it all my imagination?" I asked the kitchen walls.

Scruffy growled. *That furry face never fooled me, Toots. He didn't even stay around long enough for a good ball game.*

Esbat of the Hunter's Moon

Fiona's message on the answering machine had been both urgent and incomprehensible. Reluctantly leaving unopened on the kitchen table the shipment of some special items I'd just collected at the post office—including mandrake, Chinese skullcap root, and some periwinkle for banishing evil influences—I trudged back to the Wagoneer with Scruffy bounding with delight beside me.

"Don't you ever tire of riding in the car?"

Flying, flying . . . faster than squirrels, faster than rabbits, faster than cats, faster and faster . . . As the car gained momentum, the dog stuck his nose out of the partly opened window, narrowed his eyes, and enjoyed the air riffling through his shaggy fur. *Don't you love it!*

Fiona must have been watching for my arrival, because she hurried out to meet me, holding her coat sweater closed against the damp wind. As I left my companion to complain at being shut in the car, the last leaves of autumn, the color of dried blood, whipped around us in her unraked front yard.

Scruffy yelped. *Help! You forgot me . . . I'm trapped in the car.*

"Do you remember how you behaved the last time I brought

you into Fiona's house?" I reminded him through the four inches of open window.

I promise I won't chase that miserable, lying cat this time. You can trust me, honest.

"Just stay like a good boy, and I'll get you a burger on the way home."

With a reproachful sigh, Scruffy settled down to wait, nose between his paws.

"I've found him, Cass! We've got him now, " Fiona exclaimed in triumph, tugging me away from the car toward the house. "Clayton M. Quicksall, Sachem Road, Carver."

"That's wonderful! Are you sure? How did you manage it?" Fiona steadied me as I stumbled over a broom that seemed to be weighing down a pile of sweepings in the entry. Omar Khayyám barred the living room door, arching his back and crooking his tail to protest this interruption to his nap. With Fiona still guiding my elbow, I stepped over Omar and around several piles of books on the floor near the door.

"First let me get our tea." With an industrious sweep of her hand, Fiona cleared off the newspapers festooning the sofa.

I sat down out of harm's way, grateful to have traversed the obstacle course. Omar jumped into my lap with aggressive purring that had more to do with reclaiming his rightful place than with showing affection.

"Oof! He's a heavy baby, isn't he?' I said to no one in particular, since my hostess had disappeared into the kitchen, a room I avoided whenever possible rather than spoil my appetite for whatever delicacy Fiona was preparing.

The laden tray Fiona brought back held a fat pot of tea, a basket of delicately fragrant miniature scones, and an open jar of homemade strawberry preserves. One black cat hair clung to its rim, catching the sunlight streaming in the window behind me. Fastidiously, Fiona plucked it off before pouring our tea into thistle pottery mugs. She sat opposite me in her favorite chair, judging from its accoutrements: a stack of journals with variously earmarked pages, an overflowing knitting bag, a wineglass half tucked under the chair's skirts, and a footstool, against which was leaning the ever-useful green reticule.

"Now!" she said, obviously relishing the moment. "I don't know if you remember that I was to attend the South Shore Librarians Conference in Duxbury last Friday? Well, I brought the photo you gave me—showing the man you thought might be called Q standing at Angelo's meat counter—and passed it around among my friends from other towns, just on the off-chance. Actually, I had a feeling in my bones. You know how I get these hunches sometimes. Cass, you must have some of these scones while they're still warm—an old MacDonald family recipe. I was a MacDonald, you know, before I married Rob Ritchie. Half heavy cream, half buttermilk—that's the secret, but don't tell Phil. I love to see her expression when she tries to figure out what's in them without coming right out and asking."

"So you were at this conference . . ." I prompted, accepting a scone but waving off the preserves. "No, thanks, Fiona. Scones this rich and good ought to be savored plain."

Fiona beamed at me. "I add a pinch—and I do mean, a *pinch*, less than one-sixteenth of a teaspoon, mind you—of mace. Now, I defy Phillipa to ferret that out. Also, I glaze them with heavy cream to get that beautiful color. Yes, it was Candy. Candy DeFrees. Circulation manager, Carver. Took one look and knew him instantly. Well, not exactly *knew* him, as in *knew his name*. But she remembered a man who looked like Q because he'd made rather a fuss when she wouldn't let him take out more than three books on one subject."

"What subject—did she remember?"

"Taxidermy." Fiona looked at me meaningfully over the top of her gold-rimmed half-tracks. "Kinda gives you a shiver, doesn't it? I mean, knowing what we know—or at least, *seriously surmise*, based on our trance work and considerable psychic acumen."

Omar walked across the coffee table, tipping dangerously over a teetering pile of magazines, and sniffed the scones. If a cat can be said to curl his lip, Omar did so.

"Omar doesn't care for mace. Even the slightest bit of it," Fiona said, explaining this callous rejection. "Isn't it getting a bit chilly in here? Shall I light a fire, do you think?"

"No, no, I'm fine," I exclaimed, forcing myself not to leap off the sofa. "In fact, I'm quite warm." It seemed to me that this whole room was a firetrap that only needed one spark to go up like a bonfire. I quickly changed the subject, feeling like a coward. What would happen if she lit that match when she was alone? "How did you account to Candy for your interest in Q?"

"I said the snapshot had fallen out of a stack of interlibrary loan books and I wanted to return it—assuming, of course, that it was a photo of the patron who had borrowed the books."

"Did she buy that? I mean, did Candy think anyone would care about a picture of himself shuffling through pork ribs?"

"You never can tell. We find a lot of strange things in books that people come back looking for. Personal letters and such. I could tell you stories . . . But to make the case, I explained that the photo had been clipped to a fifty-dollar bill. I said I would mail it to him if Candy could provide me with that patron's name and address." Omar leaped into his mistress's lap, clambering around to find a comfortable position, and settled in with a proprietary glance my way, as if I were disputing his claim.

"Very clever." My hand seemed to reach for another scone of its own volition. No matter the chaos in which they were created, these buttery morsels were meltingly delicious.

"Well, maybe. The problem was, Candy immediately offered to take that chore off my hands. If I refused, it would have seemed as if I didn't trust her with the money." A tiny frown marred Fiona's normally cheerful expression.

"So, how did you handle that? You didn't give her the picture to return, did you?"

Fiona buried her chin in Omar's silky black fur.

"Did you, Fiona?"

"I just couldn't think of any way around it. I even had to part with fifty dollars to go with the photo—and apologize for not having that single crisp new bill I'd described to Candy. Oh, why couldn't I have said twenty, or even thirty?"

I was silent, appalled at the consequences, mentally flipping through a Rolodex of the horrid possibilities. Finally, I took pity on Fiona, who looked as if she was going to cry.

"It's all right. We'll think of something. And I will reimburse you, of course."

"That's okay," she said weakly.

"I insist." I began to write out a check to forestall any more insincere protestations. "All right—then what happened? Did Candy call you?"

"No, she sent a memo through the interlibrary mail."

"What did she say? Do you have the note with you?"

Fiona reached into her reticule, pulled out the folded memo, and handed it over. "I'll just go freshen the teapot while you read it." Unceremoniously, she unseated Omar and hurriedly disappeared into the kitchen sanctum.

FROM: Candy DeFrees
TO: Fiona Ritchie   *SUBJECT: Lost and Found*

Have located the patron in question with some fancy detective work through our computer records. Clayton M. Quicksall of Sachem Road. Took the opportunity to return his property when he visited us recently. (No more taxidermy—he's into building some kind of brick patio now! Rather late in the year—possibly planning for spring.) He seemed quite surprised. No faith in the honesty of his fellow readers, perhaps. In any case, he asked me all about you. I hope it's okay that I gave him your address. A nice thank-you will probably be forthcoming.

Say, what about that party! Would you ever have guessed that a quiet person like Fred Peck could recite all of Kipling's "Gunga Din" from memory? And what was it exactly that you-know-who was wearing under her skirt??? Can hardly wait for next year's conference.

Best!
C.D.F.

"Oh, my good goddess," I said, reading the memo for the third time.

"What's that?" Fiona called from the kitchen over the whistling kettle.

I waited until she returned to pour forth my worries. "What will you say to him if he shows up here and demands an explanation? If he's the crazed person we believe he is, he may view the circulation of his photo as a threat. He wasn't thrilled when I took it, if you remember. I told him I was comparison shopping, that I was photographing the end-of-aisle display behind him. Now how do you suppose his photo would have ended up tucked into a library book with fifty bucks? What's he going to think? That he's being traced, that's what. How will you defend yourself if he turns up here and gets ugly?"

"I feel sure I'll be safe if our circle concentrates on surrounding me with the white light of protection and love." Omar rubbed himself luxuriously on Fiona's tartan skirt.

"*Get real*, Fiona! I mean, that's all well and good—of course we'll throw our hearts and souls into guarding you—and guarding all of us. But what if there turns out to be something like a wee loophole in the fabric of our white light? Achilles' mother missed that heel, remember?"

Fiona drew herself up with dignity and smiled in a Mona Lisa fashion. Her crown of carroty-gray braids, into which a pencil or two was always impaled, had loosened into a frizzy halo. "You don't have to worry about *me*, dear. Rob Ritchie, rest his soul in the briny deep, taught me how to protect myself whenever he was gone to sea." Suddenly she reached into her reticule and drew forth a wicked-looking pistol. She squinted and aimed at the window behind me, in the general direction of the bird feeder. Omar uttered a sharp cry and sensibly bounded out of the room.

"Fiona! Stop!" Instinctively, I ducked down, pulling a sofa cushion over my head.

"Don't be silly, dear. Get up. Forgive me for the somewhat dramatic disclosure. I bet you never realized that I carry this at the bottom of my reticule, did you?"

"I should have. Heaven knows, that bag is heavy enough."

Fiona polished a smudge on the pistol with the corner of her coat sweater of many colors and returned the weapon to its hiding place. "I also have pepper spray. Cayenne. Guaranteed to put anyone out of commission, especially if you get him in the eyes. You really ought to get yourself one of those, dear, in the present emergency. Now, do have a nice cup of fresh tea—it will settle your nerves."

I never could decide which was better, Saturday or Sunday. Whichever morning I chose to call one of my children, I often reached an answering machine, and I'd have no idea if that child was gone for an hour or a weekend. Far beyond the empty nest syndrome, since I'd moved to Plymouth I seemed to be starting over, purged of past ties like someone in the Federal Witness Protection Program.

Still, I shared a special closeness to my elder daughter Becky, a political assistant in the office of a Massachusetts senator. She often called me around six in the evening—a moment of relaxation between coming home from work and dinner. I could hear ice clinking in her glass. When she was prepared to chat with Mother, she was a delight, full of intriguing stories and great gossip to share, which I enjoyed tremendously. But she rarely asked about my life. Perhaps she thought I could reveal no surprises. She had even decided that our circle was only some kind of feminist support group.

It's a bit touchy, telling your children you've become a witch—a word that carries such a lot of negative baggage, even in our enlightened times. And yet, those nearest to me deserved to know I was veering a bit off the mainstream. So I worded my announcement carefully but casually, and I never used the word "witch." Some friends and I had formed a circle, I explained to each of my children in turn, to practice Wicca, a kind of nature spirituality religion.

Cathy thought she knew all about Wicca. As soon as she'd graduated, she'd headed for Broadway to try her luck at the theater. When that didn't work out, she'd followed some actors to San Francisco, where she lived now, alternating between small parts in theater productions and waitressing. Apparently she was acquainted with some West Coast Wiccans whose practices were on the wild side. I had to reassure her that I hadn't taken to dancing "sky-clad" on Plymouth Beach.

My lovely, ethereal youngest child, her father's favorite, had been devastated by our breakup and, since I initiated the divorce, blamed me for it. I'd been mending our relationship ever since—calling often, but not too often—always hoping that passing time would bring Cathy understanding, without my having to tell her just how bad things had been with Gary, all that I'd shielded her from in the past. I didn't want any sad stories of mine to diminish her rapport with her dad.

Adam, on the other hand, might connect with me less often through the year—although never missing Christmas and my birthday. Nevertheless I found him quite the most charming and sympathetic of my children. The computer expertise that had caused him to be transferred to Atlanta was incomprehensible to me, nor did he try to explain it. I would like to have known more about what his real life was like. Was his career soul-satisfying? Was he in love? But instead of talking about himself, he would ask me about practical matters concerning my life, from the state of my health to how the Wagoneer was behaving, and promise again to set me up with a computer program for my herb business the first chance he had to get away. After I'd told him about our circle, he always referred to it as my Wiccan study group and advised me to take a course in computers instead.

That Saturday in early November, a week after Joe left for environmental hazards unknown, I chatted with my oldest's answering machine. "Hi, Becky! This is Mom! Everything is fine here. Just wondering how you are. And by the way, how about Thanksgiving? I'd love to see you. Let me know! Bye-bye." My tone radiated the false cheer of a telemarketer selling swampland in Florida.

Adam's voice had that deep, foggy note of someone who'd just been awakened. He said no, he'd been up already, but my motherly chitchat inspired only a few groans and grunts at the other end of the line. Maybe he had a young woman there? He explained that the program he'd been working on was almost ready to run; it would be hard to get away at Thanksgiving. How was the weather up there? Still balmy in Atlanta.

Cathy was involved in a show and couldn't fly home for Thanksgiving, or Christmas, either. I refilled my coffee cup and sat at the kitchen table looking out at the sea, feeling as if waves of loneliness were washing over me. Maybe I should have called Phil or Heather to dispel the gloom, but I was more in a mood to yank out the phone jacks and wallow in melancholy. How peaceful life must have been before long-distance calling! When a child stepped onto a stagecoach or a ship, a parent knew the loss would be forever. Perhaps that made it easier to accept.

Shaking off the image of myself shading my eyes to watch the dust of a covered wagon fade into the horizon, I decided to mix up some All-Purpose Comfrey Salve in the Cuisinart. Between on/off turns of the motor, I thought I heard a timid knock at an unusual place, the front door. Putting down the spatula, I went into the front entry and leaned against the wide, red-painted planks, listening. Silence. I might have thought the sound was my imagination if I hadn't seen Scruffy just then through the parlor window. He was bounding around the side of the house and barking a cheerful greeting, which meant that the stranger was neither the paper carrier nor the mailperson, both his mortal enemies.

"Around to the back door," I hollered through the wood. I wasn't even sure if the wrought-iron hinges on the front door were still working and made a mental note to oil them in case of visiting royalty or clergy.

A slight, dark figure moved obediently past the front windows. Following to the kitchen, I went out onto the back porch and opened the glass door on a thin, brown face and two solemn eyes. The eyes were a rare shade of gray, and the rough thatch of hair was stick-straight with glints of red where the sun bounced away from its dark brown depths. The boy standing on the porch stairs wore a Davy Crockett-style jacket with a ragged leather fringe.

"Hi. Are you the lady who advertised for a handyman?" While the boy looked up at me, one hand was patting Scruffy, who had joined him on the stairs and was jumping on his pants leg. The dog licked the hand all over in an excess of welcome.

"Yes, but . . . I'm really sorry, but I need to hire a guy who can cope with some carpentry and stonework."

"I can do all that—just give me a try," the boy insisted. He looked about eleven or twelve, sixth or seventh grade.

"This job opening is for a grown-up," I explained, wondering if the boy were hungry. His eyes had an empty, guarded look.

I like him—let's keep him. Scruffy dashed down the stairs to resurrect his orange sponge ball, then rushed back to push it into the boy's dog-washed hand. Without taking his eyes away from my face, the boy grasped the ball lightly and skittered it across the yard sideways into a pile of leaves. Scruffy scampered after it joyously.

"On the other hand, I might have a few weekly chores that a youngster could handle." I thought about the cord of wood I'd ordered, that the delivery truck had dumped in a heap by the main road. Lifting that wood onto the wheelbarrow and stacking it beside the back porch would have done wonders for my stomach muscles. "What kind of wages do you have in mind? Would five dollars an hour be all right?"

The boy grinned—big, white teeth in a determined jaw, eyes that suddenly looked Asian—dispelling his unchildlike aura of melancholy. "That'd be great. Would it be okay if I started today?"

"My name is Mrs. Shipton," I said.

The boy stuck out his hand, and we shook to seal the bargain. "I'm T. P. Thomas."

"What's the T. P. stand for?" I was immediately sorry I'd asked, he looked so embarrassed.

"Thunder Pony," he said, studying his shoes. Now I noticed they were leather moccasins.

"That's an interesting name," I commented noncommittally, not wanting to make it sound like a question. I wondered if some of his family were employed at Plimoth Plantation, recreating the roles of the early Wampanoag.

He shuffled his moccasins, offering nothing.

"What do your friends call you?"

"Tip."

"Do your parents know you're applying for this job, Tip?" I asked.

"Sure they do."

"Then you won't mind if I check. Come on into the kitchen." I handed him a notepad and pencil. "I'd like you to write down your mother or father's name and phone number, please."

He hesitated a moment, looking sideways and down as if something interesting were happening on the mopboard, perhaps an unusual insect blazing a new trail for his species. Then he wrote hastily, but more legibly than most boys his age, *S. E. Thomas* and a Plymouth phone number. I decided not to ask about S. E., but I wondered.

"You don't need to talk to my Paw, do you, Mrs. Shipton? I'm saving up to buy him a Christmas present, and if you call him, it'll spoil the surprise."

If I believed that, no doubt he'd want to sell me the Bourne Bridge next. "We'll see," I said, employing the time-honored dodge of uncertain adults. "Did you happen to notice that pile of split logs up by the road? If you want to work a few hours today, you could stack the wood this side of the bulkhead, near the house but not quite against it. There's a wheelbarrow out front, by the big oak."

"Yes, ma'am!" He grinned again, turned, and raced out of the house toward the front yard with a youthful enthusiasm that usually faded out as soon as boredom set in—after about five minutes of labor. I glanced at the wall clock—11:00. He might last until noon.

Between making batches of Comfrey Salve, I glanced through the dining room windows and noted Tip's silent, steady progress as he set about his task. I checked that the wood was being stacked the right way in the right place—and that Scruffy wasn't being a complete nuisance. Unflaggingly, the dog escorted every load of wood from the road to the house, sometimes dropping the orange ball on top. Every once in a while, Tip would suddenly throw the ball to one side or the other, and Scruffy would lunge after it. The boy had a gift for not betraying his intentions by glance or gesture—inscrutable as an old man.

By one in the afternoon, I called Tip in and insisted that he quit. "Scruffy's exhausted and needs a rest," I pointed out. The dog threw himself on the braided rug, panting, his tongue hanging sideways. "If you like, you can come back tomorrow and finish the job."

The moccasins shuffled back and forth.

"How about having lunch before you go home? I'm fixing tuna sandwiches."

Tip shook his head, looking down, his hair reflecting light like dark, polished wood.

"Okay. But hold on a minute—I'll pay you the ten dollars I owe you for today." That was it—the sunshine grin came out again.

"Could I have it in ones, please?"

"I'll see what I have. Will you take a sandwich with you? And some cookies? You must be very hungry after working so hard all morning."

"Okay, thanks."

I packed the lunch before getting the money, so the boy wouldn't get away without food, adding an apple and a can of ginger ale to the bulging paper sack. All I could find were five one-dollar bills. That and a five would have to do.

Scruffy ran from window to window, watching each step of his new friend's departure from our back door to the main road. *Why is the boy leaving? Let's get him back. I want to keep him.*

"He's not ours," I explained. "But he'll be back tomorrow." Through the kitchen's side window, I was glad to see Tip munching on a molasses cookie.

No bicycle. That's unusual, I thought. Maybe he's saving up to buy one.

I changed my mind about why the boy was anxious to work the next morning when Tip showed up with an ugly purple mark that ran from his eyebrow to the lobe of his ear. "What happened to you?" I asked. "Here—let me put some of the salve I've made on that bruise. This is miracle stuff. You'll see how fast you'll heal."

"Nothing. I fell downstairs."

Sure you did, kid. I've used that excuse myself. "I'm making griddle cakes, and if you don't have some before you start work, I'll be insulted," I said. A home where a kid falls downstairs on Saturday night doesn't often provide a hot breakfast on Sunday morning.

Over blueberry griddle cakes, Tip told me that he lived with his father on the other side of Jenkins's woods. Must be some-where near Phil, I thought. Maybe she knows the family.

"I have a special place of my own in the woods. I seen those eagles that everyone's talking about." Tip mopped up maple syrup with the last bite of griddle cake, wiped his mouth, and neatly folded the paper napkin, as if for another use.

"Saw," I said automatically.

"Yeah. I got a feather, too. The eagle left it for me." He scraped away from the table, carrying his dishes to the sink. There was something familiar about the set of his thin shoulders. "I'll finish that woodpile now."

"Scruffy's waiting for you." If Tip worked as hard as he had yesterday, he'd be finished in an hour. What else needed doing? There weren't too many outside chores left in November. I'd already laid a mulch of salt hay over the herb gardens.

"Yes, I know the family," Phillipa informed me later. We sat at the marble-topped table in the middle of her magnificent kitchen, sipping cappuccino while she considered the casual heap of squashes assembled into an impromptu centerpiece. "The mother left for Maine about a year ago—there's another boy, I think. Younger. I guess she took him with her. What would you say to a coiled braid of butternut bread? Why do you ask?"

"Make it sweet, with brown sugar and raisins," I suggested. "The older son has been doing some chores for me. Goes by the name of Tip. Actually, it's Thunder Pony, but I guess he's embarrassed by that."

"You know what kids that age are like. The others probably tease him. Maybe some of the teachers gave him grief over his name, too. The father's a drunk, you know."

"I rather thought that might be the case. Tip gave his father's name as S.E. Thomas. Steven? Stanley?"

"Soaring Eagle. Listen, Cassandra . . . don't get involved." Her olive-skinned hand with short, square nails caressed the butternut squash thoughtfully. A delicious aroma wafted from her wall oven—coconut?

"What are you doing for Thanksgiving?" I asked.

She sighed. "Deidre's invited me. I suppose I'll go. Other than that, it would be my brother's in Cincinnati. What I really want to do is to cook up a big feast myself, but I've no one to do it for. Very frustrating!" She walked over to the butcher block, pulled out a cleaver, and tested its edge. "How about you?"

"Depends if Becky's coming. Otherwise it's Deidre's for me, too. I'm sure she'll let you bring the desserts. Jess never called back?"

"No, the coward. Lost his nerve over a pot roast. Don't be shocked, but I'm thinking of putting a genteel ad in the Personals column of the *Globe.*" A buzzer alerted Phil to spear the golden loaf in the oven with a cake tester.

"Are you crazy?"

"Crazy on Cape Cod. Sounds like the signature on a letter to 'Dear Abby.' Pie-eyed in Plymouth, *Meshugge* in Massachusetts—take your choice. Do you realize that winter is coming? I'm about to be snowed in here alone with a mountain of food." Carefully, as if carrying an infant, she brought the cake to a waiting wire rack.

"That looks perfect, like Sara Lee's. I bet you've already run the ad, haven't you?"

Leaning over the cake, black wings of hair falling forward, she smiled enigmatically and inhaled. "Mmmm. Pina colada pound cake," she said. "You're getting to be a regular witch, you know that?"

"Aren't you afraid you'll get mixed up with some *Fatal Attraction* maniac?" I thought of rosy-faced Clayton M. Quicksall, probably stalking his next victim even as we sat there spooning up frothy, whipped milk. The copper windowsill planters were filled with flawless green herbs, not an aphid lurking among them. Put them outside in the real November, and they'd curl up and die in an hour. "The world outside is a killing cold place with some truly evil men in it," I said.

"That *Fatal Attraction* killer was a woman, dearie. Cold and evil or not, life goes on. You're just feeling sour on men because you haven't heard a word from Ulysses. Probably gone home to Penelope." I'd finally confided some steamy details of the affair—which everyone in the circle knew about anyway—to Phillipa. We were so routinely insulting to each other, I knew I could count on her not to embarrass me with sympathetic remarks about my Greenpeace fling.

"So . . . you ran your ad seeking a poetry lover and connoisseur of fine food, and what happened?" I asked.

"I'm meeting someone at the Boston Museum this Sunday. He sounded okay—really." Phil confessed. "The museum should be an ideal place to check him out—crowds of people milling about to guarantee my safety, fine art to break the ice and appraise his cultural literacy."

"The most successful degenerates seem innocent and sincere—they inspire confidence. Otherwise they wouldn't be successful. Look at Quicksall, with his Santa Claus rosiness. No one suspects him of whatever terrible deeds he's been doing."

"You do," said Phillipa, turning out the pound cake onto the rack. "Not only that, but you've even rallied our circle as a kind of psychic posse to chase him down."

"What will you do when Mr. Wrong suggests that you leave the museum's neutral zone and have a drink with him in a trendy wine bar nearby?"

"That depends on what he has to say about the Renoir exhibit." Caught by her own reflection in the glass-fronted cabinet, she began briskly patting the underside of her chin.

Before we gathered for Thanksgiving at Deidre's, the remains of Gerry Kirschmann had been found, but not in Jenkins's woods under rotting leaves where Scruffy had turned up his sneaker. The ten-year-old's body, minus the sneaker and his key chain, had been discovered in a remote area of Myles Standish State Forest, twelve miles away. It had been wrapped in a rubbish bag and buried in a shallow grave where it might never have come to light if it were not for another perceptive canine. A hiker's bull terrier had dug madly into the partly frozen ground to unearth a fingerbone. Decomposition was already far advanced, and little could be told about what the boy may have suffered before his death. He was identified by an arm that had been broken in a fall from a tree house, two dental fillings in lower molars, and a lucky aggie he'd carried in his pocket, blue and white, like the earth's sphere seen from space.

After reading every word of the newspaper reports, I called Detective Stern for more details, explaining that I felt involved because of the Jenkins's woods connection. I wondered if the boy had been killed there and transported to the state forest for burial.

Detective Stern was less than forthcoming. "It could be . . . we don't know," he said. "You know I can't comment while we're investigating."

"Maybe Gerry's sneaker just walked over from Myles Standish," I suggested tartly.

"Maybe so," said the detective. "On the other hand, maybe you know a bit more about this boy than you've led us to believe."

"Oh, please," I said. "That's just stupid."

One thing and another, the scholarly detective and I did not part on the best of terms. Unless I wanted to make myself look suspicious, I'd better not pester him with any more questions. But I felt helplessly burdened with information—of the unbelievable psychic kind—that I was unable to disclose without getting myself into even more trouble. I couldn't very well tell him that I was a Wiccan clairvoyant. We hadn't yet tested the waters on how our neighbors would respond to a circle of Wiccans right here in Plymouth, a town that took such pride in its uncompromising Puritan ancestry. With so many people confusing Wicca with Satanism, we five had agreed to keep a low profile until we could find a way to reveal ourselves in a favorable light.

Although I wished I could present Quicksall as a suspect to the detective without involving the Wiccan connection, no bright ideas came to mind. We would have to find another way.

* * *

"We could send an anonymous letter," suggested Fiona, when we all met at Deidre's for Thanksgiving.

"Detective work is too sophisticated these days," Phillipa objected. "Suppose the police were able to trace the letter to us? Then what?"

"What do you suppose that one sneaker was doing in Jenkins's woods?" Fiona asked.

"I think the boy was murdered in our woods, but Quicksall must have thought there was less chance of discovery if he buried the body in Myles Standish. Jenkins's woods is a small, contained area. You know what a wilderness the state forest is," I said.

"It was taking quite a chance to move that body. Maybe what Quicksall did was waylay or kidnap the boy in Jenkins's woods, and then took him somewhere vastly more private for his sport," Heather said. "Before we approach the police, however, we must have more evidence."

"We'll just have to gather what we need ourselves. Let's not wait until another kid gets tortured and murdered," Deidre whispered, hearing Will stamp in the door of their mudroom after a quick walk with Salty and Peppy. The discussion would be tabled until another, more private time. Now, it was back to the Thanksgiving festivities.

Looking around Deidre's table, I saw that we were all there, the circle complete. Facing the holiday must have been as demoralizing for the others as it was for me. Behind the merry smiles, the expressions of satisfaction, and the sentimental toasts, weren't we all wondering why we found ourselves essentially alone on this depressing family occasion? Well, yes, we were all here together in Deidre's showroom of Colonial arts and crafts, sharing her bounteous family, who had taken us to their bosoms like a cluster of orphans. But that was the emptiness of it—the turkey dressing was not seasoned in our own special way, from a

recipe passed down by our own grandmother, for the nourishment of our own kin. It was just as well to have an absorbing
problem to occupy our reflections.

"A simply beautiful dinner, dear," Phillipa said. She pushed a
spoonful of candied yams stuck with mini-marshmallows under
the turkey skin on her plate.

"Do tell us more about your date from hell," our hostess commanded Phillipa. "What was that remark about the Renoirs? I
was whipping the potatoes and missed half your story."

"What Renoirs?" asked her husband Will, who was ignored.
He grinned and reached over to tousle the reddish-gold curls of
his small son. The once-handsome basketball champion shone
through his thickening features.

"Fascino—he said his name was Fascino, do you believe it?—
Fascino said the colors were pretty but any true art lover could go
into a gallery on Cape Cod and find really inspiring paintings of
waves breaking on the rocks or seagulls flying over dunes at sunset. Nicely framed and affordable, too," Phil said tiredly. "But
that wasn't as bad as the poems he recited from memory. His own
works, of course. I don't think I can go through all the sordid details again. Listen, Cass—Dee's over at the mall every day. Aren't
you going to ask her to check out their Santas?"

"Okay—later."

It seemed a shot in the dark, but when Will went upstairs to
the bathroom, I suggested that Deidre find out what she could
about who was playing the "right jolly old elf" at Massasoit Mall
this year. Given Quicksall's deceptive mien, it was at least possible that he might use such a gambit to select his next victim.

"Gosh, now I'm going to feel nervous about having Bobby's
photo taken with some depraved beast in Santa's clothing."
Deidre cast a worried glance down the table where her youngest
was running a tiny pickup truck through the hills of mashed
squash on his high chair tray. "Oh, for goodness sake, look what a
mess Will let him make," she added sharply. "I'd better clean
that child up before he's dyed orange permanently."

"Don't worry—it matches his hair quite well," said Phillipa. "If I were you, I would forget the photo with Santa during the present emergency."

"Haven't you given him a little amulet to ward off evil?" Fiona asked as Will came back and took over the job of de-squashing Bobby.

"Are you kidding? Show your amulets, children," Deidre ordered. Jenny and Willy Jr., who had left the table and were building a car wash with Bobby's wooden blocks, obediently pulled up the gold crosses that hung from chains under their shirts. "And the ones in your pockets, too." Small, grimy hands fetched up plump little earthenware Willendorf goddesses from their pockets. "And don't you dare ask me about conflicting values, you witches. I just want my little ones to be protected. And I believe in everything. So wipe that supercilious smile off your face, Phil."

"I was just wondering . . . is this overkill? Or its opposite— oversave, maybe?"

"Well, it's certainly not oversight," Heather declared, reviving from her post-turkey slump.

Little Bobby chortled and banged a fist on his bib. His father disentangled the cross hanging about his chubby neck, which was coupled with a silver ankh. "Bobby wants you to know that he has a cross, too, just like a big boy."

Everything that falls under the table is ours. Scruffy was explaining the Thanksgiving protocol to Deidre's poodles. All three dogs had stationed themselves at the children's end of the table, the high chair evidently being the choicest begging station.

"Behave yourself! Good manners," I warned him.

"I'll try," Phillipa said with a frosty stare.

"Not you, Phil. I was conversing with Scruffy. Heather talks to her dogs, too—don't you?" I looked across the table for confirmation. Heather was beaming, glassy-eyed from too much white zinfandel, which wasn't white at all but rosy-pink, tasting like the Kool-Aid of wines.

"When I want to have an intelligent conversation, yes," Heather agreed. "Or any conversation, rattling around in the old home-stead by myself."

"Then, they talk back to you, right?" I hoped a fellow dog fancier would understand my situation.

"One bark for yes, two barks for no," she replied unhelpfully, with a dainty hiccup.

Gazing at the ravaged turkey carcass propped in front of her husband, who had been less than expert with the carving knife, Deidre asked if Heather and I would like to "take some home for your puppies," possibly hoping for a reprieve from making turkey soup.

"Oh, no thanks. We mustn't spoil them with table food," Heather demurred. "They're all fed a high-protein, nutritionally balanced dry kibble. Dogs prefer that, you know. It's their human companions who get bored dishing out the same old stuff and crave a change."

Obviously, she's never consulted her dog. From under the table, I heard a crunching sound and a smacking of lips.

"I hope that's gristle and not bone," I said.

"Of course, and good leg meat, too," Deidre replied, thinking I was impugning her kind offer. "Naturally, I would never allow a dog to have poultry bones."

"I trust that everyone has saved room for dessert," said Phillipa, who certainly had. Deidre's buffet overflowed with the largesse of Phil's invention—such meringues and chiffons and glazes as are only seen on the glossy pages of gourmet magazines. Deidre's three children bounced up and down in anticipation.

"I enjoy living alone." Fiona echoed my inner reflection. "My dear Omar is all the company I need. Apart from the fascinating people who speak from books, I don't require constant interaction. That's just me, of course," she added modestly, having succeeded in getting everyone's attention. "I don't expect everyone to feel as I do. You girls are younger and probably ought to have . . ."

Seeming to lose her train of thought, Fiona began rummaging in her reticule. She came up with a mangled *New York Times* clipping, which she thrust across the table at me. "Former Soviet Union Frees Whaling Protesters," Fiona recited the headline.

"Oh, that must be Greenpeace," I said. Jolted out of my after-dinner lethargy, I took the clipping out of Fiona's hand and read it aloud. "November twenty-fourth—this was in yesterday's paper!"

> *Six Americans and a Canadian, members of a Washington-based environmentalist group, Greenpeace USA, who were seized in Siberia for passing out leaflets to workers at a whaling station, were released earlier today. The protesters, who had crossed the Bering Strait from Nome to Siberia aboard the* Moby Dick *in order to draw attention to the killing of whales to provide meat for minks at a fur farm, were in good health and said they had been treated well.*
>
> *Immediately following the arrest of its landing party two weeks ago, the* Moby Dick, *refusing to halt as ordered, departed from Siberian waters. After several diplomatic talks with a specially deputized United States consular officer, Siberian officials decided not to treat the intrusion of the Greenpeace team as a criminal act. The seven men were returned to Nome aboard a Soviet research vessel.*

"Well, no wonder you didn't hear from him," Deidre exclaimed.

Not a phone call in three weeks. Not even a postcard. I supposed there weren't any postcards of icebergs or polar bears in the Siberian prison commissaries.

Phillipa, who was cutting perfect slices of pumpkin-maple chiffon pie with a wet knife, cast a significant glance my way and winked.

"How are the children, dear?" asked Fiona, leaning toward me confidentially across her dessert dish.

"Busy," I said.

She sighed. "Sometimes I wish . . . But then I do have nieces and a nephew. I'm especially fond of my niece Belle Mac-

Donald—Tinker Belle, I used to call her when she was small. She has that certain spark. It's possible that I could teach her some things. I've never met your children."

"They were all out on their own before I moved here. Becky promised to visit at Christmas, and Adam may be able to get away, too. You can meet them then, if you like."

"She's the one in politics? And your son?"

"Adam's in Atlanta. Computers. Becky's getting engaged, I guess. I haven't met the young man yet, but his family's Old Boston and political. She's being presented to them this Thanksgiving. And Cathy, my youngest, is in the theater in San Francisco."

"She's the one," Fiona said.

"Yes."

"The one who's healing the child within by distancing herself from the mother?"

"Right."

"It will pass."

"So will a kidney stone. Meanwhile, the pain goes on."

"Pumpkin chiffon, strawberry marscapone, pear praline, or divine decadence chocolate *gâteau?*" asked Phillipa.

"Decadence," Fiona, Heather, and I chorused. In chocolate, if not in life.

Esbat of the Laughing Moon

"How could Fiona be so dumb as to allow her address to be given away?" Deidre shook her blond curls with pert disapproval, wafting my way the scent of lily cologne that mingled oddly with the smells of lemon disinfectant and rain-wet dogs that permeated the kitchen.

Saturday morning. We were sitting across from one another in her jonquil-yellow breakfast nook, sipping coffee that was both weak and bitter. Salty and Peppy scampered around the kitchen playing tug-of-war with a soft-rope bunny Deidre had crafted for them. Lying on my feet under the table, a soggy Scruffy was expressing some extreme of canine *ennui* with repeated deep sighs.

"Well, it's done now," I said, and heard a tone in my voice sharper than I intended. "We'll just have to be on our guard, that's all. A banishing next Esbat, I'd say. Protection rites. Anything else we can think of. It's a comfort to know that if creating a surround of white light fails, Fiona does have that pistol."

"I'm not surprised. I think I almost knew there was something formidable and peculiar in that dreary green satchel she never lets out of her grasp."

"So, all I'm asking is this," I continued, broaching the subject cautiously. "Would you lend me your kids and your van—and yourself, of course—for a drive through Carver? A dark day like this—I don't think Q will recognize me in a strange car with a strange family. Strangers—that is, unfamiliar to him."

"Say what you mean, Cass. You want to use my family as a blind while you spy on a maniac killer." Deidre passed me a plate of fat-free, sugar-free Nature's Bounty cookies, in case I'd missed noticing it on the table between us.

"Well, I wouldn't put it quite that way." The sound of cartoons at full blast seemed to rise up through the floor tiles from some subterranean retreat.

"I wonder what possessed you to bring this danger into our midst, Cass. Do you really have enough to occupy your mind these days? There's your herb business, of course, and that's going quite well, isn't it? Judging by the way Earthlore has created its own devoted following at my place in the mall—and the gratifying response to your catalog. But pottering about with salves and lotions doesn't exactly fill up your life, does it? Perhaps it's time for you to think about getting married again. You don't want to end up like Fiona, do you? Rattling around alone in that incredibly dusty, cluttered cottage, which any day now I expect some concerned neighbor to report to the Board of Health." Deidre took another tiny, precise stitch in the pansy border of the guest towel she was embroidering.

"Fiona prefers the solitary life. And besides, she has Omar." Scruffy sighed even more deeply, muttering something I couldn't quite hear. I handed him a piece of cookie under the table, which he sniffed and refused. Dislodging the dog from my shoes, I brought my cup to the sink where I could dispose of the rest of the coffee and cookie without comment. Salty and Peppy bounded under the table, yapping at one another. "Why are married women such persistent matchmakers?"

"Not me." Deidre replied. "Perhaps you haven't noticed that I never advise Heather to find another husband. Frankly, I wouldn't want to have that on my conscience. She does seem to have a penchant for scoundrels, even though she's such a strong person psychically. It must be her kismet or karma or something like that. Otherwise, she'd just zing out her wish to the cosmos, and Mr. Reliable Person would come zooming back."

Now thoroughly on the defensive, I wondered if Deidre might be making the same simplistic observation about me. "It's not that easy to bring our desires into the world of form, as you well know. If it were, we would all be spiritual adepts enjoying perfectly realized lives."

"Speaking for myself, I'm not quite ready for perfection yet. I'm just working on a few creature comforts, occasional healings, and the odd malediction." Holding up the towel, Deidre assessed her handiwork with shrewd, pale blue eyes. "And now, of course, this project of yours, this Q. And the evil that emanates from the death of the Kirschmann kid. We're forced, I suppose, to confront the situation and do something about it. Without, of course, revealing . . . our abilties."

There was a barely audible snarl under the table, and a sharp yelp following. Salty rolled out from beneath the yellow Formica and leaped into Deidre's lap, while Peppy barked furiously.

"Play nice, Scruffy. Well . . . will you?"

"Will I what?"

"Help me to reconnoiter Q's place in Carver."

"Yes, that's what I'm saying. I'm for it. This rain is getting on my nerves anyway. I never thought I'd be looking forward to snow, but now that it's December . . ."

"But not the puppies, okay?" I interrupted the weather lament. "Because if we're lucky, and no one's home, I may take Scruffy out of the car to scout the area. He's quite clever, you know. He did turn up that sneaker."

I hope you don't expect me to ride in back with the Brady Bunch. They're worse than these two idiot hot dogs. Scruffy stalked out into the middle of the kitchen, deliberately sat on the rope bunny, and tried to fix me with his most powerful dominant stare.

"Look at that cute face!" Deidre exclaimed. "Is he adorable or what? Cass, have you ever noticed that Scruffy looks exactly like that woebegone hobo dog in that movie? I bet he's begging for a piece of this cookie—aren't you, honey?"

Scruffy stared at the proffered cookie as if it had been baked on a planet far, far away. He licked one corner of it, took it into his mouth, then let it fall to the floor. It crumbled into dry fragments that were instantly inhaled by the two eager poodles.

"What about Joe Whatsizname?" Deidre asked, breaking off a purple thread with small, even teeth. "Anything promising there, now that he's been released from that Siberian prison? More coffee? I'll heat it up."

"No, thanks. I still haven't heard from him. I don't know if I'll ever see him again—or if I want to." The moment I spoke those words aloud, I realized that I was indeed cherishing some fervid hopes in that direction.

"Don't try to kid me, sister! You want him, all right. The bond that ties the circle together is getting pretty strong, you know. There's no way we can keep secrets from one another." Deidre gazed out the kitchen window at the neatly hedged yard with the swing set shining in the rain, and two precisely placed, leafless maple trees. Feeling her palpable dissatisfaction, I waited silently while she traveled in some other realm of thought. When a hazy image formed in my mind, I deliberately turned away from it, not wanting to intrude. But an impression remained nonetheless—a man running to a house aflame. A cry . . . unquenchable, unbearable heat . . . a burst of searing light. Was she wishing Will safe—or consumed?

Deidre was right about that connection between us.

By the time we began our expedition at noon, the sky had cleared. A cold sun shone fitfully through small, high clouds. Sachem Road, off a desolate stretch of Route 44 studded with boarded-up ice-cream shacks and abandoned farm stands, was badly paved but passable. Quicksall's place, an L-shaped farmhouse identified by his name on a silver-colored mailbox, appeared freshly painted, a pale minty green. The grounds were tidy, bordered by woods. Beside the house stood a venerable barn of weathered shingles. The nearest neighbors were a cluster of shabby ranch houses we had passed a quarter of a mile away as we came off Route 44. On our third drive-by, we slowed to a crawl, then continued down Sachem Road as it curved through more woods, past two cottages, one peeling white and one dark red, and ended at a crossroads where there were a seedy gas station, a desolate barbershop, and Ellie's General Store. Another farmhouse beyond the crossroads bore a *For Sale* sign staked into the front lawn.

"Let's circle around one last time, maybe take an even closer look," I suggested to Deidre. "I could take Scruff out for a walk. No car in the driveway. Everything looked quiet. I don't think he's home, do you?"

Her two oldest children, Jenny, six, and Willy Jr., five—Baby Bobby had been stashed with her mother—paused in their jostling and pushing in the backseat to commence whining for lunch. It was now 1:30, and I couldn't blame them. I was getting hungry myself. Deidre's jaunty beret had gone seriously askew, and she looked as cross as I felt. Scruffy, relegated to the rear of the Plymouth Voyager, behind the children's seats, thrust his nose farther out the partially open tailgate window, detaching himself as much as possible from the turmoil.

"We'll just drive back the way we came, and then it's on to the Lobster Shack," I promised the children.

"Will they have hamburgers, Aunt Cass?" asked Jenny.

"I want peanut butter and banana," said Willy.

"Okay, one more slow pass." Again Deidre turned the van around at the gas station and headed back into Sachem Road. "I veto the walk. I'm beginning to get bad vibes. Just in case he's there, try not to be seen. Otherwise, he may add the children and me to his enemies list. Scrunch down a little when we go by."

"Can I scrunch down, too?" Jenny giggled hopefully at this prospect of a grown-up game.

"I'm hungry," Willy complained. "And I have to go to the bathroom."

"Quiet, you two. Aunt Cass and I are trying to sleuth here." While Deidre slowed at the silver mailbox, curiosity overcame me and I opened the window and leaned out, looking for signs of . . . what? A gun at the window? A frozen body sticking out of the woodpile? I longed to get out and look around. *No, this is crazy.*

"This is crazy." Deidre echoed my thoughts. "Okay, so now we know where he lives and what the house looks like. Now let's get out of here and get something to eat."

Scruffy abruptly shifted his attention to the front seat and sniffed the air, his ears pricked up. Suddenly, two black streaks shot across Quicksall's lawn, barking and snapping. The streaks metamorphosed into a pair of Dobermans frantically jumping at Deidre's front tire.

Snarling back, Scruffy tried to claw open the tailgate window. When that didn't work, he leaped over seats and children into the front, the better to parry this attack. One of the Dobes vaulted so high, he nearly reached my window. Hastily, I pressed the button to close it.

Let me out! Let me out! Scruffy was trampling my lap.

"Those sons of bitches aren't going to let me get past," Deidre swore, heedless for once of the impressionable young. Slowing down even more only gave the demonic duo a chance to rush in front of the car so that our only choices were to stop or to run them over. Now Scruffy had his paws on the dashboard, knocking the rearview mirror aside, the better to growl savagely through the windshield at these attackers.

We were so occupied with the furor that we didn't notice when the barn door opened and a man emerged—until we heard a sharp whistle. The Dobes appeared to freeze in mid-leap. They turned toward their master in unison and hightailed it back as he walked forward. My gaze followed the dogs in amazement, as startled by their flight as I had been by their assault. I found myself looking into the narrowed, angry eyes of Quicksall.

"Holy shit," I said.

"Not in front of the children, please." Then Deidre turned and saw him, too—the big, choleric man now standing in the dirt driveway halfway between the house and the mailbox, the two Dobes sitting attentively in front of him. "Wow, I think he remembers you, Cass. Let's get the hell out of here." She gunned the motor as she spoke, odd bits of gravel flying in our wake as we sped back toward Route 44.

I began to feel exhausted and depressed. What was I doing out in the wilds of Carver being besieged by wild animals? " 'Cry havoc, and let slip the dogs of war,' " I murmured.

"You forgot to scrunch down, Aunt Cass," said Jenny. "See me? I'm all scrunched down, like you said."

Scruffy lay panting across my lap. *Water, I need water. It's not an easy job, keeping you safe.*

Sam Tucker was in for a nasty surprise when he unveiled his proposal to the Plymouth Planning and Zoning Commission—to turn Jenkins's woods into a handsome, upscale community of condominiums called the Governor Bradford Estates. He'd heard about the bald eagle rally, of course, but apparently he was undeterred in his plan to acquire and develop the property. The lawyer Tucker brought with him was well known as an able fellow from an important firm. Doors always opened for Tucker, and this time would be no different.

But formidable forces were arrayed against him. The circle was present in full force, and Heather had already lobbied every environmental agency in the area.

Right at the start, members of the Inland/Wetland Conservation Commission countered Tucker's proposal with a petition to declare the Jenkins property restricted under the Wetlands Protection Act and confirm its status as a habitat of the American bald eagle. From then on, the meeting really heated up.

Tucker's face mottled from red to purple. "What do you mean, 'endangered,' " he yelled. "Those damned predators are multiplying like a bunch of rabbits. Flocks of them all over the country." The lawyer whispered in his ear, no doubt trying to keep his client from exploding.

A reporter from the *Pilgrim Times*, who had been lightly dozing in the back row, suddenly came to life. Quickly he swung his camera into place to catch Tucker shaking his fist, a photo that would appear on the front page the next day.

Heather, looking regal with her crown of shining bronze hair, jumped up to protest Tucker's outburst. "Sir, our eagles may not be, strictly speaking, 'endangered,' but they're still considered 'threatened' and their habitat is therefore protected. And what a wonderful and fitting symbol it is that a breeding pair has chosen historic Plymouth as their home."

The camera could be heard clicking again.

Phillipa and I clapped furiously while Fiona sorted through her reticule, which was spilling over with supporting legal summaries she'd printed out of the library's computer. Deidre had brought her husband Will and her embroidery, an eagle pillow cover. Her sharp little needle continually speared the material as she nudged Will to join the discussion.

Lucien Jenkins stood up and waved his cane at Heather. "What about me?" he shouted. "How the hell am I going to sell the place after you've slapped a restriction on building against it? I'm not a young man, you know."

Will lumbered to his feet reluctantly. "I propose that we look into buying the land ourselves—I mean, the Town of Plymouth. A fair offer, Mr. Jenkins. So's you'll get your money, and all these environmental folks will be happy."

We clapped and cheered as Will sat down, grinning. Deidre beamed at her husband and hugged him. A few members of the zoning board nodded in an agreeable fashion. Will's suggestion would be a popular one. Many residents besides ourselves wanted to keep Plymouth from becoming overdeveloped, and beautiful wild places like Jenkins's wood from being razed to make way for condos.

"Happy!" Tucker screamed at such a high pitch, I wondered if there were a doctor in the house. "What will *I* have to be happy about? I've invested in surveyors, architects, draftsmen . . ."

"Not to mention those expensive payoffs," Phillipa whispered to me.

"Don't you think you could have brought up this nonsense a little earlier, like before I spent a fortune?" Tucker rolled up his beautifully drawn development plan and swatted the table with it. "And what the hell *is* this wetlands, anyway? Nothing but a damned hole in the ground."

In answer, a friend of Heather's from the Massachusetts DEP got up and read the eight types of land defined as wetlands in the Wetlands Protection Act.

"Sounds like most of Plymouth," Phillipa murmured.

"Dunes! Flats! Creeks! Are you kidding me?" Tucker turned his back on Heather and the DEP representative and faced the hall where about forty residents were spread out among many empty chairs. "Might as well give up all new construction in Plymouth and turn it into a damned bird sanctuary. You know what I think? I think habitats for *people* ought to come first. People deserve consideration. *I* deserve consideration—after all I've done for this town!"

Phillipa chuckled wickedly, and that made me laugh, too. Fiona joined in, and Deidre's giggle floated across the room. Our amusement was contagious. Soon someone else snickered, and there was a burst of levity at Tucker's expense.

The lawyer sighed and closed up his bulging briefcase.

"You haven't heard the last of this," Tucker declared, casting furious looks around him as he stormed out of the hall, waving his plans overhead like a cudgel.

"Oh yes, we have," Heather announced in ringing tones.

"Wow!" Deidre said, leaning over from her row into mine. "Am I proud of us!"

"Me, too. Magic happens," I agreed.

* * *

I was still feeling our power when it was my turn to be the hostess at our December Esbat of the Laughing Moon. It should have been a time to honor births, children, and beginnings, to banish sadness and sleep, but our ceremony took a somber turn.

Deidre had brought printouts of articles about one more murdered boy and two who were missing. She'd helped Fiona cull them from the library's microfiche, reports from the *Quincy Ledger* and other newspapers in Amesbury and Portland, plus information about those same cases printed in the *Boston Globe*. "These span the past year and a half," she explained. "There were more disappearances, of course, but I ruled out those whose histories suggested kidnapping by the noncustodial parent. That left these—two vanished off the face of the earth, no trace ever found by the police or the FBI. The third, a particularly foul murder, still unsolved. Study these faces, Cass. Perhaps something will ring your inner bell."

My fingers traced the young, smiling faces, the insistent cowlicks and askew collars of school pictures. Only a pervasive melancholy. But there was a vague familiarity about the boy from Portland—Leroy Wilson. "Maybe this one," I said, reading the headline and captions, and studying the grainy photo closer. He could have been the boy in my vision. And even more chilling, with his stick-straight hair and broad grin, the boy looked a little like Tip, who had become as dear as family to me. His frequent visits "to see if any chores needed doing" were a welcome part of my day-to-day life. A terrible fear squeezed my heart in its fist.

Hundreds of searchers look for Leroy Wilson. Ten-year-old disappears en route to Halloween party.

And then, at a later date:

The body of Leroy Wilson found in woods off Route 95. Boy was assaulted and murdered.

"Maybe Leroy. I'll keep these clippings, okay?" I kept my voice steady, but I couldn't fool Fiona.

"Leroy, for sure. Trust your first impulse," she said, putting her warm, comforting hand on mine, "before your conscious mind gets a chance to equivocate. Have you read Eileen Garrett's *Awareness?*"

"Fiona is a walking reader's guide. We ought to have her bound in volumes." Phillipa arched an expressive black eyebrow and looked around the circle. "This is getting serious, isn't it? I don't like looking at these innocent faces, imagining what might have happened, whether by Q or another. But Cass *does* see Q involved in the fate of these boys, so that means the matter has come to our door. It may be up to us to stop this horror."

"Right. Let's get busy, then." I drew our circle with my athame, the sacred space in which we would work between the worlds. After the ritual invocation, we centered a photo of Q—looking quintessentially suburban at the meat counter—and called upon Hecate, lunar goddess of the underworld, to help us. We raised our energy to stop Q from preying on boys. We burned flax and ash for banishing. We sprinkled ourselves with a tincture of anise and valerian for protection.

After I opened the circle and dispersed the energies we'd invoked, we made amulets of dried avens root, *herba benedicta*, to keep us safe. I attached one to Scruffy's collar and wondered if I could talk Tip into carrying an amulet in his pocket.

While we were having sage tea, I noticed that Fiona was nervously clutching her green reticule, as if reassuring herself of the ultimate banishing power secreted within. When she reached in and drew something from its depths, I instinctively ducked, feeling like a total fool when I saw it was only a gray book sporting several disparate bookmarks.

"Listen to this!" she commanded, drawing herself up with her most authoritative fairy-godmother demeanor. Adjusting her gold-trimmed half-tracks, she read aloud in ringing tones: " 'Hecate is believed to haunt tombs and crime scenes, and to watch over crossroads. In the ancient world, her triple image frequently was erected at a crossroads, where offerings would be left and prayers made on the eve of the full moon.' " Removing a sharp pencil from her untidy knot of hair, she underlined some important phrase, breaking the pencil point, and snapped the book shut. "That's what we must do. Set up Hecate in that crossroads at the end of Sachem Road, and invoke her against Q."

"Where do you suppose we will get a statue of Hecate in triplicate?" asked Deidre, full of amused interest at this outburst. Her merry eyes sought each of us out, as if polling for clever responses "Shall we rob a museum?"

"That's an interesting idea," Heather said thoughtfully.

"Get real, Heather," I said, passing around a plate of herb scones of my own devising.

Phillipa took one, sniffed it gingerly, broke it in half, and studied the crumbling insides as if expecting my recipe to pop out, like a fortune from a fortune cookie.

"Leave this to me," Heather continued, undeterred. "Q knows too much already about Cass, Fiona, and Deidre. *I* will arrange for Hecate at the crossroads." With her shining chestnut braid coiled around her head, the supple brown suede outfit she was wearing, and the athame in its sheath at her belt, she looked like Maid Marian planning a medieval caper. Somehow she inspired our confidence.

Deidre offered to prepare a binding spell for the Hecate altar "guaranteed to tie Q's guts into knots," as she described it. Fiona insisted that Deidre keep her work on the white side—no black magic, as we had agreed.

"All right, then," I said, "if there isn't any other new business, let's open the wine!"

The day after the Esbat was crisp and windless, the Atlantic like rippled silk, the sky as clearly blue as the world before air pollution. I was restless and sick of myself for hanging around the phone waiting for Joe to call, so I decided on a foraging expedition for Yule greenery and holly in Jenkins's woods with Tip as my assistant—my excuse for paying him an hourly wage.

We followed the path of least resistance, a narrow trail where generations of walkers had found the easiest footing around half-buried rock and bulbous root. In time the beaten earth became more resistant to undergrowth than the softer, more hospitable composting layers a few inches to the right and the left. Even Scruffy naturally trotted along the winding path several lengths ahead of us, looking back occasionally to make sure we weren't wandering off. Once satisfied that we weren't lost, he allowed himself a few diversionary sprints to startle a chipmunk or tree a squirrel.

"Good boy!" I would compliment him when he sauntered back proudly. Years of child raising had programmed me to express admiration for trifles.

The woods in December, having begun in sodden burnt orange, had darkened to a dismal brown, but this day was pleasantly sunny, and we were sheltered from the chill east wind by thick walls of trees. Tip, the silent scout, walked neatly ahead carrying a bushel basket while I thrashed around at the rear. He was not a chatterer; the silence made a talker of me, like a nervous TV interviewer dealing with a laconic guest.

"What will you do with your wages?" I asked. "Buy a bike?"

"Nope."

"What then?" It occurred to me that if Tip were ten years older, this line of questioning would be rude.

"I'm saving for a clarinet."

"Oh, how interesting. Do you play?"

"I took some lessons at school."

"Are you still taking them?"

"Nope. I play the recorder now. It was my aunt's." Tip volunteered something at last, holding a low, thick pine branch out of my way.

I remembered the oddly hatted figure I'd seen in the woods

when I'd first gone searching for wetlands. "It's possible that I may have heard you—when Scruffy and I were over near the brook one rainy afternoon. Do you play there sometimes?"

"I have a place there. My own place," he explained.

"A clubhouse? A tree hut?"

"Nope. It's better than that."

I guessed it must be some abandoned bog worker's shack, but judging by my own son Adam's boyhood hideouts, I knew better than to expect an invitation. The thought of Gerry Kirschmann intruded itself, a shiver of icy fear.

"Do you happen to know a big, red-faced man that some of the kids call 'Mr. Q'? Quicksall, his name is."

He walked on without answering. Finally he said, "Maybe. I might have seen him around the track fields when school started. I think he was coaching something. But he wasn't with us runners."

"Stay away from him, Tip. He's a very dangerous man, especially to boys. I can't prove any of this—but it's something I *know*. I don't want you to get hurt."

"How do you know? What about the other kids—are we going to warn them?"

I was saved from answering when something remarkable took Tip's attention. He put his finger to his lips, then pointed to the right and upward. My gaze followed his trajectory to the top of a towering pine. A dark hunk perched on one of the highest branches.

"Uh-oh," I whispered. "Where's Scruffy?"

A single, sharp bark answered. It came from the bend in the path where clumps of thin, young oak trees were woven together like a giant basket. I glanced back at the lofty pine. The wide, black wings fanned out magnificently. The eagle rose and circled high above the furry intruder.

Untying the leash I'd wrapped around my waist, I whistled softly. It was a mistake. Scruffy, for once instantly obedient, bounced out of the screening oaks onto a length of marshy clearing, cocked his head, and looked at me. *What's up, Toots?*

The enormous bird hurtled down, circling the surprised dog's head with an angry scream, then soared out of sight behind the treetops, perhaps gathering force for another go-round.

Scruffy yelped, dashing toward me. I ran to meet him, wanting to get the dog securely leashed so I could haul him out of harm's way if the eagle attacked.

The next thing was a searing pain in my left knee. The leg buckled under me, and I sprawled flat in wet, cold underbrush. Still, I had presence of mind enough to snap the lead onto Scruffy's collar when he came nosing around. *This is no time to play games. Let's get out of here.*

With Tip's help, I got back to the path, every step shooting fire through my knee. I sat on a fallen log to consider my options. Should I send Tip for help? How long would that take? Would the eagle return in a disgruntled mood? The dog snuffled and tugged on the leash.

Taking the leash off my hands, Tip squatted down and scratched Scruffy's ears in a brusque, reassuring manner. "It's okay, old boy. We're nowhere near that big fella's nest, and you're too big to be his dinner, anyway, so I don't think he'll be coming back." Scruffy looked skeptical but sat quietly, plastered against my leg.

I wasn't convinced, either. "I think I can walk," I told the boy. "Let's get out of here."

"You can lean on me, if you want." He squared his thin shoulders. "But wait a sec—I'll make you a cane." With a quick, surprising motion, Tip reached under his fringed jacket, unsnapping a knife from his belt.

"What in the world are you doing with that?" I exclaimed.

"It's just a hunting knife. Lots of guys have them."

"You don't wear that to school, do you?"

"Nope. It's for the woods. Like this . . ." Looking around, he seemed to find what he wanted in the limb of a fallen log. "This one's good," he said, freeing it from the tree with quick, slanted strokes, fragrant wood chips flying through the air. In a few minutes, he'd trimmed off all the small branching twigs and presented me with a sturdy walking stick. Gingerly, I tested my weight on it. The stick held up well.

"Wow! I'm impressed," I said.

Flushed with pleasure, Tip hooked Scruffy's leash to his belt and offered me his arm. Since he was so much shorter, I settled for a hand on his narrow shoulder. We'd come a long way from my side of the woods, and our passage was slow. Soon I was leaning gratefully on Tip as well as the stick in my other hand, trying to do the impossible—keep my weight off my left leg. We hardly spoke; I was absorbed in putting one foot in front of the other. In the hush of the woods, a chastened Scruffy trotted quietly along with us. My painful progress triggered a crush of memory that weighed me down more than my injury.

I remembered . . . that heavy arm over my shoulders. "Help me up to bed, honey."

The fetid breath in my face, his body sagging against me, pushing me into the side of the stairwell. I put my arm around his waist. He was dead weight, immovable.

"Help me, honey."

Somehow, dragging and pushing, we got as far as three or four steps up, then he began to fall backward, taking me with him. I was on the inside without a railing, not letting him go, my other hand slipping helplessly against the wall with nothing to hang onto.

He slumped down on the stairs. "Help me to bed. Please help me, honey."

"Get up, then."

He sobbed and sniffled. Finally I got him on his feet again. The higher we climbed, the more treacherous the slide down. What if I fell under him? How would I get help?

"Mommy?"

"Everything's all right. Daddy's just not feeling well. Go back to bed now."

"Daddy? Are you sick again, Daddy?"

"Becky, go back to bed, dammit. Do as I tell you this minute."

Scared face, screwing up tearlessly, she pattered back to her room.

"Help me, honey. I don't feel good." Throwing up over the stair carpet, over me.

Falling on the bed. Half unconscious but still his hands moving over me, pinching and squeezing, unable to complete the act, rolling on his back and snoring. Slowly, carefully, I unclenched myself from him. Washing up the vomit on the stairs, I almost scrubbed the color off the carpet.

Taking a shower, 3 A.M. Afraid to go to bed in case Gary would wake up, afraid to go downstairs and leave the children. Sleeping on a blanket in the hall.

"Why are you here, Mommy?"

Another night. And another night. How many years? "Help me, honey. I need you." Looking down at him, lying in a heap at the foot of the stairs. Smelling the sourness. Stepping over him and going up the stairs by myself.

For what seemed like hours, I could hear him calling me faintly. "Help me, help me, please." But only the youngest, Cathy, woke up.

"Daddy's playing a game. Go back to sleep." Put the pillow over my ears. Let the bastard die down there.

"Am I too heavy? Are you all right?"

"Sure. We're almost there, Miz Shipton. Then you can rest. I'll make you a cup of tea."

"That's okay. You've done enough."

"I know how!"

I bet you do know how to take care of the stumblers, I thought. "I'm really grateful. I'd love a nice cup of tea. Have you ever had ginger spice? It's one of my specialties."

I'm tired. Who's going to make my dinner? Scruffy growled.

"Quiet, old boy," said Tip. "I'll fix you something, too."

I looked down with some amazement at the boy trudging

along, Scruffy hooked to his belt and me leaning on his shoulder. My knee was on fire but I couldn't help smiling.

"You seem to understand Scruffy very well."

"He has his own way of talking."

"Right." I wondered how much of a bonus I could give Tip for all this without insulting him. We limped and walked the rest of the way in silence while I mulled over the money question.

Once I'd sunk into the kitchen rocker, wrapped in a terry robe, and elevated my leg, giving it a good rub with my homemade menthol salve, I said, "I don't know how much trouble this knee is going to give me, but judging from the way it feels right now, I'll probably need some extra help this week. Are you ever available after school as you are on weekends?"

Tip's melancholy look faded instantly; his face brightened. "Sure, Miz Shipton, I'm available practically all the time."

"This would be for tiresome indoor tasks—not macho outdoor stuff," I warned him.

"I can do everything," he said, puffing up his thin shoulders like a matador. "Don't you worry."

"Okay. How about that tea, then? You can have milk, though, if you'd rather."

The phone jangled, out of reach across the room. Scruffy, who'd thrown himself into a dead heap on the braided rug at my feet, sat up with a start and trotted over to lean against the refrigerator while Tip answered. "Just a minute, Miz Gold. She's hurt her knee and can't move, but I'll see if the phone will reach."

I almost wished Tip hadn't said anything as I defended my woodland foraging to Phillipa.

"You were looking for *what?*" Her tone was incredulous. "Scotch pine? Juniper? Holly? I can't believe this! Well . . . I'll be right over to take you to the emergency room. You have to make sure it isn't something worse than a sprain. And don't worry about supper. I've been testing soups."

* * *

Although I convinced Phillipa that I didn't need to be rushed anywhere, there was no stopping her from taking over the kitchen. At least, with Tip there to help me, Phil, who gloried in her own efficiency, which was indeed honed finer than most people's, didn't feel the need to take over management of my household during the crisis. Soon we were filling bowls from fragrant pots on the stove.

"Ugh!" said Phillipa, eyeing Scruffy with disfavor. "Does he always make such a mess?" Having enjoyed a Portuguese beef soup mixed with his chow, Scruffy had left pieces of kale in a neat circle around his dish, like seaweed washed up on the shore.

I think she's trying to poison us. Some of this stuff smells strange to me. The stubborn canine gourmet tossed a piece of celery out of his dish.

The boy caught my eye, chuckling behind his hand, and I smiled, wondering . . . did he hear what I heard?

The phone rang again. Oh, who else? I thought ungratefully, scraping up the last bit of the chili-chicken soup. Being taller and bigger, Phillipa beat Tip to answer it, two efficient caretakers clashing in my muddled life.

"Just a minute, I'll see if she's here," was Phillipa's response, as cold as if it were the IRS calling for an audit. "It's Gary," she whispered, her hand over the mouthpiece.

I motioned for Phillipa to hand me the phone. She started to leave the kitchen, but I shook my head at her, so she busied herself at the sink, rinsing dishes, while Tip, discreet for a youngster, took Scruffy out for a stroll.

"Hi, Gary. What's up?"

"Sandra . . . it's been a long, long time," he said. He had the deep, resonant voice of an old-time radio announcer—how I hated those oily, soap-selling tones.

"Cassandra," I corrected him. "And it's a legal change, the same as my return to Shipton."

"I'll never get used to that. Small world, Sandy. Here I am

posted to Pilgrim—actually booted up to the higher echelons—
the kids probably told you that I finally got a master's, nuclear
engineering at MIT—and I thought, hell, there's Sandy only a
stone's throw away. Chatted with Becky about her engagement—
can you believe it?—and about Christmas, which she tells me she's
spending right here in Plymouth with you."

"So?"

"So, we—Becky and I—thought it would be real nice if you
and I went out somewhere special to dinner with Becky and Ron.
Presenting a civilized front, so to speak. Maybe even rope in his
parents. I hear you haven't even met Ron yet."

"No."

"Aw, Sandy . . . what do you mean by that?"

"I mean, no. No happy family dinner."

"Now, Sandy, you don't have to worry. I've been dry for two
years."

"It's nice to know you won't disgrace Becky."

"Come on now, honey. Never mind you and me . . . try to
think of Becky. His people are a big deal in Boston politics—it
wouldn't hurt to reassure them."

"Right. Great idea. You meet Ron and Becky's future in-laws
whenever, wherever you like. Just leave me out of it. Becky will
bring Ron to meet me at Christmas. And I'm sure there will be
plenty of opportunities for me to be presented to Ron's family
sometime between now and the rehearsal dinner."

"But won't you join us now? Not even for Becky?"

"We'll all be together for the wedding, Gary. Becky's day
ought to be as lovely and serene as we can make it. But that's it."

"No compassion. No forgiveness. What kind of example are
you setting for the children?"

"They're not children anymore. That's why I'm free now. But
if they ever need an example of a clean, absolute break with the
past, perhaps thinking of me will help them to be resolute without guilt."

"You've become really hard, Sandy, a regular ballbreaker. I hear you're running with a weird crowd, too."

"Do you indeed?"

"Don't use that bitchy tone to me. The children are concerned about you. They think you're into some kind of deviant cult. Environmental terrorists or Moonies or something like that . . ."

"Listen, Gary . . . " I interrupted.

"Yes? What?"

"Don't ever call me again. Write a letter to my lawyer, or send a telegram if it's urgent. If you value that new position at Pilgrim, you'll take this as a friendly warning." Before he could reply, I hung up and handed the phone to Phillipa. "Shut off the answering machine, too, will you?" The phone rang again. "Don't answer that."

"Not a chance. How about a drink? Got anything?"

"Just wine. There's an open bottle in the fridge."

The phone rang twelve times. By then, Tip and Scruffy had returned, and I repeated my instructions to the boy, who listened solemnly without a change of expression.

It's too noisy here. I need some peace and quiet for my evening nap. Scruffy stalked into the living room. I heard him hitting the hooked rug with a thump and a sigh. Tip looked heavy-eyed, too.

"It's late. Want to stay here for the night?" I asked him.

"No, thanks, Miz Shipton. Dad might need me later, so I better get home. But tomorrow's Sunday, so I can come by early, if you want."

"Yes, Tip, I sure do. Come as soon as you're up. You can help me get breakfast. But it's dark, and I don't want to worry about you short-cutting through Jenkins's woods now. Just hang around for a few minutes—help yourself to the cookies—and Miss Gold will give you a ride home."

"Okay. Thanks." The sound of the cookie jar lid instantly brought Scruffy to life, and he trotted into the kitchen. *Did someone call for a faithful pet?*

"Come on, old fella—I'll share. Let's watch TV."

When Tip and the dog had disappeared into the living room, Phillipa said, "He seems to make himself right at home here, doesn't he?" She handed me a glass of wine and sipped her own.

"I wish he were."

"Are you crazy?" she hissed. "You just finished with all that, and you're still young enough to have some life left in you—a promising future. So what are you going to do, tie yourself down again?"

"Freedom is greatly overrated," I said. "I *do* want to start again, I *am* starting again—but for what?"

Phillipa stopped scolding and merely looked concerned. "Don't cook anything," she ordered. "I'll bring over some casseroles tomorrow, and while I'm at it, how about if I read your cards?"

"Perfect. I hope I don't begin to enjoy being laid up." What a wonderful thing this circle is, I thought. Women friends are so supportive.

After talking with Phillipa, however, two of those supportive friends called me the next morning to inquire about my knee and to psych out my interest in Tip.

"If the boy needs a job, I could find something for him at Animal Lovers," Heather offered. "We always need someone to muck out the cages and exercise the animals."

I knew such a job would be perfect for Tip and for the abandoned animals as well—someone who would really play with them. And I wished she hadn't thought of it, even though, once my knee was healed, I'd have nothing much for Tip to do at my place until spring. "I'll speak to him," I said. "Nice of you to be so helpful. What about the child labor laws?"

"I have a cousin at City Hall who knows how to fix anything. Would you guess that the zone where I live only allows three dog licenses per residence, and no kennels?"

"You don't say! Well, it's hard to count noses the way they all mill about at your place. So what exactly did Phil tell you?"

There was a pause, during which I was treated to a background chorus of yapping and snapping. Finally Heather said, "Phil says you're feeling at loose ends these days, so you're fantasizing about adopting a kid."

"That's what friends are for—half-assed psychoanalysis."

Deidre called up next, to ask if I'd like to stay with her until I was up and about.

"You're a dear, but no thanks. You wouldn't want me to miss out on Phil's gourmet meals-on-wheels, would you? And she's promised to read for me." Actually, I would rather have walked the plank into shark-infested waters than be laid up in the bosom of Deidre's little family.

"Has she? That traitor. She never reads for me."

"What's to read, Dee? There you are, happily married with a lovely, growing family, and you're expressing yourself creatively in the crafts." I finished sifting the ingredients for cranberry muffins and limped over to the refrigerator with the phone cradled on my shoulder.

Deidre sighed. "Apparently you've forgotten how much work and worry there is for a woman with a young family. I suppose you have that little Indian boy to fetch and carry whatever you need. Just be glad it isn't a permanent arrangement. No braces, no music lessons, no PTA meetings, and no failing marks in Health Habits."

"Native Americans," I corrected Deidre while measuring milk. "Some of them prefer that. And you don't have to worry about me. I'm just tucked up on the divan with a racy novel, living vicariously as usual." I cracked two eggs into the milk.

"I don't see you on the sofa. I see you at the kitchen counter. What was that?"

"Is this phone-a-vision? I would have combed my hair."

"No need to change your *au naturel* style for me. I heard a cracking sound."

"My joints, probably. Listen, Deidre . . . you don't need anyone to read the cards for you. I bet Will never gets away with anything."

"Never." She sighed again, deeper this time.

I smiled and blended the batter, liquid into dry, then threw in a cup of chopped frozen cranberries. As it turned out, the muffins were cooked and cool before Tip arrived, late, limping.

"I fell on the stairs," he explained. "But I'm all right, Miz Shipton. I can get around to help you, no problem."

"Listen, Tip—are we friends, or what?" I began to make scrambled eggs, butter sizzling deliciously in my old cast-iron frying pan.

"Sure." He washed his hands at the kitchen sink. "Should you be standing up that way? Want me to cook those eggs? I know how. My mom showed me."

"I'm leaning against the stove, so my weight's off the knee. Now, if we're friends, Tip, suppose you start telling me the truth. Do you expect me to believe that a strong, graceful boy like you just falls down every Saturday night?"

He looked at me with those clear gray eyes. There were dark smudges under them today. "Friends don't ask stuff like that."

"My friends sure do, but okay, Tip. I respect your privacy, up to a point. But I want you to know that I understand what's going on with your dad. I've been in your situation myself, and if you need me, I'm ready to help. You can call on me or come here anytime it seems like a good idea to get out of the house. And right now, you can pour milk for yourself and coffee for me. Better let Scruffy in, too." I limped over to dish out the eggs, and we sat down.

Tip applied himself to his plate, generously dousing muffins with butter and honey. "Thanks, Miz Shipton, but I can't leave Dad when he needs someone to watch out for him. Sometimes he gets sleepy and forgets he's holding a cigarette."

Smells good, Toots. The dog stationed himself under the kitchen table with his paw on one of Tip's moccasins.

"You can give Scruffy some plain muffin. And not all at once, or you won't have a moment's peace with your own breakfast—or

I guess we should call it brunch now. So, you stay up, do you, in case your dad wakes up and decides to smoke another cigarette?"

"Yeah, sometimes." Tip drank his milk down to the last drop. He glanced at the fruit bowl. "Can I ask you a question, then?"

"*May* I ask . . . Sure. Have some more milk, and help yourself to a banana or a tangerine," I suggested.

"What have you got against this Mr. Q, anyway?"

That caught me off guard. I'd thought he'd simply accepted my warning to watch out for this man. I sipped my coffee, shuffling through plausible explanations, deciding finally on a version of the truth, as I'd so virtuously recommended to Tip. "Well, to explain about Q, first I have to tell you something about myself. Occasionally I have what you might call a 'vision.' It's something like a dream, only I'm awake, So . . . in these visions, I might see or learn something I wouldn't ordinarily know. I might not be able to prove it, but I *know* this thing, whatever it is."

I looked up from my cup to see how the boy was reacting to all this. His gaze was intent on the banana he was peeling. There was no change of expression on his thin, brown face.

"This is how it happened with Q. One evening, I bumped into Q at the supermarket. He was a complete stranger, and yet he wasn't. I saw, in a vision, that he was an evil kind of person who could harm others, and who had harmed youngsters already but hadn't got caught. I was very upset by this, because although I knew he might hurt boys in the future, I didn't have any proof. If I told the police about my vision, they would just laugh and think I was crazy. I bet this sounds crazy to you, too, doesn't it?"

Tip got up and began to rinse and stack dishes into the dishwasher. "Nope. Want me to take Scruffy for a walk?"

Run! Run! Let's all go for a good run. Scruffy barked joyously, trying to tug his leash off its hook by the door.

"Okay, old fella. Take it easy. My uncle Winter Hawk was a shaman, and he had visions, too," Tip said. "Our people would ask him for advice and listen to what he had to say. They say that once my uncle was out hunting with some white men who were careless, and one of them got shot in the jaw. They were far up in the woods, and the man was bleeding bad. When my uncle put his hands on the man's face, the bleeding stopped. No one thought Winter Hawk was crazy. Don't those witch ladies who come here believe you?" He took the leash down from the wall.

"Witch ladies?" That made me smile. "Yes, they do. They're as worried as I am about Q. We're all trying to learn more about him, hoping to prove what I already know. Why do you call them witch ladies?"

"Someone said it, I forget who. Maybe at church. I'm not sure now."

Scruffy caught hold of Tip's pant leg and tugged. *Come on, boy! You're wasting a good morning.*

"Which church do you attend?" Guiltily I remembered that it was Sunday, and here I had the boy working on the Sabbath. Well, not exactly working. So far, we'd just eaten a meal together and chatted.

"Garden of Gethsemane. Right up here at the corner. But I don't have to go anymore, since Mom left." Tip snapped the leash on Scruffy's collar.

"Well, Peacedale should know," I said, feeling a bit uneasy. Petitions. They were probably taking around petitions from door to door against me. Maybe they'd organize a block-party exorcism.

Don't be such a ninny, I scolded myself. It was just a chance remark. They probably saw Phil wearing her black straw hat and toting in baskets of goodies. Or Fiona, with that carroty hair standing out all over her head, although she looks more like a fairy godmother. Or they heard the chanting. Or maybe it's the herbs—herbs have always been very suspicious. No, no—this is silly. There's nothing strange about any of us. And besides, we can protect ourselves, if need be.

"You okay, Miz Shipton?"

"Of course. You go ahead now, before that dog scratches through the door."

As soon as the boy left, I called Phillipa. "There's been some talk about us at Gethsemane."

"Let's not worry about Peacedale. We have enough problems right now. We have Q to hunt down, possibly some kind of ugly murder to prevent, and we have our eagles in Jenkins's woods to protect. Our personal lives could certainly use some work, as well. What happened to Joe Ulysses, anyway? As for me, I haven't had a date since the museum fiasco. Heather's given up everyone who doesn't have fur or a cold nose. I know it seems as if Fiona and Dee are happy with their respective lots in life, but I don't believe it for a minute."

"Thanks," I said. "I feel a lot better now. You do have a way of making my little problems pale into insignificance. If we're so adept, how come we're not rich and beloved?"

"We must be doing something wrong. I'll be over later today with your dinner, and we'll read the cards. Maybe dream up some new strategies. We just have to work harder and figure which path to take. The trouble is, we have no authority to consult—no rabbi, no priest. Is the kid there?"

"Yes."

"Well, if he hasn't gone home by the time I get here, we'll find something to keep him busy while I lay out the Tarot. He's a noticing kind of boy, don't you think?"

"Not to worry. His uncle was a shaman. Anyway, I want to keep Tip here until his father sleeps it off."

"And forever. You don't fool me."

Having nothing to do but wait for Tip and Scruffy, I threw on the lumber jacket I keep on the same hook with Scruffy's leash and limped onto the chilly porch with its deceptively bright sunlight. Gulls rose and fell, catching those glittering rays on their wings. The green-gray waves moved toward me, cold, salt, and pure. An oil tanker steamed across the horizon. One of the gulls swooped across my rotting beach stairs, dropped a clam on the rocks below, and screamed when it smashed open. A long, white wing feather tinged with brown fell and caught on the railing as the gull disappeared down the slope. A message from the goddess. I hobbled out to collect it. On the beach below, Tip ambled along with Scruffy, who was nosing every weed and shell, the two of them seemingly impervious to the freezing wind off the water.

Holding my prize, leaning on the railing, I let my being glide mindlessly with the gulls, roll thoughtlessly with the waves, embracing nothing and everything. Why all this striving? None of this matters. That letting go of everything was a moment of great freedom and power.

Dimly, somewhere on the left side of my brain, I realized this was the connection we kept seeking—that only came unsought. When the moment had passed, it occurred to me that this was some kind of ultimate paradox, impossible to sort out rationally. Wanting, needing, reaching only caused the goal to float farther away, like trying to grasp a log in the water. One should simply step into the stream of light and let the thing happen, whatever it was. I would tell the others. Meanwhile, my knee hurt more than ever. So much for the healing touch. Where was Uncle Winter Hawk now that I needed him?

Yule—The Winter Solstice

I'd answered the phone on its first ring, wildly hoping it would be Joe. But before a word was spoken, I knew from the complaining canine chorus at the other end of the wire that the caller was Heather.

"If that boy of yours still wants a job, Animal Lovers can use him to open up and clean the kennels on Sunday mornings. How's the knee? Are you able to get about yet?"

"Pretty much. I wouldn't say I'm spry enough for any strenuous nature walks yet. I keep a cane close by—Tip made it with his trusty hunting knife, the clever kid!—but it's mostly for reassurance. He'll be ecstatic, I'm sure, and you'll find he's great with animals."

"If it were up to me, no one would be tramping through Jenkins's woods, especially not any little Hiawatha with a hunting knife," Heather said.

"Oh, come now—you can't be including us. Our Wiccan circle, I mean. That would be rather ungrateful, considering the psychic sweat we put into saving the place."

"I suppose I would make an exception for us, providing you promise not to frighten our eagles again."

"It was the other way around, Heather, so get your belligerent feathered friends to sign the treaty first. And about Tip's hunting knife—try to remember that hunting is a Native American survival skill as well as a religious and social tradition. Did you call merely to berate me?"

"Not at all. I called to invite you to lunch. You can meet my new greyhound, Holmes," she replied.

"Oliver Wendell or Sherlock?" I asked. "Come to think of it, that does sound like the Baker Street Irregulars yowling in the background."

"Don't be a smartass. Holmes is a lean, intense, unsociable fellow, like the consulting detective. I thought some company might make him feel less a loner and more like a family member. Why don't you clean up Scruffy and bring him with you? It will do him good to hang out with his own kind for a change."

"Will it? He seems to prefer people. Are there going to be goodies for the dogs?" No doubt a retired racing greyhound could use some fattening up.

"Now, Cass—you know I wouldn't feed junk food to animals. It's like giving them poison. They feel much more secure on an unvaried diet of nutritious dog chow. But since this is a special occasion, there will be some liver fudge treats. Ashbery makes them with strained baby-food liver and wheat germ. Saturday. One o'clock. A good chance to fill you in on how I'm handling the Hecate at the crossroads in the Carver project. Don't dress up."

If I weren't personally acquainted with the redoubtable Ashbery, who might be ranked with some Vanderbilt nanny or butler in old-fashioned family loyalty, I would have worried what equally weird treat she planned to whip up for Heather and me. But having had Ashbery's perfect New England fare before, I accepted without hesitation. Not so my four-legged companion, however.

A bath? In water? It's against all nature. Scruffy yelped, but Tip and I already had him closeted in the bathroom. His pleas and threats were vociferous, but they went unheeded as we scrubbed and rinsed. We finished by fluffing him up with a hair dryer, scenting him with essence of pennyroyal, and tying a sporty red bandanna around his neck. The bathroom may have been wrecked, but Scruffy was now party-ready.

"Liver fudge. Dog pals, some of them surely females. You're going to have a wonderful time," I assured him. He slunk into a corner to chew off his scarf while I got myself cleaned up and Christmas-wrapped a jolly package of my natural herbal flea powder for Heather's gang.

Clean jeans and an L. L. Bean sweatshirt had seemed okay to me, but I reconsidered when I sized up Heather's safari suit from Bloomingdale's. Earth tones suited her; she looked bronzely beautiful in that flawless way that only the very rich can achieve. A ragged, furry crew from the other side of the tracks swirled around her faux alligator boots—no lizard died so that Heather could be shod. I lost count, but there must have been eight or more mutts—losers and outcasts all. Leaning against my side in utter disdain, Scruffy could sum up his feelings in one caustic word—*dogs!*

"Well, you're a dog, too," I reminded him.

Yes, but I'm more than just a warm, furry body. I have a mind, too. I exhibit personality, opinions, and occasional witticisms.

"Have I ever denied it?"

"Denied what?" asked Heather as we took our places at the table and lifted the silver domes that protected our lunches.

"Denied that dogs are an admirable species." I eyed my plate with respect, appreciation, and lustful appetite. "Please tell Ashbery that her lobster salad is to die for. I mean, what I like best about it is that it's entirely composed of lobster and some kind of homemade lemony mayonnaise."

Lunch had been served in what must have once been the conservatory of this spacious mansion but now had degenerated into a romping room strewn with more plastic bones than a desert movie set.

"I find dogs to be a cut above humans morally," Heather confessed while refilling our champagne glasses. I was thankful that she opened the French doors to allow these superior beings to disappear into her large fenced yard and relieve themselves among the trees instead of slobbering on our shoes and begging for lobster. I booted Scruffy after them with a muttered "Play nice."

It was a crisp, sunny day, perfect for creatures who are never without their fur coats—not such a chilling wind as swept shore properties like mine. In this posh neighborhood, prosperous sea captains of early Plymouth had built their handsome houses where they would be protected from the elements. But if one climbed to the third floor or out onto a widow's walk, above the decorative trees that surrounded these mansions, one would discover a commanding view of the harbor.

"If I could find a man as loving, loyal, thoughtful, and cheerful as, say, a golden retriever, I'd marry him on the spot," Heather said, continuing her tribute to dogdom.

"But you did find someone like that once or twice," I recalled.

"My first husband Chet was no puppy dog. More like a bull-frog. Full of self-advertisement, quick to leap from female to female. Rather a slimy character, especially in matters of finance. Fortunately, I was still too young to ravage my trust funds for love. What about yours?" Heather topped off my glass with the last of the champagne. Then she pulled another chilled bottle out of the silver ice bucket and began to open it with practiced finesse—probably some course taught at Vassar.

"Yes, Gary was a reptile, all right," I said, getting into the spirit of ex-husband bashing. "Snake, lizard—something like that. Cold-blooded and unpredictable."

"Then there was Roberto the Hyena." Heather seemed as bemused as an opera heroine, wandering among her tragic memories. "I never liked his laugh right from the beginning. But I figured he wouldn't laugh all that much once he married me. 'My Melancholy Baby,' he called me. At first, it was divine—he danced and made love so very well. Then he appointed himself my financial planner. That jackal . . . what did I know?"

"Hyena," I reminded her while I buttered another flaky biscuit. "You said, about his laugh."

"Same difference. Cunning bastard, gorging himself."

"This is better than daytime TV. *In vino veritas.* Was it Norman after Roberto?"

"Norman the CPA only wanted to straighten out the mess Roberto had left, he said. A clever owl, Norman. Gray and hollow eyed. Stayed up nights figuring how to divert dollars to his account on some tiny island with three palm trees and a bank. I shall never, never marry again." Heather sighed and burped softly.

"I can imagine that you'd enjoy a rest from all that." Glancing over at the French doors, I saw that Scruffy was pressing his nose against the glass, wearing his most plaintive expression. I waved him away and refilled our glasses. "But why do you suppose we speak of these predators in the past tense? They are all alive and kicking, more's the pity. I wonder what our circle could do if . . . Oh well, I guess that's why we have rules, isn't it? Did you know that Gary's working at Pilgrim now?"

"Phil told me. Surprising they'd hire him with his history, however talented he may be as an engineer. Your dog seems to be scratching at the glass. Shall I let him in?"

"No, Scruffy's just fine where he is." I pulled my hostess back into her chair. We dog-parents deserved our quiet hour. "My daughter Becky tells me that Gary has twelve-stepped his way to sobriety. I guess he asked her to throw his hat in the door, because the next thing, he called up and wanted us all to get together at Christmas."

"So what happened to his hat?"

"I kicked it back out the door. I only wish his head had been in it. Now the children will blame me because we're not going to have a Cratchit family Christmas."

"They're all coming for Christmas?"

"Becky and Adam, for sure. Cathy's just too far away and too involved in the theater right now. But to tell you the truth, Heather, I'm a little anxious about Christmas. I'd like us to forget

the unhappy holiday memories that loom over the feast like
ghostly guests. It's time to make jolly, warm new memories. I really want to start over, and to include Tip, too—to have a close,
loving family again."

"Good show. You can divorce a husband, but children are forever, Cass. I envy you and Deidre—you're both real earth moth-
ers. My only kids are the canine kind." Heather stood up a bit
unsteadily, pulled a small silver whistle out of her khaki jacket,
and stepped out the door. When she blew the whistle, all of her
dogs, even the new greyhound, ran to her and sat at perfect attention. Scruffy gazed at them in some amazement, but when he
saw that Heather was passing out liver fudge, he seemed suddenly to comprehend the drill and got into line. She patted each
head in turn and doled out the treats, like a priest handing out
wafers at communion.

"Positive reinforcement," Heather explained. "Too bad they
don't have obedience training for children. I think about having a
child a lot lately, but I certainly wouldn't want another husband."
The horde of dogs surged into the conservatory with her.

"That shouldn't be much of a problem," I said. "Adopt or get
laid."

"Excuse me, madam—did you call?" Ashbery appeared at the
door, a tall, stoop-shouldered woman in a black dress. She carried
a coffee tray from which wafted the scent of a strong Kona brew.
Her long face was heavy with disapproval, whether of the dogs or
us I couldn't tell. Despite my lavish praise for her culinary skills,
her scowl never wavered. Several of the animals scampered after
her toward the kitchen while we humans drank our much-needed
coffee, accompanied by tiny chocolate eclairs. It had started to
rain, fat drops hitting against the French doors and zigzagging
down.

"When I said I wanted to start over, I guess I was thinking of
Tip," I confessed.

"Ah, the little hunter. Don't worry—they'll raise his consciousness at Animal Lovers. But what exactly do you mean?"

"I have this fantasy that I get him away from his drunken father—that he comes to live with me."

"That's just nostalgia for the days when your own children were small," Heather said.

"Maybe you're right," I agreed, pouring us a second cup of coffee. "Now tell me how you managed the Hecate business."

"Wouldn't you rather see for yourself? We could drive over there in twenty minutes or so."

"Not unless Ashbery wants to turn her hand to chauffeuring. Don't you realize that between us we've consumed two whole bottles of the bubbly? Have to wait for the glow to wear off before I drive myself home." And Heather had drunk twice as much as I, but no need to mention that.

"Very well. I'll order a taxi, then."

"A taxi? To Carver?"

"Sure, why not?" As her hand reached for the phone, the sleeve of her safari jacket slid back to reveal a diamond tennis bracelet. Why not, indeed? I headed for the powder room tucked under the grand staircase, unaware that my expensive friend was actually ordering a limousine.

"Black," she explained when it arrived a few minutes later. "Blends better. Less noticeable."

Accompanying us in grandeur were Holmes, because he was new and needy, and Scruffy. With expressions of sheer bliss, they thrust noses out of their respective windows, lounging between-times on leather upholstery with appreciative sniffs. The driver had been well tipped—or bribed—to allow this ragged couple on board.

"I have this artist friend named Flora Durer," Heather told me as we sped smoothly over the back roads of Carver. "She's created a Hecate triptych for me, oil on wood, ever so evocative. Oh, look—there's a split of champagne in this cooler!"

"Forget it, Heather. How big is this triptych? Where did you put it?"

"Not a very good vintage anyway," she said. She opened the minibar, inspected its contents, and closed it again. "The shrine is not too big, not too small—you'll love it. Here we are!"

Heather knocked sharply on the glass panel. The driver pulled up onto the dirt shoulder of the crossroads, beside the deserted gas station, facing Ellie's General Store and the Barbershop at the End of the World.

"Now look straight ahead toward Sachem Road," Heather commanded, opening the panel between us and the front seat. "Driver, do you see that dark wooden plaque nailed to the pine tree, just off the road from the telephone pole? Pull up right beside it."

The limousine moved slowly forward, majestic as a black swan, until we were parallel to the triptych.

Out! Let's get out! Scruffy yipped.

"Just be quiet for a moment, Scruffy, while I look at this marvelous creation." The triptych was painted on dark wood panels about eighteen inches long. Hecate in three incarnations: a wild, dark-browed girl; a sensuously inviting woman half-hidden in leaves; and a powerfully visaged old lady with a crow on her shoulder. The three panels enclosed a narrow shelf.

"Heather, it's so beautiful! What a shame to leave that work of art out here in the woods where some yahoo will be certain to deface it." Glancing in the side mirror, I saw a lanky woman step out of Ellie's and stand staring at us, her eyes curious and suspicious, her hands folded under a carpenter's apron.

"Hecate can take care of herself. Now let's make an offering and get out of this dismal place." Heather took a small silk drawstring purse out of her pocket and opened the limousine door. Immediately the two dogs jumped out as if they had been sprung like a jack-in-the-box, disappearing among the trees.

"Oh, great. There go Scruffy and Sherlock. How will we get them back into the car?" I wailed, trailing after Heather.

She ignored me and began to murmur an incantation. Opening

the silk bag, she took out the stump of a black candle, fixed it to a nail point on the triptych's shelf, and tied a red thread around it. She sprinkled some ashy stuff over everything.

"What's all this?" I wanted to know. The driver seemed to be paying no attention, gazing off into space in a bored fashion. I supposed he was no stranger to eccentric behavior.

"Better you shouldn't ask," she warned. "I'm taking chances with this. It's supposed to send a strong negative impulse toward Q."

"Listen, Heather. Let's get the pups and get out of here. I'm beginning to have this weird feeling . . ."

She lifted the silver whistle that hung around her neck and blew a startling, shrill note. A few minutes later, Sherlock and even Scruffy came bounding noisily through the leafless underbrush.

Now that's what I call magic, I thought, vowing to get myself a whistle and try this at home.

The driver came out of his coma, stepped out smartly, and opened the door with a flourish. Anticipating their next fun ride, the dogs jumped inside. The woman at Ellie's had stepped into the road, and two men now stood in front of the barbershop, gawking—one evidently the barber, the other his crudely shorn customer. A third man emerged from Ellie's carrying a brown paper shopping bag. He froze in the doorway, his cold gaze raking over me. It was Clayton Quicksall.

Heather, who was just ahead of me, looked up with a smile at this assembly and would have waved like touring royalty if I hadn't at that moment given her a swift push into the limo. I clambered in after her, grateful for the smoked glass windows.

Looking back, I saw Quicksall writing something on his shopping bag. It must be the plate number. Now he would call the service and find out who had rented this monster. "There goes *your* anonymity," I said. "That was the devil himself coming out of Ellie's, my dear."

"Don't worry about a thing." Still smiling beamishly, she opened the minibar and took out two nips of brandy. "Everything is going to work out just fine now that Hecate is in charge."

I closed the panel that shut out the driver. "Don't you suppose that Q will have her off that tree and smashed to splinters before our footprints are even cold?"

"The car was between him and the shrine. He probably thinks we stopped to let the dogs run for a few minutes." Heather wrestled the cap off one of the nips. "Remember that I've obscured the triptych. Now, do we believe this stuff works, or what? It's important that we have faith."

Our Yule celebration would take place on the winter solstice—conveniently a few days before Becky and Adam arrived for Christmas Eve. They would stay until the day after Christmas and then return to their real lives. My two guest rooms under the eaves were charming and cozy, one Wedgwood blue and the other rose—all of us remembered them with affection from the days when Grandma welcomed us here. Her tranquillity and the ocean's excitement always had worked a healing magic. Also, Gary rarely came with us. Family vacations were not his style.

As I arrived at Heather's on the twenty-first, fat, lush flakes were falling, frosting the trees and roofs.

Thanks to the Spirit of All Creation for the beautiful snow, my four-wheel drive, and every other blessing, I thought warmly as I parked the Wagoneer. Heather's Mercedes stood in her circular drive, unhoused and forlorn since the three-car garage had been converted to a comfortable kennel for her animal companions.

Heather—or maybe it was Ashbery, that dedicated housekeeper—had outdone herself in decking the halls with holly, mistletoe, and other sacred greens. The huge Yule log was resplendent with twists of red berries and evergreens, elegantly ensconced in the Italian marble fireplace in the red parlor. Next to it was the unburned portion of last year's log saved to light the new one, to grace us with continuity. The wassail bowl stood ready, along with an abundant array of liquor on a sideboard. And the immense, aromatic fir tree—as tall as the high ceiling, adorned with tiny yellow candlelights and apples wrapped in gold or silver paper—was a marvel. Flocks of tiny glass and ceramic birds were perched on its branches, to encourage the coming of spring.

"Awesome!" exclaimed Deidre, mistress of homey arts and crafts that she was. She examined the apples in the twists of shining paper with a discerning eye.

"Where are all the little doggies?" asked Phillipa, holding a linzer torte in one hand and a vast tray of canapés in the other as she looked around for the stampede to begin.

"Tucked up in their little beds . . ." said Heather.

". . . while visions of marrow bones danced in their heads," recited Fiona.

". . . and I've found just the perfect companion animal for you, Phil," continued Heather, taking the torte and the tray out of Phillipa's hands and setting them on the sideboard. "A sweet little greyhound rescued from owners who raced but never socialized the poor thing. Just like my Holmes. She wants proper feeding and cuddling, so naturally, I thought of you."

"Phil would be a cat person if she were an animal person at all," Fiona declared.

"Leave me alone, you two," said Phillipa. "I don't want a dog. I don't want a cat. But if you come across a good-looking, two-legged male creature with those same feeding and cuddling needs . . ."

"He'd be fun for a while, but you'd soon tire of cleaning up after him," Heather assured her. She lit the kindling under the old Yule log and held a fireplace shovel ready to push it under the new log. As flames leaped up around the old and the new, Heather's chestnut hair shimmered in the light.

"Will introduced me to someone, a state police detective

who's really quite literate and absolutely unattached . . ." indefatigable Deidre began, but Phillipa's raised eyebrow gave her pause.

"A cop? Surely, you jest."

"A funny thing happened to Omar today," Fiona said, rummaging through the reticule stashed beside her chair. She drew forth and unwrapped from protective tissue a large dark, moldering book with no title. "Look at this. I found it in some boxes of books donated to the library sale. It's seems to be an antique *Book of Shadows*—now isn't that an extraordinary thing! Surely no one would deliberately give away such a book. All those valuable recipes and spells. I'll bet that batch came from someone's grandmother's attic. This old treasure is my Yule gift to us all."

"So, what happened to Omar then?" Deidre's mind stayed on track while Fiona's wandered off.

"Oh, yes—Omar went out for a walk, despite the snow. Sat in a tree near the bird feeder, thinking long thoughts, I guess. He looked quite picturesque, black on white. I was sorry to discover no film in my camera."

"What's odd about that?" Deidre pursued the point.

"Nothing. I usually do forget to buy film. Consequently, my life goes largely unrecorded." Fiona sighed wistfully. "Today everything's camcorders, though. Memories tidily packaged for the VCR."

"Don't tell me you allow that beautiful Persian to go tomcatting around the neighborhood," Heather remonstrated tartly. "Cats should be kept indoors for their own protection. You know that, Fiona!"

"Omar is his own person. Anyway, I heard this tiny sound— something like a *ping* against the side of the house. Omar jumped down out of that tree in a flash and commenced clawing at the door in a rather frantic manner. I opened it immediately, of course. He raced past me, and as he slid under the sofa, I saw there was a tiny nick out of his ear. Wouldn't let me treat it properly, either. When I pulled him out, he jumped away and hid under the armoire where he knows I can't reach him."

"Now you see what I mean?" Heather asked us all, summing up the prosecution's case on this corroborating evidence. "The world outside is too full of hazards and pitfalls for cats."

"As it is for all of us, which is why we have agoraphobics," Phillipa said. "But a person or a cat who doesn't want to roam about in the real world could be rightfully labeled neurotic. Omar was in a cat fight, that's all." She followed Heather's tray of champagne flutes with the delectable canapés.

"No," said Fiona, thoughtfully licking a bead of caviar off her upper lip. "There was fresh blood on the snow. It hadn't been there before, when I was imagining how I'd frame Omar in the camera lens, if I had any film."

Heather sat on the floor and took the book from Fiona, opening it at random, seemingly oblivious to the moldy green stuff that was smudging her cream silk blouse. "Hey, this is really intriguing, if I'm reading it right. Seems to be a recipe for invoking spiritual energy. Any of these ingredients familiar to you, Cass?" She laid the heavy book on my lap. Fortunately, my velvet pants were also green.

"Fenugreek. Unicorn root. Dragon's blood," I read the spidery handwriting aloud.

"Ugh," said Deidre, circling with another bottle of Moët. "Don't be alarmed." I held out my glass for a refill. "They're all simply herbs, my dear. Yes, I'm familiar with them." Turning the page, the wavering letters read *Binding Spell*. This could be a real treasure.

"Take good care of this," I said, handing it back to Fiona. "Perhaps there's something here we can use."

She took the book from my hands and rewrapped it in tissue. "You think it will help us to stop Q from going after some other poor youngster?"

"Say, don't be in such a hurry to stick that book away. I want to have a look at it myself," said Deidre.

"Yes," Phillipa agreed. "Maybe there's a good old love potion."

Thousands of bayberries had given their wax for the half-

dozen candles in silver candelabra that Heather now lit to celebrate the passing of the year's shortest day and the coming of the
new year. Symbolizing growth and prosperity, the candles had
been my gift to the circle.

We held our brief ceremony of healing, holding hands, whis-
pering wishes. Some arid place in my heart conceived a tiny
green sprig of hope, and I thought the others must feel the same.
Gleaming with firelight and candle glow reflected in every shining surface, the room appeared to be dancing around us. We
beamed at each other, our smiles mirroring the radiance. All our
petty criticisms of each other, often voiced when we were apart,
had faded away like shadows.

When the shot rang out and the window shattered, it was such
a jolt to our mood that we were transfixed in our places. With a
heavy thud, the bullet imbedded itself in the beautiful old sideboard, splintering its pattern of inlaid wood. The crystal punch
cups crashed around the wassail bowl. A few of them fell to the
floor and smashed.

At first when we moved, it was as slow as if we were under
water. Yet, somehow Deidre managed to crouch toward the library in search of a phone, and I fumbled for the wall switch,
which doused several of the lights, including the tree. Fiona sank
to the floor, collapsing into her thick wool skirt like a fallen pup-
pet. Heather, too, dropped down, duck-walking to candles,
putting them out with a silver snuffer as she went, and snapping
off the remaining lamps. One would think we had choreographed
our defense in advance.

"Well, well," Phillipa said. "Merry Christmas from the neighbors."

"Just stay low, everyone. They're on their way," Deidre whispered from the library door. Even as she spoke, we could hear a
distant siren wailing through the snow-insulated night.

"Thank goodness, a patrol car must have been cruising nearby," Fiona murmured. The firelight glistened on something metallic in her hand.

"For heaven's sake, put away that damned pistol," I murmured. "I bet you don't even have a permit . . ."

"It's Q. It's Q coming after me," she muttered back angrily, but she did stuff the pistol back into her reticule. "And it's all your fault, Cass."

"Okay, Fiona—was it I who blabbed my name and address to Q's librarian friend? Had you thought that it might have been Q who took a potshot at Omar today?"

The pistol came out again and waved wildly. "Omar—my Omar? I'll shoot the bastard right through the heart, if he has one."

A strong hand clamped down over Fiona's. Phillipa had crawled over and was trying to wrest the weapon out of Fiona's grasp. They struggled, and the pistol went off, taking out another pane of the big bay window. The patrol car skidded into Heather's driveway. Heather's dogs, tucked up in garage pens, apparently unperturbed by the earlier attack, now set off a fearful racket of barking and howling. Deidre began to scream, not loudly but in short, shrill shrieks like a tin whistle.

I took Deidre by the shoulders and shook her to stop the noise. I needed to be heard before we had cops in our midst. "Listen, you guys," I said between her diminishing squeals, "*not one word about Q.* And that means you, too, Fiona."

"Is that some kind of sportsman's handicap we're giving the officers of the law?" asked Phillipa. She removed the smoking weapon and dropped it into the melting contents of the ice bucket. "So that we can be the first to nab the murdering sniper? Those of us he doesn't take out first can have the credit and glory."

"Chill out, Phil. You're getting hysterical. Do you think we should explain that we've unmasked a killer in a psychic vision? *Think!*" Meanwhile, the patrolmen, having knocked loudly once, were throwing themselves against the door. Heather ran to open it before they could break it down.

"You mean, *you* have. It was *your* psychic vision, dearie. The rest of us were just being supportive," Phillipa hissed. "Well, I, for one . . ."

"Cass is right, *not a word*," interrupted Deidre, suddenly calm and collected. "We have to guard our circle's secrets. People just don't understand this kind of thing. Remember, *I* have children to protect."

From the look in her brilliantly dark eyes, I thought Phillipa was about to throttle Deidre. Fortunately, having finished her hasty explanation at the door, Heather brought the two police-men into the darkened living room to survey the damage. I snapped on the wall switch. One of them was a young redhead with a coalescing mesh of freckles across his forehead and nose. The other was older and rounder, with a Neanderthal brow that overhung his eyes. They introduced themselves as Officers Not-ley and Bronk.

The redhead whistled through his teeth as they inspected the two blasted panes in the bay window. "Looks like a sniper," he said cheerfully, as if glad of this break in an otherwise boring pa-trol. "Don't get many snipers this time of year. Spring and fall are the sniper seasons usually."

"Thank you for sharing that professional insight," said Phillipa. I trod gently on her foot to remind her to be civil. After all, these men were strangers, not friends who were accustomed to her insults.

The room reeked of gunpowder, but the officers didn't seem to notice. Perhaps the scent of the Christmas tree and the herbal incense I'd added to the fire had confused their olfactory senses.

"Two panes of glass blasted. Must have been two shots," grunted the caveman Bronk. This intense analytical effort fur-rowed his heavy brow.

"I think I'll just slip away and get a glass of water while you chat," said Fiona, dabbing at her forehead and throat with a red bandanna pulled from her reticule. "I trust I won't be disturbing Ashbery?"

"Ashbery deserted me early this afternoon. She's spending the holidays with her sister in Vermont. So . . . perhaps you'll get us some fresh ice while you're in the kitchen?" Heather handed her the ice bucket, which Fiona whisked out of the room in an instant, looking all roly-poly and bustling, like Mrs. Rabbit in a Beatrix Potter book.

"No doubt you'll want to bring the state police into this. For all we know, the sniper may be planning other hits in the near future. Is Detective Stern on duty this evening?" Deidre asked. I shook my head, but she kept her eyes on the two officers, informing them of their responsibilities.

Meanwhile, as Heather told us later, Fiona was draining the ice water from the pistol and stashing it in a crock of dog chow.

Officer Bronk studied the two broken panes of glass. "Funny," he summed up his conclusions in a bemused fashion. I confess to not having a great deal of faith in the law's efficacy, dating back to the days when various police officers proved unable to protect me from what they called "domestic disputes." I doubted that Bronk would change my opinion.

"Not so funny if you were us, singing 'Silent Night' around the piano and being targeted by some bloody fool with a rifle," snapped Phillipa.

I glanced at the piano. Perhaps they wouldn't notice that it was closed and had a couple of champagne flutes standing on the lid.

"They aren't broken the same way," Bronk plodded along his deductive trail.

"What's different about them? *Smashed* and *smashed*, I'd say." Using a fireplace tool to point out this similarity, Heather hit a shard of glass in the second, lower pane. "Oops!"

"Now, you shouldn't have done that, ma'am," Bronk remonstrated, taking the poker out of her hand. "That's evidence, you know. The detective is going to want to see what's what here, and you've gone and knocked out the glass."

"Sorry," said Heather.

"I think you ladies had better just sit down quietly in those chairs over there while I have a look around the house. Notley, you call this in. And you'd better rope off the area outside the

window. Might be footprints. They'll want the footprints secured. Okay, then—let's get busy." Bronk lumbered off into the
cavernous hallway.

"I do hope Fiona has taken care of everything," said Heather,
as we fell into the easy chairs near the fire, avoiding the handsome but unyielding Victorian museum pieces that were dis-
played here and there about the parlor.

A cold wind accompanied by blasts of thick, wet snowflakes
was blowing into the room. Removing the glasses from the piano,
Phillipa threw a protective afghan over it. The dogs, who had
quieted down after the arrival of the patrol car, commenced barking and yowling again as Notley encircled a trackless expanse of
snow with yellow warning ribbons. I thought it possible that the
window glass from Fiona's wild shooting, which must have fallen
outside, had disappeared without trace under the soft, heavy
snowfall.

"I'll go out to the kennel in a minute," Heather said. "I just
want to catch my breath first. They can smell anxiety, you know.
I wouldn't want them to catch a whiff of the way I'm feeling right
now."

Fiona returned with the freshened ice bucket and helped herself to a stiff Scotch from the sideboard. "We'd better think about
a group saltwater purification here," she said. First taking a gen-
erous swallow, she set the glass down and dug out a tube of hand
cream from her reticule. After vigorously rubbing a squirt of it on
her own hands, she offered it to the others like a dish of candy.

" 'Salt and water, inner and outer, soul and body, cast out all
that is harmful,' " quoted Deidre. "Yes, this definitely calls for
some cleansing. Do you really think Q is stalking us? So he knows
we suspect him of whatever it is that he has on his conscience,
not that we actually *know* what that may be. Shouldn't he be
afraid of giving himself away, shooting up the place like this?"

"Just a warning shot across the bow, I'd guess. It certainly wasn't
Santa Claus out there tonight." Phillipa threw a log on the fire in

her decisive way and raked out an unburned piece of wood to save for next Yule.

"Sociopaths don't have what you'd call a conscience," I corrected Deidre. "I know in my bones it was Q. Don't you?"

"Yes," said Fiona, taking another swig of Scotch and making a face. "And we simply have to finish him off before he hurts my beautiful cat—or somebody else."

"You mean, bring him to justice, right?" I asked nervously.

"Of course, justice. Absolutely, bring him to justice. That goes without saying. One way or another." Fiona took out a travel-size bottle of cologne and sprayed her wrists. The aroma of gunpowder that had clung to her was overwhelmed by some ladylike floral scent—lily, perhaps.

When the detectives arrived, the uniformed officers went outdoors with Detective David Moretti to canvass the grounds. The snow had ceased to fall, and there was hope that some evidence of the sniper might not have been obscured.

Detective Stone Stern, who remained inside to question us, examined the sideboard and then sniffed the air. "I'm wondering why I smell gunpowder inside this room," he inquired, turning first to the two of us he knew, Deidre and me. "Mrs. Shipton, perhaps you will be good enough to explain that."

"Maybe the odor drifted in through the broken window. Also, we've been burning some rather pungent herbs with the Yule log," I suggested. "You've noticed the mess the bullet made of the sideboard, Detective Stern. Any one of us could have been killed, standing here to ladle out a cup from the wassail bowl."

The rest just looked dumb—even Phil, who normally scorned that sort of automatic female response to unnerving questions. I got the feeling that Detective Stern didn't miss much and wouldn't take kindly to being deceived about the second shot. Despite his easygoing expression, the eyes behind those trendy metal-rimmed glasses were ice-blue. His fine, rather long brown hair constantly fell across his forehead and was pushed back by tapered, artistic fingers. I wondered if Deidre had said a summoning spell for this particular detective to be called here.

I asked her as soon as we were alone, making a restorative pot of coffee in the kitchen. Ashbery had left a silver coffee service and Lenox coffee cups at the ready.

"What's the good of being a witch if we can't pull a few metaphysical strings?" she asked with a sly smile as I measured out coffee for an extra-strong brew. "Don't you think he's a looker? Lean, mean, and those chilling eyes! Isn't he simply *made* for Phil? Wasn't she just a teensy bit impressed with him?"

"He looks so teacherly, like a young Mr. Chips—what makes you describe him as 'mean'? Can he tell bouillabaisse from bouillon? If Phil invites him to share her braised loin of veal, will he ask for ketchup?"

Deidre winked broadly. "Did I plan this or what? According to Will, Stern is known for being quite the gourmet—and a great chef, as well. Believe me, he can talk soufflé and syllabub with Phillipa to her heart's content. As for the 'mean'—I hear he's rather aggressive in his investigations."

"Haven't you ever heard the adage 'too many cooks,' Dee?"

We brought the heavily-laden coffee tray into the living room. Detective Stern was questioning Phillipa in a cozy corner. A dazzling smile made her sharp features look elegant and enticing, She didn't exactly look as if she were being grilled.

When I finally plowed home in the Wagoneer through drifts and depressions wind-carved from the soft snow, it was nearly two. I don't know if dogs can tell time, but I often had the illusion that Scruffy glanced at the kitchen wall clock whenever I came home late. He was waiting for me at the door, sitting up alertly as if he hadn't slept a wink the whole time I was gone.

Where've you been, Toots? I should have had my last walk hours ago. If this keeps up, I'm going to have to insist on indoor accommodations.

"You've been a really good boy," I said, which was a euphemism for not peeing on the furniture.

As I escorted the dog out to break through the snowdrifts and find a tree, I discovered a curious package that looked as if it had been hurled onto the porch in haste.

The delivery man must have been working late to catch up with Christmas. I turned the parcel over in my hands. There were stampings over stampings and inked index fingers pointing this way and that. Exotic Malaysian stamps were peeling off the dilapidated box. It had come a long way to lift my heart with exultation. A letter and a gift from Joe.

The letter said:

"Beautiful Cassandra!
I want to be with you so much. The thought of you kept me warm in a Siberian jail when we were taken into custody for passing out leaflets to whalers. After being released and debriefed, I had to ship out immediately on the Rainbow Warrior for a short-handed mission to Singapore. Greenpeace is holding a worldwide conference here while a documentary is being made aboard the ship. But I'm coming back to you as soon as they get someone to replace me. It must have been love at first sight, because I can hardly wait for a second encounter. Merry Christmas, darling, and a thousand kisses."

Enclosed was a Greenpeace press release about the Soviet affair, with a grainy photograph of Joe and his colleagues grinning broadly after their release. I touched his face, no bigger than my fingertip. He was halfway across the world. But not too far for me to summon him back to my arms.

After I'd read the letter again, I opened the tissue-wrapped gift, an exquisite silk shawl with a deep fringe. It was embroidered with a border of leaves in vivid shades of green with tiny pink and yellow flowers. On the card that fell out of its folds Joe had written: "Something to go with your lovely green eyes." I wrapped it around me and twirled around the kitchen while Scruffy watched me warily.

I guess it's time to go through my closet, I thought, and throw out the really grungy stuff.

Our sniper was a hot front-page item in the *Pilgrim Times*.

. . . No other attacks have been reported. While admitting that holiday celebrants may have been responsible, Detective Stern said the incident is being treated as a felony, and the investigation will continue until the sniper is apprehended. Anyone with information about the shooting should notify Detective Stern or Detective Moretti at the Plymouth County State Police Detective Unit in Middleboro or the Plymouth Police Department.

But when nothing further was reported, interest soon turned to seasonal stories of shoplifting sprees, space heater fires, and nativity scene disputes.

Those of us who *did* have knowledge of the shooting and the shooter agreed that this wasn't the time for such revelations. Only Fiona was reluctant to keep quiet, especially about the attack on Omar, until we reminded her that the laws were lenient in regard to crimes against animals. However reprehensible, shooting a cat probably would not put Q in prison. Unless we could offer proof that Q was a serial killer, and that he knew we were after him, it would seem that he had no motive to stalk us. He might very well claim that we were stalking *him*.

"Explain a psychic vision to the state police? Get real, Fiona," I said as we shared a coffee-conference at Phillipa's on the twenty-third.

Phillipa backed me up for her own reasons. "I'd rather that interesting Detective Stern didn't think me absolutely bonkers. Button it up, Fiona."

* * *

On the twenty-fourth, Becky met Adam's plane at Logan, and the two of them traveled down to Plymouth in her Volvo, arriving just before sunset at 4:20 P.M. The purple-and-gray strata of twilight came much too early for me, but I comforted myself that the days would be getting longer now, dating from the winter solstice we had just celebrated. For now, I basked in the joy of welcoming my children "home."

After our traditional Christmas Eve dinner—my mother's special baked, stuffed shrimp—we exchanged not only gifts but also our good memories of the past, especially of my parents and Grandma. I'd always tried not to dwell on the dysfunctional aspects of our family life. Maybe that had been a mistake. Would Cathy have blamed me for her chaotic childhood if she knew more about her father? As the youngest, she remembered least.

Becky had given me a glorious, gleaming bread machine, now standing under the Christmas tree looking like a little robot that had wandered off the set of *Star Wars*. Adam's gift was an Asian jewelry chest of carved wood that was probably worth more than all my baubles put together. He seemed to like the Native American rug I'd bought to warm up his Spartan apartment, furnished for the most part with electronic gadgets and computer equipment. For Becky, I'd chosen sumptuous satin nightwear from the Victoria's Secret catalog. I'd also ordered a little something for myself—in case!

What about my gift, Toots? Scruffy pawed through the heap of Christmas wrappings on the floor, and then at Becky's knee. She screamed, pushed him away, and examined her cashmere tunic top, thread by thread, for damage.

"Here, you rascal," I commanded, lunging for Scruffy's collar. He eluded me deftly and jumped up beside Adam, who was sitting on the window seat. Eye to eye, the dog fixed Adam with his dominant stare. I hauled Scruffy off unceremoniously and made him lie down beside my chair. "You'll get yours on Christmas morning, as usual," I muttered.

"I usually wrap his gifts," I explained, "so he gets all excited when he sees tissue paper and ribbons." Becky rolled her eyes heavenward and glanced at Adam.

I don't know why you're making such a big fuss over them. His nose between his paws, Scruffy looked as dejected as a dog peering through a crate at the pound. *A fat lot they ever do for you around here, while I'm out patrolling the property night and day. Unrequited loyalty.*

"All right. *All right.* You can have *one.* Choose which you want from the packages with your name on them."

Scruffy sprang up in an instant and sniffed all the packages remaining under the tree. He snatched up one in his mouth—the one that was gift-wrapped with Disney Dalmatians.

It was small, but it contained Ashbery's dried beef dog biscuits, a gift from Heather. Holding the package down on the floor with one paw, he ripped off the paper with his teeth.

"Good Lord," said Adam. "He seems to understand every word you say."

"How does he know which packages are his?" asked Becky.

"I always put a few drops of cod liver oil on the bow. He knows if a package smells fishy, it's his." While the dog was contentedly munching a biscuit, I took the opportunity to remove the rest before he made himself ill.

"I wonder, Mother, if it wouldn't be better for you to have someone in to live with you," Adam said cautiously. "You know, like a companion. Someone who would look out for you in exchange for a good home."

"It's one of the new lifestyles for older people these days," Becky agreed. "It must get a little eerie here all by yourself."

So, what do they think I am—chopped liver? Scruffy looked at my two earnest children with disdain. I smiled, wondering how Adam and Becky would feel if Joe moved in to keep Geriatric Mom from going off her rocker.

* * *

Heather was entertaining blue-blooded aunts, and Deidre was knee-deep in gleeful children with new toys—but Fiona and Phillipa, having no special plans other than avoiding the charity of well-meaning relatives, had been glad to accept an invitation to join us for Christmas dinner.

Christmas Day brought a brisk nor'easter with freezing sleet. Adam looked often and anxiously at the sky. "If this keeps up until morning, we ought to leave an hour earlier than planned," he muttered to Becky.

"Don't worry. I'll get you to the airport on time," she assured him.

We weren't far into our cocktail hour in the living room, snug and cheery despite the frenzied winds beating against the house, when Becky began raising her eyebrows and nudging Adam at Fiona's vagaries. Building up the blaze in the fireplace to a roaring pitch, Adam proceeded to drink rather more single malt whiskey, his own contribution, than I would have wished. Ignored by his siblings, Scruffy sulked jealously in the kitchen, keeping a solitary guard on the savory bird in the oven. But otherwise, I felt the day was going well.

I pulled the silk shawl around my shoulders, a shimmering reminder that Joe was still in my world somewhere.

"That's pretty. Where'd you get it, Mom?" Becky asked.

"It's a Christmas gift. A friend sent it to me from Singapore."

Adam and Becky exchanged a *Mom has weird friends* glance. Fiona smiled and winked at me. Later I got the questions. After the apricot-stuffed goose I'd generously allowed Phillipa to roast for our feast, the young people retired early to ready themselves for the icy morning commute. We three witches settled down in front of the dying fire for some serious wine-mulling.

"What did he say?" Fiona demanded. "Surely there was a *billet doux* tucked in with that beautiful wrap."

"Oh, the usual," I replied more casually than I felt. "He loves me. He'll return someday. I only hope Greenpeace runs out of toxic waste alarms."

"I read that Greenpeace is planning to expose some American chemical manufacturer's practice of shipping mercury waste to South Africa," Phillipa informed me.

I groaned. How far—how long—was it from Singapore to South Africa? This fragile relationship was straining my patience—and my geography, never a favorite study topic. Suddenly I had a vivid mental image of Joe—the Aegean-blue eyes, square jaw, and neat beard, the strong Greek profile, the deeply bronze skin and compact, agile body that smelled of sensuous herbs growing by the sea. I was pleasantly lost for a few moments until Fiona brought me back with talk about my children.

". . . rather a handsome pair, especially that Adam. And quite agreeable to us intruders on the family scene. I had a nice chat with Becky about poisonous herbs while you and Phil were hovering over that goose. She hadn't realized how many of our common plantings were toxic, like foxglove, lily of the valley, and even rhubarb . . . not to mention the mushrooms. That's how the subject came up."

"What subject?" I wrenched myself back from a passionate daydream . . . Joe and I on a moon-drenched, deserted Mediterranean beach . . . the rhythm of warm, powerful waves throbbing against the curving, white shore . . . *From Here to Eternity.*

"Those delicious mushroom-stuffed mushrooms you served as an appetizer. Wild ones are so much tastier. Those were dried wild mushrooms in the stuffing, weren't they? I would never dare harvest those myself. I don't have your foraging expertise. Perhaps Becky hadn't realized what a genius you are in that field, no pun intended."

"Thanks so much, Fiona."

"She'll probably warn her father, your atomic-ex," Phillipa said, sipping her mulled wine and smiling wickedly. "If Mom sends you a jar of marinated mushrooms, you'd better watch out, Dad."

"True enough," I admitted.

"I thought the Indian kid would be here."

"Native American kid. Gone to spend the holiday with his Ma

in Maine. Lit up like a Christmas tree himself. He was about to spend his clarinet savings on a locket for her, but I talked him into one of my dream pillows instead. He says she likes herb things."

"Those are the parents that get the devoted children, I've noticed. Will he come back, do you think?" Phillipa wondered.

"Oh, yes. I gather that Ma has some new boyfriend who doesn't care to have another youngster around on a long-term basis. The younger brother is there, but there's no place for Tip. And Tip says his father needs him."

"Son of a bitch. They're all the same. No compassion for defenseless children and cats." Fiona's chin was resting on the cinnamon stick in her mug.

There was a sharp bark from the kitchen, where Scruffy had been collapsed on cool tiles, recuperating from a surfeit of roast goose. A scraping of paws on the bare floor. More barks and scratchings at the door. I jumped up, thinking this was some kind of gastrointestinal emergency. But when I flung open the kitchen door, Scruffy backed up instead of rushing out, adding a low growl to his barking. And there on the porch was a Christmas-wrapped hatbox, its glossy red ribbon frayed, as if it had been exposed to the raw blustery wind off the ocean. Scrawled on the star-spangled tissue in uneven letters were the words *Merry Christmas, Girls* written with a black marker.

"Don't touch it," ordered Phillipa, who had come into the kitchen behind me and was looking over my shoulder.

"Well, what do you expect me to do . . . leave it there? Or call for the bomb squad to defuse what will probably turn out to be a fruitcake from Mrs. Peacedale?" Brave talk from me, but actually I was trembling inside. Was it better to be blown up than to be considered a foolish woman?

Get rid of it. I don't like the smell of it. Scruffy had come a little closer.

"Oh, look—a lovely present!" cried Fiona, appearing suddenly and pushing right past us. Before I could stop her, she'd rushed out and picked it up. Phillipa and I ducked and threw our arms over our heads. "What's the matter with you two? Don't you want to see what's inside?"

"Put that right down," ordered Phillipa. Startled, Fiona dropped it on the porch floor.

"That blows the bomb theory out of the water. We may as well open the damned thing," I said.

"It's curious that the dog allowed someone to enter your porch and leave this parcel," Fiona commented with a worried frown.

Scruffy assumed a hurt expression and commenced scratching his ear. *Everyone always blames the dog.*

Finally, after much discussion at the open door while the chill of December seeped into the kitchen, we fastened a carving knife to a broom handle and gingerly sliced through the wrappings of the package where it lay on the porch floor.

It *was* a fruitcake!

Cautiously, I leaned over and sniffed at it. It smelled like a fruitcake. I ran a finger over the sticky surface and licked it. It tasted like a fruitcake. When I brought the package into the house, Scruffy seemed to feel the coast was clear for him to dash out onto the porch and bark heroically at the vanished intruder.

Now Phillipa smelled the cake. "A lot of brandy and something else, something strange," she said. She unfastened the carving knife and whacked into the cake with it, succeeding only in slicing halfway through. Looking at it more closely, she took hold of the two sides and lifted. The top half of the cake came off as if it were a lid. Nestled inside the hollow cake lay a small coiled poisonous-looking snake, quite dead.

"You and Scruffy get top honors for noses that know," I said.

Fiona opened her mouth in a perfect O. "Don't scream!" I ordered, shaking her slightly. "Adam and Becky will come running down here, and what will I tell them?"

We stared at the two halves of the evilly glistening serpent cake as if it were a meteor fallen from outer space.

"What the hell are we going to do about this?" Phillipa asked. "Do you want me to call that sexy detective?"

"I guess so," I said halfheartedly. "Let's just say that someone seems to be stalking us—we can't imagine who it would be. At least we'll be on record with a complaint, and the police will take charge of the evidence. At this point, I wouldn't want to throw the nasty thing out, but I don't want to have it around the house, either."

Scruffy sauntered back into the kitchen. Things are at a low point indeed when the dog says *I told you so*.

Since Stone Stern was in Vermont visiting his mother, I did have to keep the cake for the next two days. By then, although they were mildly interested in this ugly prank, Stern and the other state police detectives had more serious matters to pursue. A Wareham boy had disappeared from the Plymouth Theater.

His name was Daryl Hendler, twelve years old, the youngest of three Hendler boys. His two brothers had accompanied him to a Christmas vacation matinee showing the new Bruce Willis film. Brian Hendler, seventeen, had driven the family station wagon to Plymouth. Daryl's brothers sat separately from him, with two Plymouth girls of their acquaintance. When the houselights came on, the older boys stayed a few minutes, horsing around in the balcony until the manager made them leave. By then, Daryl was nowhere to be seen. The ticket seller, who was the manager's wife, said she'd seen him hanging around the front while she was packing up her things to go home and cook dinner, but then he'd gone around the corner out of her sight. No one working that day in other places along Main Street, which included an ice-cream shop and a video arcade, could add any information about Daryl's disappearance.

A major snowstorm barreled in from the northeast, making driving that week suicidal, but the phone lines burned between our houses while we argued about this new development. It was

Heather, finally, who insisted on our voicing our full suspicions to Detective Stern immediately.

"Either you tell Stern whom we suspect, or I will. The boy may still be alive. Our information might save him," she declared. And so it was that I pushed through the snow in the Wagoneer—with Phillipa and Heather riding shotgun, so to speak—to have a chat with Stern at the Plymouth State Police Detective Unit in Middleboro.

Despite his benign expression, the ice-blue eyes regarded me thoughtfully for some time after I'd finished my story. "You're asking me to interrogate a man named Clayton Quicksall, a resident of Carver, in the matter of the missing boy Daryl Hendler because you had a vision while shopping at Angelo's," he repeated.

"Listen . . . she's really uncanny . . . you have to believe her," Phillipa pressed our suit urgently.

"It's not the sort of evidence that will get me a search warrant, you understand. But since it's for *you*," Stern said, looking only at Phillipa, "I will check out Quicksall very quietly."

Not one to let an advantage slip through her fingers, Phillipa reminded Stern of the loathsome fruitcake we'd received. "Maybe it's an old Quicksall family recipe," she mused. "Reeked rather heavily of brandy for my taste. Not to mention the crunch of scales."

"And let's not forget the incident of the sniper shooting out my bay window," Heather reminded the detective, who dragged his attention away from Phillipa's dark eyes with visible effort. "We all feel certain that Quicksall is trying to frighten us away. He knows we're onto him."

"Two shots, as I recall," Stern said. "But only one shell was found. It seemed to me . . ."

"Well, that's of no matter now," Heather interrupted quickly. "The important thing is to save the boy. What you *should* do is to break in there and search the whole place from attic to cellar. And dig up the lawn, too. Find out where the bodies are buried."

"Not until the spring thaw, they won't," Phillipa said dryly. "But you must act right away, Stone. What if Daryl is in Quicksall's cellar at this very moment!"

While agreeing to investigate, Detective Stern refused to share any details of how thorough he was prepared to be. We drove away in a state of mingled anxiety and frustration.

"See, I told you how it would go," I muttered, while babying the car over a particularly slippery patch of roadway.

"At least we've finally brought in the authorities. Heather, you were so right about that. I feel certain that Stone will do something wonderful. He's just not telling us what he has planned," said Phillipa.

Hardly an objective opinion, I thought. "How very John Wayne of him," I said. "Meanwhile, let's continue to do what we can among ourselves."

"I've been trying to think of a way to get into Quicksall's place if the law won't do it," Heather confided. "Since when do witches wait for warrants?"

Esbat of the Wolf Moon

The new year arrived without any word from Stern about Quicksall and Daryl. "He's working on it," Phillipa assured us, looking rather sleek and smug, like a cat with a dish of cream. Inviting the attractive detective to an elegant New Year's Eve supper *à deux* apparently hadn't frightened away this hero. Now Phillipa had become our liaison with the law. "In fact, Stone is satisfied that the boy is not in Quicksall's house. He's checking every possible lead."

"And I'm working on it," Heather said with a serene smile. "Just give me your energy and your faith."

"I'll give you a punch if you keep on with this secretive nonsense," Deidre declared.

But somehow none of us came up with a plan of action on which we could all agree—until our next run-in with Quicksall.

January continued to wear away our energy and faith with howling winds, freezing rains, and the need to wear life-support clothing as heavy as an astronaut's. I kept an eye on Tip through winter's onslaught, making sure he was hatted, scarfed, mittened, and booted to my satisfaction. He would demur that he was "just fine, thanks, Miz Shipton," of course, while shivering in his moccasins. Knowing he'd be embarrassed by constant gifts of new clothing, I would root around in the Good Will store for boys' heavy winter wear and then claim the item was some castoff of Adam's. But I had the impression that those direct gray eyes often penetrated my little smokescreens.

"Indians never bothered about bad weather," Tip told me. Since his father had gone to Waterbury to visit relatives, I'd invited the boy to spend the weekend—with the usual offer of chores he could do. "Their skins were tough from being outdoors all year."

"You want everyone else to say Native Americans, so why don't you do the same? What about those blankets they wore over their shoulders in winter?" I asked.

"Oh, sure, but that was only the women and old men. You wouldn't see a warrior all wrapped up that way."

Pleased to hear him say something positive about his people, I simply handed him the navy blue turtleneck sweater I'd found at the church rummage sale and leaned over to scratch Scruffy's ears. "We should all be as well equipped against the cold as this fellow," I commented.

Scruffy sighed at this disturbance of his afternoon nap and got up from under the kitchen table, stretching his back legs and tail in a blissful manner. *I suppose you've never considered what it's like to have to relieve yourself outdoors in a January blizzard or to have ice slivers tear into your paws.* He jumped up on the storage bench under the window and stared out disconsolately. *Don't you think I'd like to pee right now but I'm holding it until the wind dies down? I don't like the way big stuff gets tossed around the yard. I got hit on the head once with a folding chair.*

Tip smiled as if he'd understood Scruffy's complaints. "I'll take him out when he's ready," the boy offered.

The phone rang. "Okay. Put on your boots first," I said with my hand on the receiver. *Phil*, I thought.

"This is a good day to learn how to make grilled pizza," she said without preamble. "You never know when you might be out in the wilds with some Greenpeace type and want to rustle up a pizza to share with the rabid raccoons. So why don't you come over here and we'll play with my indoor grill."

"Sounds warming. Is it okay if . . ."

"No, do *not* bring the kid and the dog," Phillipa interrupted. "Just bring your love philter herbs. Because what I have in mind is a sharing of expertise here. I'll demonstrate the grill technique—and you'll do the Tristan and Isolde spiced juice. Okay?"

"Best offer I've had today." I would leave Tip to keep an eye on the fire in the fireplace and heat up some stew for himself and Scruffy when they got hungry.

"We'll watch the auto races together," Tip said happily.

By the time I arrived at Phillipa's, the kitchen was fragrant with her herb-rich tomato sauce and the dough had risen like a magic mushroom. After showing me how to punch it down and roll it out thinly for the grill, she said, "Your turn."

" 'To know, to dare, to will, to keep silent,' " I recited the age-old rule of spellmaking as I took out the silk bag in my carryall. "Have you considered your objective with care?"

"I never thought I would be remotely interested in anyone Deidre dragged in, but this guy is clever and personable and appreciates fine food."

"So . . . you're very attractive and you *create* fine food. Why do you need a love potion to bewitch Stone Stern?"

"Because some evil fate may be waiting in the wings to squash my fond hopes, just as it always has before. Call it psychic insurance, if you will." She laughed. Phillipa had a deeply wicked, whiskey laugh that often made men nervous. Not Stern, though—he seemed to be made of stronger stuff.

"You wouldn't want to close the door on some unknown but marvelous future love," I warned. "Still, it will be a comfort to all of us if you get an enraptured detective on board."

"Right. No closed doors to the future, but let's have a surefire love potion for the present. Did you bring the right herbs?" Phillipa began opening jars and sniffing. "Hey, cilantro and anise. Is this some kind of California potion?"

I laid out a triple thickness of linen and added a pinch of each of a dozen herbs, tying the bag together with a dark red thread. "Infuse this as you would a tea bag in boiling water. Add the liquid to hot mulled wine, and drink it with Stern, preferably from the same cup. Then, watch out! 'Beware of your heart's desire . . .' "

Having carefully put away the philter in the back of her spice cupboard, Phillipa oiled a thin rectangle of dough and flipped it onto the grill. As she demonstrated when to turn it and delicately spread on the sauce, I poured the red wine. The finished pizza was a thing of lopsided beauty and seductive fragrance. We consumed it while it was scalding hot, cooling our mouths with sips of wine.

"So, why don't you do this kind of thing yourself, Cass?" Phillipa asked.

"The pizza or the love potion? Because I'm not ready yet. I'm too busy with the herb business. And I'm obsessed with this Q thing, and Daryl. Then there's Tip. I worry about him constantly, and there's so very little I can do. Maybe all this is happening because I'm at that awkward age, bouncing between PMS and hot flashes."

"Stop right there," Phillipa commanded. "You're getting rather hysterical. I'm sorry I asked." She looked at me shrewdly. "Maybe you're right. The Tarot I read for you when you were laid up with a sprained knee was all Swords. Action, storm, battle. You do recall, don't you, the Knight of Swords in that spread? Keep an eye out for a daring rescuer . . ."

But I was not exactly paying attention anymore. "Don't turn suddenly, Phil," I said. "Just get up casually and walk over to the grill. Then glance out the window. It isn't my imagination—there *is* someone standing out there by the beech tree?" He had on a gray coat with the collar turned up, a gray hat pulled down to his eyes, and was leaning against the tree, almost looking a part of the gnarled, gray bark against the pearly sky. A heavyset man with an ominous aura.

Phillipa's dark eyes took in the situation instantly, and the next moment she'd pulled out a great, long knife from the knife block. I'd once seen her split a Hubbard squash with one whack of this wicked-looking machete. She waved it purposefully at the window, up to the sky, and down to the earth. "Begone, unwanted guest!" she screamed. Having no idea that her voice could reach that shrill pitch, I was chilled to the marrow. "Be cast out and banished, evil one!"

I don't know if he heard her through the triple-paned window, or simply saw the sword-like knife waving his way. Whichever— he stepped back, a gray shadow among the gray tree trunks, and faded into the icy woods beyond the lawn. But I felt him still lurking there, and I was afraid to head out to my car in the early dusk, afraid of what might happen to Phillipa if I left her alone and drove home.

"Do you think we should call Stone?" Phillipa asked.

"And confess how craven and cowardly we are? Absolutely."

"Never mind. Let's call Deidre instead. Maybe she can send Will over."

"All right. Say, Phil—where did you get that banishing thing?"

"Can't remember. Maybe Fiona's old book. You know—the dilapidated, moldy one. You call Deidre, will you?"

I picked up the phone from the kitchen desk to dial and felt the blood rush away from my head. I sank down into the desk chair. "No dial tone . . ." I whispered.

Phillipa's pale olive skin drained of its slight color, and her dark eyes turned glittering as she grabbed the phone receiver from my hand and listened. "What do we do now?"

"Do you have a cell phone?"

"No. What about you?"

"Left it home. I'm going out to the car," I said.

"You're not leaving me here alone!"

"There's a built-in CB in the Wagoneer. I've never used it, but there's a booklet about it with the owner's manual in the glove compartment."

"I'll come with you." She was already shrugging into an old fur jacket by the door. "After this, you can bet I'm going to buy a cell phone."

"Bring that awesome knife."

"You bet." She picked up the kitchen machete with a flourish that made us both giggle. Maybe it was nerves, but we couldn't stop giggling while we crept into the car, locked the doors, and struggled with the CB instructions.

"Breaker . . . breaker . . ." I called to the world at large, while peering out the windows for the intruder.

"What's that mean?"

"How should I know? I've heard it in the movies. Maybe we should just drive out of here."

"No way. Suppose he decides to take out his revenge on my house. I just got my Viking range installed. Or he could hide somewhere and jump out at me right when I step into the shower, that psycho. Just tell whoever answers to send in the cops."

I tried several more times, adding that there was an intruder and giving our address. Amazingly, someone must have heard my repeated calls for help, because ten minutes after we'd run back inside and barricaded the doors, a cruiser rolled into the driveway, blue lights flashing on the rapidly darkening scene.

"Someone was stalking us," Phillipa explained to the two blue-uniformed women. I found it rather embarrassing that our would-be protectors were females like ourselves, but then, they did have those nice big guns to back them up.

"A man in a gray coat and hat. He went that way, into Jenkins's woods. We couldn't get a dial tone," I added.

One of the officers shone a flashlight on the telephone wire and followed it to its connection to the house. It was no surprise to learn it had been cut. The officers radioed headquarters, and soon we had a detective—not Stern, who was out working a case, which I hoped was Daryl's—enjoying a piece of Phillipa's spiced-apple pie and asking questions, some of which we didn't exactly answer. After that, the telephone repairman arrived. Then Deidre with Will, who'd heard the police call on his scanner. Deidre offered to leave Will for the night, like a guard dog on loan.

The detective finished his pie, closed his notebook, and comforted Phillipa with "Not much we can do about this unless he tries to break in." The officers promised a cruiser would check back often, and they probably would. This was the kind of slow winter's night when crime on the South Shore was hardly rampant.

So I felt Phillipa was in good hands—or at least, many well-intentioned hands—when I finally drove home. I felt guilty to find Tip and Scruffy curled up together, asleep on the living room floor. I had to wake them up to finish the night in the blue bedroom upstairs that I thought of as Adam's, although Adam had only slept there twice in three years. Scruffy sighed heavily but nonetheless decided, as a host, that his duty lay in keeping the guest's feet warm in bed. It seemed natural to have Tip at home here, lifting a sadness I'd been carrying like some old infirmity so familiar as to be half-forgotten.

Phillipa called at dawn. "Guess what I found!"

"What?" I asked without interest from the deep fog of my dreams.

"Kerosene-soaked rags under the porch. I smelled them as soon as I opened the door."

"Oh, shit. *Now* will you call Stern?"

"Yes. I mean, I already did. He's on his way. Perhaps now he'll believe us about Q. I think the bastard must have returned after the detective decamped. Then, of course, the cruiser did patrol quite often during the rest of the night, so perhaps Q got interrupted again. Somehow his plan to torch the witch went awry."

"When Stern hears about the telephone and sees those rags, he'll know we must be on to something."

"I look a wreck," Phillipa sighed. "I hardly slept a wink. How about you?"

"I slept alertly. Listen, I'll call the others. We'll pin Heather down on her mysterious plan. It's time we took those serious measures we've been threatening."

Phillipa's house in peril! Trailing about the kitchen in my faded L. L. Bean cords and flannel shirt with dawn's early cup pumping caffeine into my bloodstream, I looked around my own snug little home. Grandma's rocking chair by the fireplace. The shelves of neatly arranged, if dusty, jars of dried herbs and tiny dark bottles of essential oils. Bunches of aromatic plants hanging from the kitchen beams. I tried not to imagine flames licking up the walls and ceiling, a sharp mingling of scents as glass containers exploded.

"Banish the thought!" I recited nervously, and went into the lav to throw cold water on my face. Catching sight of my wild hair, like a tangle of wheat, I attacked it with a hairbrush until it stood out all over my head with winter electricity. A regular crone!

After Tip and I had consumed bowls of steaming oatmeal, he ran off to catch the school bus, not looking back, eager for the day ahead and, most likely, for his father's return from Waterbury. I stashed the dishes in the dishwasher and stood for a long time at the window fronting the ocean. Sun broke through the gray wall of clouds and shone like a searchlight on the far boats. It was deadly still, deadly cold out there. Had Stone really looked for Daryl? Or had he simply dismissed our alarm as female, midlife craziness? Could we get in to search Quicksall's place ourselves? Was Heather's mysterious magic going to help? Was Hecate manifesting from her crossroads shrine?

My inner dialog was beginning to remind me of a soap opera. *As the Wheel Turns*, perhaps. Quicksall was on to us, all right—or rather, he knew we were on to him. What terrorism could he not devise? Thinking about protective herbal charms for all of us, I took down my largest hardwood mortar and pestle, giving it a cleansing swipe with my flannel shirttail, and set it on the kitchen table.

Thistle, fennel, wood betony . . . Drifting around the kitchen, I began to feel somewhat airy and unrooted, gathering herb jars as if in a dream. My ears buzzed; that familiar flutter unsettled my stomach. A vision flashed across my inner eye. I was on a sidewalk watching a car careen through a red light, narrowly missing a truck. Deidre's Plymouth Voyager! Faster and faster, a blur of blue metal. Something about the brake—a child screamed. I almost screamed myself as the vision broke into a thousand pieces, like the reflection in a smashed plate glass window.

Sternly pulling myself together for quick action, I glanced at the clock. It was almost eight already! I grabbed the phone and pressed that convenient single digit labeled "D." On the third ring, a sleepy Will answered.

"Have Deidre and the kids left for school yet?" I demanded without preamble. Deidre often drove Jenny to first grade before delivering Willy Jr. to kindergarten. Some time passed during which I could hear Will stumbling around, calling for his wife.

When he returned to the phone with an affirmative murmur, I screamed at him, "Go after her right away! The brakes are going to fail. I think Q may have done something to them." There's something to be said for a fireman's training—instantly he was alert, ready to rush into action.

"Call me," were my last words before he slammed down the receiver. I was relieved that I hadn't had to explain to Will that he was sprinting out of the house because of one of those dizzying visions of mine. Unable to do anything besides pace around the downstairs while I waited to hear from the Ryans, I caught sight of my grandma's rifle over the living room mantel. Suddenly that weapon made a lot more sense to me than herbal charms. I almost felt the feisty little lady's spirit standing beside me, urging me to take the rifle down and defend myself—and her home.

This same rifle had been the cause of considerable discussion between me and Heather, who was anti-gun, anti-NRA, and probably anti-bow-and-arrow or slingshot. False-friend Phil had sided with Heather. "It really doesn't fit the rest of this primitive nest of yours," she'd said, surveying the living room with an artistic eye while her long fingers, scarred from paring vegetables, caressed the polar bear, one of the Inuit sculptures I'd arranged on the mantel. "A bone harpoon would work, perhaps."

"What's the difference? They both mean business. And this rifle has great sentimental value to me," I'd said. "My dear departed grandma used it to discourage woodchucks and the occasional intruder. I don't even know where she kept the bullets or how to load the thing if and when I locate the ammunition."

Yet, standing here now, looking up at the rifle, two thoughts sprang to mind. One—there was a cobweb gracefully draped over the butt of the old weapon, and the whole ceiling needed to be gone over with a pillowcase-wrapped mop, and two—I knew exactly where the bullets were—in my grandma's handkerchief case.

I raced upstairs with renewed energy to find Scruffy ambling out of the blue guest room, lazily stretching his hindquarters. Catching sight of me rummaging through the armoire in the hall, he began to cavort around in an urgent manner. *Let's go, let's go—I need to pee!*

"You had a walk already, so hold your water for a minute," I barked at him. "Ah, here we are. Good old Gran." I tossed several bullets into my shirt pocket and ran downstairs to let Scruffy out the kitchen door. The instant the cold air hit him, he began an uproar of barking, which I ignored.

Dragging a side chair over to the mantel, I removed the rifle and dusted it off with my already grungy shirttail. Possibly it would save wear and tear on my clothes if I simply carried a duster in my pocket at all times. Without getting down from the chair, I loaded bullets into the rifle without a bit of a problem— funny how my hands seemed to know just what to do. Perhaps it was a skill remembered from a previous existence, a life on some frontier shooting rampaging natives, maybe Tip's very ancestors.

So now was I trying to make amends by harboring Tip? Or maybe it was an early memory of watching my grandma prepare to murder a few woodchucks with her .22.

May she journey through Summerland in peace! I swung the rifle around and aimed it at various items in the room.

There was a small, scratching sound at the bay window. I turned to investigate, the rifle wedged against my shoulder. It was Joe Ulysses looking in at me—those Mediterranean features, so strong and handsome! He threw up his hands and disappeared from view.

"Don't shoot," I heard him shout. "I can explain everything." Scruffy was growling ferociously somewhere nearby.

I leaned the loaded rifle against the fieldstone fireplace, then jumped off the chair. "So . . ." I said as I threw open the seldom-used front door, "Couldn't you have sent me a postcard from that Russian prison? Scruffy, let go of that man right now! He's our friend. More than a friend." Joe's arms went around me, and I drew him out of the January chill into my warm living room.

Is he hurting you? Scruffy hunched uncertainly on the granite doorstep, having released his grip on Joe's duffel bag but still growling.

"No. Go chase seagulls." I shut the door on Scruffy before he could take it into his head to leap to my defense.

The kiss was deep and sweet. Joe's hands went under my shirt, caressing my bare back. I had a strong urge to sink onto the sofa and pull this beautiful man after me. It was a pure wonder that I ever remembered Deidre, who, at this very moment, could be wrapping herself around a telephone pole on Route 3A.

Lingeringly, I broke free and whispered, "Wait, Joe. I'm expecting a call from Will. I mean, my friend Deidre's husband Will." He looked at me with a wise grin and a raised eyebrow. "Whether she's cracked up the car with the kids in it," I explained.

"Sounds serious. What's going on?"

I moved away, but not too far away. He still held onto my hands with a firm, ardent grip. "It's a *really* long story, Joe."

"I have a few hours. How long will it take to tell me?"

"Are you laughing at me? How much time do you really have?"

He had the grace to look guilty. "I'm to rendezvous with the *Rainbow Warrior* in New York tomorrow for its annual U.S. tour. Receptions for major donors in major cities from New York to Houston. We returned from Singapore two days ago and have been taking on some new crew members and supplies. I got the shuttle to Logan as soon as I was free. Drove a rental straight here. I have to drive back to catch the noon shuttle tomorrow. But, hell, we're on the same continent at least. I'll fly here every chance I get, providing you want me."

"Oh, I want you, all right," I sighed, pressing against his marvelous body. One glorious day together—perhaps it would last forever. But a little part of my mind remained aloof from my elation and remarked, *Typical sailor, Cass. Are you planning to be his girl in Plymouth, like the girls he has in other ports?*

Quiet, I said to my critical self. *Just leave me alone, will you?*

Joe and I kissed again. His hands, under my shirt again, moved around to my breasts. I would soon forget everything. We'd be the way we were before—unbelievable enchantment. The phone rang, jolting me out of my melting mood. Gently pushing Joe away, I scrambled into the kitchen, answering breathlessly—and not just from my dash to the phone.

"Do you think that son of a bitch tampered with my car?" Deidre demanded. "The brake was okay when I backed out of the driveway, but then all of a sudden it went completely. Will's having it checked."

Hearing her voice brought such a sense of relief. "You're all right, then—what a blessing! Were the kids shaken up?"

"Everyone's fine. Willy Jr. asked me if we could drive like a racer again tomorrow when I take them to school."

"I'm so glad. What happened exactly?" Joe had followed me

into the kitchen and was holding me around the waist, kissing my neck. This was going to be a short—and guarded—conversation.

"Apparently, you already know."

"I had a glimmer."

"A vision?"

"You could say that."

"What happened was, I found myself driving through Plymouth Center without brakes. The first light was green, so that was okay. I stepped up on the gas since we were running late for Jenny's first grade, as usual. Then suddenly I was sailing through the second light, which was red, pumping the brake in vain. What an awful feeling! Say, are you all right? You're breathing funny."

Unashamedly listening to Deidre's excited voice, Joe chuckled.

"I'm fine, Dee. How'd you stop the car?"

"Ran it up on the Town Hall lawn and through the hedge. Nice, soft landing. You know, they really ought to take down that nativity scene at the new year, don't you think? Well, I guess they'll need a new one next year. Will said you were yelling something about Q."

"We'll see what Will discovers when he checks out that brake."

"Right. Listen, let's not waste any more time getting our healing circle together to zap that murdering creep. How about tonight—my place?"

"Ah . . . make it tomorrow, okay? Listen, I'm really thankful you were so quick-witted. But we'll have to talk later. I have a delicate decoction on the fire."

"I bet," said Deidre. "Well, if we have to postpone until tomorrow, we'll have to meet at Phil's. Will and the boys will be playing poker here. Who've you got with you, anyway? Don't tell me he's back!"

"Good-bye, you witch," I said, and softly hung up the receiver.

We almost made love against the kitchen counter but managed to find our way to the bedroom without ever letting go of one another. The second time was even more amazing. That man knew more about driving my body wild than Gary had ever learned in all our years of marriage.

Scruffy wasn't speaking to me when I finally let him inside and rubbed him down with a heated towel to melt the little icicles on his fur.

Fiona the librarian was our finder. Whatever was lost, sought, needed, or barely dreamed of, Fiona, on one of her good days, would probably conjure up out of the serendipitous stew of her normal environment. So it was not surprising that she had unearthed a promising avenue of investigation.

"Clayton M. Quicksall of Sachem Road, Carver," she announced to us all, "has only recently retired from being an independent trucker. Owned his rig and traveled the highways and byways of New England with whatever goods he was hired to transport. He might load up with Massachusetts widgets for Maine shipyards, then turn around with a truckload of Maine fiddleheads for Massachusetts grocery markets. I came across this feature article about him, you see, in the *Wiscasset Weekly*— "The Last of the Independents.""

"How in the world did you come by this little tidbit?" Phillipa exclaimed, taking the ragged page out of her hands. "This woman is a wonder, an absolute wonder . . ."

Joe had departed for the Greenpeace U.S. fund-raising tour. I was still feeling a bit dazed, as if from an overdose of sunbathing, only it was January. My dreaming self remained lost in Joe's sea-muscled, sun-warmed arms, while my sensible self tried to connect with reality, which at this moment was our gathering at Phillipa's for dinner and to plan a serious offensive against Q.

The circle was complete, except for Deidre, who would join us as soon as her buffet for the firehouse poker players was "out of the way," as she put it, in a tone of motherly forebearance. It was the night of the full moon, making this evening the traditional Esbat of the Wolf Moon, although no moonlight would be seen through the heavy cloud bank looming ominously above us, shutting out all but a few high, cold stars.

"Actually, it was Omar," Fiona explained. "As it happened, there was a family of field mice in the stacks, chewing up old pamphlets for nesting fodder, so I'd taken to bringing Omar into the library to scare them off. Maybe the 'wee, cowering, timid beasties' could be persuaded to find fluffier digs in the basement quilting room." The small branch library run by Fiona was located in a building owned by the Women's Cooperative for Folk Arts.

"I hope you didn't let Omar snack on any of those dirty little creatures." Heather was immediately up in arms at the thought of Fiona's negligence. "Talk about intestinal parasites!"

"Let's not," Phillipa suggested. She refilled our wineglasses and stirred some more fragrant broth into the risotto. As always, we were hanging out in her resplendent kitchen where shining copper pots cast a benign glow on our winter pallor. "Dinner will be ready in eight to ten minutes. Do you think you'll be able to get to the point of this story by then?" We all understood that conversation would have to turn to unstinting praise when Phillipa served her risotto followed by osso buco. I felt life returning to my taste buds.

"So Omar was out back stalking and pouncing to his heart's content one day last week when he jumped into an old wooden chest and the lid slammed shut," Fiona continued, unperturbed by the timing of Phillipa's risotto. She wandered over to the window and looked out fretfully at the wind-driven blasts twisting and turning. "Do you think this snow is ever going to let up?"

"Occasional flurries only," Phillipa declared. "Absolutely no accumulation, the weatherman guaranteed. Do you think I'd have taken the chance of having you all snowed in here?"

"So, what happened then?" I prompted Fiona. "Did Omar read a few old weeklies while waiting for you to rescue him?"

"Stuck to his claw, would you believe it? When I opened the

lid, Omar just jumped out into Mommy's arms and delivered the goods!" Fiona pointed to the mangled article in triumph.

"If this maniac Quicksall has been traveling up and down the northeast coast for years, he could have been preying on children from any state in New England," Heather said.

"How do you know Q has recently retired?" I asked, feeling just a tiny bit miffed at having our investigation topped by a Persian cat.

"The town council, you may recall, has decided to move that big wooden cow from the defunct How Now Brown Cow Dairy to a playground in Manomet, and they consulted the fire department about transporting it. I remembered Deidre mentioning the matter at Yule. After this article came to light, I suggested that Deidre get Will to call Quicksall, inquiring if he still owned his rig and would be available to help tote the cow. Which he didn't and he wasn't. Simple, really." Looking pleased with herself, as well she might be, Fiona drained the last of her wine as a discreet buzzer summoned Phillipa to the range.

"Quicksall may have brought some of his victims back to that secluded house of his in Carver," Heather continued her train of thought. "He may have buried bodies right here on his home ground. Gerry Kirschmann, of course, was dug up in a deserted part of Myles Standish—but I bet there are other remains to be found at Quicksall's place. The thing to do would be to turn over his entire property, don't you think?"

"Makes sense to me," said Fiona absently as she searched through her reticule, looking for heaven-knows-what. A pick and shovel? A bulldozer? I wondered. Was it my imagination, or did I hear a bell tinkling somewhere in the depths of her green carry-all?

"Are you mad?" I asked. "We'd have to wait for the spring thaw. March at least, maybe April. And besides, we know from our earlier research that other missing boys have been found tied to trees in remote woodland locations in New England coastal towns. Exactly what I saw in my vision, by the way."

"Yes, but I feel strongly that there must be evidence of some of his local crimes on Q's property. We just can't wait until spring while some other youngster gets tortured and murdered. We'll get into the house itself right now," Heather said. "After all, if we can't dig until the spring thaw, neither can Q. So what did he do with Daryl? Surely there's something in the house itself to incriminate Q. Stern never actually went in, you know. Staked out the place all right, but since there was no sign of Q that week, they concluded that Daryl couldn't have been imprisoned there."

"Stone investigated the matter *thoroughly.*" Phillipa defended her detective sharply while getting us all seated at her marble kitchen table and setting plates of steaming, creamy risotto before us. "He learned that Q was in Atlantic City all Christmas week, gambling with cronies. So what excuse could Stone possibly use to obtain a search warrant from a judge? Cass's supermarket hallucination?"

"Oh, thanks. If Q was in Atlantic City, who left us that snake-stuffed fruitcake?" I demanded. "I think you'll find those cronies were covering up for Q, at least for some of those days."

"How the devil are we going to get in?" Fiona pounced on the salient point.

"My first thought was some sort of household emergency. Anything that would take him away from the house for a reasonable amount of time. I've been summoning Hecate to create a domestic crisis," Heather finally confessed.

"Gas!" Fiona declared triumphantly. "Why doesn't Hecate simply blow up the house with him in it?"

"With those poor, helpless dogs trapped inside? Never!" Heather said.

"I wouldn't describe those bloodthirsty Dobes as helpless, my dear," I murmured. "They are *dogs*, however, so naturally I agree that we mustn't harm them. But what about a nice little gas leak instead? I wonder if he's a customer."

"Oh yes, indeed he is." Fiona fished in her reticule and pulled out a wrinkled, spotted computer printout of names and addresses that proved to be a list of the Plymouth Gas Company's customers on Sachem Road, including C. M. Quicksall."

"I hardly dare ask," I said, passing the printout to Heather. "Fiona's amazing. I've been working on this for days," Heather sighed. "But gas is much too volatile. What do you say?"

"I say, table it until after dinner," Phillipa ordered, sweeping grandly to the table with a platter of osso buco. I followed meekly with a dish of roasted vegetables, like a postulant after a saint's statue.

Later, when we were all sipping cappuccino topped with mounds of cinnamon-flavored steamed milk and lolling about in front of a roaring fire in Phil's baronial fireplace—the centerpiece of a gray-upholstered conversation pit, like a fifties movie set— Deidre appeared, jolly Mrs. Snowman with apple cheeks and a peaked red hood, to assure us that the roads were getting impassable. Phillipa groaned.

"No need to get frantic," Deidre assured our hostess. "One of Will's buddies in the highway department dropped me off on his sanding route. If need be, he'll pick us all up and take us home later."

"You see, Deidre has all the contacts we need to do some actual digging in the spring," Heather pointed out. "When the ground thaws, we can probably scare up an urgent environmental hazard—seepage of dangerous chemicals into the groundwater, perhaps."

We filled Deidre in on the plans of action under discussion. "Interesting. A delicate instrument—such as, say, a gas meter— should be especially vulnerable. I think I've read that the CIA's been studying the use of psychic energy to fiddle with machine controls." Deidre shook out her yellow curls, which had been flattened by the elfin hood. "But if we succeed in causing a leak, speaking personally, I wouldn't go anywhere near it, nor would I want any of you, my dear friends, to fall victim to your own clever craft. One spark, and you're off to Eternal Summerland. There must be some better—or at least, safer—ideas."

We waited politely, savoring the spicy cinnamon—which is noted in my herbals for stimulating the mind and purifying thoughts.

"There are three concerns we need to address here, as I see it," Deidre continued. "The first is getting Q elsewhere. The second is breaking in—where and how? And the third is those vicious dogs of his—if he leaves them on guard in the house, how can they be tranquilized or neutralized, or whatever?"

"Oh, is that all?" Phillipa's dark eyes gazed heavenward. "Duck soup."

"I won't have those animals hurt," Heather warned. She sat cross-legged with easy grace, her back to the fire, the light burnishing her hair with a halo.

"By the way, the garage mechanic found a slice in something or other that caused all my brake fluid to leak out," Deidre told us. "Looked to him as if it just happened, a nice, fresh, even-edged cut. Will found a little pool of brake fluid on the floor of the garage, but the hose must have really let go when I was well on my way with the kids."

"You don't lock your garage?" I asked.

"We do now, that bastard. How did he sneak in there without any of us hearing him—not even Salty and Peppy? All right, let's see. Let's focus this intention of ours through the four elements." Deidre got down to business. "The gas caper is an air idea, but it's too volatile for us to manage. Digging up the grounds is an earth notion but not practical in winter. That leaves fire and water, both certainly capable of causing a domestic crisis at Q's place. Since water is distinctly the more manageable of the two, why not concentrate on that first?"

"You mean, create a flood somewhere? That's a bit daunting!" Phillipa complained while passing a plate of buttery shortbread. "And how will that get us into the house?"

Deidre was silent for a moment. Finally she said, "I don't

know exactly how a water spell will work for us. We'll simply use water as a focus, and leave the details to the Goddess. Let Q somehow be washed away from his place long enough for us to jimmy a cellar window or whatever. And we'll need some kind of psychic protection, I guess—from Q, and from the law. We're talking breaking and entering here."

"Glamour! It's a glamour we'll need!" declared Fiona in her low, raspy voice. "An enchantment to transform appearance." As if to illustrate her point, she stood up and raised her hands above her head. The sleeves of her coat sweater fell back, revealing pale, plump arms aglitter with silver bangles. With a flourish, her hands described a figure in midair—perhaps a pentagram—causing the bracelets to tinkle like a wind chime. She smiled enigmatically, gracefully lowered her arms, looking suddenly younger and even taller, commanding, unquestionable. Was it some trick of the firelight?

"I didn't know you could do a glamour, Fiona," I said. "You'll have to give us a few pointers . . ."

"With a magical presence, you can look the way you want for any occasion." The usually frumpy Fiona warmed to her subject. "Capture every gaze, if it suits you—or disappear into ordinariness and be an invisible woman. In fact, you're sending out some sort of visual vibrations all the time, unconsciously. Just look at Cass today, for example. Aglow with sexuality, isn't she? But you must all learn to gain control over these impulses you emit, my dears, and shape-shift into the image you desire—with practice, practice, practice."

They had all turned to me. I stifled a strong urge to study myself in the oval mirror I knew was behind me. "I guess my life is just an open *grimoire* to you guys," I moaned.

"Do you think we could claim to be rescuing his pets from some dangerous situation?" Heather hauled us back into our war scenario.

"If you'd seen those two hounds from hell, you'll never call them pets," I muttered.

"So, what *are* their names?" asked Fiona, having become herself again, slumped into her sweater of many colors.

"I don't know. Killer and Diller, probably," I replied testily.

"Doesn't all this seem unnecessarily complicated?" Fiona complained. "I'd vote for a nice, clean explosion myself. Of course, that's only my opinion."

"We'll have to work in teams, watching Q's place for the magic moment, so to speak. We can keep in touch by cellular phone," Heather said.

"So the object now is to precipitate some crisis of a watery persuasion," Phillipa said thoughtfully. "This is a real test. I like it. But Stone is going to be pissed with me if we're caught at Q's."

"Do you suppose Stone would believe that we went in that house to rescue the Dobes?" I wondered.

With one incredulous glance from her dark eyes, Phillipa squelched my hopes.

But Heather had the last word. "Yes—because in the meantime, I'll have several anonymous complaints of animal cruelty phoned in by the staff at Animal Lovers," she said.

A snowbound Esbat seemed to be the perfect atmosphere for our incantation that evening. As hostess, Phillipa drew the circle with her athame, a no-nonsense nineteenth-century dagger, and spun out crashing, watery words from her poet's imagination. Fiona unearthed her moldy *Book of Shadows*. I laid on the herbs. I could swear I felt the tides of power rise in us, and it seemed a fortunate omen that the snow turned to a drenching rain before we all left to creep home on the wet, icy roads.

"We don't know our own strength, Cass," whispered Deidre, lowering herself cautiously through Q's cellar window and onto the workbench below it. I wriggled through next, and a pretty tight fit it was in rain jacket and jeans. We jumped down into the four inches of water below on the cellar floor. Deidre carried a heavy-duty flashlight, and I had my cell phone, freshly charged, the wrench we'd used on the window, and several plastic baggies in my pocket, in case we found any evidence worth filching.

Early that morning, Q had phoned the firehouse looking for a sump pump he could borrow. By luck or magic, Deidre had been in the station house when Will took the call. She'd heard her husband say, "Sorry, Mr. Quicksall. We don't have one free at the moment. They might have one over in Halifax, or you could try Duxbury." Then Heather, on watch in the woods—in a rent-a-wreck loaner she had parked in an overgrown side road—saw Q leave his place at 8 A.M. in his black-paneled van, a dog sitting beside him in the front seat. That's why Deidre and I were at this very moment breaking into Q's cellar. We'd left Heather as lookout down the road. Her mission was to call us if she spotted Q returning.

Water was spewing through cracks in the old stone foundation, and more water was rising in the set tub, spilling onto the floor. The set tub water smelled putrid. The heavy downpour that had continued all night had melted accumulated ice and snow into a river that, besides seeking out weak places in the cellar wall, was also running into Q's cesspool and backing up into the tub. With Q on his way to Halifax, I figured we had an hour at least, of which we'd used up twenty minutes hightailing it over here.

"Let's look for a freezer or refrigerator," I said. "We should be safe wearing these rubber boots, but don't turn on any lights."

Deidre swung the flashlight around the sodden, dark cellar that smelled, I imagined, like the sewers of Paris. "Ugh. What do you suppose . . . ? Oh, look over there, Cass." Her searching beam arrived at the freezer locker in the corner of the room. It was still above water, resting on some kind of wooden platform. "You lift the cover. I just can't . . ."

"Well, then, you take the phone—and give me the flashlight. Why don't you slosh over to the window and just have a fast look at the driveway." With some trepidation, I opened the coffin-shaped freezer and peered inside, shining the light from end to end. I was relieved to observe it contained not a frozen dead body, but packages of meat wrapped in butcher paper, labeled "horsemeat" or "venison steaks." Q probably fed raw horsemeat to those dogs. That should bring out the vigilante in Heather!

"Nothing here," I said, clapping the freezer shut. Shivering, I wondered what might have gone on in this evil-smelling cellar.

"Coast is clear outside. Want to have a look upstairs?" Deidre suggested. "Let's try the hall closet. You never know what you might find in one of those."

It made sense. I trudged upstairs in my rain boots and cautiously opened the door into some sort of laundry workroom—about six feet wide and ten feet long. With the cellar at my back, it had to be the kitchen door at the other end. On my left side, a washer and dryer. On the floor, two baskets of dirty clothes. On the right side of the room, a stained butcher-block bench, a knife block with chef's knives, and a cleaver. A lab could tell if those bloodstains were animal or human. Grabbing a boning knife from the block, I scraped up a tiny amount of the stained wood, wrapped it in a baggie, and stuffed it into my pocket. The place I'd scraped looked entirely too clean. I rubbed it with my muddy glove.

There was a sound at the kitchen door. At first I thought it was a loud purr. Wondering if Q kept some kind of big cat in the house, I listened more closely. I was actually hearing a low, menacing growl. Q must have left one of the Dobes at home! The growl got louder and more anxious as the dog commenced scratching at the door—which moved open about an inch.

With a flash of pure terror, I saw it was a swinging door. But it seemed to be barricaded on the other side by some heavy cartons propped against it. I could see red printing through the slitted door—beer cases, I guessed. The Dobe must be trying to paw his way around them and push open the door. Slowly I backed away, never looking away from the shaking and scratching. Damn it! I'd been hoping to have time to go through that laundry for evidence.

"Hi! Any problem there?" Deidre had come up behind me, her whisper making my heart jump wildly.

"One of the Dobes," I explained.

By then Deidre could hear for herself the animal's frantic attempts to get through and attack us. It took Deidre, with her young mother's quick reflexes, only an instant to snap back with a plan. "Let him run straight to the cellar," she whispered. "I'll stand behind the cellar door, you open the swinging door and stand behind that. When the Dobe barrels through, I'll slam the cellar door after him. *Voila!* Dog in cellar, witches in house!"

"Worth a try," I agreed hastily. "You throw something down the stairs, a sound for him to follow."

"Okay, on the count of three. You count . . ." Out of the corner of my eye, I saw her pick up something from behind the washing machine.

"*One . . . two . . . three . . . GO!*" It was a miracle of good timing. I flung open the swinging door with myself flattened behind it. The Dobe hurtled over the stacked cases. Shielded behind the cellar door, Deidre reached around and threw something down the stairs, then whipped back to safety. Down the stairs the dog flew after his prize. Deidre slammed the door shut. There was a most satisfactory click as it latched. Also an old-fashioned key in the lock. Deidre turned that, then sank to the floor, panting.

Coming out of my hiding place, I flashed back in my mind's eye to what I'd just seen. Something was nagging at me. "Dee, what was that you threw downstairs?"

"I don't know. Some sort of bag with stuff in it."

"What sort?"

"Cloth."

"What was on it?"

"Something like a badge or an emblem."

"Could that have been a kid's book bag, by any chance?"

"Mother of God!"

"Well, we'll never get it now. Probably it was nothing. Still, let's go through this laundry. Maybe we'll get lucky."

But our hasty search yielded only oily shirts, dirty underwear, grimy jeans, and behind the washing machine, spiders. "Who's been rifling through my laundry?" I muttered.

"What?"

"When Papa Bear comes home," I said, "isn't he going to wonder about a few things, like the cellar window propped open, the Dobe dog-paddling in the flood, this table scraped raw, and now the dirty clothes messed about."

"So? Make him sweat, I say. How much time do we have left? If you're nervous, we could steal something to make this look like a genuine robbery." Deidre continued to be a fund of improvisation.

"About fifteen minutes, tops. Never mind the grand larceny—let's look in that hall closet, like you said. Got the phone?"

"Ah . . . no . . ."

"NO???"

"Ah . . . I think I left it on the cellar workbench."

"Oh, great," I hissed. "Don't you realize that we're in danger here? And that we're probably leaving more clues than we're finding? Now what!"

"Sorry," she said jauntily. "Look . . . you get into that closet, and I'll run around the outside of the house to see if I can fish that phone out of the cellar window. How high do you think a Dobe can jump?"

"Right up onto the table and through the window. The best thing would be to listen at the window to see if the phone is ringing, warning us to run. In any case, slam the window shut to keep the Dobe in the cellar. And *hurry* . . ."

Cautiously, we crept into the kitchen. After struggling for a moment with the lock, Deidre let herself out the back door. Glancing down at the floor, I realized with horror that we were leaving muddy footprints on the tile floor. I grabbed a hand towel hanging on the oven door to swipe at the marks as I backed out of the kitchen.

When I turned around, I was facing a short hall leading to the front door, with a living room on one side, a dining room on the other, and a predictable closet under the stairs. I opened the closet door; there was a pull-chain light, which I turned on to view an array of heavy coats and boots, a couple of basketballs, footballs, and chewed Frisbees, hockey sticks and pucks, a baseball bat. I tossed the towel I'd been carrying in the back of the closet and picked up the bat, examining it carefully.

There was a clatter behind me. I jumped out of the closet, bat at the ready. It was Deidre, throwing her hands protectively over her head.

"Don't swing that thing! I had to throw your flashlight to that killer Dobe. Nearly lost a hand, but I got the phone—just as it began to ring! Q's on his way home." Deidre was pulling at me urgently as she spoke. "Let's get out of here . . . the kitchen door is our best bet—it faces the woods."

We dashed out the back door and dove into the rain-sodden underbrush. Glancing back through the trees, I glimpsed a van pulling into the driveway. Deidre gasped as she saw it, too. Breathing heavily, we thrashed our way toward the cranberry bog road where Heather should have the motor revving.

Fortunately, she'd done more than that. She'd driven out of the woods and was waiting just at the point where we would emerge on Sachem Road. We jumped into the backseat of the inconspicuous Chevy a heartbeat ahead of a frenzied Dobe, fresh from his ride in the van, racing after us, drooling in anticipation of the kill. As we lay back against the seat, gasping, I realized that I was still holding the baseball bat.

"Don't worry. Your flashlight didn't have your initials stamped on it, and I doubt that Q is a fingerprint expert," Heather declared cheerily while debriefing us in Deidre's shining yellow kitchen. She failed, however, to smooth away all traces of her own worried frown.

"Are you kidding me or what?" I scoffed at her lame reassurances. "Q doesn't need to mess around with the flashlight. He already knows *exactly* who broke into his house. Maybe not that Deidre and I were the break-in team, but he doesn't have to be Einstein to figure out that our circle is responsible. What will he do to us now?"

"Do you think he'll make a complaint to the police?" asked Fiona, wringing the hem of her coat sweater as if to bleed it of its many colors. She and Phillipa had been summoned by phone for a council of war while Heather was still driving us out of Carver.

"We wish!" Phillipa said vehemently. "A complaint would give the police a chance to get into his house, ostensibly to look at the damage, but maybe to ferret out the evidence you two didn't. Q will never risk that. No, whatever measure he takes will be a private and personal vendetta. Our only hope is to get him before he gets us." She waved away Deidre's offer of tea and cookies, accepting a shot of Irish whiskey instead. "And you know what that means."

"What?" Deidre said nervously, pouring whiskey into her teacup. She broke a cookie in two and held half in each hand down beside her chair where they were snapped up by the exuberant Salty and Peppy.

"We have to break in there again," Phillipa decreed in a firm voice. "And this time, we have to get the goods on him."

"You're beginning to sound like a James Cagney movie," I said.

"Who's he?" she asked with a wicked grin.

"Well, I'm letting someone else have all the fun this time." Deidre tasted her tea, made a face, then stirred a spoonful of honey into the cup. "What about you, Fiona? You always manage to find what you're after."

"Don't look at me!" Fiona said, clasping her reticule. "My heart is willing, but my nerves are weak. I'd be glad, however, to do a nice little finding spell for you girls."

"Never mind the finding spell, Fiona. We'll settle for your gun," said Phillipa. "But the problem is, I doubt that any evidence we bring out will be admissible. Besides, Q isn't crazy enough to leave anything lying around after the stunt we just pulled."

"But if we *do* find something damaging," I reasoned, "Stone may be able to get a warrant on the strength of it."

"Surely Q will leave the Dobes on guard all the time now," Deidre pointed out.

"What about the barn?" Fiona asked, gazing beyond us with an absent expression. "I feel you ought to be looking in there."

"The barn!" Phillipa and I cried in unison.

Heather got up and strode around the kitchen, swinging her braid and munching a peanut butter cookie. "Sure, why not?" she said gamely. "But if we can't bring out any evidence or even tell Detective Stern what we find, what will be accomplished by another dangerous raid?"

"I can't believe this is you talking. Where's your faith?" I demanded. "We're going to find something important . . . something we can use . . . can't you just feel the promise of it? The real question, the only question is—how are we going to get rid of Q this time?"

"Well, our water spell was certainly a success. I wish the rest of you could have seen Q's cellar," chuckled Deidre. "This time, let's use the element of earth. Personally, I'll be fascinated to see what we can conjure up."

Following an afternoon of whiskey and peanut butter cookies, I drove home feeling exhilarated by a combined alcohol and sugar high—eager to wash off the scent of Q's septic system and whip up a robust dinner for Scruffy and me. Relief from danger brings on quite a lust for life, I noted, gazing with real awareness at the clearing sky, pale crystalline blue with touches of gold on the eastern horizon, dark clouds overhead moving steadily westward, an extravagant effect.

What a surprise—and an enigma of pleasurable prospects—to find Joe and Tip sitting on my back porch, chatting companionably as if they were old friends! A disconsolate Scruffy was whining and nosing lonesomely at the kitchen window—dogs are so often on the wrong side of a door.

I felt as if I were coming home to a real family—my two new loves—after a hard day's housebreaking. I kissed Joe quite chastely, holding him slightly away with the palms of my hands on his shoulders so that I wouldn't melt into his inviting body, and saw his faint look of surprise at my aura of *eau de wet cellar.*

"Where did you two spring from?" I asked breathlessly. "A maiden's prayer?" He looked wonderful, the strong lines of his tanned face so reassuring and his Mediterranean eyes so thrilling.

"The *Rainbow Warrior* is docked in Charleston for a long weekend of entertaining rich benefactors, for which they don't need an old salt like me," Joe said. "Kelly gave me a lift to Atlanta, where her folks live, and I was able to get a direct flight to Boston from there. I've been having a most interesting talk with your young friend here."

Remembering tawny Kelly, the Greenpeace girl with the dazzling smile, I became increasingly aware of my disreputable gray sweatpants and shirt. "Well, I'm glad to see that you've met the clever handyman I count on to keep things shipshape around here."

"Thought I'd stop over to see if you had any chores that needed doing before I gotta go back to school Monday," Tip volunteered. His level gaze was both sad and hopeful. I wondered what kind of Christmas he'd had in Maine with his wayward mother. Didn't his face look thinner? Who was there to feed this boy properly?

"I sure have," I said, ruffling his straight brown hair and unlocking the kitchen door. Joe and Tip together! An embarrassment of riches. At least he'd have a good dinner before I sent him home to whatever awaited him with his father. An irrepressible surge of joy rose in my heart as we went inside to a disgruntled dog who curled his lip at Joe, then greeted Tip effusively.

I tore myself away for a quick shower, pausing only to throw a package of frozen chicken into the microwave to thaw. As the hot water steamed away the remaining scent of our adventure, I began to wonder what Tip might have said to Joe. The boy knew about my visions, after all, and about the circle—a side of my life I intended to break gently to Joe when the right time came, if ever.

Of the several herbal after-bath splashes I had concocted, I chose the essence of rejuvenating rose and seductive jasmine to waft away all memory of our escapade. Deciding on a leafy green tunic and dark green tights—an outfit inherited from Heather's closets, which overflowed with such Sherwood Forest garb—I summoned Fiona's glamour technique to surround me with an alluring twilight mist. I brushed my hair with ritual slowness and, for a change, liked what I saw in the mirror. Perhaps this precarious enchantment would not be dispelled by the need to do something constructive with the raw chicken. Greek . . . Joe was Greek . . . that meant oregano, lemon, and garlic. Feed a man the herbs of his mother's kitchen, and he will trust you in all things. Reconstructed and heartened, I went downstairs to prepare a feast for four.

Scruffy was plastered against the refrigerator door, looking betrayed. *How long will a loyal dog have to wait for his dinner this time?*

We drove Tip home at eight, with the promise that he could come back in the morning to clean out and hand-wash the Wagoneer in the warm haven of the toolshed garage. On the way back, I could hardly keep my clothes on and my hands off Joe. It hit him as hard as it did me. Although it was only two miles, he drove my car into a shoulder halfway back to kiss me and run his hands over my breasts and thighs.

"We'd better get out of here before the cops come by," I murmured. With a groan, he moved away and started the motor.

At three the next morning, Joe and I were hungry enough from all that sexual exercise to raid the refrigerator for leftover chicken *à la Grecque* and apple cobbler. The overhead kitchen light was much too bright. I turned it off and lit the candles on the harvest table. The gold cross hanging around Joe's neck glinted in its nest of curly black hair. Watching me with an unreadable expression, he said, "The boy tells me you're a witch, which he says is like a shaman."

Don't forget me. Scruffy trotted into the kitchen from the blue bedroom upstairs, a place he enjoyed retiring to for a few hours since it had become enriched with the scent of Tip's visits. The rest of the night he would sleep on the hooked rug outside my bedroom door. I shredded some chicken wing meat and fed it to the yawning dog, giving myself time to consider an answer.

"How do you mean 'witch'?" I countered, striving to sound amused. "What exactly did Tip tell you?"

Joe related the substance of their talk on the porch. From my vision about Q—what Tip knew of it—to the gossip at the church to the unusual holidays celebrated by my circle of friends, Tip had spilled everything. Whoever said Native Americans were stoically silent?

"When I first moved here, Joe, I was recovering from a terribly depressed period in my life. After my divorce, I supported myself and my family by running my parents' garden shop in Salem, but when my children graduated and went out on their own, I felt completely alone. Then I inherited this place, and it seemed like a heaven-sent opportunity to make a fresh start. The warm little ghost of my gran hovered in these rooms—less so now, though. Selling the garden shop brought me a little money, so I started a business in what I loved best, herbs. Just wait until spring when you'll see what sweet gardens I've planted here."

"I noticed the brick walks and all that salt mulch hay," Joe said, taking my hands in his, which was slightly embarrassing since I was holding a chicken bone in one of them. "And, of course, I care very much that you've had a bad time—although you seem positively blooming now—but are you really answering my question?"

"Yes," I said, disentangling my hands and the chicken bone from Joe and handing him a napkin. "Just be patient and let me explain in my own way. I began to spend time at the Plymouth Library, studying Asian herbal medicine. Phil was often there, too, researching wild foods native to our region, a subject I happen to know very well. She introduced me to Fiona at our local branch. Fiona was organizing a woman's study group that Phil and I joined. Heather and Deidre, too. Heather was already delving deeply into the ancient matriarchal religions while recovering from her divorce from a larcenous financial advisor. It was she who talked me into adopting some love at the animal shelter . . ." I scratched Scruffy's head under the table and gave him the rest of the wing meat. "Then Deidre was kind enough to take my first herbal products to try in her natural vitamins franchise—Nature's Bounty. Deidre is very clever with her hands, and between customers, she was sewing little good luck poppets for her friends. So she wanted to know more about herbal lore, its magic uses. Somehow the whole study group thing coalesced into the five of us forming a healing circle, which is something like a consciousness-raising group without the politics. Heather was eager to celebrate some of the high holidays of the pre-Christian era, and we found when we followed some of those ancient rituals we were raising a lot more than our consciousness. We found there was a power in it."

Was it my imagination or was that slight humoring smile on Joe's handsome face slowly fading? I busied myself getting out the good brandy Phil had given me and two snifters. The house was chilly at this hour, and I shivered—I was wearing only the tunic of my green outfit.

"What kind of power?" asked Joe while I poured us each a healthy belt of brandy.

"It's not easy to explain. Things began to happen. Deidre, who'd been having trouble conceiving another child—her heart was set on a family of three—got pregnant with Bobby, her youngest. A major New York publisher decided to make a big advertising

splash with Phil's sumptuous *American Desserts* cookbook.
Heather got back the fortune her ex had stolen while managing
her finances. Well, actually . . . he met with an accident while flying his Cessna to that island bank where he'd stashed the money.
Their wills hadn't been changed yet, so Heather simply inherited his purloined nest egg—minus legal fees, taxes, and payoffs,
of course. Now you may think all this was simply chance or coin-
cidence, but . . ."

"But you think it was witchcraft," Joe said.

"We prefer the term *Wicca*, actually. Meaning *wisdom*. Wicca
offered each of us something she'd been looking for. It's a modern equivalent of the old nature religions."

He sipped his brandy thoughtfully. "And what gift did this
new power give to you? Did some inconvenient person in your
life conveniently meet his doom? And how did what's-her-
name—Fiona—make out?"

Words poured out of me. I wondered if Joe would run away
from me this very moment or wait until morning. "It's funny
about Fiona. She simply doesn't want anything. Apart from
friends, that is—and now she has us. We all have each other. Oh,
and my herbal products took off like a rocket—so fast that I had
to labor, literally, night and day to keep up with the orders.
Really . . . with several Boston salons, some spas, and the catalog
. . . The bottom line was, if I'm willing to work my ass off, I won't
have to worry about paying the taxes on this place anymore. No,
we don't devise spells to harm inconvenient persons, none of that
so-called black magic. Maybe we *could* do it, but we won't, because everything we've read tells us it's dangerous to ourselves.
Otherwise . . ."

*I suppose you and the furry one are going to keep me up all night with
your noise.* Scruffy sat up suddenly and scratched a hindquarter,
shaking the whole kitchen table. Then he sprawled out again
with a groan.

Joe stood up and stretched sleepily. Salt-faded jeans, which
were all he was wearing, slipped down slightly below his navel.

"Otherwise, what? This Q person?" he asked, taking my hand and blowing out the candles. Apparently he wasn't terrified of my powers after all. "According to young Tip, you have the notion that this Q is some kind of psychopathic devil."

"It's a true dilemma," I admitted. "I suppose I am some kind of witch, visions and all, with absolutely no assistance from hallucinatory herbs. Right out of my head—do you mind?"

"No wonder you're so fascinating," he said, putting his face into my tangled hair and his hand on my exposed thigh. "How sure are you about this Q? I'm worried about you. Perhaps I should jump ship and stay here until the matter is settled."

What a lovely offer! Of course, I couldn't allow it. I resolved to put him off with a few palliative lies. "I promise to stay far away from Q, whatever kind of devil he is . . ." I began.

Imbolc—First Stirrings of New Life

Why were there no instant repercussions after our intrusion into Q's private world? We had expected another assault, steeled ourselves against it—and were made all the more nervous by the uneasy quiet of the next few days.

"Perhaps he's gone away," Fiona suggested. "Perhaps our water magic inspired a cruise."

"Get real, Fiona," Phillipa said. "Q is not the cruise type. Clearly, he's holed up in his house going over any traces of murder and mayhem, scrubbing them clean with a toothbrush. And contriving some dreadful fate for us."

But if he were plotting revenge, nothing surfaced as January continued, wet and wild. We planned a dark-of-the-moon ritual at Deidre's—earth magic its theme, and Q the target. The north, the most powerful direction, corresponded to earth, to midnight, to dusky colors. It welcomed silence, allowing earth forces to gather and work in darkness. The earth signs were the sacred bull, the pentacle, and the North Star.

At the end of the rite, Deidre gave us moist, earthy clay to mold into shapes of our imaginings, which we fired in Deidre's oven. As they cooked, they smelled like a month of drought in a heat-hardened land. The next day we buried them—at Fiona's, so that Deidre's children wouldn't dig them up. The ground was still frozen, but we opened bags of potting soil and created an earthwork mound in the corner of Fiona's yard. I don't know what her neighbors thought we were doing—as always at Fiona's, I sensed curtains twitching nearby. We all put our hands into the dirt, digging little graves for our artworks, then patting soil over them until not a gleam of pottery showed through the blanket of earth.

"There," said Deidre, briskly brushing her hands against each other as if dusting off flour. "That should do it."

"Regular patrols past Q's place," Heather decreed, "until we see how this spellmaking is going to play out in new opportunities for investigation."

Before we were to see the fruits of our spellmaking, however, Q made his malevolence felt in a new and unexpected way.

"Willy's first-grade class made a Saturday morning field trip to the Whale Discovery Center," Deidre said before I had even removed my green down jacket and boots or Scruffy had given himself a good shake. She'd sounded so upset on the phone, I'd driven over to her house immediately. A light snow was falling from a pale gray sky, but the misty flakes didn't amount to any accumulation. "It's open on weekends, practically the only place at this time of year. Thirty youngsters, six parents, the teacher—young and enthusiastic—and a hired clown. Not me, of course. I was at the store taking inventory. But they don't know who hired the clown."

"That's weird," I commented. At the yellow Formica table, she filled two cups with her usual weak coffee. I could see Jenny and little Bobby playing with blocks on the living room floor. Scruffy trotted right in to nose the baby, who often trailed a half-chewed zwieback in one grubby hand.

"Yes, isn't it? Say, do you want some whiskey in that? I think I'll have some." She poured a shot of the Irish into each cup. It did wonders for Deidre's coffee. "The clown explained to Miss

Hurley that one of the first-graders' fathers—Miss Hurley thought he said Brittany's father, Garth Adler—had hired him to entertain the children on the bus. Jane Weeks, Timothy's mother, seemed to know the clown, said he'd been so clever making balloon animals at someone's birthday party. The clown had an instant rapport with the children and was such a delight, Miss Hurley said, that she accepted the situation at face value, making a mental note to scold Mr. Adler for taking so much on himself without asking her permission."

"I'm surprised. I would have been slightly suspicious myself. Something about the clown upset Willy?" I heard blocks crash in the living room. Scruffy sauntered back to the kitchen and threw himself under the table amid cries from Jenny and Bobby.

"Not then. The trip was a huge success—the center has a lot of hands-on activities that kids enjoy—and the clown continued to be a big hit. Junie Hurley is barely twenty-six, idealistic, energetic, and belongs to the Quaker church."

"Oh. So she's not a paranoid type, like ourselves. Did the clown have a name?"

"Henry. Happy Henry. Paranoia is a survival instinct." Deidre got up and went to the window, looking out at the jungle gym, its bright metallic colors polished by the wash of snow. "After the excursion, they all got on the bus, which returned to the school. Then Sue Rigotti, the driver, took home the youngsters who hadn't come with a parent. Happy Henry, however, didn't get off at Massasoit Elementary. He got off at the Little League field where he'd left his black-paneled truck. Apparently, he'd parked there this morning and walked to the schoolyard."

"Black-paneled? I'm beginning to understand your concern."

Golden-haired Jenny appeared in the doorway, the very image of her mother, and shook her finger at Scruffy. "That dog deliberately knocked down the castle I made for Bobby."

Deidre turned back to the warm yellow kitchen, leaning against the window. "It was an accident, dear. Dogs don't mess up deliberately. They can't help being clumsy."

There was a snort under the table. *Let's get out of here. I'm getting bored with these kids.* Scruffy yawned hugely, then rested his nose on my shoes.

"You can't play with us anymore, you bad dog," Jenny said, returning to the living room to soothe Bobby with a new masterpiece.

"And that's not all," Deidre continued. "Before he got off, he gave Willy a little package. "Don't open this until you get home," Happy Henry said. "It's a present to share with your mommy."

"What was it?" I asked apprehensively. I began to realize that I hadn't seen Willy this afternoon. "Where's Willy?"

"Willy was so upset, I put him to bed. Salty and Peppy are up there with him. He's sleeping now. It was a dead kitten. Tiny thing, looked newborn. Black. With a swizzle stick through its heart. From the Carver Arms bar."

"Ugh—that pervert! How terrible for poor Willy! I gather you've already called Miss Hurley. Did she check with Adler?" I felt sick with anger and dismay, but I didn't want to upset Deidre more than she was already.

"Garth Adler said Happy Henry *had* contacted him—by phone, he never saw the man—offered his services for free, gave the Giffords as references. Adler said, sure, if it's okay with Miss Hurley. You want another whiskey?"

"No, thanks. I have to drive home, and the roads may be getting messy." I put my hand over the top of my cup for added emphasis, since Deidre was definitely distracted. She poured whiskey into her own cup, minus the coffee. "And the Giffords?" I asked.

"Hired Happy Henry for Beverly's birthday party, out of an ad in the *Pilgrim Times*. He arrived in costume. Made balloon animals and did magic tricks. They never saw him without his makeup. Of course, I immediately checked with the *Times*. The phone number turned out to be an answering service. Happy Henry, claiming to have no phone of his own, called in for his messages. Leaving no trace, naturally."

"What are you going to do?"

"Miss Hurley has already notified the police. Some wacko, the cops said, but, hey, no harm done to the kids. A stern warning to Miss Hurley not to be so credulous from now on. They're checking on the ad the Giffords answered. But they won't find a trail, will they? Just in case we were in doubt, he left that calling card from the Carver Arms." She looked at me, her eyes narrowed. "And I'm going to kill the bastard."

Scruffy stirred restlessly from his nap on my feet. "Maybe we've smoked out Q's MO—this clown disguise. He's a big, cheery-looking guy. Are you going to tell your husband that you think you know the clown's identity? How about Detective Stern?" I asked.

"I haven't decided. If I tell Will, he'll go over there and beat up Q, just on my conviction alone. And then Will lands in an undeserved mess of trouble himself. But I *could* tell Stern. Yes, that's the thing to do. Stern may want to look into this clown angle in connection with Daryl Hendler or some of the other missing boys."

"Now we're getting somewhere," I said. Looking out the kitchen window, I saw Heather's Mercedes pulling into the driveway, followed by Phil's BMW. Good—we would have a council of war.

The next morning at 6:03 A.M., an earth tremor occurred in the Boston area, classified as 4.2 on the Richter scale. The small quake was preceded by a rumbling sound as if loaded trucks were passing nearby, followed by the sensation of a heavy body hitting the side of the house. Windows and dishes rattled and house frames groaned in the Back Bay. In Plymouth, the effects were slighter—so slight as not to wake any but the lightest of sleepers. Some breakfasters heard walls creak and saw the coffee in their mugs betray the disturbance with an unexpected swirl. Hanging objects swung sedately, not wildly.

At the time it happened, I had been sitting cross-legged, meditating, and thought I was having an unusually uplifting experience. Then Scruffy bounded into my bedroom and jumped on me excitedly, licking my face. *Run! Danger! Run!* he yelped, and nothing would comfort him. He dashed from room to room like a mad dog, but when I opened the kitchen door, rather than running outside, he tried to hide in the fireplace. Still, like many other people, I was unaware that a quake had occurred until I heard about it on the morning news. No damage was reported, but civil defense teams were activated anyway as a matter of protocol. Not much was required of civil defense these days, outside of the hurricane season, so this was an opportunity not to be missed.

Heather, who had been out with her dogs at the time, called me excitedly a few minutes later. "Truth be told, I might not have known anything was going on if the dogs hadn't gone ape. You remember my new greyhound Holmes? Jumped straight up from the ground into my arms! All right. I know we shouldn't take credit for this seismic activity, but it's damned coincidental, isn't it?"

"Scruffy went ballistic, too. Let's not talk about it, though. Keeping silent is part of the spell. Especially an earth spell."

"Okay, but we have to scout around Q's place to see if anything's happened there."

"By now, he might recognize any of our regular cars after all our trips up and down Sachem Road."

"I'll borrow Ashbery's Dodge, and leave her to comfort the dogs. Be there in a jiffy."

I was thankful that the leaden skies dulled everything below, including us as we crept past Q's place in the old black car. Heather wore a navy blue anorak with the hood hiding her hair, and Ray-Bans that seemed incongruous on such a gray day. I disguised myself in a dark green parka and Whittaker cap with the earflaps pulled down.

How did I let myself be talked into this? I wondered, perhaps ungratefully, since this was only one more reconnaissance in the offensive against Q personally generated by me. Still, the whole affair was making me a nervous wreck. I glanced at my watch. It was just past seven, a time of morning when country people tended to be up and about. How could Heather look so cool? Her patrician profile had a stony quality this morning, like a queen engraved on a coin.

The pale green, L-shaped farmhouse was as quiet and neat as ever. As far as I could see, every weathered shingle was still in place on the old barn. Heather continued to sputter down the heavily wooded road, then turned around at the cluster of ranch houses we'd passed on our way in from Route 44, and headed back toward Q's property.

"Listen," she whispered, rolling down her window as I slunk down as low as the seat belt would allow.

"Nothing to hear but the birds." But even as I said that, I did hear something faint above the wheezing motor and crunching wheels—the howl of a dog, of two dogs in chorus, then alternating back and forth. "Oh, it's the Dobes! Do you suppose the quake set them off?"

"Absolutely. Animals are much more sensitive than we are to earth vibrations. And the Dobes you described sounded rather high-strung to me. I'm heading back to those ranch houses. I don't think Q will notice if we park there. That way, if he heads out toward Route 44, we'll see him pass."

Pulling myself together, I agreed to go along with this scheme despite my heart palpitations. Heather pulled into a curved side road that led to the cluster of ranch houses and parked in front of the sand-colored one. A face appeared in the picture window briefly, then disappeared behind a hanging spider plant. I expected the salmon front door to be flung open at any moment and the lady of the house to demand an explanation for our presence, but for some strange reason no one appeared. All was silence. Not even a child in sight, just quiet swings and abandoned bikes.

It was a shock when we heard, then saw, Q's black-paneled van passing by at high speed, pebbles bursting away from its wheels. A Dobe's nose was thrust through the window on the passenger's side.

"My guess is that the dogs were nippy with each other because of the quake," said Heather as she started the motor, "so he's keeping them separate. There'll still be one on guard at the house, and not in a good mood. But this might be the right time to get into that barn. We'll park on the same side road where the car won't be seen and walk in."

"Phil was supposed to be your partner in the barn raid," I whined.

"I called Phil first. She told me to get lost—she wouldn't be available until noon."

"What do you suppose she's up to? Baking a breakfast brioche for two?"

"Very likely. Besides, you wouldn't really want to miss this foray—it's your quest, after all."

"How do you know Q won't be back in ten minutes?"

"I talked to Fiona, too."

"What was her excuse?"

"I wouldn't have invited her along. She doesn't have the nerve for commando action. I just wanted her input. Know what she came up with? Quicksall is a volunteer member of the Carver Civil Defense, and as you know, those guys have been called in. Apparently, she's assembled a dossier on Q. Isn't she fantastic?" Heather swung the Dodge into the old cranberry bog road and turned it around in a wide place to face outward, poised for a getaway.

"Fantastic . . ." I said lamely. Such a tidbit hardly guaranteed our safety. As we got out of the car, I did my best to visualize a protective sphere of white light surrounding us—something like a giant soap bubble. Heather picked up some tools from the floor of the backseat, tucked a jimmy into her pocket, and handed me a wrench.

After we had negotiated the woods as quietly as was possible for two suburban females in heavily padded jackets and chunky boots, we sprinted across the open area of Sachem Road and Q's front yard, ducking behind the barn. Peeking around the corner, we surveyed the side door, which bore a padlock. Heather took the jimmy out of her pocket and wielded it meaningfully, but on closer inspection we found that the padlock wasn't snapped shut. As we slipped into the building, I closed the door carefully so that it would appear undisturbed. I heard the padlock, still in place, clunk against the door.

The barn smelled of pine and dust. Its centerpiece, looking old but still usable, was a dark red pickup truck facing the big barn doors. The stalls were empty, the floor bare, and there was no hay in the mow. The walls were hung with old farm tools, rusted and draped with cobwebs. Subdued by anxiety and the emptiness of the scene, we tiptoed over the scarred pine floor as quietly as if we were entering a church. A slight rustling sound suggested that some critter was hightailing it for cover. Two new rubbish barrels stood near the door; I opened each cover with trepidation to find they were filled with forty-pound sacks of dog food.

"Never saw him drive that truck, did you?" Heather whispered.

"Nope. Not to say he hasn't. Let's look it over. And then, let's get out of this mausoleum," I whispered back urgently. An uneasy aura hovered around that truck that both attracted and repelled me. It was more than I had time to explain to Heather.

She set to work in the cab while I went over the bed. Not much there—a toolbox full of ratchets and other items unfamiliar to me, a gas can, empty, and an old canvas that might once have been a sail. The canvas had brown stains on one corner. Could be dried blood, I conjectured. Should I take it with me? I jumped out of the truck, dragging the canvas, and began to roll it up, then stopped. Would it still be legal evidence if I removed it from the scene? Perhaps Heather would know.

I leaned over the right side of the cab. Heather's legs were stuck out the door. I thought she must be examining the floor under the seat. But as I began to speak to her, I noticed a slight change in the light to the left behind me and an ominous sound. I glanced back. A small scream surprised me, even though it came from my own throat. Quicksall was standing in the open door, his big body dark against the outdoor light streaming around him, a Dobe straining at its leash beside him. The animal was growling with quiet menace.

Hearing my squeaking cry of alarm, Heather's head popped up, then ducked down again. Quicksall seemed to be grappling with the leash while his Dobe strained forward, pulling it taut, snarling. I clutched the canvas against my chest. A moment later, Q succeeded in unbuckling the leash from the collar. The Dobe lunged toward me.

I don't remember thinking anything, but evidently my hands had their own plan of action. Instantly, they threw the heavy canvas over the dog, who began barking and snapping as he attempted to free himself. I took the wrench out of my pocket and held it up in the air, hoping the gesture wouldn't look as impotent as it felt.

Quicksall laughed and took a step forward, then he looked beyond me, surprised. Evidently, he had just caught sight of Heather. I didn't dare take my gaze away from his steady, threatening advance, but I heard Heather struggling with something heavy and creaking. Suddenly light flooded the barn. She had opened one of the big doors.

Just as Q's big body thrust itself toward me, the Dobe emerged from the canvas. In their mutual confusion, the man stumbled. One of the truck doors slammed. "Get in! Get in the truck!" Heather shouted at me.

I jumped into the passenger seat and slammed the door. Heather was turning the key, neither of us knowing if the motor would really start. But it did! Amazingly, it leaped into life at her touch.

Quicksall sprang for the door handle, but Heather gunned the motor. We shot forward through the open half of the barn door.

Instinctively, I ducked as we hit the closed side, splintering it
and knocking our attacker off the cab. Heather aimed the red
truck straight as a spear across the lawn toward Sachem Road.
Looking back, I saw Quicksall dashing toward his black van
standing in the circular driveway. It wouldn't take him long to
catch up with us.

"Think good thoughts!" Heather yelled at me over the racing
motor. "Lucky thing he left these keys in the truck, wasn't it?
Recently driven, I'd say, from the way it responded."

"Stuff the analysis—what are we going to do now?"

"Can't imagine!" Heather's words came out in jabs as we
bounced along at high speed. "This is Q's territory. There can't
be a side road he doesn't know from one end to the other."

I turned to look out the back window. "I don't see him following yet."

"That's what I mean. He's probably going to cut us off somewhere up ahead. The way this road curves, there may be a
quicker route through the bogs."

"Yeah? So why don't we double back the other way?"

"Why not, indeed." Apparently, I didn't need to draw her a
map. Heather immediately stepped on the brake hard, flinging
me into the dashboard. The wheels squealed in protest as she
swung around, crashing through underbrush to make a quick
U-turn on the narrow road. Soon we were hurtling back the way
we had come. By now Q must have figured out our scheme, I
worried, and was coming after us. When we passed the ranch
houses in a blur, I glanced at the speedometer. I never would
have believed a person could drive eighty miles an hour on
Sachem Road.

"Hey, are you crazy?" I yelled over the noisy motor. Before I
could form a more suitable protest, Heather was driving the truck
back into the barn, bumping over the splintered remains of the
door.

"Keep low," she yelled back, slamming on the brakes and
jumping out of the cab. What could I do but follow? I could hear

a dog barking somewhere nearby. "And watch out for that deadly Dobe—he may be loose!"

Without further discussion, we both dove into the woods behind Q's place, weaving our way through tangled, leafless birch saplings and bushy pines until we came to a place that was just across from the bog road where we had parked the Dodge. Cautiously, we peered up and down to see if it was safe to dart across Sachem Road.

"Okay, let's do it," Heather whispered hoarsely. But just then we heard the van motor—it was coming at us fast. As we saw Q rounding the turn, we faded back out of sight. The van went barreling past his own property.

"Foiled by his own cleverness," Heather muttered with satisfaction. "Come on, let's get out of here."

As we puttered away in Ashbery's Dodge, I told Heather about the stained canvas. Meanwhile, Q must have figured out what we'd done, but by the time he caught up with us, we were on Route 44 again. Traffic was unusually heavy for ten in the morning on that quiet route. We could see Q's van coming behind us, slowly passing car after car, while he looked over each driver.

"He doesn't know what we're driving. Got to change our look." Heather shrugged out of the anorak, took a beige scarf out of its pocket, and put on the Ray-Bans. "Help me tie this scarf over my hair, then get down and pull this over you," she ordered. It's not so easy, I found, to wedge a full-size woman on the floor of a Dodge, but I managed. Heather tucked the anorak around me.

"Whatever you do, don't stop the car," were my muffled words of warning. "And for mercy's sake, tell me what's going on out there."

"Don't worry. He's about six cars back and bottled up by a septic system truck. Do you think he'll recognize me?"

I stuck my nose out of the anorak. "For sure. You don't exactly blend, you know. That snooty profile of yours."

"I have an idea. Pull that thing over your head and leave this to me."

I could feel the Dodge take a sharp left. "What? Just tell me what."

"I'm turning onto Route 80. The Kingston Police Headquarters is only a few miles ahead."

When I felt the Dodge speeding up, I peeked out again. We were passing a bakery van. "Oh, sure. Let's pull in at the police station and make it that much easier for Q to have us arrested for car theft."

"What car theft? His red truck is back in his own barn. I never took my gloves off, so there aren't even any fingerprints, if it ever gets to that, which it won't because he's no fool." She passed a station wagon, sighing. "I only wish we could have grabbed that canvas. He must have used it to transport a body he couldn't bury because of the frozen ground. Maybe even Daryl's body. Uh-oh."

"What do you mean, 'uh-oh.'" I stuck my head up again, just enough to see over the back of the seat. "Is he gaining on us?"

"Don't get hysterical. He's still three cars away." This time she gunned the motor, passed a heavy lumber truck. "And . . . we're over the hill and into Kingston Center now. There it is! You can sit up, if you want."

I threw off my cover just as we fishtailed into the station drive-way. Three little banners were flying above the side door. I felt like waving one myself.

Heather swung the Dodge around to the parking lot in the rear of the building. "We'd better get inside. I don't know if he saw us or not."

"What will we say?"

"I'll think of something. Maybe we're lost and need directions. Meanwhile, you keep a lookout to be sure Q hasn't followed and parked beside us. If push comes to shove, I'll call Stone Stern."

While I paced the hall, looking out the front door and then the back, Heather disappeared inside the reception room. Later, when there was no further threat from Q, I located Heather in a smaller office, having a cup of coffee and leaning over a map with a rugged, blond, uniformed officer. Her cheeks were flushed a pretty shade of pink, and she was laughing.

"I don't think Q recognized me at all," Heather said while we were driving back to Plymouth. "He only saw me for a minute or two in the barn, and then I was partly disguised by the hood. I probably looked quite different in the scarf and sunglasses, an unknown woman in an unknown vehicle. That means we can use the Dodge again, if need be."

After a leaden start, the morning had turned even darker and more foreboding with a gunmetal sky that presaged snow. But the subtle fragrance of cinnamon that emanated from the seat cushions was quite cheering. I wondered what baked delicacies Ashbery had been transporting. Life after danger is very sweet.

"No, thanks. I don't ever want to find us in such a threatening situation again. I'm retiring from my criminal career. Do I have the nerve to admit to housebreaking so I can give Detective Stern the blood scrapings from Q's butcher block? It's time we gave everything we have over to the law—not that we have much."

"Don't be too certain." Heather's smile was enigmatic. Taking one hand off the wheel, she fished in the pocket of her anorak. With the points of two fingernails, she extracted a crumpled ticket stub and handed it to me gingerly. "Hold it by the corner in case there are fingerprints. This was under the seat of the red truck."

I examined it, wishing I had my reading glasses. Although I am rarely ever without a handbag, such niceties, it seemed, must be abandoned during forays into the enemy camp. I was able to make out, however, that this was a stub from the Plymouth Theater and might be connected to Daryl Hendler's disappearance. In fact, holding that stub by its grimy corner, I felt sure of it.

"We ought to be able to find out when this ticket was sold. There must be a code of some kind," Heather said. "What do you bet it was Christmas week? There's a box of tissues on the floor in back. Fold a tissue over the stub lightly, and put it in the glove compartment."

"What are you planning to do with it?"

"Shall I take it right to Phil's? If Stone is still there, I can hand it over to him. Why don't you come with me?" We had reached Jenkins's woods. Heather idled the Dodge at the stop sign, waiting for my answer before turning one way or the other. A Toyota behind her honked impatiently.

"You go ahead. But drop me at home first. I'll join you as soon as I've cleaned up." But even as I spoke, I realized I was nervous about being alone—what if Q were there waiting for me? Then I had a horrifying thought of Scruffy attempting to guard the place against a merciless attacker. Still, everything looked peaceful as we drove into the drive. Too peaceful. I jumped out of the Dodge and raced around to the back door.

"What is it, Cass? Is anything wrong?" Heather called after me, turning off the motor. I heard her quick step on the gravel behind me.

Running up the stairs, I found Tip on the porch, shivering, holding a large, brown-wrapped package in his lap. At the kitchen window, Scruffy began his most scolding bark. The package! I snatched it away from Tip and threw it out the porch door. It did not explode.

"It's not your fault," Heather told the startled boy. "Everything's all right. Mrs. Shipton is just worried about what may be in the package. She's in an excitable mood."

Meanwhile, I went after the package and had a closer look where it had landed sideways in the crook of a lilac bush. Postmark: Atlanta. Return address: Greenpeace. I plucked it out of the bare branches and hugged it, beaming at the two of them. "It's from Joe!"

"She'll be all right," Heather said to Tip. "When you get into the house, give her a nice, hot cup of camomile. With lots of honey in it. Cass . . . I'll see you later." She ran back to the

Dodge with long, graceful strides, as fresh and lithe as the huntress Diana running through the woods.

I was surprised by the gladness I felt in seeing Tip, a warm feeling that rose in my heart like the first sign of spring. But I only said "hi" and unlocked the door. "I want you to have a key," I added. "I can't have you sitting out here on the cold porch, waiting for me."

"That's all right. It's glassed in. Indians aren't bothered by the weather much. Maybe it would be okay if you hid a key some-place and told me where to find it."

We were in the kitchen, shaking off our jackets, hanging them up on the hooks by the door, with Scruffy jumping ecstatically between us. *Let's go out . . . let's go out!*

"Go out by yourself this time. Tip is freezing and needs to get warm." Suddenly, everything seemed so normal, I felt foolish. Gently, I shooed the dog out the back door. After one reproachful look over his shoulder, he trotted off in search of a bush. "And come right back!" I called after him.

Tip was already putting on the kettle.

"The trouble with a key under the mat is that any fool would look for it there. I'd rather you had it in your own pocket," I said. Tip turned around, and I had a better look at him than I'd had on the shadowed porch. He had dark circles under his eyes, a cut over one of them, and a torn shirt.

"Things are bad at home, aren't they, Tip?"

He looked down at his feet, causing me to notice that he was wearing thin moccasins instead of winter boots. "Could I stay here for a while, Miz Shipton, and do chores for you and sleep in the room upstairs?"

"Sure you can," I said, wondering if he would, in fact, be jump-ing from the frying pan into the fire. I would have to be even more guarded against Q for Tip's sake. And Scruffy's. I opened the back door and whistled.

The dog strolled in at his leisure, ignored me, and nosed Tip affectionately. As the boy leaned over to scratch Scruffy's head, the dog sniffed the wound with concern. *This hurt place needs a good licking.*

"Come into the bathroom, Tip, and let me wash that cut. I have this great eucalyptus salve for abrasions."

"My uncle used plantain leaves." Tip winced while I cleaned up his forehead but stoically endured without complaint.

After we'd had camomile tea together, I opened the package from Joe, peeking inside to be certain it was something decent before I spilled out the contents. Between the boy, the tea, and the gift, I was in such a good humor that the problem of Q faded into the background, a pleasant respite.

Chaste enough—a magnificent forest green cape, ankle-length, with a luxurious hood and two pewter clasps. I drew the soft wool folds around me, loving the romance of it, loving Joe for picturing me just this way.

"Wow!" said Tip, while Scruffy tore at the wrapping paper, looking for a new ball or a bone. It had been a mistake to teach that dog to unwrap his own presents.

I opened the white envelope and read the card.

Darling . . . our fund-raising festivities were interrupted by an emergency trip. Saving the ozone layer from Florida fruit growers' methyl bromide. Also interrupted, my plan to fly to Boston this week. But I'll be with you as soon as possible—perhaps next week. Meanwhile, here's something to keep you warm until I get there. Also, look underneath—for your ménage!
I love you,
Joe

Despite all the beautiful, sexy things Joe had said to me on other occasions, this was the first out-and-out "I love you." Words of commitment for which any woman's ear is perpetually listening—yet they made me uneasy, signaling as they did the end of playtime. Well, I would think about that when things calmed down.

I reached under the tissue paper and a cardboard liner to find two other items. A boy's *Rainbow Warrior* sweatshirt and a soft Hug-a-Planet ball, presumably for Scruffy. Tip seemed delighted with his shirt and retired to the bathroom to change from the torn one into the new navy blue with a brilliant ship sailing across it. His shyness made me wonder if there were other marks of abuse he was hiding. And what would I do if his father showed up, drunk or sober, to demand that the boy return home? I heard myself sigh as if the weight of the world were sitting on my chest.

Scruffy pushed his soft cotton world around with his nose and licked it disinterestedly. Putting one paw on it for leverage, he tore at it with his teeth. *It doesn't have any bounce.*

I removed it from his grasp and rolled it around the floor. "A lot of life is like that," I said, although generally the dog wasn't keen on my philosophical musings.

The grand new cape called for a bath and a change of clothes before sallying forth to Phillipa's. Although I knew she would be less than delighted, I was nervous about leaving Tip and Scruffy on their own. So the three of us arrived on her doorstep at lunchtime, unfed, which is the best way when visiting a dedicated cook. Sure enough, she and Heather were putting out "a few snacks," buffet-style. The copious kitchen table was soon crowded with delicacies like homemade bread, paté, and herbed cheese.

"Good manners," I muttered to Scruffy as he made a complete round of the table, sniffing rapturously.

"Out!" Phillipa decreed firmly. Scruffy ducked under the table and hunkered down. "What a great cape! Positively in character, Cass."

"Did you give Stone the movie ticket stub? How did you explain our having it? What did he say? Have you told Fiona and Deidre?" I addressed my tumble of questions to both Phillipa and Heather.

"Stone is very upset with the two of you," Phillipa said severely, putting a plate, fork, and napkin on a small tray and handing it to Tip. "Fill it up, dear, and then you can watch television in the study. Milk or cider?" As Tip left the room, having helped himself mostly to sweets, Scruffy sidled out after him.

"I told him everything," Heather added. "Well, a *version* of everything. We were driving by and saw Q leaving. The barn door was standing open, and we noticed a strange red pickup, so we stopped to have a quick look. The stub caught my eye, so I palmed it."

"Breaking and entering. Tampering with evidence," Phillipa intoned, filling our glasses with Pinot Grigio. "Q could have shot you both and got away with it, defending himself against intruders. Other house owners have been acquitted under similar circumstances."

"I've given up my life of crime," I said, helping myself to veal paté, fragrant black bread, and Greek olives. "From now on, it's strictly up to the law to solve these child slayings. What's Stone going to do about the stub?"

"If it's from Christmas, as we believe, he'll try to get a warrant. At last," Phillipa said. She sat down in the rocking chair by the window where perfect herbs flourished in copper planters, her feet propped up on a small blue footstool, and sipped her wine delicately. She was wearing a pink cashmere sweater, her cheeks were flushed in an attractive way, and she wasn't eating. It looked to me as if things were moving along nicely between her and the detective. Finally, someone she couldn't scare away with her accomplishments.

I raised an eyebrow and smiled. "You look all rosy today."

"Oh, be quiet," she said, but the old vitriol was missing. "I'm just using my charms to keep you all out of jail. By the way, you know that clown thing? Stone found a vague kind of connection. A little over a year ago, in Portland, Maine, there was a particularly nasty murder. A boy on his way to a Halloween party. Witnesses reported that a man wearing a clown costume was seen in the area. Riding a bike."

I felt as if a jolt of electricity went through me. "That was him. I know it."

"We'll have to tell Deidre when she gets here, but she's going to be even more upset," said Heather.

Tip appeared beside me with an empty plate, followed by Scruffy, who had an air of secret satisfaction. "Is it okay if I have some more of those chocolate things?" Tip whispered. With a pang of fear, I wondered if Q knew about Tip's connection to me. I'd have to reinforce my warnings to him. He was a bright, re-sourceful boy—I prayed that would help to protect him.

Later that night, I did talk to Tip again about Quicksall, this time more explicitly. I hoped to tread the fine line between strongly advising the boy of his risk and not giving him night-mares.

"I'm not scaring you too much, am I?" I stabbed a fork into the block of chicken soup I was thawing in a saucepan. The noodles were turning to mush, but the carrots were standing firm. We weren't very hungry anyway.

His thin face paled under the olive skin and his eyes grew even more wary than usual. "Naw, I'm not scared, Miz Shipton. But if this Q murders boys, why haven't the police put him in jail?"

Why, indeed? "Because they still don't have enough evidence. Everything has to proceed according to the law. Sometimes that makes the process seem slow, but it's the only way to get a con-viction to put away an evil person like Q for good."

"Is that what you and Miz Morgan were trying to do today—get more evidence?" Tip asked slyly while he laid out placemats, napkins, and silverware. It was remarkable how eager he was to do small chores—much more so than my own children had been.

"So you were listening, were you?"

"When the other two ladies came for lunch, you were all talk-ing real loud. And once I came through the kitchen to take

Scruffy for a walk. He was getting jumpy, you know. And Miz Morgan was telling how she stole Q's truck and crashed through half his barn door. I guess no one noticed me and Scruff. Indians can walk real quiet."

"So I see. Well, yes, we were looking around the barn." I turned away to slice some tomatoes and mozzarella.

Tip leaned two scrawny elbows on the kitchen windowsill, looking out at the bleak January darkness. "Do you think Q will attack us while we're asleep? Or maybe throw a bomb into the house?"

"Those things only happen on TV. I don't think he'll dare. He will guess that we've told Detective Stern everything. And even if Q does show up in the middle of the night, we have Scruffy to alert us." I strove for a confident tone, while whacking frozen Italian bread with a meat cleaver so I could fit the loaf in the microwave to thaw it.

"I bet you wish your friend Joe was here. He looks like he could beat up that Q if he tried anything."

"Great idea. I'll suggest it to him," I said, ladling some chicken broth onto Scruffy's dog chow.

Later, I turned on the six o'clock news while we ate our soup, bread, and salad. The storm that had been off the Carolina coast was barreling our way, turning from icy rain to snow. There was nothing about a police search of Q's premises. How long could it take to get a warrant?

"Maybe I could help you find some clues," Tip said, wiping off a milk mustache with the back of his hand.

"Don't even dream of it!" I warned sternly. "Why do you think I've been putting you in the know with top secret official police information? So you wouldn't act like a naive kid, that's why."

Where's the chicken? Scruffy was nosing his dish with a grumpy, critical air.

"We ate the chicken before. This is the broth," I said, garnishing his dish with a little diced mozzarella. Tip was chuckling. I smiled, and was still smiling when the phone rang and I picked up the receiver.

"I've had enough of you fucking witches," snarled the caller. "I tried to warn you off, but you weren't smart enough to listen. Now I'm going to cut you up into pieces and feed you to the bluefish. I know who all of you are and where you live. I'm going to do it to all of you. I don't care how long it takes."

I didn't reply. I just stood there listening, immobilized with terror. I hoped he would keep talking. Because after the first few words, I had pressed the record button on the answering machine.

"I'll take care of that blond whore's brats, too—but first, I'm going to do that cute Indian kid you got there. I'll have some fun with him."

He hung up. I shook myself out of my frozen stupor and called Deidre. After I'd related the gist of the call, I played the recording so she could hear it over the phone.

"This is all your fault," she screamed at me. "Our circle was getting along just fine, enjoying our harmless little nature rituals, and you had to come up with this foolhardy *cause célèbre*. Now you've put us all in danger. And the children—that's the worst part! That's what I can't forgive!"

I waited. After a few moments, her angry breathing slowed, and she said, "No—I'm sorry. This is Q's evil we're dealing with here. You've only done what you had to do—must be your karma. I'll get Will home and keep the kids close. You go find Stern, and let me take care of calling the others."

"Will you impress them with the seriousness of the threat?"

"Damn straight, I will."

Tip's gray eyes got bigger as I took down the rifle from over the living room mantel and loaded it. "Don't worry, Miz Shipton. I have my hunting knife." He tapped the sheath attached to the beaded belt on his jeans. I didn't lecture him this time about not wearing the knife to school. Time enough for that later, I thought.

"We're going for a ride to the police station," I said, slipping the tiny tape from the answering machine into my pocket. I put a fresh one in its place in case Joe called.

A ride! A ride! Scruffy grabbed one more mouthful of chow, letting most of it drop and scatter as he raced across the room, then leaped up and scratched on the door where the wood panel was already clawed bare. But nothing is that quick and easy in January. Opening the door, I let the dog go running through, then shut it while we got into our involved winter gear. I took satisfaction in seeing Tip put on the heavy jacket I'd given him. Outside, Scruffy barked impatiently until we finally joined him. People never move fast enough to suit dogs.

Seating Tip in the back with Scruffy, I locked the doors and put the rifle beside me in the front passenger seat. If Q attacked us now and I had to shoot him, would I need to open the window first? If I shot through the glass, would the splinters kill us all?

Men always knew about rifles—it just came naturally with the genes or some early brush with the military. Gun savvy should be taught to every girl in Home Ec, I thought bitterly, instead of wimpy skills like how to make Eggs Goldenrod. As I raced through the quiet streets of Plymouth, I wondered what the actual odds were between women who would need to fire rifles from closed cars and women who would be moved to make creamed hard-boiled eggs on toast. At least twenty to one, I decided.

I pulled into a well-lit spot right near the door, not really a legal parking place but safer for Scruffy, unless Q wanted to break into the Wagoneer while standing on the police station steps. I threw a car blanket over the rifle.

When I actually got inside—with Tip in tow—I felt I could stave off my nervous breakdown after all, as long as I was in the midst of these cocky big guys in blue with black-holstered guns strapped to their belts. True, more of them were big in the gut than were wide in the shoulders, but still, I inhaled the odor of maleness—sweat, nicotine, after-shave, hamburgers, dill pick-les—with a renewed sense of security.

I gave my name and asked the desk sergeant if he would call Detective Stern. I explained that I had some important evidence for the detective. Sergeant Jacobi, a tired-eyed officer with frizzy black hair, raised an eyebrow and studied my face. I hoped I was looking sensible as well as desperate.

"It's about the kid murderer," Tip volunteered. I pressed my elbow into his ribs, but the down jacket worked against me. "He's after us, but it's okay. We have a piece."

The sergeant leaned over the counter to have a better look at the boy. "And what's your name?"

"Thunder Pony Thomas. Call me Tip."

"Your son? Grandson?" the sergeant asked me.

While I paused, thinking how I would explain the boy, he piped up himself, "I'm the handyman."

The sergeant looked down at his deskpad, revealing a thin-ning spot in his curls. Moments went by, and I was beginning to wonder if he'd nodded off, when he raised his head again and said, "You'd better wait in one of the offices. I'll get in touch with Detective Stern."

Tip had been sent out of the interview room with a woman po-lice officer who'd offered to get him a can of soda. Leaning back with eyes closed, Stone Stern listened to the answering machine tape for the third time. Then he pulled his long body upright and reached for my hand, looking so much like the ideal of a country doctor that I expected him to check my pulse. "Do you identify that voice as Clayton Quicksall?" His tone was deep and compas-sionate. He wore those cool wire-rimmed glasses.

Not bad, Phil! How fortunate to have found this strong, charis-matic man. I hoped Phillipa would marry him soon so we could always have him nearby for such emergencies.

"I do identify Quicksall's voice," I assured Stone. "There's ab-solutely no doubt in my mind about it. But don't talk to me about a restraining order. I know all about restraining orders—they're absolutely useless. And what about Dee's kids, and Phil, Heather, and Fiona? How will they be protected?"

He patted my hand, let it go, and sat gazing at the featureless wall for a long time. Deciding, I discovered, whether or not to inform me of the latest developments. Apparently his reflections came up affirmative.

"The Plymouth Theater stub checked out to Christmas week, but there were no retrievable fingerprints. The Hendler boy might have been wearing mittens. The stub wasn't much to go on, but I took it to Judge Hendler, who just happens to be the missing boy's great-uncle. He disqualified himself and sent me to Judge Lindman. Possibly Hendler gave Lindman a call, telling her to expect me. I don't know. Whatever happened, a restricted search warrant was issued by Lindman this afternoon, for the red truck and the barn. Even as we speak, the forensic people are still at it. That's where I was when the desk sergeant called to say you were waiting for me. Not surprisingly, no blood-stained canvas such as you described turned up in the barn." Stern smiled at me but his expression was still distracted. He drummed his long fingers on the table. "But there was a spot of blood on the front seat of the pickup. It will probably turn out to belong to Quicksall himself. Nevertheless, we have sent the sample to a lab for DNA testing. We don't have Daryl's body, but we can compare the DNA to that of his brothers. Maybe there will be enough of a match for another, less restrictive warrant. If a boy was murdered in that house, there's no way Quicksall could have cleaned up every trace of it. And with this tape you've just given me—illegal though it may be—we may be able to make an arrest.. The man is obviously guilty and threatening. Did you realize that it's against the law to record someone's phone conversation without his permission?"

"I was in a panic. My hand must have hit the record button by accident. What about the scrapings from Q's chopping block? Didn't Phil pass those on to you a few days ago?"

"Animal blood. Venison, mostly. I don't want to know anything more about how you collected those splinters. Come on—let's get ourselves a cup of coffee. And find Tip before he drives the officers out there crazy with his questions."

"What if Q skips while you're going through all these careful legal maneuvers?"

"We'll go after him. We'll catch him," the detective assured me.

But *disappear* is exactly what Q did do—and he was not to be found that easily. Meanwhile, another, more comprehensive search order was issued. Scene-of-the-crime experts went over the house, barn, and grounds like a team of hounds. They found traces of human blood that might be Daryl Hendler's on the wall and floor of the cellar. A close DNA match with Daryl's brothers' blood would help identify Q's victim. The Dobes were in the cellar, too—shot through their heads. Strong evidence that Q wasn't planning to return.

Heather wanted the death penalty invoked for anyone who would shoot a dog. She couldn't imagine any reason why human life was counted more precious. "The least he could have done was to let the Dobes run free. Animal Lovers would have picked them up, rehabilitated them, found them homes," she wailed when she saw photographs of the shambles in the *Pilgrim Times* under the headline: "*Missing Carver Man Wanted for Questioning in the Hendler Case.*"

S. E. Thomas sobered up after his long binge and came looking for his son after school a few days after Q's place was turned over. Whatever he promised Tip, the boy insisted that everything would be all right at home now. I knew differently, but there was nothing I could do. Tip packed up his things in a brown paper bag and moved back home.

Two or three days a week, he came by after school. I was provisionally pleased to see no signs that he'd been pushed around. Tip said his father was going to AA meetings again. At Heather's suggestion, Tip had been hired by Animal Lovers for a real weekend job, mucking out the kennels and exercising the dogs. I found as many other tasks as I could to keep the boy busy and supplied with pocket money. Perhaps Tip would be safer living at home than with me, I told myself.

Meanwhile, I maintained a constant state of stomach acid-producing vigilance through my days, and when I slept, it was with the loaded rifle beside me. Dee had Will, Phil had her resident detective, and Heather her army of mutts to attack an intruder. But Fiona and I relied on our firearms. Not to disparage Scruffy's protective instinct, but for an experienced killer like Q, one shaggy dog wasn't much of a deterrent. Besides, if danger came, I'd probably find myself throwing my body in front of the dog. As a mother, I'd been thoroughly trained in instinctive self-sacrifice.

The rifle beside the bed was certainly a surprise to Joe, who arrived the following weekend, looking even more tanned and mythical with his crisply curling black hair and Aegean eyes. Reassured by his broad-shouldered male presence, this time I told him everything, not only about the evidence against Q and his threats, but also more about the Wiccan connection. I even described the Hecate shrine Heather had mounted at the crossroads to foil Q, and our water and earth spells that had proved so productive. Then I added a disclaimer on Satanism. What would he think!

"I guess if you can abide a roving sailor, I can live with a touch of witchcraft," he said. I was relieved that he didn't cross himself and wave a silver crucifix between us.

What could harm me when his arms surrounded me? All right—I knew better, but it was a welcome fantasy. But that relief from self-reliance is never a lasting one. After a long weekend of not-so-careless rapture, on Monday evening, Joe drove back to Logan in his rented car.

Before he left, he said, "You can't go through this alone. Why don't you pack a bag and go stay with one of your friends until the cops bring in this maniac? What about the librarian—what's her name?—Fiona? Meanwhile, I'll see what I can do about taking a leave of absence. There shouldn't be any problem during this fund-raising stint. The *Rainbow Warrior* won't really need me until there's another global emergency."

The idea of staying with Fiona was a laugh. I thought about her firetrap of books and magazines. I imagined Scruffy chasing Omar through the dust balls. I wondered how greasy the kitchen really looked—it was a room I always avoided entering. My expression must have registered some of these thoughts.

"Well, I see you're too independent to cut and run," he said—but I thought I detected a slight tone of approval. "I suppose having a loaded rifle makes you feel more secure here, but I'm worried that you'll have some sort of accident."

"Shoot myself in the foot, you mean?"

"Cass, you have a smart mouth, you know that?" But he softened the criticism by kissing—and silencing—the defensive mouth. After a while, he said, "What about Tip? Boys generally can't keep their hands off firearms."

"Tip's been taught to hunt by his father and various uncles. From what he's told me, Native Americans pride themselves on not behaving like gun-crazy white 'sports.' More weapon safety and animal conservation has been drummed into his little head than I'll ever learn."

"Okay—so you're both as tough as tigers and need no protection whatsoever. Nevertheless, I'm going to take this leave. I'm going to stay with you. That is, if you want me here."

"Yes, darling, of course I do. And please make it soon." I felt as glad as if he were proposing a lover's tryst, not a cavalry rescue. But then, why not both? I found myself stopping short of saying *I need you*, but that's what I was thinking.

We heard nothing more of Quicksall's whereabouts until Imbolc, the beginning of February, feast of the waxing light, first stirrings of life in the dark earth. Our circle gathered at Phillipa's for this ancient high holiday. A celebration of the sacred fire and the holy well, Imbolc was a time of inspiration and rededication, traditionally associated with the goddess Brigid of Ireland, whose worship was so popular in her native land that the Christians adapted and adopted her into the sainthood.

As she cast the circle, Phillipa said, "We meet here tonight to share the seeds of inspiration, which will flourish with the growing year. And here we rededicate ourselves to ending the evil career of Clayton Quicksall."

By the light of many candles, we chanted, we passed the energy from hand to hand, and we danced. A fire blazed on the great hearth, throwing our moving shadows on the creamy walls. Fiona really threw herself into the dance, kicking off her shoes, coat sweater swirling, taking on the unconstrained "glamour" of the flower child she'd been in the sixties. Finally, we raised a cone of power and let it fly moonward. "He is finished," cried Phillipa. "So must it be!"

Deidre's face was flushed with excitement. "This has been the best ever," she declared. In the naming of our wishes, she had called for a renewal of her marriage, which had seemed to surprise even herself. Generally so absorbed in mothering, Deidre often treated Will as just another kid in need of being taught good health habits.

Fiona had astonished us, too, with her whooping, "I'm going to get organized!" Now, there was a Herculean task.

And Phillipa had proclaimed her desire to unchain herself from the stove. "Enough with food. My life should be a poem, not a paté."

Possibly not any less sweeping a change, Heather and I had declared ourselves ready to take on a new life companion. With all this wildness coursing through us, we were pretty well drunk with the spirit before Phillipa opened the first bottle of bubbly.

"Where on earth do you suppose he's run to ground?" asked Fiona, all of us quite clear on whom she meant. "Why don't we guess and see which of us proves to be on target?"

"Atlantic City," said Phillipa.

"Mexico. Or Canada," said Deidre.

My hand knocked over my glass and I nearly blacked out. Leaning over with my head between my knees, I managed to say aloud the words that had shrieked in my head. "He's here. Q is back."

Ostara—The Spring Equinox

Stone Stern met with our circle at Phillipa's big living room, which was all apricot and cream, with golden Afghan rugs on a slate floor, a copper-hooded fireplace where wood coals glowed, and Moroccan brass bowls. Phillipa served us a tea that would have done Buckingham Palace proud. I observed that our detective, like Lord Peter Wimsey, seemed perfectly at home juggling a cup of Earl Grey and a tiny salmon sandwich—and that Phillipa must have dazzled him indeed if he had agreed to share the progress of his investigation with his friendly neighborhood witches. Although he was suave and charming about it, he took the opportunity to deliver the anticipated lecture.

"There's no doubt in my mind that Quicksall is our prime suspect in the disappearance—and murder—of several Massachusetts boys," Stone said, "and we're making every effort to bring him in for questioning. We've taken several separate samples from his house and barn, and we're awaiting results from DNA tests. As soon as the ground thaws, we'll have a go at his yard. Meanwhile, I need to know that all of you will be extremely discreet and cautious."

"Cass says Q's back in the area," Fiona offered, clutching her ragtag coat sweater more closely around her. No reticule beside her chair. That was odd.

Stone turned to me questioningly. "You have some evidence of his whereabouts? Or are we talking about another vision here?" He may have striven to keep his tone neutral, but the underlying sarcasm seeped through.

"Since my first vision about Q apparently was on target, perhaps you ought to give this one credence," I said tartly. At the same time, I noticed that Fiona's reticule was lying on its side near the entry hall, and it appeared to be moving. What did she have in there this time—gerbils?

"Of course, of course," Stone said smoothly. "I have the utmost respect for your powers. In fact, for all of you—and whatever it is you do." His long hands gestured to include all of us in the awkward compliment. "It certainly has stirred the waters, and many suspicious facts have floated to the surface. And I mean that in the best possible sense. Sincerely." He looked pleadingly at Phillipa.

"Sure you do," she said, taking his cup for a refill from the Mimosa-patterned teapot. "Because you know this bastard would have tortured and murdered God knows how many other boys if we hadn't got on to him. Not only that, but we conjured up some real evidence."

Stone seemed about to rebut, but Heather jumped in to ward him off. "I know . . . I know . . . some things we did were risky and illegal, but you have to admit they got action."

"Indeed they were . . . and they did." Stone ran his fingers through his fine, brown hair. Then he looked at each of us with a teacherly expression of firm but kind disapproval, his gaze finally resting on me. "So . . . Miss Cass . . . can you describe Quicksall's present whereabouts?"

"I saw him lurking. He *was* lurking," I mumbled. It is always difficult to verbalize a vision, a wordless impression that comes and goes like a flash of lightning. "Let me see . . . there was this chain-link fence, some pine trees, not too tall, and a bright metal thing . . . red and yellow . . . or maybe orange and yellow."

"That could be a schoolyard," Deidre whispered.

"How did you know the scene was local?" Stone asked.

I focused on the scene in my mind's eye. What was beyond the fence? Some little sign . . . yes. "The pilgrim sign. There was a sign on the telephone pole with the Plymouth Pilgrim motif. That was it."

"Hmmm," said Stone. "I wish we had the manpower to . . ."

"If you can't guard all the schools, the least you can do is to give some kind of official warning to the teachers. Better yet, a poster with Q's picture on it," Deidre said sharply. "Otherwise, we . . ."

"No . . . no. You ladies are not to do *anything more*. I'll have a quiet word with the school principals, I promise."

"But maybe, if we scouted around, we could find out exactly which schoolyard fits Cass's description—if it was a schoolyard," Heather suggested. "Then you could alert the patrol car in that area. Maybe even station an officer at the school."

"How can I put this so that you'll understand?" Stone mused, resuming a severe professorial manner. "Stay out of the investigation completely. Suppose, for instance, that we're staking out a place, such as a school, and you wander through the scene and unintentionally tip off Quicksall."

"You wouldn't be staking out any local place if Cass hadn't told you about her vision," Deidre pointed out. Stone ignored this reasonable remark.

"The investigation is moving forward, and we must have your cooperation in staying clear," he said firmly, putting down his teacup and unfolding his long frame into a standing position. "Phil, you're getting low on wood. I'll bring in some logs."

Striding toward the front door, he disturbed the reticule. A cautious pink nose emerged. Then a whisker. It certainly wasn't Omar, the fat Persian, but still decidedly feline. Stone watched with some surprise as a disheveled black kitten, yawning cozily, emerged from Fiona's commodious bag. I was glad I'd left Scruffy at home.

"Oooh," said Deidre. "What is that dear little thing?" She pounced with maternal abandon on the woebegone orphan. Stone went out the door, shaking his head.

"Eeek," Phillipa echoed.

"I'm surprised at you, Fiona," Heather said severely, immediately suspicious of animal abuse.

"Oh, dear," Fiona wailed. "Well, I just didn't know what to do. As I was driving here this afternoon, I saw this wee thing crawling around the Dumpster on High Street. Now, I know how you feel about pets, Phil, but surely he would have frozen if I'd abandoned the darling to his fate. So I just picked up the little fellow and brought him with me. All he wanted to do was to curl up in my bag for a comfy snooze. But I bet he's really hungry now. He must have been trying to scavenge up some scrap of food in that Dumpster."

Fiona had hit on the magic words. Phillipa snatched the kitten out of Deidre's arms. "Hungry! Why, he's nothing but skin and bone," she called back to us as she disappeared into the kitchen, the kitten's head of wispy black fur and rosy nose bobbing over her shoulder.

"Oatmeal and warm milk," Heather called after her. "None of that exotic stuff, Phil. No smoked salmon. No liver paté."

Deidre was laughing. "Fiona, you devil."

Fiona assumed a quizzical, innocent expression. "All of you know I would gladly give a home to that sweet thing if only Omar wouldn't torment any other animal I attempt to introduce into our household. He simply prefers being an only child. I mean, only cat. If Phil won't offer a tiny corner of this huge place to a discarded animal, I guess Heather will have to dump the kitten on Animal Lovers' doorstep."

Stone returned with an armful of wood, carefully placed two logs on the fire so that no spark was disturbed, and stashed the rest in the brass log carrier. With admirable persistence, he turned and said, "So, do I have your collective word that you'll refrain from interfering with my investigation?"

"Oh, absolutely," Fiona assured him. "None of us would want to do anything that might hinder your efforts, you can be sure of that."

Deidre caught my eye. I didn't have to be a mind reader to know what she was thinking. Tomorrow, first thing, we would drive around in Will's Cherokee, looking for the scene I'd envisioned and described to the circle.

I smiled and nodded reassuringly to Stone. "I hope you like kittens," I said. "I think there's one being adopted into this house even as we speak."

He smiled enigmatically. "There's a certain appropriateness to a black kitten's sudden appearance here today. Whatever Phil chooses to do is just fine with me. In every regard. And that extends to your entire circle. Providing you allow me to handle my business without encumbrance. I don't want to be tripping over one of you at every turn I make."

"Oh, you won't be," said Deidre—whatever that meant.

"Very well, but let me warn you, Detective Stern," Fiona said, drawing herself up into a commanding glamour, "that if Q comes after us, we will be prepared to defend ourselves. And if he attacks one, all of us will descend upon him."

" 'All for one, one for all'—you see, Stone, we are rather like the Five Musketeers," Heather said lightly. "It just so happens I have some kitty litter in the trunk of my car. I was going to use it on my icy paths, but I can buy more on the way home. I'll just pop out and bring in the bag for Phil."

"Bag of what?" asked Phillipa, who was just coming back into the room, the black kitten prancing lovingly after her. She put a small silver tray on the floor beside her chair. On the tray were a tiny bowl of cereal and milk, a demitasse of broth, and a single sardine with a sprig of parsley on a Lenox saucer.

Fiona had the grace to look just a bit guilty.

"Heather will find you a nice home," Phillipa assured the kitten, watching with approval as the waif dug in.

"A bit young for the rigors of the shelter," Heather said smoothly. "He might get banged about by the others."

"*She,*" corrected Deidre, who had investigated the matter earlier. "Black, too. A perfect familiar. How I wish I could take her home with me, but my little hellions would have her for lunch."

"Which little hellions—the poodles or the kids?" asked Phillipa crossly.

"Judging by the way Scruffy goes after Omar, I guess you'll have to count me out, too. And Fiona tells us that Omar won't tolerate a roommate, either. Do you think you could keep her for a few weeks, Phil—just until she's big enough to hold her own in the shelter?" I suggested, keeping my eyes on the tea leaves in the bottom of my cup. The arrangement looked like a house in flames. When I turned the cup around, I saw a pitchfork sticking into a torso.

I looked up to tell the others but was distracted by Phillipa, who was leveling a snapping, dark-eyed look at each of us in turn. "Is this some kind of conspiracy, or what?"

Stone laughed. "What are you going to name her?"

"How about Piewacket?" I suggested.

"Hepzibah?" Heather offered, perhaps reminded of Hawthorne's cautionary tale of the cursed Pyncheons.

"Thirteen O'clock. Blacker than midnight," said Deidre.

Fiona, with her usual literary inspiration, came up with Scheherazade—who had lived from night to night on her ability to charm.

"I shall call her Zelda," Phillipa declared. "Just until she's strong enough for the shelter. Then it will be up to whoever takes her home to name her appropriately. I just hope it won't be something bourgeois, like Blackie."

Stone was smiling broadly, but the rest of us avoided each other's eyes lest we break up into chuckles and put Zelda's fate in jeopardy.

Driving home, I enjoyed the good guffaw I had been suppressing.

* * *

"Are you *positively* certain this isn't the schoolyard you saw?" Deidre pinned me down again.

"The fence isn't right. The trees aren't right. There's no pilgrim motif on the telephone poles. Yes, Dee, I'm sure."

As we drove away from Massasoit Elementary, where Jenny and Willy Jr. were enrolled, I spread out the map of Plymouth County on my lap. Deidre had marked the location of every school, private and public, with red crayon. I studied her route as she drove. Bobby, the youngest member of the Ryan family, sang a tuneless motoring song to himself in the backseat, small hands turning the car seat steering wheel in wild swings around the racing track of his imagination.

"I had no idea there were so many schools in this county," I said later in the morning, having become a veteran of some twenty-odd sorties around playgrounds, recess yards, and sports fields. I gazed out the window dreamily, looking for willow branches beginning to turn golden-yellow, one of the first signs that the crisp New England spring was on its way.

"The rest will go faster, I promise. We'll just drive around the grounds slowly. You can take a good look without our even getting out of the car," Deidre said. "But we'll find the place . . . don't worry about that. You just keep that vision sharp in your mind's eye."

Deidre didn't realize, and I didn't tell her, that that vision was fading fast—not as quickly as the features of a dream, but just as surely. Most of what I remembered now were the words I'd used to describe the scene. I made a mental note to write down the details immediately the next time I had a troubling vision. Which I hoped would be *never.*

A quick swerve of the Cherokee offered instant distraction. Bobby chortled gleefully, and I grabbed the dashboard with both hands as Deidre made a fast left to avoid a police cruiser circling the Bright Horizons Early Learning Center.

"On the chance that Stone Stern is actually out following this great lead you gave him, we'd better keep a low profile," she explained. The potato chip van we'd cut off honked long and insultingly, and a man out walking a golden retriever shouted at us as we sprayed our way through a deep puddle. In the side mirror, I noticed that the cruiser had stopped, and the officer inside was looking after us thoughtfully.

"There's no real schoolyard here anyway. Just that little bit on both sides of the front walk. Why don't we head over to our next target," I suggested.

"Which is?"

"Cedar Hill Middle School. Do you know it? Keep on this route for three miles past Jenkins's woods. Right near my place. That's Tip's school." I had planned to check out Cedar Hill first thing, but Deidre had arrived at the crack of dawn, while I was still too groggy with sleep to assert myself, and carried me away in the opposite direction.

Deidre raced to our next destination, the Cherokee making the most of every bump. She slowed as we approached the school zone. The long, low building fronted on Route 3A, the school grounds located in back, the playground level with the school, the sports field larger and lower, down past an embankment studded with glacier-rounded boulders.

It was the sports field that drew my attention. Goalposts painted fluorescent orange and yellow struck a familiar note. I saw a twelve-foot chain-link fence, rounded at the top to catch balls. The field was bounded on the right by a narrow parking area on the shoulder of the road and a separate entrance to the field. On the other side of the road there was a small picnic area, with three wooden tables and benches chained to the pine trees.

"Drive around the ball field, and we'll park there for a minute," I directed. The sign read *Cedar Hill Road*. Driving alongside the field, Deidre turned onto the broad shoulder beside another car, whose driver was reading a newspaper and eating a sandwich, reminding me that it was almost lunchtime and I'd had only a banana for breakfast.

I got out of the Cherokee, leaving the door open, and surveyed the area from different angles. And there it was, *déjà vu*. When I lined up the goalposts, the pines, and the fence in relation to one another, I zeroed in on the telephone pole on the other side of Route 3A. Fixed to it was a bright metal sign with the black silhouette of a pilgrim and a black arrow with the words *Plymouth Center* printed below.

A lurch of fear went through my body. My breath stopped for a moment. Then the air came back into my lungs with a rush. "This is it!" I cried out to Deidre, who was hanging over the backseat to pacify Bobby's hungry whine with a Milk Lunch biscuit.

"Oops," she said as she sat back down. "Cool it, Cass."

"Didn't you hear me? This is the place where Q has been hanging out, this school, where Tip is! It must be Tip he's after!"

The man in the other car had stepped out of it and was folding his newspaper. "Well, well . . . good afternoon, ladies," said Detective Stern. "I thought this might be the place. But what surprises me is to find you two here. Only yesterday, you promised me, on your word of honor, to stay out of police business." He looked at me gravely, the displeased professor facing down an upstart student.

I was literally speechless. I hadn't recognized the car because it wasn't Stone's silver-gray Audi but some anonymous rusty Chevy.

"Oh, goodness, you misunderstand entirely," Deidre piped up. "We just happened to drive by to have a look at the field where Cass's protégé practices with the track team. He's a runner, you know. Incredibly fast. And then, I guess, the vision just came back to Cass in a flash. Didn't it?" She leaned out of the driver's side window and stuck me in the ribs with the biscuit tin she was holding.

"Yes, that's right. The vision came back to me—yes, it did." I had no trouble speaking now. The words just rolled out of my mouth without passing through my brain. "Now, are you, like, on a stake-out or something? I certainly hope so, because this is indeed Tip's school. He's in the sixth grade, by the way. A very bright boy. Despite his home life, or lack of it, he still gets very good marks. A wonderful boy. And that devil Quicksall has been hanging around on this very spot, watching the players. I can feel him in the air here. An evil, evil man. A torturer and a murderer. Lovely boys like Tip. So what I want to know is, will there be someone on watch here at all times? Can I have your assurance of that? Convince me of that, Stone, and we'll leave at once. Because I really love that boy Tip, and if anything happens to him I won't be able to stand it. I'll murder Quicksall myself. And I can do that, you know. I have a rifle and I know how to use it. Or I might use Fiona's pistol. That's big enough to blow his head clean off."

"There, there," said Stone, putting an arm around my shoulders and patting me. "Everything will be all right. You just leave it to me, Cass. Dee, why don't you take Cass home and give her a nice cup of tea?"

Deidre's "nice cup of tea" was insipidly weak, but hot and sweet and accompanied by a bologna-and-mayonnaise sandwich on a soft, white bread that was like a time machine hurtling me back to childhood. Just the ticket, though, to boost my blood sugar—and temporarily energize my brain.

"Was I babbling to Stone? I had the feeling I was just rattling on about Tip and Quicksall."

"No, no, you were simply showing your concern. That's a perfectly normal hysterical reaction," Deidre said, putting some Oreos on a plate. "He understood completely. Perhaps it would have been better not to mention the guns, though. Especially Fiona's pistol."

"Did I? I can hardly believe it. I guess my porch light dimmed back there for a moment."

"It was more like an electric surge. No matter. I like Stone. He's a really nice man, isn't he? And so sort of mature and intellectual." She sighed deeply, and I knew that Will, the ex-basketball jock and now beefy, beer-drinking fireman, was suffering by comparison. Putting her chin in her hand, she looked out the kitchen window at her neat backyard, the swings and gas barbecue, carefully shrouded in a plastic cover, with apparent dissatisfaction.

With a rush of affection, I said a few "power words" silently for Deidre. I hoped she would be guided to recognize Will's goodness and bravery, that these fine qualities would be enough and would be valued by Deidre. *If it be for her good and harms none, let her be fulfilled by Will's love*, my spell concluded.

Turning her attention away from the window, Deidre looked at me sharply. "What are you up to now?" she asked irritably.

Before I could think up a suitably misleading reply, the phone rang. Deidre answered and listened quietly for a few minutes. "Keep calm. Cass will be right there," she said.

"That was Ashbery," she explained as soon as she'd hung up. "Heather's in a frenzy. Some of her animals have been poisoned. Heather says it was antifreeze in the kennel drinking water. Fortunately, she'd kept the smaller dogs in the house last night. Ashbery's been calling both of us all morning. She says Heather is crying and lighting black candles."

"That rotten bastard! Poor Heather . . . but those black candles worry me."

"Yes. I'd go with you, but it's nearly time for me to pick up Jenny and Willy Jr. I won't trust them to the bus these days. I've been driving them to and from school. Fortunately, my assistant manager is quite competent, and we've worked out a schedule between us. I've been leaving the store early during this current emergency, and today, of course, I took the whole day. After Will gets home, I'll go back and take the evening hours."

"Very wise." I wondered if I myself shouldn't be driving Tip to school and back, and whether that independent boy would allow it.

"Come on. I'll take you home to pick up your car. Shall I call Stone first, to fill him in on the latest? This could only be Q's dirty work. See if you can get Heather to snuff out those black candles."

"You can call Stone when you get back, Deidre. Grab the kid, and let's step on it. I need to make sure Scruffy's all right. Maybe I'll just help Heather light some more death candles. If ever there was a time for some good, old-fashioned black magic . . ."

Hugging Scruffy once more, I left him for safekeeping in the Wagoneer, which I had parked in Heather's circular driveway where I could keep an eye on him. *Hey, Toots! Wait up, will you? You've forgotten me again.* He sniffed anxiously at the partly open window as if he were being deprived of oxygen. But I needed to evaluate the situation before I could allow Scruffy out, so I murmured my usual assurances.

Right back? Right back, my right paw! Does that mean hours from now you'll remember your loyal dog fainting from thirst and heat prostration?

"In March? I do wish you'd stop reading *Dog World*," I said, my gaze scanning the bushes for intruders. Everything looked quiet— abnormally quiet for a place where a dozen or so dogs were always in residence. I found the redoubtable Ashbery dragging a malamute out of the kennel toward the toolshed, using a blanket to pull his body over the frozen ground. While I gave her a hand with the grisly clean-up operation, she told me more about the morning's tragic events.

Heather had decided last night that it was still too cold for the shorter-haired and smaller dogs to sleep in the three-car garage that had been converted into kennels, lavish but unheated. But before bedding everyone down for the night, she'd taken all the dogs for a run through the fields and woods surrounding the house. This nightly ritual must have given the intruder his opportunity to enter the kennel. Early in the morning, when Heather went to let the three kenneled dogs into the dog yard, she'd discovered their bodies.

After she stopped shrieking, Heather had observed a green

tinge in the drinking water. Antifreeze! A sweet taste but deadly, an agonizing death. Immediately, Heather had called the Animal Lovers Shelter and shouted at the young man in charge not to allow the shelter animals into the outdoor runs until their drinking water had been changed. Ashbery thought there had been some kind of problem at the shelter, too, but she didn't know the details. She and Heather had been occupied with walking each of the remaining animals on leash and returning them to the safety of the house.

Dick Devlin, a local veterinarian and the owner of Plymouth Animal Hospital, who donated free services to the shelter, had been hastily summoned to join Heather in checking over the dog yard and the rest of the grounds to make certain there were no other poisons or traps. Alerted by Ashbery, the police had arrived, and in their usual frustrating response to violence, made a few notes and departed.

"Be sure you report these murders to Detective Stern," Heather had screamed after them.

As soon as Devlin had gone, Ashbery told Cass, Heather had fallen into hysterics and fled upstairs to the turret room, a small octagon surrounded by a widow's walk on the roof of the Federalist mansion. Following her with a pot of tea, Ashbery had discovered Heather lighting black candles and chanting death threats.

At this point in her narrative, Ashbery's thin lips tightened with disapproval. Since we'd finished dragging the last corpse out of sight into the shed, until Devlin would rent a van to pick them up for burial in the Forever Friends Pet Cemetery, I brought Scruffy inside the house to mingle with Heather's nervous gang and left him in Ashbery's charge.

What's all this doom and gloom? Scruffy sniffed one of the females with interest. *This place smells like trouble.*

"Exactly," I agreed, and hurried to Heather, up three flights of stairs to the little glassed-in retreat some early sea captain had thoughtfully provided for his wife's lonely vigils. At this point, I was dragging myself along on sheer nerve power.

Hearing the soaring chant going on in the room overhead, I knocked and opened the trapdoor without waiting for a reply.

"Oh, you can see the ocean from here!" I exclaimed, emerging to a rapturous view not observed from any other room in the house. "No wonder you work in this turret." I was looking around at broad windowsills holding an assortment of incense sticks and candles, a brass cauldron, a crystal ball, an ivory-handled athame, unlabeled bottles of oils, and various goddess statues, including a duplicate of the Hecate we'd nailed to the tree in Carver. Actually, I was feeling a little hurt not to have been invited before to see this sanctum.

Heather stopped chanting when I entered the room but continued to stare fixedly at the three lit black candles, all melted about halfway into pools of molten blackness. She was pale and red-eyed, her hair uncombed. "Did Ashbery tell you what happened?" she whispered.

"Yes, of course, dear. A terrible tragedy—that evil man!" We hugged, still without her turning away from her watch. "Ashbery called us, but Deidre and I were both out scouting the schoolyards or I would have been here sooner. Do you think all this black stuff is wise?"

"*Damn straight!* Only it might not work right if I leave the spell unattended. And I really need a break in the worst way. Ashbery and her tea, you know. So would you mind taking over for a few minutes?"

"Yes, of course I'll help. You run along and freshen up." I pushed Heather gently away and took her place on the blue velvet floor cushion, assuming the same cross-legged position, hands on knees, palms upward, staring into the flames. "What a great place this is for spellmaking!"

But Heather was in no mood for chitchat. "Just keep conjuring death to Quicksall and I'll be back in a few minutes."

"Sure. Now don't you feel rushed. I'll take good care of everything here."

As soon as I heard her footsteps descend to the third floor, I gently snuffed out the candles and evoked my strongest protective white light to surround Heather and myself. Then I included Ashbery, Heather's remaining pets, and Animal Lovers Shelter. On third thought, I threw in everyone else: Tip, Scruffy, Joe, Deidre and her family, Fiona and Omar, Phillipa, Stone, and even little black Zelda. Then I relit the candles and resumed my unswerving attention. The black candles with their wavering lights somehow looked less ominous now. I believed I had pretty well blunted the harm Heather might have brought on all of us.

But in truth, I wouldn't mind Q and his murderous plans melting into a puddle. Nevertheless, I'd never intentionally done this black kind of thing. It was a mercy that I hadn't known about such possibilities in the fearful days before my divorce.

The decision to get a divorce had been the most difficult I'd ever had to make. But as our family life, or lack of it, had grown more and more painful, I knew it was up to me to make the tough changes. The breaking point was the Christmas morning when Gary dropped in to a neighbor's for a drink, and, apparently, into oblivion, because he never returned to share the festive dinner I'd prepared. Finally, when the excitement over their gifts had paled and the children became ill-tempered with hunger and anxiety, at last I brought out the overcooked turkey and fixings anyway and tried to put a brave face on it. But inside me, a little voice began chanting, *never again, never again, never again.*

With only a few semesters of plant science to my credit, and no job experience that had paid more than minimum wage, the notion of creating a new life with the children, even with the help of child support, had been daunting indeed. Somehow, though, I'd found the courage to confront Gary with my intention. How surprised and furious he was! The only way I'd leave with the children, he declared, would be in a pine box—so I'd felt physically threatened as well.

Yet, piece by piece, I'd put together my tenuous plan. Of course I would have to go to Mom and Dad, at least in the beginning. They offered me every encouragement—a place to live and a job all in one. It did feel a bit like going "back to the future," but I had faith that eventually I'd make my own way without relying on their help. Meanwhile, it meant the world to have their support.

And then the unthinkable had happened—the terrible accident that had taken the lives of both my parents one icy morning in February. Everything else had to be put on hold while I made funeral arrangements. Although the shock and sorrow were nearly unbearable, I didn't have the luxury of giving in to grief— there was no one else to handle the complicated aftermath of a double tragedy. Grandma was much too frail and needed care herself.

Then, after the funerals, there were a thousand details to sort out—what to do about their house, the accumulated possessions of a lifetime, and their business, which had to stay open while the will was probated and the shop's future was decided. All these decisions and difficulties required my presence in Salem for an extended period of time. Naturally, I took the children with me. Then, right after the February vacation, over their protests and their father's, I enrolled them in the Salem school system. And I never returned to Boston.

A wild March wind rattled the little octagon of glass while my thought drifted, idly stirring past with present, black moments and white light. Less than twenty minutes later, Heather returned, her thick chestnut hair neatly coiled into a single shining braid, her face looking as if it had been splashed with cold water. Immediately she took over her velvet cushion and resumed her contemplation of the candle flames.

I sat on the other floor cushion, a rich crimson, the only guest accommodation. "Ever been out on the walk?" I asked, as the wind whipped fiercely around the windows. I suffer from a touch of vertigo myself and wouldn't have put a toe out the diminutive door leading to the wrought-iron walk.

"Not lately. Often when I was a youngster, unbeknown to my

parents. So exhilarating on a fine day—the town and the harbor like a toy village. Then this little room fell into disuse, just cobwebs and yellowing scraps of paper. I rather discovered it again recently when Holmes raced up here in one of his paranoid fits."

I kept making light conversation, thinking to divert Heather's concentration. The black candles still had about an inch to go a half-hour later when Ashbery arose like a stage prompter from the trapdoor in the floor. She brought sandwiches, brandy, coffee, and a warm, spicy cake, the heavy tray poised on the outstretched fingers of one hand. There was no place except the floor to put down the tray, the low altar being taken up with candles, incense burners, and such. With one last frown of censure, Ashbery descended the way she had come and shut the trapdoor behind her.

Hungrily, I dug into the platter while Heather sipped a large brandy. Finally, she pulled some corned beef from between slices of rye bread and nibbled at it. I counted this as the greatest distraction of all. Surely no black spell could stand up against the pure physical pleasure of a great corned beef sandwich.

I must stay strong, I thought, stirring the potpourri in Grandma's Meissen bowl. Deliberately, I relaxed in her favorite chair, a small woman's rocker with pale green cushions, which I kept, as she had, at my bedroom window where I could look out at the gulls lifting and gliding over the waves. I closed my eyes and imagined summer. When I opened them, the window reminded me that the world of March was still stark and bare, but surprisingly, along the border by the garage, I noticed flecks of purple and yellow. I picked up her bird-watching binoculars and studied the tiny patches, saw they were crocus blossoms poking up through the dead and rotted leaves.

Believe in magic, and it is everywhere. Most people know that magic works and demonstrate their belief in subliminal ways. Why else do they cross their fingers? Play their lucky numbers? Wish on a falling star? Fear witches?

Magic works because the entire universe in all its glorious

forms is composed of nothing more than energy and information. The precise arrangement, the pattern of these two elements, creates all the differences between, say, a butterfly and a rose, a person and a star. Essentially, all are one. The craft is simply to tune in and hook up to the one humming energy that runs the universe—and then to manipulate the information that shapes it. That's what witches do.

These shifts in reality may occur suddenly, or they may materialize in small increments over a period of time. I had to trust that that craft we exercised against Q would eventually bring him down . . . but the wheels were turning much too slowly to suit me. And Heather and Deidre.

Something vivid and fearful intruded into this quiet reverie— a hot, choking vision smothered me, a house in flames, a terrifying flash consuming rooms crammed with books. *Fiona's house!* I dropped the binoculars and jumped from the rocker, my thoughts in a conflicting tangle of impulses. Grabbing the phone, I dialed her number. No answer. I called Deidre, who had just walked into the house with her children. "Fiona's house is either burning or going to burn," I screamed in her ear. "Can you get Will over there with a fire truck?"

"Without an alarm?" she replied dubiously.

"Trust me, it's real. I just saw it, heard it, smelled it. If the fire hasn't happened yet, maybe Will can prevent it. We have to do *something*."

"Right," she agreed. "Don't worry. I'll think of something. Meet us at Fiona's."

What Deidre came up with was to call in an anonymous fire alarm for Fiona's cottage. As she explained later, this seemed the quickest way to get a fire truck to rush to the scene without her having to answer some uncomfortable questions.

Meanwhile, not wanting to leave Scruffy alone, I hurried the dog into the Wagoneer and raced the car out of the yard. Scruffy whined and complained that the wire pet barrier had been left closed, but I was much too distraught to stop and slide it open as I usually do. My mind was full of terrifying images of what a fire-trap Fiona's place was, all those magazines and books in every room. I pictured Fiona napping in her chair, surrounded by cascades of journals and newspapers . . . Omar crying out as the first few flames licked up the wall.

A few minutes later, when I screeched into Fiona's street, my heart pounding, a chaotic scene greeted me. Fire trucks, the fire chief's car, and police cruisers had already arrived and seemed to fill the whole area. I saw fire hoses in use; a plume of smoke or steam was rising from somewhere, but I did not see flames. Swerving into a side street, I parked and ran toward Fiona's cottage.

The bulkhead door lay open while two firefighters in yellow slickers were shooting water into the cellar. The front door appeared to have been smashed open, and there was a hose snaking into the interior of the house. Acrid steam rose from the cellar windows, which were also broken.

"Fiona! Fiona!" I yelled into this melee, elbowing my way through a shuffling wall of onlookers.

"They took her off in an ambulance a few minutes ago," said a thin woman with button-shiny eyes. She spoke dispassionately, never taking her searching gaze away from Fiona's front door. The fireman inside emerged and was rolling up his hose. "I'd like to have a look in there, wouldn't you?" the woman said eagerly.

"What happened to her? Will she be all right? Was it Jordan Hospital?" My questions tumbled over each other.

"You a friend of hers? They didn't say where they were taking her. She must have been alive, because they were giving her oxygen. What do you suppose happened in that cellar?"

I brushed her aside without answering and went to find Will. I located him astride one of the trucks, flushed and sweaty, a streak of soot across his forehead. He was helping to roll up the hose that had been inside the front door. "What happened to Fiona?" I called up to him through the din.

Just at that moment, Deidre hurried up behind me and shouted, "Will . . . Will . . . it's me. Where's Fiona?"

He grinned foolishly, waved us away, and finished his task before jumping down. "It's okay. She's okay. Damnedest thing I ever saw. Are the kids with you, Dee?"

"They're right over there in your Cherokee. We can see them from here. I told Jenny to lock the doors and keep everyone inside. Tell us what happened, for heaven's sake."

Bouncing up and down on the front seat, Will Jr. waved excitedly at his dad. Will waved back, smiling amiably as if we were gathered at Fiona's for a picnic. "Damnedest thing, like I said. When we first turned into this street, I thought it was another false alarm—would have been our third this week—but just then some kind of incendiary device exploded in the cellar. If we hadn't been right on the spot, the whole house would have gone up in minutes. I had to break in for Fiona. She'd been asleep in her chair, didn't even know what was going on. Really muddled. Then when I got her outside, she began to scream for her cat. So I had to go back in. Looked everywhere, but the damned critter had disappeared. It's not too bad in there. Jim had to wet down the floorboards, but it could be worse. At least she'll have a house to come back to."

"Listen, you idiot," said the hero's loving wife, "what's with Fiona? Heart? Smoke inhalation? What?"

"Don't know, exactly. Wasn't smoke, anyway. Most of that was contained in the cellar. Nerves, maybe. What you call an anxiety attack. Fiona was running around back there like a chicken with her head cut off, except she was yelling for that cat. All of a sudden, she just keeled over. Rescue was already here, gave her oxygen right away. Decided the best thing was to ship her off to Jordan, in case . . ."

"Dee, why don't you get over to the hospital while I try to find

Omar," I said, dividing up the emergency agenda. "Call the others from there. And call Stone, too. You'll be sure to take the children into the hospital with you?"

"Of course. They'll have to stay in the waiting room, but usually there's a Friend of the Hospital volunteer on duty. I'll ask for her help. Will you be all right, beating the bushes alone here?"

"I don't think Omar's gone too far. I hope. Anyway, do me a favor? Call Tip and get him to meet you at the hospital. His number's in the phone book under S.E. Thomas. Use any excuse. I just want to know he's okay."

"You bet." We hastily parted company on our separate missions. Neither of us even bothered to check with the arson investigator, who was now poking around the cellar. First things first.

Half an hour later, I was still calling plaintively through the neighborhood when I finally spotted Omar at the top of an electric pole on the corner of the side street where I'd parked. Scruffy was at the back window of the Wagoneer, barking wildly, one more jarring note for my jumping nerves. Afraid to coax the Persian down the pole, certain he would be fried if he got tangled in those wires and tore one loose, I ran in search of Will. Obligingly, without asking anyone's leave, he hopped into one of the trucks and backed up a considerable way into the side street, close enough to get a ladder up the pole.

"Talk to him soothingly," I instructed, as Will clambered up toward the hissing cat. I didn't like the way Omar's back was arched. While I got a blanket out of the car and stuffed the dog back in, Will reached for Omar, caroling softly, "Here, kitty, kitty, kitty . . ."

The rest happened very fast. Omar screeched and leaped toward Will's face. Will teetered back and forth on the ladder, holding a gloved hand over his cheek. Omar skittered down the pole, and I threw a blanket over him, holding on tight. Then Will fell at my feet with a mighty thud. I think I screamed good and loud because they heard me back at the other truck still parked at Fiona's.

I have no recollection of tossing Omar into the Wagoneer—fortunately, into the front seat—or of the ensuing no-holds-barred confrontation, which shredded large patches of my car's red shag upholstery. There was Will, lying flat on his back, groaning in pain. Covering him with my down jacket, I held his hand and murmured over and over, "You're all right, you're going to be fine," until the rescue team arrived and the ambulance, summoned for the second time. A hypnotist had once explained to me that if you can convince people they are unharmed after an accident, while they are still in a state of shock and very impressionable, you can effect miraculous cures. I don't know if it's true, but ever since, I have adopted that harmless but hopeful policy. I even use it on myself when I fall.

I hoped Deidre and the children wouldn't see Will being rushed into the trauma unit on a stretcher. I would try to break the news to her gently.

After the ambulance left, I decided to give Fiona's place a quick once-over so that I would be able to allay some of her worst fears. Or would I? The first floor of the house proved to be a disaster area, much more damaged than could possibly have been necessary. While wetting down the floor, the firefighters had soaked several bookcases as well and crashed into the china cabinet. Fiona's reticule, however, somewhat soggy but essentially undamaged, was still beside her chair. Holding onto it gingerly, I made a mental note of the bookcases that had escaped the deluge and other intact items I could report to Fiona to lift her spirits. The big thing, though, would be that Omar was safe in my care.

When I peeked into the kitchen, which was relatively unscathed, I noticed a cat carrier tucked behind an overflowing wastebasket. This I took with me also. Omar would have to camp out at Animal Lovers for a few days while we got Fiona straightened out, a prospect made even more daunting by the clutter that prevailed at her place in the best of times.

Since my down jacket had disappeared, I was shivering in the blustery March wind when I got back to my car. My gloves were still on the dashboard, however, and that made it a bit easier to install the spitting Persian in his carrier.

If a canine can be said to use profanity, Scruffy swore like a sailor's dog all the way to the hospital. *All cats are sneaky, conniving creatures, and this fat, black hairball is the meanest of the lot.* He complained with a series of sharp, high barks that were literally earsplitting in the confined area of the car. Inside his carrier, Omar hissed menacingly, his eyes narrow, yellow slits. One sharp claw tried to poke through the wire mesh. I ignored their cacophony as best I could while I circled the hospital parking lot until I spotted Heather's car. Fortunately, it was unlocked as usual. With a sigh of relief, I transferred the incarcerated Persian to the Mercedes and locked it before running into the hospital.

I felt like a fleeing refugee who had been dodging bombs in a war zone for days—and I must have looked like a war victim as well, coatless and shaking with cold, disheveled and wet, slacks covered with long, black cat hairs and shredded red upholstery. It was cheering, however, to see the whole crew waiting for me in the emergency waiting room—Heather, Phillipa, Deidre and her children, and especially Tip. He stood stiffly while I hugged his thin shoulders, but he grinned, his eyes taking on their Asian look.

"Ah . . . have you seen Will?" I began lamely with Deidre.

"Why . . . did he drive over here with you?" she asked.

So I did have the chore of breaking the news that Will had fallen while rescuing Omar, because Deidre had not, after all, been in the right place at the right time to see him wheeled through the emergency room. But I also had the pleasure of telling Fiona that Omar was safe and sassy, that he would be the guest of Animal Lovers during the current emergency, and that she would still have a roof over her head once we had cleaned up the mess.

With a glad cry when I gave her the damp green reticule, she checked its contents without taking anything out, using one knowledgeable hand, like reading Braille. I wondered if she still had the pistol in there. Perhaps I should have looked, but what would I have done if I found it? It was Fiona's business.

We'd been lucky so far. Will was to go home the next day in a neck brace and with a bandage on one cheek—the object of much tender concern, for once, from the little blue-eyed wife who so often dismissed as boyish bravado his efforts to impress her. It was he who had carried Fiona out of the burning house, who had gone back in there to search for the missing cat, and who finally had come to grief because of Omar's ingratitude. I hoped no helpful spellmaking of mine had been responsible for his mishap—good magic can be so tricky!

Fiona, drowsily full of tranquilizers but essentially unharmed, left the hospital that same night to stay with me. Will could not rest easy when Deidre was alone with the children; an off-duty fireman was asked to stay with her until Will was released. Stone was worried, too, and moved in to guard Phillipa, as well as arranging for a police cruiser to keep a close check on my place and Heather's.

Driving home, I convinced Tip to stay with me for a few days "to help out"—with his father's agreement and Tip's transportation to school provided by me. He said permission from Dad wouldn't be any problem because his father was pretty busy anyway.

Out on a binge, I concluded.

After such a strange day, I wasn't even surprised to find Joe patiently waiting in a Hertz Chevy for my return home. A cruiser had pulled up next to the rented car. An officer was standing by the window, examining Joe's license with a suspicious expression. I pulled up beside them and jumped out of the car, Scruffy following me. "It's okay, Officer. I know this man," I assured him.

Joyous as dogs always are when their companions are excited, Scruffy leaped and cavorted beside me, then stopped short when he saw Joe. The dog barked and backed up as if Joe were a stranger. *It's that furry-faced person again. Let's scare him away before he tries to move into our place.*

"New York license, rented vehicle," the rotund, red-faced officer said dubiously. "You know this man? He claims to be on the premises at your invitation. But that mutt of yours doesn't seem to agree."

Scruffy turned his attention to the officer, snarling, curling his lip, and holding his tail stiff. *Here now—who's he calling a mutt? No doubt he's never seen a French Briard before. Want me to grab his arm and give it a good shake?*

"No, Scruff! Don't you dare." I took hold of his collar firmly. "Oh, yes, Officer. This is Joe Ulysses, my friend. But thank you, anyway. I feel quite reassured to know you're checking."

Fiona, leaning heavily on Tip's shoulder, moved past us with a half-wave at the two men and headed for the porch stairs as if she feared to pause even for a moment. The big policeman took another long look at Joe's license and made a note before driving away. Joe and I grinned at each other like a pair of fools while Scruffy stalked off in disgust and lifted his leg against the rented Chevy's rear wheel.

"Good thing you arrived when you did. You might have had to bail me out," Joe said, swinging a duffel bag out of the Chevy's backseat.

I must have looked a frizzy, sooty, bedraggled fright—but as soon as I'd opened the door, and Fiona and Tip had stepped inside the house, Joe pulled me back onto the porch, into his sturdy arms and the comforting aura of his spicy scent. A sigh and a shudder of relief went through me. Everything would be all right now. Everything would be wonderful. I kissed him back with melting abandon that nearly cast away my fears and my new responsibilities.

It was a houseful! Flustered and feeble, Fiona was installed in the dusky pink bedroom, and Tip took his usual nautical blue bedroom.

I thrust tomato sauce, aromatic with summer herbs, into the

microwave to thaw and laid frozen sausages, still welded to-gether, in a pan with a little water to bake untended. A tray of broccoli spears. Crusty garlic bread. A chocolate cheesecake and raspberries from my garden. *Semper paratus* was my freezer. While the food emerged from cryogenic sleep, Scruffy scrambled about, excitedly escorting every guest around the house. For the sake of appearances, I would toss a quilt and pillow on the living room couch for Joe.

Not wanting Tip to take Scruffy for a walk alone, Joe and I bundled up and stood on the walkway that led to the rickety beach stairs, watching while boy and dog ran along the shore below. It was a good opportunity to tell Joe all that had occurred since last we were together. In the sheltering circle of his arms, words tumbled out to describe the evidence that had been found in Quicksall's place, his flight and suspected return, the poison-ing of Heather's dogs, the arson at Fiona's house, all tied together with Quicksall's threatening call to me. Joe listened without in-terruption, not stemming the flood of incident with questions and lectures as Stone would have done. Yet his silence wasn't at all passive. His embrace tightened when I related the perilous parts, such as our escape from the barn. And when I cried over the dogs, his warm lips against my forehead calmed me.

"You've never seen this man. He looks perfectly cheerful and harmless, like someone you'd see at a Shriners' parade. Unless you've seen the evil in his eyes. Or been the object of his rage, as Heather and I were in the barn. Did I tell you that they found human blood on the wall of the cellar? It's too much to contem-plate. It's bad enough when children have to die, but to die so horribly, to be tortured and fearful and uncomprehending. I can't stand it! I could kill him myself."

As soon as I said that, I thought of Heather's unwavering gaze as the black candles sputtered into a pool of congealing wax. My words slowed as my mind began to race. Perhaps that was the way, after all. Whatever the repercussions, they would be worth it to rid the world of this maniac.

"Honey, I'm going to stay right here until this matter is settled," Joe said. "You've taken on too much, alone the way you are. We'll see this one through together."

With his Greek fishing hat set at a jaunty angle and his confident smile, he looked so very reassuring. My gloved hand whisked away warm tears starting from my eyes; I was embarrassed at feeling so needy.

"You won't lose your place at Greenpeace or anything like that?"

"I've taken a leave of absence. 'Family emergency.' They make allowances for that sort of thing. There's a support system of extra personnel to fill the crew roster."

"Won't you miss all the high drama? Only last week I read that four Greenpeace activists hung off the rafters of the World Bank meeting to drop mock dollar bills in some kind of protest against ozone destruction. So colorful!"

Joe smiled ruefully. "I don't want to disappoint you, but my work is seldom that glamorous. I simply keep some ship or other running to wherever a protest action is needed. Other ship's engineers can do the job as well. And besides, if I were hot for high drama, I couldn't do better than to visit your little world of murder and mayhem, now could I?"

Laughing, we clung to each other and braced ourselves against the merciless gusts from the east. Finally, when Tip and Scruffy trudged up the stairs from the beach, winded and merry, all of us went inside to a warm kitchen filled with the spicy scent of sausages on the point of burning. It was a pleasant time, as if I had a new little family around the table that night. Fiona shed a few tears into her pasta—mourning over the wreck of her cottage and being parted from Omar. After drinking too much wine, she had to be helped to bed, armed with her beloved reticule, rescued from the flames.

Sometime after midnight, just as Joe and I lay back in a lazy cocoon of pleasure after making love, we heard a gunshot and a crashing of glass, the sound coming from my rose bedroom. I grabbed my bathrobe and ran upstairs. Fiona crouched against the wall, a pistol dangling from her fingers. The window was smashed through, shards of glass glinting on the floor.

"I saw a face . . . I really think I saw a face at the window," Fiona said between sobs.

Gently and gingerly, Joe removed the weapon from Fiona's damp clutches. Tip had come to the door of the blue bedroom, sleepy but alarmed. Scruffy dashed halfway down the stairs, turned back toward us, and began barking from the stairwell.

"Just an accident," I told Tip. "Why don't you take Scruffy downstairs and shut him in the kitchen until I get this glass cleaned up off the floor."

Joe closed the bedroom door, turned out the light, and studied the yard outside for signs of an intruder. Just before he doused the lamp, I noticed that Joe had put on my big pink shirt by mistake—it had been lying next to his jeans on the bedroom chair. *Oh, well . . .*

"Anything?" I asked, while Fiona collapsed on the bed and yawned.

"I guess not. But I'd better look around outside."

"I'll go with you."

"No way. You stay here with Fiona. I'll borrow her pistol." He checked that it had not been emptied. "Could be military issue . . . is it? Do you have any more clips in your bag, Fiona?"

"It was my husband's. Navy shore patrol until he took up commercial fishing." Fiona reached into her reticule, then handed Joe a box secured with an elastic band. He took out an extra clip and stuck it into the pocket of the shirt he was wearing. Noticing at last that it was pink, he raised one eyebrow and smiled at me.

After Joe opened the bedroom door and went downstairs, I got a dustpan and brush from the linen closet and quickly cleaned up the glass by the light from the hall lamp. Then I stuck a beach towel over the broken window to cushion the jagged edges of glass temporarily. Moving from window to window, I watched while Joe toured the grounds. He should have put on a jacket—

he'd surely catch his death. The wind was whipping the branches fiercely. Perhaps it had only been a spray of leaves against the window.

Another shot whizzed through the trees and thudded against something. I ran downstairs into the kitchen and switched off those lights. "Tip, you get under the table and hang onto the dog until I tell you to come out," I said as calmly as I could. Then I eased my way through the back door into the yard. I'd better not call Joe's name, I thought.

Nevertheless, "Joe, Joe—are you all right?" I heard myself holler through an uproar of wind. I crept around the side of the house and found Joe crouched behind the big old rhododendron bush near the front door. The pistol was in his hand. "Maybe you shouldn't shoot at something you can't see," I suggested.

"I didn't," he whispered. "Look at your door. I must have made a lovely target in this shirt, but the bastard missed. What the hell are you doing out here?"

"Disobeying orders." The red front door was splintered, show-ing flecks of early green paint and freshly peeled oak. Actually, it had taken the shot rather well. A sturdy Colonial door. "It's Q. He must have thought it was me. Do you think we could crawl around to the kitchen and call the cops?"

At that very moment we heard the sirens heading in from Route 3. Tip had called 911. "I knew it was a rifle shot," he ex-plained later, enduring my hug. "Not Miz Ritchie's pistol. It was someone outside shooting at us."

"That's the last time I wear pink," Joe said, after the bullet had been dug out of my front door for evidence and the police force finally cleared out around three in the morning.

"Clothes call," I agreed.

The next day Joe bought glass and repaired the window while I drove Tip to school. Later in the morning, we took Fiona home to see the damages. Deidre and Phillipa joined us, and we began cleaning up. By afternoon, Joe had the house tight and secure, except for the cellar, and the rest of us had hung carpets out to dry and scrubbed woodwork and floors. Deidre had to leave early, but Phillipa and I continued the sad work of sorting out ruined books to be put out with the trash, with Fiona hanging over us to be sure nothing that could be salvaged was tossed.

"See this! See this!" she exclaimed bitterly over a soggy yellow pamphlet. "This is a magical weight loss program. At least I have to copy as much as possible."

"I'd like to read that myself," I murmured. "What's the gist, do you remember?"

"Jasmine, quartz crystal, and some business about a key word—that's all I remember. Oh, this is terrible!" Fiona sank down on her favorite chair in tears again and had to be comforted.

"What's Stone doing about this?" I demanded of Phillipa as I mourned over the ruin of a rare English herbal. "We're just a flock of sitting ducks waiting for the hunter to pick us off as long as Q is on the loose."

"He's doing the best he can," Phillipa answered tartly. "But I think there's something more we—the circle—can do. Something a little different from our usual white light thing, which hasn't been all that successful at protecting us lately. This Q must be psychically powerful indeed. Can you tear yourself away tomorrow evening? Saturday, the dark of the moon. If you remember your table of correspondences, Saturday's the day that criminals can be bound over for justice. We're meeting at Heather's."

This would be a sacrifice, but at least I'd have Joe at home to watch out for Tip and Scruffy. "I can come for an hour or so. What time? What should I bring?"

"About nine-thirty. Bring periwinkle, St.-John's-wort, frankincense, and sandalwood, if you have them. I suggest you wear something strong and dark—if not black, purple, or dark green. And bring a banishing stick."

"So . . . what do I say to Joe as I whip out of the house at nine wearing my forest green cape—which, incidentally, was his gift to me—carrying my grandmother's walnut walking stick, with a basket of herbs and incense tucked under my arm?"

"Oh, I don't know. D.A.R. meeting? Camp Fire Girls' council? You'll think of something." She smiled suddenly, transforming her fierce look with a soft warmth.

After school on Friday, I drove Tip to his house, which was on Phillipa's side of Jenkins's woods, to pick up some school clothes and to check with his father before he stayed with me for the weekend. It was a strange-looking place, too tall and Gothic to be called a cottage, yet surely no more than one room on each floor, with narrow windows to match—one of those New England curiosities. Tip looked so uncomfortable, I offered to wait in the Wagoneer. He ran into the house and was gone only a few minutes. When he returned with a bag of clothes, Tip said his father was sleeping and couldn't be wakened.

"He's not sick, is he?"

"Nah, just tired. Paw will be okay. I left him a note, so he can call if he needs me for anything. I said you had some extra work for me to do this weekend."

"Good enough. So I do. Joe's going to do some more repair in Mrs. Ritchie's cellar, where the fire was, and you can help him while I work upstairs."

"So you see, Joe, after the dreadful things that have happened to Heather and Fiona, not to mention shooting up my front door, Phillipa felt we should have a little conference on our own." We were in my bedroom getting dressed, fresh from showers to wash off the soot and grime of Fiona's place. Having recently spent an irrational afternoon at Victoria's Secret buying lingerie—in case!— I was able to slip into a green silk chemise instead of my usual grunge. Around my neck, I fastened a chain with the gold eagle pendant Joe had given me in memory of where and why we'd met. I'd added a very small pentagram. Putting my arms around Joe's waist, I leaned my head on his shoulder. "You won't mind staying here with Tip and Scruffy while I just run over to Heather's place for a couple of hours, will you?"

"How could I possibly deny you anything in this outfit?" he said while his hand smoothed the silk appreciatively. "But if I understand what's actually going on here—and I think I do—there's some magic afoot tonight, isn't there?

I sighed and thought of several dodges, but decided it was too late in our relationship for anything but the truth. "It's a kind of protective thing we do. Not black magic, if that's what you're thinking. Our spellwork may be helping us. After all, our circle is still alive and well, despite Q's attempts to destroy us. And he himself is on the run from the law. Certainly, he now sees us as his nemeses."

"That's why you're in all this trouble, getting poisoned, set afire, and shot at," said Joe.

"Now here's the plan," said Phillipa, as we sipped the excellent sherry that Heather had provided for our warm-up. "Tonight we construct a psychic wall between us and Quicksall. Let's face it—we have some serious gaps in our protective auras. Heather's dogs . . . Fiona's cottage . . . and every one of us has been threatened in some way. But a wall now . . . all Q's evil impulses and acts will rebound from a wall."

Looking quite dramatic in her plum slacks and sweater, standing in front of the marble mantel, Phillipa placed her glass down next to a Venetian vase and raised her arms to describe the circular wall of her imagination. "And the beautiful thing about this is, we won't have to resort to any black spells that may harm ourselves." Lowering her arms, she looked pointedly at Heather.

"Well, I don't give a damn," said our hostess, tossing her head, swinging the shining chestnut braid, her expression defiant. "I've taken my chances. That man deserves anything I did to him. With all I put into that spell, it's a wonder to me that he hasn't keeled over by now. I only hope he's breathing his last this very minute."

I couldn't help agreeing and felt a bit guilty for having secretly blunted her death spell.

"It's a wonderful plan," Fiona said. Rising from her chair to stand beside Phillipa, she no longer appeared wispy and frightened as she assumed the majestic *glamour* we all admired. Her raveled coat sweater seemed to flow away from her like a short, richly-colored cloak, and her crown of braids gave her a royal demeanor.

"How *does* she do that?" I murmured to Heather.

"I don't know. It's some inner vision thing. She looks at least three inches taller, doesn't she?" Heather whispered back.

"Phil, you're a genius. I like this a lot." Deidre's blue eyes narrowed and sparkled malevolently. "Q could be made to destroy himself. How do we work this spell?"

It wasn't unusual for Phillipa, who had an evocative way with words, to script our ceremonies. We listened quietly as she explained the ritual, and then began. Drawing the creamy velvet drapes in the bow window, Heather turned off the many lamps in the Victorian parlor, leaving only the warm glow of lit candelabra on the mantel and sideboard. As hostess, and therefore priestess, she drew our ceremonial circle with an ivory-handled athame. As we entered the circle, we stepped "between the worlds" where magic is accomplished.

Fiona, still regal in her glamour, lit the frankincense and sandalwood incense sticks and blew out the flames. The heady scents whirled around us, inducing a calm, meditative state.

While Phillipa summoned the powers of East—the air, South—the fire, West—the water, and North—the earth, I tossed into the fireplace garlands of dried periwinkle, "the sorcerer's violet," and woody stems of St.-John's-wort, oily leaves and dried yellow blossoms still attached, causing the flames to leap and snap. Carrying a crystal goblet of consecrated salt water, Heather sprinkled a few drops on each of us, touching our heads, our breasts, and our hands.

"Now with our banishing sticks," Phillipa continued, "let's take turns visualizing the wall of protection that will surround us and our families. We'll go around the circle from oldest to youngest. Fiona . . ."

Waving the witch hazel branch she had brought, Fiona rapturously imagined a great, curving wall made of crystal. Phillipa followed with a carved rowan cane, describing irregular crystal stones that had been cut to fit together perfectly. Then it was my turn. With my grandmother's black walnut walking stick, I added a guardian to our vision of the wall, the Greek messenger Iris who travels on a rainbow.

Laughing, Heather declared that she had forgotten to bring her banishing stick down from the turret room. She grabbed a brass fireplace tool instead and gestured toward the scrolled plaster ceiling, devising a wall of infinite dimensions that nothing wicked could circumvent. Last, Deidre swept into the circle with Jenny's toy broom, brushing away all countercharms.

We raised our banishing sticks toward the center of the circle, sharing the remarkable vision we had created. "So must it be!" said Phillipa, her voice deeply dramatic. Later, after our ceremony had been completed, it was like a splash of cold water to return to the mundane world. We drank sparkling white wine, toasting each other, talking and laughing loudly. But I could hardly wait to rush home to Joe and was the first to leave. "Merry meet and merry part!" I called hastily, as I wrapped myself in the long, green cloak and swept grandly out of Heather's front door.

The clock in the Wagoneer read midnight, the witching hour. I checked in the vanity mirror, noting that my face was flushed in a rather attractive way, and my eyes sparkled with excitement.

Surely Joe's not asleep, not yet, I thought. Perhaps I'm getting the hang of this glamour thing.

But as I drove away, I had the uneasy feeling that the car following me might be Q. I stepped on the gas, skidded around the corner, and raced home. After a while the lights behind me turned off onto another road.

* * *

Not only was Joe awake, he had been waiting for me, sitting on a cold chair in the enclosed but still frigid porch, holding my grandmother's rifle, with Scruffy hunkered down at his feet. By the time I got out of the car, Joe was beside me, ruggedly handsome and very macho, my personal armed escort to the kitchen door. We looked like a pioneer couple, he with the confidently held rifle, I in the swirling, ankle-length cloak, the dog dashing around us, making three trips out of our one.

"Everything quiet on the home front?" I inquired, slipping my hand into Joe's unencumbered left arm.

"Seems to be. How'd the witching go? You certainly look enchanting." We paused for a lingering kiss.

Save the nuzzling for inside. It's freezing out here. Scruffy made use of the delay to relieve himself against the old white birch.

"Quiet, you mutt. No, not you, Joe. Scruffy. As for the 'witching'—we prefer Wicca, by the way—we built a psychic wall against Q tonight. I only hope it holds, because I feel he's in the neighborhood." As soon as we had double-locked the back door, I took off my cloak and picked up the kettle. "Would you like a cup of tea?"

"Would you?"

Scruffy sat pointedly in front of the cookie tin; *How about a snack for me, Toots? After guarding the house all evening.* I handed him a biscuit. Grabbing it, the dog immediately ran into my bedroom, no doubt hoping he could stake a claim in there. Wrong!

"Guess I'll pass on the tea," I said, moving easily into Joe's embrace, as if we had known each other for many lifetimes. "Let's just go to bed. Notice anything different about me?"

"Let's see." He held me away from him and pretended to study my face and figure. "Yes . . . there's a kind of mischievous glimmer, a wild glow of energy. Some new spellbinding, or just 'the same old witchcraft that I know so well'? No wonder I can't get enough of you."

I smiled. Was I going to tell Joe that I'd practiced a glamour on him? Not a chance.

Finding Scruffy behind the rocker in the bedroom, I caught hold of his collar and hauled him, protesting, into the kitchen, firmly shutting the door. Then I slipped off my sweater and slacks, down to the admired green silk chemise and the gold pendants, eagle and pentagram. Joe was already undressed, wearing only the small gold cross that always hung against his chest.

I slept a little later than usual the next morning, Sunday. It was after eight when I started the coffee, turned on the oven to pre-heat, then noticed a note on the kitchen table.

> *I walked Scruffy. We ate. Gone home to check on Paw. Be back soon for chores.*
>
> Yours truly,
Tip

"Do you have anything to add?" I asked Scruffy, who was idling beside the refrigerator, cleaning a paw.

It's fun with the boy. Good rotted fish on the shore, he sighed.

"I can smell that. But I wish you'd waited for me. I didn't want you two out by yourselves, or Tip walking home alone." I broke eggs into a bowl and chopped tomatoes, avocado, and chilies to make crustless quiches. Cradling the phone while I worked, I dialed Tip's number, sprinkling bread crumbs and cheese into two pie plates while it rang and rang. On the ninth ring, a man answered. *Paw*, I assumed. S. E. Thomas.

"Hi! Mr. Thomas?" There was an affirmative grunt at the other end of the line. "This is Cassandra Shipton. As you know, Tip has been working here for me this weekend. This morning— probably about seven—he walked back home, and I wondered if he's arrived there yet."

Another grunt. "Tip!" he yelled loudly, not bothering to cover the mouthpiece and save my ears. "You here? Tip?" There was a long pause, punctuated by some stamping about. You wouldn't have to go far to search that tall, thin dwelling from one end to the other. A scrape and a crunch. "Not here."

My heart thumped painfully. "Mr. Thomas, would you do me a favor and look around outside, too? He should be home by now. Maybe he's in the yard."

"He was home, all right. Made a pot of coffee and fried the cornmeal mush. Breakfast for his paw, I guess." Thomas chuckled at these boyish antics. "Wait a minute, and I'll give a yell."

This time I held the phone away from my ear. A sound that might have been a door opening, then Thomas bellowed into the crisp March morning. Someone answered. I couldn't distinguish the words, but I recognized Tip's voice. Relief flowed through me from head to toes.

"Yeah, Tip's coming in now with the wood. You want to speak to him?"

"Yes, please."

I heard the wood being set down, then Tip's voice. "Is everything okay, Miz Shipton?"

"Yes, fine now. Listen, Tip . . . I don't want you to walk back here by yourself." Joe wandered in the room sleepily and kissed me on the neck while reaching for a coffee mug. He seemed to fill my prim New England kitchen with Mediterranean sunshine. I stroked his bare shoulder while he poured coffee.

"That's okay. I was going to bring my bike."

"*No*, don't do that. I'll drive over. It won't be safe for you on the road until the police pick up Quicksall. Do you understand?"

"Sure, right. I'm supposed to be at track practice this afternoon, but it's mostly for the relay team. I can skip it if Joe's going to need me over at Ritchie's again," he said hopefully.

"Wait, I'll ask him," I said, turning to the man himself, now sitting contentedly at my kitchen table, sipping scalding coffee and gazing out at the choppy, gray waves. "Shall we finish up at Fiona's today?"

"Good idea. She'll have found more things in need of fixing now that she's moved herself back home. Anything we can do to lessen that burnt-out smell will help, too."

"Yes, Tip. Ritchies it is. We'll be having breakfast soon," I said, pouring whipped eggs over the chopped vegetables and crumbs. "So . . . I'd say we'll pick you up in about an hour, or an hour and a half. Then we'll all head over to Fiona's. You stay right there with your father until we arrive."

"Okay. I understand."

"And, Tip . . . is everything all right over there? No problems?"

"Yes, sure. I just brought in the wood for Paw and some other stuff. Don't worry, Miz Shipton. See you later."

We said good-bye. Scruffy had perked up his ears. *Take me, too. Take me, too.*

Gingerly, I put the well-filled pie plates into the hot oven. "Will you be a good boy with Omar there?" Actually, I had no intention of leaving Scruffy by himself.

"I'll try," said Joe.

"I'm talking to the dog. Living alone does that, you know— you begin to communicate with other kinds of sensate beings."

"Don't worry. We're into that sort of thing at Greenpeace. Signing with chimps. Whistling with dolphins. Respect and understanding for the intelligence of animals. Most of us don't even eat 'em," he teased.

"I really do want to become a vegetarian," I defended myself from an indefensible position. "I've given up veal, beef, and pork. All I have left are free-range chickens and fish."

Scruffy growled and flopped over on his side in disgust.

"Don't give up lamb yet," Joe said. "At least, not until you've tasted my mother's *arni kapama*. Lamb shanks braised with tomatoes, garlic, wine, and spices known only to her."

"Your mother who lives in Athens?"

"The same."

"Sounds great to me."

* * *

"I feel safer after last night's ritual," Phillipa admitted. "Don't you?"

Reclining on Fiona's sofa, she sipped sparkling water from a cobalt blue bottle while we took a break from the exertions of washing smoky walls that may never have been washed at all during Fiona's haphazard tenure. I wiped my wet forehead with a sooty hand, giving Phillipa a chuckle. She handed me an immaculate white linen handkerchief from the pocket of her tweed slacks.

"Yes, but I'm not relaxing for a moment, especially with Tip and Scruffy. How does Dee stand the worry?"

"She's had enough, actually. When she called this morning, she said Will was driving the kids to her mother's in Albany. They'll be safe there. Sorry—I meant to tell you earlier, but we got sidetracked into Fiona's hysterics." Phillipa capped the blue bottle of sparkling water and wedged it back into the enormous hamper of goodies she had brought for the nourishment of the disaster-relief team. We had all lunched almost too richly for a work party.

There was a crash, a shout of profanity, and laughter from somewhere below where Joe and Stone were installing a dead-bolt lock on the cellar door leading to the backyard. Phillipa smiled her Cheshire-cat smile. "Shall we have a detective in the family, do you think?"

"Ah. He's asked you, then." I hadn't wanted to intrude with questions on such a delicate subject, but I was dying to know.

She sighed. "His work hours are erratic, and many a good dinner will be ruined, but other than that . . . Do you know how old I am?"

"Old enough to wear diamonds."

"Exactly. All those years looking for Mr. Right."

"There is no Mr. Right. There are only men—plain, imperfect men, some of them more lovable than others."

She ignored me and continued. "Then, with one fateful shot, Fiona summons him into my life. She always has been our best finder."

"It was Dee who had him marked for you. Don't you remember? She kept suggesting a blind date. As I recall, you would have none of it."

"Fiona's technique was much more colorful."

"What's that about me? Are you gossiping again? Is there any paté left?" Fiona had wandered downstairs from a meditation break in the privacy of her bedroom. Omar came with her, stretching and preening with all his natural insolence. I congratulated myself on having closed Scruffy in with the cellar work team. The cat jumped up on his rightful sofa. Not one to stand on ceremony, he stuck his sensitive nose right into the hamper. Normally, Phillipa would have given him a quick shove away, but life with the waif Zelda had mellowed my solitary friend. She took out the container of paté.

"I was just saying that it's thanks to you that we have Stone down cellar doing good works. Remember at our Yule celebration, when you shot out Heather's window?"

"You misremember, my dear. It was Q who brought you two together. Q shot at us first," Fiona corrected, the lingering aura of her meditation giving her a serene authority. Phillipa looked startled and unsure, also a rare event. Watching them, I felt they had suddenly changed personae. "From evil comes good—from good, evil," Fiona continued her motherly lecture. "The great lesson is that all events have an opposite or neutral aspect, all things are made of the same interchangeable stuff, we ourselves are all connected to one another. That's the natural explanation for Cass's visions, don't you think? As opposed to *super*natural. Now you girls, I know, have been wanting to know how I mastered the glamour, such a useful technique. But first you must understand, somewhere deep down at the level of your bones, the plastic nature of the universe. Ask any chameleon." With that, she trailed out into her kitchen, coat sweater flapping, speaking over her shoulder. "I'll make tea. Now, don't you stir, Phil. I think I can manage this without your persnickety overseeing."

Phillipa and I looked at each other, chagrined. "Now there's a lesson in plastic, if ever I've seen one," she said. "Is she a typical Pisces, or what?"

"I *have* been working on the glamour," I admitted. "Have you?"

"Remember, it works two ways," Fiona called from the kitchen, where water ran and a kettle clanged. Coming back into the living room, she carried a tray laden with mugs of dubious origin and cleanliness. "You can assume the center of attention or slink by unnoticed. In the sixties, I used to be able to penetrate government buildings. You know, to burn draft records. Either I would be mistaken for a cleaning woman or a legitimate delivery person or not seen at all, depending. Do you think those guys downstairs will have some tea?"

"1'll ask," said Phillipa, giving Omar a spoonful of paté, then shutting the hamper firmly. Omar draped himself across it protectively.

Joe stayed in the cellar, banging something together with Tip's help, while Stone came upstairs for a restorative mug of Earl Grey. I brought cold drinks to the cellar crew, enjoying the sight of Joe's body at work, muscles of arm and thigh moving so casually and smoothly, and with a particular grace, beneath his guernsey sweater and jeans.

"I have to be home by seven," Tip said reluctantly. His gaze at Joe was nearly as worshipful as mine.

"Okay, honey," I said. I wasn't happy to let him out of my care, but what could I do? "You two have certainly done an amazing job down here."

"Tip's been a great help. He really knows his way around carpenter's tools." Joe tousled Tip's hair. The boy flashed his winning grin and flushed with pleasure under his olive skin.

Scruffy, who was curled up in the driest corner of the cellar, looked up with a disgusted expression. *This furry-faced person is really boring. Just banging around in here so that I can't even get a decent nap. And Tip hasn't been any fun, either.* He jumped up to nose my hand affectionately. *Why don't you take me upstairs with you for a while? I promise I won't chase that miserable cat.*

"If I believed that, soon you'd be selling me the Bourne Bridge."

"Cass, how can you say that?" Joe looked shocked. "You know what a great handyman Tip is."

"Naw, that's all right, Joe. Miz Shipton doesn't mean me. She's talking to Scruffy. He promised to be good if she took him upstairs, but she doesn't believe him."

At that, I merely lifted an eyebrow, smiled, and left without further comment. Just as I got back upstairs, Stone's beeper began clamoring. Immediately, he called the station on the kitchen wall phone, while we all listened in unashamedly to a conversation that sounded excited but was too guarded to understand.

"There may be a break at last," he said after hanging up. "An accident victim brought into Jordan Hospital, unconscious. His pickup ran into a brick wall over at the school. Possibly some defect in the steering mechanism. The admitting nurse found that he was carrying a bogus insurance card and identification, so she checked with us. In general, he answers to Quicksall's description. An officer is on his way to the hospital, and I'm going right now. Phil, I'll call you later, here or at home, wherever."

"Which school?" I asked, knowing already.

"Cedar Hill Middle School. The track team is working out there today." he replied.

"And Tip might have been there. That bastard Q!"

After Stone ran out the door, refusing to answer any more of our questions, we hugged each other gleefully and danced about.

"We did it! We did it!" Fiona caroled.

"It couldn't be a clearer manifestation," I agreed. "It almost seems as if he crashed into our psychic wall. I'm glad it was good, solid brick."

Phillipa thought to call Dee right away, with me listening in on the study extension, but Will had already left with the children, delivering them to a safe haven at his mother-in-law's.

"Gee, the kids are so looking forward to the visit! But Jenny and Willy *really* should be in school. I suppose I could call Will back on the car phone," Dee said uncertainly.

"No!" I heard myself scream. What *was* the matter with me? "Not until they have him locked up, Dee. I'm sensing something . . . I don't know . . . a glitch." A cloud passed over my vision, obscuring Fiona's cluttered study. "He's slipping through the net. He's hurt, though. We've accomplished that much."

"Are you sure? Damnation!" exclaimed Phillipa. "Hang up, both of you, so that I can alert the hospital."

"He came to, got himself dressed in a lab coat, and walked out the back way while the officer was running in the front door," Stone told Phillipa when he called at six, while she repeated his words to us. We were still at Fiona's, unable to tear ourselves away until there was some news. "We're searching the whole area. He's on foot and pretty well banged up, so there's a chance we'll nab him. I'll keep you posted, but I have to go right now. For God's sake, *be careful*, Phil. Stay with the others."

We'd been trying to reach Heather ever since the first call came in to Stone, but she was out for the evening, Ashbery said, reluctant to provide any details of her employer's whereabouts. Eventually I managed to pry out of the closemouthed woman that Heather had gone to dinner with her old friend Dick Devlin.

"Keep an eye on the dogs," I warned, hearing them bark and scuffle about in the background. "The man who poisoned two of them is on the loose and in a very bad humor."

"Do not be concerned, Mrs. Shipton. The dogs are all indoors with me, and I am well-armed against intruders." For a moment,

I envied Heather, picturing Ashbery whipping up one of her marvelous mayonnaises with one hand and toting a semiautomatic in the other.

"Well, some good is coming out of this bad business," said Deidre, who had driven over to join the Q watch. "Heather is out on an actual date. And the man is a real teddy bear, too—although rather too old for her."

"Fiona will not be surprised," Phillipa said. "She was lecturing us on the interchangeable nature of good and evil earlier. I bet you're sorry to have missed *that.*"

Fiona smiled enigmatically, and Omar on her lap seemed to mirror her expression. Suddenly, I could see not a wisp of gray in her hair—a trick of the light?

I went to ask Tip to walk Scruffy again. "Hey, what are you two building, the Taj Mahal?" I said as I walked gingerly down the cellar stairs. Joe and Tip had finished replacing the part of the cellar paneling that had been burned and were sitting together, deep in conversation.

"I gotta get home now," Tip said as soon as he saw me. "I could walk—it's not far."

"Not a chance. We'll drive you—we're going home now that you've finished. You'll probably be safer with your dad than with me."

"Let's get started then," Joe said.

"I guess we're not going to get any good news about Q in a hurry, anyway. Fiona and Dee are going to stay with Phil. Ashbery's on the watch at Heather's. And I have you to guard me, darling," I said to Joe, who had slipped an arm around my waist. Looking into his dark blue eyes, his gaze so intent with tenderness and desire, had a mesmerizing effect on me. Despite my concern about Tip, I couldn't help but contemplate with pleasure the thought that Joe and I would be alone together.

Listen, Toots . . . I've about had it with this disgusting cellar. Scruffy broke the spell with his complaints, getting up from the discarded tarpaulin where he had been napping and shaking himself with distaste. *Nothing down here but fried mouse turds. The least that lazy fur-ball upstairs could do is to keep the field mice out in the fields.*

I suppose I must have nagged Tip all the way back to his house on how to protect himself from Q. Most of all, I urged him to explain matters to his father and stay close to him until the school bus came tomorrow. S. E. Thomas had more than one hunting rifle at his disposal, if he wasn't too drunk to use them. I reminded Tip to lock every door and window. I asked what time he headed for the bus stop, so that I could call before he left, just to make sure he was all right. I thought I'd covered just about every eventuality.

That night we made love by candlelight and firelight, moving together with leisurely grace at first, and then with increasing abandon. Joe's mouth explored those places in my neck and back that gave exquisite pleasure, and I searched his body for its most sensitive pulses. I was not afraid to be open and vulnerable to his gentle strength. We came together in that magical way that opens the world of spirit to lovers.

Afterwards, thinking about our sharing, I couldn't imagine that he would ever leave me, or that I would want another. It seemed as if something had been settled between us beyond the simple words of love we murmured to each other.

But in the deepest part of myself, I still knew that everything changes, that change is the nature of life, that even this profound union between us would stretch, weaken, tear, and be rewoven into new patterns. What I imagined him to be as a man and what I thought he felt for me were constructs of my own devising. I knew these things—I had been in love before—but looking back through a filter of all that had gone wrong afterwards in my marriage, that other relationship seemed a pale imitation. Now, right now, I had been taken out of myself, the small querulous, everyday self, into a spacious oneness with Joe, and through him, with life itself.

I slept deeply until near morning, when an insistent and trouble-some dream began to pry at my consciousness. In a wild, rising rainstorm, I was running through a wilderness calling Tip's name, but the wind was carrying my voice away. No one could hear my soundless cries. Wet branches like living hands tore at my face and arms. Great, gnarled roots caught at my feet. Stumbling, I ran forward until I found myself at the edge of a black, wet swamp that was pulling struggling small animals into itself.

I must have cried aloud. I woke with Joe's arms around me, his lips caressing my hair, soothing me as if I were a baby. "What time is it?" I asked when I realized I was safe in bed, my face buried in his bare shoulder.

He rolled over and looked at the small digital clock on the bedside table. "Five," he groaned, sinking back on the pillow. "That must have been some nightmare. Want to tell me about it?"

Dreams are never as menacing when you put them into words. You can describe the action but it's impossible to conjure up the frightening atmosphere, the awful feeling of powerlessness. I felt better for the telling, but talking about it didn't dispel my anxious need for action. I waited until Joe went back to sleep, then carefully disentangled my body from his. Wrapping myself in a warm robe, I took my jeans, a turtleneck sweater, sneakers, and underwear in case I needed to get dressed before Joe woke up again. I tiptoed into the kitchen and fell into the rocker. *Five-fifteen. Too early to call anyone.*

What's up, Toots? Scruffy, who had been napping on the braided rug on which the rocker stood, rose groggily and nosed my lap.

"It's not time for your walk yet. Go back to sleep." Quietly closing the door that led to the living room and my bedroom beyond it, I started a pot of coffee. Scruffy stalked over to the refrigerator and settled himself with a sigh on the cool tiles, stretching his legs out full-length and straight.

Soon I was sipping the good, strong brew I'd made while I rocked and watched the clock impatiently until it crawled to six-fifteen. Native Americans, I told myself as I dialed the Thomas number, surely must be early risers, *singing their dawn song* or something like that. S. E. Thomas answered, sounding groggy.

"Oh, is it you, Mrs. Shipton? Tip's gone already."

"How do you know? Have you looked around for him? It's too early for the school bus."

"There's a note here on the table."

"Do you mind telling me what the note says?"

"It says,

Ate breakfast. Tell Mrs. Shipton I got an idea where Q might be, and I'm going to track him. Say that I'll call her. Don't worry, Paw. I'll get to school later.

> Love,
> Tip.

I screamed. The coffee mug fell out of my hand and rolled across the braided rug, leaving a trail of brown liquid.

"That crazy kid," said the kid's father. "What's he up to now?"

I told him, as briefly as possible. Thomas, drunk and abusive though he might be at times, was entitled to know the seriousness of the situation—and besides, he might be a kind of tracker himself. Where else would Tip have got this insane notion?

"I'll go after him," Thomas said. "Any idea of where he figured to find this Quicksall?"

"Not yet. I'll be working on that. If you don't have any luck in the next hour, call this number and ask for me. It might be wise to take some kind of weapon. Do you have a hunting rifle?"

He coughed slightly and laughed. The same kind of quiet, almost secret laugh as Tip's. The way a person laughs among strangers, amused by their odd ways but not wanting to offend.

"I'll be looking for him, too," I said. "And my friends will help."

"The medicine women?"

So that's what Tip had told him. "Yes."

It took me fifteen more minutes to call everyone, arranging to meet at Deidre's before she went to work. With Will and the children gone, we'd have a clear field. It's not that I didn't want and need Joe's help, but first I needed the circle to conjure up a strong, quick finding spell.

Letting Scruffy out to run by himself, I woke up Joe. The hot cup of coffee I handed him dribbled on his bare stomach and brought him to complete attention while I explained.

"You take the Hertz car and look for Tip on the main roads between his house and the hospital. Let's see—that would be Clifford and Old Sandwich. And anywhere else you think he may be. His father's out tracking, too, so don't let him mistake you for Q. Or vice versa. If you find Tip, call me—here's the number of my cell phone. But right now I'm going to Dee's for a few minutes. Then I'll be out searching, too. And we'll alert the police, of course. Oh . . . you take Scruffy, okay? And there's an omelet sandwich that I wrapped up for you on the kitchen table. Thanks. 'Bye!"

Although I left Joe shaking his head and gingerly sipping coffee, I knew he'd be all right as soon as the caffeine got to his brain—better than all right, think of that Greenpeace training, like some kind of environmental special forces! When I opened the kitchen door, Scruffy heard the rattle of Jeep keys and ran in expectantly, but I skipped out on him. As I ran down the porch steps and around the house, he followed from window to window, barking canine profanity.

At Dee's, we drank a strong, hot infusion of mint and put our heads together over divination. Well, not together *precisely*, since we each followed different paths.

Dee read drops of oil floating in a basin of water. "The short one is following the tall one," she said. "They are at a distance from one another."

Phillipa laid out three Tarot cards—The Fool, the Six of Swords, and the Page of Swords, reversed. "Travel over water. Or maybe near water. An impulsive action nears its conclusion. The cunning imposter is exposed. Do you think they're in Jenkins's woods? Tip knows that place like the back of his hand."

Heather drew a single animal card from a blue deck. It was a beaver. "A building near water. A warning to watch your back. Cass, didn't you tell me once that there's an abandoned cranberry worker's shack in Jenkins's wood?"

Fiona swung a pendulum over a map of Plymouth County. "Oh, for heaven's sake, it's swinging right here over Myles Standish State Park. Between the campgrounds and College Pond. Now what would make the boy think of looking there?"

When a finding was needed, my money would always be on Fiona. I had been lying on Dee's rosy sofa, letting all these impressions wash over me. Suddenly I could see quite clearly in my mind's eye the place where Q must be holed up. I sat up and swung my legs to the floor. "Because of the outbuildings, of course. No one's in there at this time of year. A perfect place for Q to hide if he could get himself there. He's injured, but he could have hitched a ride or hot-wired a car. Tip and I went to Myles Standish together last fall to cut some witch hazel wands. There's a nice little stand of witch hazel near College Pond. The place is less than five miles from Jordan Hospital, which may be why Tip would expect Q to hide in there. Listen, Phil! Tell Stone to get some men out to the forest."

"Cass, Myles Standish is so huge—not to mention eerie and deserted! And there's more than one crop of outbuildings. How will anyone find anyone?"

"We have our cell phones. Just tell Stone to check wherever there are closed-up buildings. Fiona, let me have your pistol. Is it loaded? Good. If Tip is there, I'll try to get him out before he gets too close to Q."

"Not alone, you won't," Heather declared, and added that she would just dash home to get Trilby, her bloodhound, and meet me across the road from the entrance to the campgrounds.

"What would Trilby need for scenting?" I asked.

"Do you have anything of Tip's in the Jeep? Otherwise, I'll go back to your place and collect some item of clothing."

I thought a moment, going over the contents of the backseat. "Yes, some old gloves he wears when we're digging roots or cutting branches." She said that would do nicely.

Fiona was to stay at Dee's to handle messages, because Dee had no choice but to go to work, at least until she could get her assistant to cover for her at the store. If Tip's father called, Fiona would be able to tell him where we were searching.

"What about your Greenpeace person?" Fiona asked me. "Should he be told if he calls?"

"Yes, okay. But Joe isn't familiar with that park at all. Maybe it would be better if you connect him with whatever Stone's doing. Phil will know." I put on my leather windbreaker, tucked my phone into one pocket and the pistol into the other, hoping I wouldn't shoot off my foot. I'd never actually handled a pistol.

"I'll join the hunt at Myles Standish, too, as soon as I've spoken to Stone," Phil chimed in. "I wish I could go with you now, but this is not a message I should entrust to anyone but Stone himself. Just promise me that you won't do anything crazy because Tip is involved. The boy may have gone somewhere else entirely. For that matter, we don't know for sure that Q is there. Although, it does feel true, doesn't it?"

"Damn straight." At this point, I was headed out the door with Heather and Phil following me to impress upon a moving target a few last words of advice. Quick hugs all around, and I ran for the Jeep.

From Dee's, it was quicker to take Route 3A, then cut off at Watercourse Road, twisting and turning toward Myles Standish, one of our state's more depressing, if not downright foreboding, natural preserves. I parked the Jeep on Rocky Pond Road, just outside the forest, and tapped my fingers nervously on the dashboard for a minute or two before deciding I was too apprehensive to wait for Heather or Phil to accompany me.

Avoiding the main gate, I went in through the woods on foot.

The scrub brush was still leafless, but here and there a young pine or fir tree provided some real cover. The ground exuded the rich aroma of wet, rotting leaves, which helped to muffle my awkward progress.

Cautiously, I advanced to the campground clearing. Surrounding the parking lot was a garage for forest vehicles, a long building housing rest rooms and showers for campers, and a small cottage serving as headquarters for the forest rangers—all of which appeared to be completely deserted. On a central bulletin board, shredded notices flapped in the wind. Hunching down behind a conveniently placed threesome of Christmasy fir trees, I studied the situation. A crow spotted me and squawked an alarm, buzzing some companions in nearby towering oaks. The raucous sounds soon faded away into a profound silence, except for my thudding heartbeat.

Fighting the urge to call Tip's name, I waited and watched for what was probably ten minutes, although it seemed much longer. Had Fiona's and my perception been wrong about Q hiding out at Myles Standish? How many hundreds of other places could Tip be right now, perhaps in trouble or only on a wild-goose chase?

A soft clanging behind the ranger headquarters interrupted my ruminations. After I had heard the sound a second time, I began to duck-walk around the perimeter of the clearing to survey the back of the building, keeping well behind the slightly obscuring screen of crisscrossed brush. Slowly, I edged my way along this wild border until finally the back door and two trash cans came into my view. A raccoon was standing on one closed trash can, and with long, sharp claws, was lifting the cover of the other to look inside at what must have been a disappointing lack of decent garbage. Noisily, he dropped the cover and scurried away.

I let out the breath I had been holding.

"Stand up," said a man's voice behind me, "and put your hands in the air." In that frozen moment, I wondered how he'd been able to sneak up on me without my hearing even a twig snap. It was Clayton Quicksall.

I was sitting on my haunches, my hands on my knees. As I moved them up toward my waist—as if for balance in getting up from that awkward position—I hooked one finger into the pistol, flipping it out of my jacket pocket into my right hand. When I stood up and turned around, I held the pistol, facing Q.

I should have fired right then, the moment I saw him. He wasn't even armed. All he held was a thick branch like a club, which he swung at me without hesitation, knocking the pistol out of my grasp. Jolted off balance by that powerful blow, I tried to throw my body over the pistol. He hit me again, this time on the side of the head. I almost blacked out from the pain. He pushed me aside and grabbed the pistol.

Now he *was* armed. What a fool I was! A fool taking her last breath. At least the pain in my head would stop.

"Stand up," he said for the second time. I did as I was told. His round, red face was sweaty with exertion. I saw now that his shoulder and arm were bandaged, and that he had a mean cut with several stitches over one eye. He must have discarded a head bandage when he sneaked out of the hospital. No splint on his arm. Probably he could move as freely as he wished.

"You'd better let me go," I said. "The police are on their way. They'll be here any minute."

"Is that so? Well, Ms. Nemesis, in that case, you and I are getting out of here. I have some unfinished business to take up with you. Walk ahead of me over to that garage."

When we got nearer the garage, I saw that the padlock had been smashed and the door was an inch ajar. He opened it and pushed me inside where there were various yellow machines—a bulldozer, a snowplow, a wood chipper—and a dark green van bearing the legend Myles Standish State Forest. That was the last thing I remembered before there was another explosion of pain in my head and then . . . nothingness.

* * *

When I woke up, the pain was excruciating—the mother of all migraines. My hands were tied behind my back. There was a cruel piece of duct tape over my mouth. I heard a Country and Western tune playing as the van jolted over bumpy dirt roads. Looking up, which was the only way I *could* look, I saw the back of Q's head wearing a forest ranger's green cap. He must be listening for a news report. The slanting sunlight was hitting him in the eyes, which he shaded with his left hand while he drove. He was probably heading toward Wareham. Maybe that's where he planned to kill me in some slow, nasty way. Would he cut me up alive as he had his other victims? Would he rape me first, or did he only fancy young boys? I had to get away before he got to his destination.

After a furtive struggle with my bonds, I looked around for something to cut the rope, which didn't feel all that thick. More like cord, thin enough to cut into my wrists severely. The back of the van was strewn with odds and ends of tools, all of which looked too smooth for the job. My head pounded with every bounce of the van. After a few moments of hopeless searching, I saw the edge of something metallic and rusty stuck under the driver's seat—it was a pair of grass shears! Slowly and quietly, I turned my body around so that I was facing the back doors of the van.

When I felt my back pressed against the driver's seat, I reached down with my fingers to pull out the shears. Someone had carelessly left them unlocked and they snapped open easily. I held my breath and waited. Had Q heard that sound? No, the local news broadcast had begun, and he was leaning forward as if to hear it better through the rattles of the van bumping over rough roads.

I began to saw the cord back and forth against the shears. Nothing seemed to be happening, other than the blades nicking my wrists. I kept at it. There was, after all, not another thing I could do.

We drove for what seemed to be many miles. Because I was

now facing backwards, I couldn't tell if we were still in Myles Standish, but the van began to ride more quietly and smoothly, as if we had left the dirt roads. Just as one of the tightly twisted cords began to shred, I was knocked forward onto my face when the van thumped up and down for several minutes, lurched, and then came to an abrupt halt. I felt the cell phone slip out of my windbreaker pocket, and there wasn't a thing I could do about it. Q jumped out of the van and came around to the rear.

The rear doors opened—his sweating, wounded face loomed over me. The eyes were narrow, cold blue blades looking directly into mine. I had decided not to play dead, since I hoped to avoid being dragged or dumped. I couldn't afford any more injuries if I was going to fight back.

"Get out," he ordered. All I could see behind him was a thick stand of pine.

It's not easy to get out of a van without the use of one's hands, and I couldn't prevent myself from falling when I jumped out, but I hastily stood up again, facing my tormenter. I thought of making a run for it. I was a lot lighter on my feet than Q. But I saw he had taken Fiona's pistol out of his belt—and I knew I wasn't faster than a speeding bullet.

Then I realized with a shock where I was. We had left Myles Standish far behind us, and we were now in a place I knew very well. Q must have driven the van out of the forest, circled around toward Black Hill Point, and turned into an abandoned cranberry bog road that traversed Jenkins's woods. He'd pulled off the dirt road into a space between the trees, and the forest green van was now camouflaged by low-growing pine boughs. Whatever hopes of rescue I still cherished washed out like a child's mud dam. Stone and his men would take hours—maybe days—to search all through Myles Standish. Joe, with Scruffy in tow, would have joined Stone. Phil would be there—and Heather, following a yelping Trilby to a dead end at the garage. They would all beat the bushes for me and Tip in vain.

Tip! Where was Tip? I had the overwhelming sense that he

was nearby. I didn't know whether to be glad or sorry. Q was looking at me silently, menacingly—deciding, I feared, how to kill me in the most unpleasant way, settling the score. I eyed the hunting knife on his belt. Would he slice me up or skin me alive? Or would he tie me to a pier at low tide and let the ocean drown me, wave by wave filling my mouth and nose? If it were not for me—my visions, my insistent persecution—he might never have become the wounded, hunted animal he was now. He bared his teeth in a grin that chilled me to the marrow. Blood rushed to my head, making it pound painfully, leaving my hands icy. Since they were behind my back, out of his direct vision, I cautiously worked them back and forth, straining at the partly shredded cord.

He stepped toward me, and I froze in terror. With a quick movement of his left hand, he grasped a corner of the duct tape and, in one cruel jerk, pulled it off. Half my facial skin seemed to go with it, and I cried out.

"Shut up, you bitch, or I'll finish you now," he said. "First, I need food. You will walk ahead of me toward your house, and we'll see what's going on there. I suspect the whole posse is at Myles Standish by now, isn't that right?"

"Yes, they are all over at the forest." Every motion of my mouth felt as if I were stretching burned skin. I didn't try to dissuade him from this new plan with some lie. It seemed to me that I would have a better chance—or even *some* chance—of getting away from this maniac on my own home ground.

Frantically, I pictured the weapons I might use, if I got the chance. Kitchen knives, of course. Would he want me to cook something? How I'd love to have him turn his back when I had my old cast iron frying pan in hand! If he raped me in my bedroom, was there any chance of my getting the loaded rifle that I kept under my bed? He motioned with the pistol for me to get started. Before I turned, I clasped my hands together as tightly as possible, hoping he wouldn't notice how I'd been weakening the cord.

It would be a half-hour's walk. We were at the south side of Jenkins's woods, nearer Phillipa's place than mine. I led the way to a familiar footpath that branched off the old cranberry bog road. From that passage, I could cut across the new wetlands preserve and pick up another route that led home. It was slow, treacherous going without the use of my hands, which I kept closely clasped together. When I stumbled the first time, it occurred to me that it would be a good idea to make as much noise as possible to alert Tip in case he was tracking through the woods somewhere. From time to time, I deliberately crashed into low, dead branches hanging off the pines—until we came to the wetlands, which was open territory. At our awkward approach, black ducks and snowy egrets rose from the reeds with a satisfying clamor. Tip would surely hear the commotion if he was anywhere near.

"You're being a little too docile, bitch," said Q, lumbering behind me. "I wouldn't try anything fancy, if I were you. Remember that it would be quite easy for me to kill you right here and dump you in that swamp."

Yeah, well, I'm going to die anyway, I thought, so what do I have to lose?

"You and your friends have been so terribly stupid," he continued, as if deliberately baiting me. He kept at it, with pauses to catch his breath, for he was now panting from exertion. "I warned you last Christmas—bang! Nice little warning shot right through that big bay window. But you ignored the message. Then I showed you how easy it would be for me to get my hands on that blond bitch's kids. You still didn't get it. Thought I'd burn up the old lady in her rat's nest for fun, but I guess she's got nine lives, just like her fat cat. You don't, though, do you? Just one life."

"Please . . ." I said. I felt unable to listen to any more, and straightened up for a moment from the task of pulling one boot after another out of the spring mud. Hearing Q still struggling to follow, I thought he probably hadn't seen the pinecone drop from a tree on the other side of the wetlands clearing. But I had. And when I looked up, I saw Tip's ashen face peering around the trunk.

He was about three-quarters of the way up, as far as he could go before the branches would be too thin to bear his weight. I shook my head slightly, willing the boy to remain silent and un-detected. Unfortunately, we would have to pass right under that tall pine in order to pick up the second path, the one that led to my house. I hoped Tip would wait quietly until we were gone—then, when he was out of danger, run to the nearest phone to sound the alarm. Maybe the police would arrive in time. After all, Q wanted to eat something before commencing with the torture. Maybe he'd order me to make coffee and sandwiches. Or maybe he'd want whiskey. I thought about what poisonous herbs I had on hand. Maybe I could mince henbane into the food. How I wished for belladonna—or hemlock. If I lived through this, I vowed never to be without some quick, dependable poisons on hand.

Not wanting to draw attention to the boy, as I moved ahead I kept my head down, eyes fixed on my feet—sometimes sloshing through the swamp, sometimes using flat rocks or fallen trees as stepping-stones. So when the crash came, it was almost as much of a surprise to me as it was to Q. Tip jumped off his perch just as Q was passing under it! No doubt he'd seen this tricky maneuver in some adventure film—but it wasn't so easy to pull off in real life. Catching Q with a glancing blow, the boy cried out with the shock of falling. Q fell forward, screaming and cursing, Tip on his back. With all my might—and much painful effort—I thrust my arms apart and broke the cords that bound my hands together. Thinking to grab the pistol while Q was down, I rushed forward. But I had been walking too far ahead of him. Q rolled over onto his back, taking Tip with him, pinning the boy beneath him. He pointed the pistol directly into my face.

In a heartbeat, I'd stopped right in my tracks, swaying from the momentum. I heard someone yell, "No!"—and realized it was myself. Now Q had both of us. I couldn't stand thinking about what he would do with Tip—what he had done with the other boys. It must not end this way. I wouldn't let it. Suddenly, my whole being was one silent, screaming call for help.

There was a fierce cry in the air above us, and one of the eagles who'd nested in the tallest pines came careening down with a savage beating of wings, diving at Q. Grabbing Tip's shoulder, Q pushed the boy between himself and the angry, predatory bird. Then he took aim. I saw him smile in that instant—his wet lips curving in sensuous enjoyment. There was an instant explosion of sound and another furious scream from the eagle. Instinctively, as if knowing a man with his arm raised was too formidable an enemy, the canny eagle had already risen like a rocket through crackling branches when the shot sounded. He escaped into the air beyond, with obscuring pine branches between him and his attacker.

"Fucking bird!" said Q. "Did you call him, you witch?" He looked at me murderously. I heard a popping sound. Light seemed to come from everywhere, a super nova. Then a godfist slammed me back into a tree, and I slumped into oblivion.

When I woke up, Scruffy was licking my face and whimpering. *Get up, Toots! Come on now, get up!* Joe was there beside him, his concerned face leaning over me, calling my name tenderly, holding my hand. He looked terrible.

"What are you doing here?" I asked, then, without waiting for an answer, went on to my central concern. "Q's got Tip. Call the police. Find Stone. And Tip's father. No time to lose."

Scruffy began circling us in a distracted fashion, yelping. But Joe was silent for a moment, running his hands over me gently, looking for the injury. When he put his hand on my head, it came away sticky and red. He parted my hair. "Looks like a graze," he said.

"Feels like hell," I replied. "Get to a phone. I'll be all right. I'm not going anywhere."

"I can run to the house in five minutes. I'll contact Stone and get an ambulance for you," he said. Taking off his jacket, he tucked it in around me. "I'll be back in ten. Can you hold on? Will you lie still until then?"

Scruffy lay down and stretched himself full length beside me, licking my hand and chin alternately. *Don't you worry, Toots. I'm staying with you.*

I lifted one hand painfully and scratched between his ears. "Good boys," was all I could manage. "I'll be fine."

"Scruffy suddenly became impossible to control at the forest," Joe explained, quietly holding my hand after I'd been released from the trauma room and x-ray.

I was lying on a stretcher in the hall, with a bandaged head and wrists, waiting for a room assignment. Joe hadn't been able to ride in the ambulance with me, because he'd needed to bring the Hertz car with Scruffy. So this was our first chance to talk.

"He ran around in circles, barking and howling, even foaming a little at the mouth, as if he'd gone mad," Joe explained, while softly smoothing wet tendrils of hair off my forehead. "Frankly, I was afraid one of the officers would think he was rabid and shoot him. At first, I tried locking him in the rental car, but he continued to bark frantically and to claw at the upholstery. I suppose, now, that he was trying to get me to do what I finally did—bring him back home."

"Poor Scruff," I said. "Living with me has made him what we call 'a familiar,' supersensitive to my feelings and wishes. It's only natural that his sixth sense would be alerted that I was in danger."

"As soon as I'd opened the door, Scruffy jumped out of the car and dashed into the woods," Joe continued. "I ran hollering after him, carrying the leash. By that time, I was ready to strangle him with it. All I knew about your whereabouts was that your Jeep had been abandoned at Myles Standish. I desperately wanted to lock the damned nuisance in your house and get back to the search for you. But then, of course, Scruffy found you in an entirely different place."

I was struggling to sit up. "I've got to get out of here," I said.

Gently, Joe tried to push me back onto the stretcher. "The doctor wants you to stay here overnight, in case of complications."

"No way. You heard what she said as well as I did. 'If there is a concussion, it must be a slight one.'"

"She only said that because of the noisy and uncooperative way you were behaving. It was a wry comment, not a diagnosis."

"Are you going to help me off this rolling trap, or do I have to struggle alone?" I wasn't going to rest until Tip was rescued. Q couldn't have gone far. Jenkins's woods was no Myles Standish wasteland. It was a small, contained area that could be cordoned off and searched foot by foot. While I limped purposefully toward the swinging doors, Joe told me that Stone had been on his way to the woods before the medics arrived to take me to Jordan Hospital. Tip's father, too, went with one of the boy's uncles to track Q.

"Q will have his hands full, trying to get away and keep Tip under restraint," I said through tight lips. The skin around my mouth still hurt to move. "I only hope that Q will want to keep Tip alive to use as a hostage."

Unfortunately, as it turned out, Q had managed to escape from Jenkins's woods before the net tightened around the area. It was Tip's father and uncle who found the trail Tip left as he was dragged away.

"You look awful," Phillipa said, her dark eyes kinder than her words as she handed me a cup of strong, black coffee, refusing my request for aspirin in case I did, after all, have a slight concussion. I could have dosed myself with my own willow bark tea, its salicylic acid being the source of aspirin, but brewing herb tea didn't seem feasible at the moment. Since Stone and his men,

plus the various teams he'd called in to assist, were using my little house as a kind of unofficial base of operations, Phillipa had
commandeered my kitchen as well. A box of bakery rye loaves
stood on the floor, and she was making sandwiches with the
quickening fervor of The Sorcerer's Apprentice.

"Do you really need that bandage around your head? You look
as if you'd been mummified by an overenthusiastic first aid
trainee. Why don't you take a nice, hot shower and shampoo that
mop, only be very gentle around that graze. Then I'll stick a
Band-Aid on it when you're through."

It was an appealing idea. Suddenly I could feel every bit of grit
and grime that was stuck to my skin from the top of my scalp to
my scratched ankles. And I was famished as well. "All right. May
I have one of those Brie and smoked turkey things you're slapping together first? Will you promise to call me if there's any
news at all, even if I'm soaking wet?"

"Yes, of course." The kitchen wall phone jangled even as we
spoke. "Messages for Stone Stern?" she asked, in lieu of "Hello."
Listening a moment, she made a note on the kitchen blackboard,
which she had efficiently washed clean of my personal reminders.
"Okay. I'll tell him when he calls in."

I jumped up anxiously, a wave of hot anxiety traveling from
my battered head to my aching feet. "Have they found Tip yet?"

"No, not yet. That was Police Chief Hurley over in Carver.
Just to say they're staking out Quicksall's place, in case he's crazy
enough to return there. I've been rather a clearinghouse for messages, but they're mostly functional. If a real breakthrough oc-
curs, of course I'll alert you instantly. So finish your sandwich and
get upstairs."

I brought a quarter of my sandwich upstairs to Scruffy, who
was closed into the blue bedroom under the eaves.

Although my life was in an entire upheaval, and had been
since the holidays, my three children knew nothing about Q or
Tip or even Joe, other than my wearing an expensive embroidered shawl at Christmas. And I knew little about their concerns,

beyond the simple fact of Becky's engagement. I hadn't even met her fiancé's family, the Lowells, a name well known in Boston circles. I vowed to remedy all those lapses, to do whatever loving things were needed to make us a close family again, and especially to reach out to Cathy. But for now, I had to let Becky, Adam, and Cathy go from my thoughts, like candlelit prayer boats floating out on the tide. Tip! Right now I had Tip to save!

Scruffy was not to be mollified by a smidge of Brie. *How can I protect you like a proper guard dog if you keep locking me up?*

"Okay. As soon as I've dried my hair, you can go downstairs with me, but you'll have to stay on leash. There's too much confusing traffic in and out, and I need to keep track of you. I can't be losing my other little love."

He perked up at once and ran to the pine commode, opened the door with his teeth, and pulled out an old leash that Tip kept there. *It's a deal, Toots.*

It hit me just a few minutes after I'd stepped into the shower and was gingerly shampooing my hair around the bullet graze—a fear so overwhelming that I simply sank to the floor of the tub, oblivious to the hot water streaming over me. Tip would be killed horribly, and it would all be my fault!

No wonder he hadn't grasped my warning to stay hidden while we passed under the tree! How could I expect him to understand what he should do from that slight shake of my head? I must have been crazy to think that he would. I should have said something clever that Q would have thought I was addressing to him. Or I should have led Q in a different direction, not on the path under the tree but around through the brush, so that Tip might not have had the notion to jump Q in the first place.

How deranged and depraved I'd been to allow such a sweet boy to become entangled in my foolhardy crusade. It should have been me, not Tip, whom Q dragged away to a terrible fate. That was what I deserved. How could I ever face Tip's father? Or his mother, wherever she was. Probably on her way here this very minute to stick the knife in my grief and turn it. Lost! Tip was lost, and it was all my doing. And after he finished with Tip, Q would come after me. There would be no hiding from Q's revenge. No one could save me. Or should save me, since I must pay for Tip's death with my own . . .

When Phillipa came upstairs later, concerned about my non-appearance at the center of activity, I was still crouched in the tub, crying, although by then the water had turned cold, my skin was wrinkled and puckered, and I was shivering badly. Turning off the shower, she put her slim, warm arms around me, heedless of the wet, and little by little unclenched my limbs until I could stand.

"It's an anxiety attack," she explained reasonably to me and my racing heart. "Perfectly natural."

As she swathed me in towels and carefully dried and brushed my hair, the acute palpitations eased to nearly normal. Finding that my wound was somewhat too much for a Band-Aid to handle, she gently bandaged it with a gauze pad and tape, arranging my hair over the odd-looking lump. Then she found clean underwear, brown wool slacks, and a creamy cashmere pullover—a gift I'd been saving for a special occasion and so had never worn—laying out the ensemble on Tip's bed for me.

Scruffy hunched on the floor, feigning sleep, with one eye slightly open to follow my every move and one ear cocked to hear those certain words that are meaningful to a dog.

"Look, just give me some old sweats, will you?" I said to Phillipa, recovered sufficiently to be querulous.

"Nonsense. This will be comfortable yet stylish. I expect there will be TV camera crews swarming around here as soon as Stone allows the roadblocks around your house to be lifted. After all, you are the heroine of the moment. 'Local witch shot by suspect accused in missing children case.' I'll wager at this very minute Dee and Heather are trying to talk their way by some stolid local policeman who doesn't know Will. Fiona, of course, should be able to just walk through—invisible, so she claims, in her glamour. Now get these clothes on and, if you're up to it, put on some blusher and lipstick. You look like the ghost of the Gray Lady."

After I'd followed these orders, she handed me the gold pendants, eagle and pentagram, to hang over the sweater. "This will give you strength, and it adds an air of mystery, too," she declared. "See you downstairs. You'll be needed to give information and help in the search. Are you reasonably recovered now?"

I nodded for yes, feeling tears wanting to start again, this time because it was so comforting to have good friends.

When I came into the kitchen a few minutes later, Fiona was seated at my table with a cup of tea. She'd brought a plate of those tiny, creamy, delectable scones one couldn't imagine emerging from her chaotic and none-too-clean kitchen. "Let me have a look at you," she said, coming over to examine my wound, her motherly face crisscrossed in kindly wrinkles, her braids wispy with escaping curls. She touched the bandage gingerly. "Does it hurt, honey? Don't you worry. Q can't get away this time. He won't be maiming anyone else ever again."

How often comforting words have an opposite effect! Her choice of the word 'maiming' gave me gooseflesh. "But he's taken Tip . . . he's holding Tip hostage." I could hear my own shakiness, the catch in my voice.

"Now don't drown Cass in sympathy," Phillipa ordered, tasting a corner crumb of scone. "Can't you see that she's barely got herself pulled together? What do you put in these things, anyway?"

"Oh, various things . . . I never measure," Fiona said vaguely, winking at me.

"Where's Joe? Did you see Joe when you drove in?" I asked.

"The police aren't letting cars through, my dear. I walked in through the trees. Apparently, no one saw me. I didn't dare wave at Heather. She and Dee were in the Mercedes, arguing with some young officer. And there were two TV vans, as well, and a bunch of our neighbors. It's quite a zoo."

"What did I tell you . . ." Phillipa commented.

"But I did see Joe with some other men." Fiona continued. "It looked as if they were being instructed in how to assist the search parties. My own thinking, however, is that the police ought to give up on Jenkins's woods. Q is long gone out of there. And I intend to tell Stone so."

She did, too. Stone came in a few minutes later to question me again, although I'd already told him every detail I could remember when he'd encountered me in the hospital parking lot, making my escape.

"Q won't be able to help himself," Fiona interrupted Stone's quiet questioning by shaking his shoulder to get his attention. He looked up, startled—possibly because Fiona's hair stood out around her head as if electrified. "He's like an animal now, at the end of his strength. He'll just naturally head back to his hole. There's probably some hideout in Carver that he knows very well—other than his house, which is being watched. He'll drag Tip to this secret place and make his stand. By the way, you ought to call down to the roadblock and tell them to let Heather and Dee through. Say that it's the Mercedes. But no TV people, please."

Fiona loomed over Stone in her queenly glamour until he made the call to lift the roadblock for the rest of our circle. He was impressed enough to call Chief Hurley in Carver also. But there had been no sign of Q in the area around his property. Satisfied that her plan of action had been put into motion, Fiona settled at the table over a teacup refreshed by Phillipa, and was simply a frowsy little librarian again.

As always, it had been amazing to watch Fiona take command of a situation. I believed, at these times, she was infused with powerful intuitions as well. But my intuitions were strong, also. My course of action, then, should be to get me and my intuitions over to Carver right now.

After Stone had gone and Heather came in with Dee, I said, "Don't take off your jackets. I need you to get me out of here.

Fiona's convinced me that Q is in Carver, so I want to touch base with Chief Hurley. Fiona, will you keep an eye on Scruffy? There's too much traffic in and out of here to let him run." I handed her the end of his leash and avoided the dog's baleful glance. *So . . . running out on me again! And this one always smells of cat.* I patted him absentmindedly.

"Maybe there will be something we can do to help the search," I urged. "Heather . . . think . . . when you were nailing up Hecate at the crossroads and otherwise running around those woods, did you come across anything that might prove to be a good hideout for Q?"

While we walked back to her car, Heather puzzled over that problem. She retraced her course through the roadblock, while I ducked down in the backseat so that neither the TV people nor Stone nor Joe would see me depart. There was no time for a lot of foolish argument about safety, and besides, the Carver police could serve us for protection just as well.

Finally, as we sped away, Heather said, "Do you remember that deserted crossroads where we turned the car around that day? There was a grungy barbershop . . . and a seedy general store, but the whole place had the air of a ghost town? Well . . . opposite Sachem Road—I forget the name of the street—I happened to notice a farmhouse set back near the edge of the woods with boarded-up windows and a *For Sale* sign stuck in the lawn. No other houses within sight. Gave me the shivers just to look at it. The image of that farmhouse has been flashing before my mind's eye. Do you suppose . . . ?"

That felt right to me. It wasn't a vision, exactly, but a moment of certainty, like when you know in your bones that you've just bought a winning raffle ticket. "Let's get over there."

"Thanks to me, Q is now armed with Fiona's pistol," I explained to Dee and Heather. The Mercedes snaked over the twisting secondary roads from Cedar Hill Point to Carver. Only someone born and brought up in Plymouth, as Heather had been, could have found her way so smoothly through the many unmarked connecting roads that wove between little bodies of water picturesquely named Grassy Pond, Bloody Pond, Long Pond, Little Long Pond, Halfway Pond, and Gallows Pond—and then cut across part of Myles Standish State Forest to come out with perfect accuracy in South Carver.

"According to my count," I concluded, "he has only three bullets left. I found it loaded with four. Then, of course, he used one when he shot me."

"Oh, swell—one for each of us," Dee interrupted. "I'm calling Hurley." She didn't bother with Information but went directly through the operator to the Carver Police on Heather's car phone. The dispatcher at police headquarters did not impress Dee with her grasp of the emergency nature of the situation.

"The chief can't be interrupted at this time. He's in pursuit of a dangerous criminal," intoned the nasal voice of the dispatcher, loud enough for all of us to hear.

Dee tried unsuccessfully to explain that we were pursuing the same desperate man that the chief was, and that Q had taken a child hostage.

"Listen, I'm holding down the fort here with the desk sergeant. We have no available officers to delegate to a missing person search this afternoon. Come in and fill out the forms, dearie."

Dee made a rude suggestion to the dispatcher about what she could do with those missing person forms, hung up, and called the firehouse. "Will, listen to me carefully," she ordered. "Somehow you've got to get through to Chief Hurley. He and his men are staked out at Q's place. Tell him to investigate a house for sale just off the crossroads at the west end of Sachem. We think Q may be holed up inside. Cass, Heather, and I are on our way there now."

There was a pause, during which I could hear Will yelling into the phone, something about "the mother of my children." Dee replied calmly. "Get a grip, Will. Did you expect Cass to sit home while Q has his hands on the kid? Could we allow her to go off on her own again and have to bury the pieces later? Okay . . . Okay . . . maybe you'd better talk to Stone, too. And Joe," she added as an afterthought. "But we're not going to do anything risky, Will. We're just going to see if Q is actually there. No, we will not approach the house. We'll just—what do you call it?—reconnoiter."

"Speak for yourself," I warned her.

"For the first time in my life, I wish I owned a gun," Heather whispered, taking a crowbar out of the trunk of her car. "I mean, I would never wish to harm any living being in the greater family of consciousness—except, I find, for some men. I don't know why that death spell I put on Q didn't take effect. It would have solved so many problems. He must be a powerful sorcerer himself."

We had parked the Mercedes on Sachem Road and ducked across the street into the woods where we could approach the farmhouse on what we hoped was the blind side. A row of scraggly pine trees had been planted along the property line, providing some puny cover. We crouched behind them and watched for any sign of life inside the house. No forest ranger van was in sight, but Q would certainly have ditched that in the woods where it wouldn't be spotted.

"Where the hell is Hurley?" Dee murmured.

"Will may have run into the same dumb dispatcher that you did," I whispered back, peering between low pine branches. "But Will is resourceful. He'll get through to Stone, and Stone will have no problem contacting Hurley. Now be quiet, both of you. I thought I heard a sound."

We waited and listened for an eternity—maybe ten or fifteen minutes—when I heard it again. A faint hammering sound. "You stay here to connect with Hurley. I'm going to creep around behind that shed and see if anything's going on in back of the house."

"Be damned quiet," Heather warned. "Here, take this." She handed me the crowbar. "Holler if you get into trouble, and I'll run to the car and call Stone and the state police. These small-town cops are more used to bringing truants to school and collecting overdue library books than tracking murderers."

"The place looks absolutely deserted," Dee muttered. "I hope we're not leading everyone on a wild-goose chase here. This *is* a bit of a shot in the dark, isn't it?"

It took a long time to crawl from the pines to the back of the woodpile to the rear of the shed and behind the broken old tractor abandoned to rust and weeds. One high window at the back of the house—probably the bathroom—had not been boarded up. Undoubtedly the water had been turned off to prevent the pipes from freezing last winter, so chances were that the room was not in use. I thought about dashing across the yard, standing on a wheelbarrow without a wheel that had been abandoned near the house, and taking a quick look inside through the accessible window. But I didn't believe it was possible to do that without attracting the attention of anyone who was in the house. I waited to hear that faint sound again, but everything was as quiet as a cemetery.

Then the silence was broken by a single hurt cry, faint, but to my ears, unmistakably the voice of Tip. It acted on me like a gust of gale-force wind, lifting me right up into the air so that I felt myself winging across the open backyard, light as a paper airplane, without volition. Jumping up on the wheelbarrow, I simultaneously lifted my palm against the window to shove it upwards. Miraculously, it was unlocked. I couldn't say how I managed to push myself over the sill and slide my hips through that small aperture, down over a dank, rusted sink, holding one hand in front of me to take the shock as I tumbled onto the floor. The other held the crowbar as if hand and weapon were welded together. I scrambled to my feet and, somehow, got myself behind the bathroom door just before Q flung it open. Heather had been dead on target, some part of my mind exulted!

Instantly, I swung at Q's head with the crowbar, awkwardly upward because he was taller than I. The metal connected with a satisfying thud. He grunted and fell forward onto the sink, a trickle of blood running down his forehead. He was not moving.

Jumping away, I ran through the door into a kitchen, calling Tip's name. It was only then, as I was rushing to rescue Tip, that I began to worry about the whereabouts of the pistol. Why hadn't Q carried it in his hand when he charged into the bathroom? I should have checked his belt while he was down. But there was no time for self-recrimination.

Tip was in the corner of a small, empty room next to the kitchen, tied up and gagged with duct tape. I knew I had heard the boy's cry for help, but how? Had his silent anguish reached me as sound? His shirt had been torn off, and there were some kind of sores on his chest. I pulled off the tape, sympathizing with the hurt Tip must feel, but in a hurry to communicate with him while we made our escape.

"Ouch," Tip cried out. "Boy, am I glad to see you. But that man will be coming back. He's going to kill us. He hurt me real bad with his cigarette. And he has a gun." His face was streaked from dried tears, and I could tell he was trying hard not to begin crying again.

I murmured encouragement as I struggled to free him. The knots were tight and difficult to loosen. If I had any fingernails left, they were broken in the process of tearing away those ropes. "I hit him over the head, and he went down," I explained to the boy as he rubbed his wrists. "But we'll have to run fast. I don't know how long he's going to stay unconscious."

Suddenly my stomach lurched in fear and Tip cried out. Q loomed in the doorway of the little room, the blood now running in a thin stream over one eye. The hand he used to wipe his eye held Fiona's pistol.

"Am I never to be rid of you?" he growled savagely, swinging the pistol down to press it against my left nipple. His eyes looked dazed—whether from fury or his wound I didn't know. I fought against the urge to vomit as he leaned down over me with a breath that stank like a decomposing animal. In that moment, I was feeling, smelling, and seeing my death. What was left for me to do but to thrust out with a surge of all my reserves of strength against him? Pushing away my fear, I took one good, deep breath—possibly my last—and felt spiritual lightning come out of nowhere, infusing me with energy. At the same time, not to leave any stone unturned, I brought my knee up smartly into his groin, while hitting the pistol away from my breast with my right hand, expecting this would be my last living act.

As I struck, I yelled, "Run, Tip, run!"

I'll never know why Q didn't pull the trigger right then. He shouldn't even have had to think about it—just a reflex action against the pain. Instead, he crumpled onto the floor, clutching his crotch and screaming. I must have delivered a direct hit. I felt a momentary glow of triumph. But he still had the pistol. Even in his agony, he didn't let go.

Tip rushed forward with the crowbar. Holding it in both hands, he yelled like a small warrior and swung it down over Q's head. But Q was not too far gone in pain to roll away from the blow. The crowbar struck harmlessly, splitting a floorboard. Still holding his groin with his left hand, Q aimed the pistol at the boy.

"*No!*" I screamed.

Something like a wrecking ball crashed through the window with a great splintering of wood and glass. The ball unfolded. It was Joe! He hurled himself at Q as the pistol fired, throwing off his aim just enough so that the bullet whizzed harmlessly past Tip's ear.

Joe grabbed Q's right wrist and struck it against the floor, trying to dislodge the pistol from Q's hand. Another shot was fired that struck the wall. Q rolled over onto Joe, the two of them still wrestling over the pistol in a sea of broken glass. Freeing the pistol but not himself from Joe's hold on him, Q slammed it against Joe's head. Shaken loose from his grip of Q's gun hand and looking stunned from the blow, Joe still managed to wrap himself around the man's waist. I grabbed the crowbar from the floor and lifted it into position, but I couldn't find a clear field to strike as the two men grappled, crushing glass into snow.

Q fired a third time just as two policemen in protective gear and assault weapons rushed in the door. I heard and felt a sharp *ping* as the bullet struck the crowbar. Q screamed, and a spot of blood appeared on his shoulder. The deflected bullet had found a target.

Like magic, I thought. "It's okay now. The pistol's empty," I said to the police team—rather calmly, under the circumstances—hoping that, in all the excitement, I'd counted right.

Two more helmeted and shielded policemen lumbered through the broken window, pulled Joe away, and handcuffed Q, not without smashing the killer against the wall a few times in the process. Sobbing with relief, I threw one arm around Joe and the other around Tip.

"Oh, darling, your face is cut, and just look at your hands! Are you all right? How did you roll in the window like that? I have never been so glad to see anyone in my life."

Joe grinned at me. "Something I learned with the paratroopers," he said. "My hands got into the glass a bit, but I'm all right. This leather jacket took the worst of it. Hey, Tip, what's this on your chest? What did that scum do to you?"

We explained everything to one another over and over, with more hugs that wouldn't let go for a moment.

Hurley had cordoned off the area and waited for Stone to arrive with a SWAT team. But Joe had arrived first, ignoring procedure and Hurley's direct orders, quietly issued to preserve the surprise of attack. Now as four members of the team marched Q past us, the face he turned my way was suffused with palpable hatred and malice. I would need some spiritual cleansing after this, I thought. Still hanging on to Joe and Tip, I watched out the broken window as Q was escorted to the waiting van, surrounded by enough police officers to arrest an army of villains.

When we emerged, it was surprising to see how many people

and vehicles had gathered around the farmhouse while we had been battling for our lives. No scavenging newspeople had arrived yet, which was a tribute to Stone's adroit management. As we walked past the detective where he was leaning against a police vehicle, I managed to murmur my thanks for the rescue.

Stone saluted Joe and me with a wry grin. "What a pair of heroic fools," he said. "You two deserve each other." Looking Tip over closely and warmly, he added, "You're a very brave young man. We're all proud of you. Now, have those wounds tended to at that medical rescue van parked at the crossroads—burns, are they? That son of a bitch! Afterwards, you and I will talk about what's happened here." He lifted his gaze to us. "I'll catch you two at your place in an hour or so."

"No way," I said. "I'm not leaving until Tip goes with me. You can talk to the three of us at my house when you're ready. But first we'll check in at that medical van you suggested and have a doctor put something on Tip's burns and pull the glass out of Joe's hands."

Then I could see Heather and Dee beyond the cordoned-off area—snatched away from their hiding place to safer ground. Tip's father was probably there, too. I realized with surprise that I'd have to clear it with him before I brought Tip home with me. I'd almost forgotten that Tip wasn't, after all, my own son. We headed toward their anxious, loving faces.

When Tip had bathed as best he could without disturbing the burns on his chest which the medic had dressed, he joined us in the kitchen. Plastering down his stick-straight, dark hair wetly, he'd succeeded in dousing its red highlights. Despite his wounds, he looked fit and fine, eager for the next thing to happen. How resilient children are! I was pleased to see him help himself to a glass of milk. He felt at home here. I wished again that he could stay forever. Would Tip want to live with me—perhaps if his father's drunken abuse got worse? Or would he only feel more responsible for his father's care?

"Stone spoke for all of us when he said that you're a brave young man," Joe said to Tip. "Why don't you keep this as a well-earned memento of the occasion." He handed the boy an exquisitely tapered and marked eagle feather. Fortunately, this one was arguably legal; Joe had found it weeks ago near the new swampy area in Jenkins's woods.

"Wow, what a neat one! This is as perfect as any Paw has in his war bonnet," Tip said proudly, his grin turning his eyes aslant. He glanced at the little mirror that hung by the back door. If we hadn't been there, I think he would have stuck the eagle feather into his hair to see how it looked. "Thanks a lot, Joe."

You can thank me *for rustling those ducks.* Scruffy finally came out of his gloomy disapproval of important events that hadn't included him. *The ducks ought to thank me, too. That eagle was swooping down to grab his dinner. Almost snapped off my head. But I gave him a real good scare. He's lucky he got away with the rest of his feathers.*

Tip and I smiled at each other. From my collapse into the kitchen rocker, I reached down weakly to scratch Scruffy's head. Having made his feelings known, the dog sighed and went back to feigning sleep, lying on the braided rug at my feet in an unforgiving heap. With my other hand I lifted the cup of hot, sweet tea that Joe had handed me and sipped it gratefully. My whole being was concentrated on a hot bath. "I'll take this with me," I said, and crushed a few dried sage leaves into the tea to restore well-being before I limped upstairs. Lighting a lily-scented candle for its uplifting fragrance, I piled my hair on top of my head and sank gratefully into a delicious, restorative thyme-and-jasmine soak. Cosseted and soothed by nature's balms, I began to feel my spiritual energy lifting, lifting, practically up to normal.

When I came downstairs, Stone was sitting at the kitchen table. He seemed to be struggling not to look pleased with himself. I guessed that pride was an expression his kind face wore uneasily. His light blue eyes studied me in their usual quizzical fashion. "I'm glad to see you looking so glowing. Perhaps you won't be sorry to learn that, between Quicksall's earlier accident—for which Phillipa unaccountably claims full credit, by the way—and his run-in with you Musketeers, not to mention his encounter with Joe the Human Cannonball, the suspect is in tough shape. But we managed to have a medic fix up his shoulder and assorted injuries well enough to keep him out of the hospital, where there would have been a certain risk, no matter how well he was guarded. The marshal took him into custody. No local jail. Since he *was* rather foaming at the mouth—rage and frustration, I don't doubt—we sent him down to Bridgewater for a psychiatric evaluation. He'll be all nicely secure with the criminally insane for a few weeks, and looked after by an excellent, although not coddling, medical staff. After that he'll be arraigned and stashed at Plymouth County Correction until his trial. Best we can do. I hope you'll feel easier in your mind knowing he's locked up."

"I won't relax until he's dead," I said, but instantly regretted my meanness of spirit when Stone was trying so hard to reassure me. "Sorry, Stone, but you have yet to uncover the full scope of his crimes. Take it on faith that I've seen them, although not in any legally useful way. Where's Phil?"

"Phil's coming over later with some fantastic soup she's conjuring up even as we speak. Heather's standing by, with Dick somebody, her companion vet who's checking over Zelda to see what's causing a touch of jaundice. Too much poached salmon and chopped chicken liver, says Heather. Personally I think that little black minx is thriving just fine after a youth misspent in Dumpsters. Dee went home, hanging on Will's arm. Fiona I haven't seen all day, which is surprising."

"Not if you knew Fiona as we do. She walked right through your roadblock earlier and was here looking after Scruffy. Now she's gone home for a "wee rest," as she put it, before her niece-in-law arrives. Belle MacDonald. Sounds uncompromising, doesn't it?"

"Belle in Bedlam," Joe said. He poured boiling water into the coffeemaker and took a bottle of whiskey out of the liquor cabinet.

Stone had turned to Tip. "Nice feather, young fella. Where did you get it?"

"Legal fall," said Joe shortly, perhaps because Stone was occupying the place at the table where Joe himself usually sat. "Coffee? Whiskey?"

"You wouldn't happen to have any Earl Grey tea?" Stone inquired. Joe gazed at the ceiling for a moment. For all our sakes, it would be better if these two men could be friends. I closed my eyes, imagining a wise, beneficent light encompassing them both.

Then Stone proceeded to take us through the entire encounter with Q, prodding us with questions when we faltered, sorting out facts when we engulfed him with impressions, methodically making notes throughout.

When Joe handed Stone his mug of tea—which should have been served in a china cup, tea bag removed—I had the distinct impression that this man I loved had been catering to everyone's needs as long as his ego could bear. Joe the warrior might need to return soon to some environmental battle or other. In another age, it would have been the Crusades. But could I deal with those long, dull stretches without him, enlivened by the occasional ardent rendezvous?

Phillipa and Heather arrived a heartbeat ahead of the TV people with their vans and mikes, who were made to cluster outside the unused front door waiting for an interview with Tip and me. Stone stayed away from the windows, not wanting to be coerced into giving a statement until he was ready.

"I'll fix your hair," Phillipa declared. "I guess what you're wearing will do."

"Oh, thanks," I said. After my bath, I'd donned the green cashmere turtleneck I'd been saving to wear with my camel's hair slacks on a special occasion. Perhaps I wasn't all that indifferent to media attention.

"And I'll write a few words for you," Heather added, taking the kitchen clipboard off the wall as Phillipa yanked me into the lav and set to work instantly. "Of course, I'll leave space between the lines for your corrections."

"You look like a sleepwalker, Cass," Phillipa said, cruelly wielding the hairbrush. "It's over, my dear. Keep telling yourself that. We've won. We've finished him."

A short time later I wedged open the front door, recently repaired but still rusty at the hinges, and stepped out with Tip. Joe came out, too, and stood behind us on the stone step, glowering as if ready to defend me. Heather's neatly printed words said exactly the right things, after all. Mostly about what I couldn't say, not wanting to prejudice Quicksall's right to a fair trial. That was a laugh. It wasn't a trial I wanted but a summary execution.

When my part was over and Tip had smiled shyly into the camera and said he was okay, a pert young reporter who looked like a college kid shouted out, "Is there any truth to the rumor, Ms. Shipton, that you belong to a local witches' coven?" Joe's hand on my shoulder tightened.

I looked at the page in my hands. No answer had been provided by the redoubtable Heather. When I looked up I could see the Reverend Peacedale and a herd of other neighbors shifting about among my trees.

"I'm not sure I know what you mean. Where did that notion come from?"

"But your friends . . ." The intern reporter's voice was fading.

"Oh, surely you can't mean our Great Books discussion group. Good heavens!" I laughed.

A short clip of the story was aired nationally as well as the longer interview shown locally. Becky called right afterwards to say she was relieved that I was all right, dismayed at what her fiancé's family might infer from the reporter's questions, and hopeful that I would try to lead a normal life from now on. I said I appreciated her concern, and I'd had enough excitement to last me a while. Then she asked, who was that tough-looking man with dark, curly hair who stood with me, some kind of body-guard? Just a close friend, I said. Very close.

Adam and Cathy called later, with similar remarks and questions. How wonderful it was to hear from all three of my children in one day!

So all it takes is a little notoriety, I thought. Perhaps that can be arranged more often in the future.

It was a fine, warm Saturday in early March, but the earth was barely thawed when digging began. Heather came over to wait with me for news of what would be discovered. None of us had the stomach to stand gawking with Q's neighbors. Heather brought a list of cleaning products I should boycott, produced by a manufacturer who still employed animals to test caustic substances. She stuck the list to my refrigerator with a *Stop the Cruelty to Crustaceans* lobster-shaped magnet. I supposed that meant we would get no more of Ashbery's perfect lobster salad.

"When and how will we know what the diggers find?'

"Stone will call Phil if there's anything, and she'll call us," I said.

While Joe, Tip, and Scruffy took a long walk through Jenkins's woods, Heather and I drank camomile tea with a hint of catnip, a great calmative. Afterwards, I busied myself mixing up my flea powder special for Heather's family of mutts: wormwood, rue, rosemary, pennyroyal, lemon peel, and citronella. As always, using a mortar and pestle soothed my nerves and focused my scattered energies. With Q's gruesome handiwork in the forefront of my mind, the mixture of dried herbs was soon pulverized to a fine powder to which I added silken white diatomaceous earth.

There was always an animal drama in Heather's repertoire, and while I worked, she regaled me with the latest, a daring rescue of puppies from a local laboratory. Dick Devlin's name figured often in these escapades, which I took as a good sign that

Heather's resolve to live a celibate life, after three failed mar-
riages, was weakening. Now that I'd rediscovered sex myself, I
was feeling downright evangelical about it.

When Heather had run out of canine capers, we hashed over
Fiona's predicament. The pregnant niece-in-law Belle Mac-
Donald had been foisted on Fiona by militant Pro-Life relatives.
The young woman was to stay for the next six months while
awaiting the birth of a child. Then the baby would be put up for
adoption so that Belle could return to her law studies in Texas.

"Law and *order*," Heather chortled. "Not only has she shov-
eled out Fiona's kitchen, she's even alphabetized the herb and
spice jars. She's talking now about the need to catalog Fiona's
books, pamphlets, and ephemera. Just wait until Belle starts
browsing through Gurdjieff, Ouspensky, Madame Blavatsky, and
Fiona's other favorites. Will she have a buzz for her parents! But
the really big battle came when Belle attempted to bathe Omar.
That cat jumped out the bedroom window, right through the
screen—came home three days later with a torn ear and an air of
secret satisfaction. With Belle and her Dust Buster underfoot,
Fiona's like a fish out of water. Well, come to think of it, she *is* a
Pisces. Remember that old *Book of Shadows* she unearthed at
Yule? Last time I was there, she wrapped it up in a *House
Beautiful's Cuisines of the Western World* dust jacket and pressed it
into my hands, begging me to hide it in my turret room. Now she
claims she's too upset to conduct a workshop in how to assume a
glamour, as she had promised."

"I'm not so sure that was a truly sincere promise. Fiona enjoys
our amazed envy whenever she wraps herself in a glamour, you
know. When is Belle's child due?" I asked, leafing through my
kitchen calendar.

"October or November, I think. Wouldn't it be nice if it were a
Halloween baby!"

I thought about Belle's baby, the reality of her, rocked in the
comfort in her mother's womb, the perfect tiny fingers and toes
flexing, the eyes waiting under silken eyelids to wake to the

phantasmagoria of the world. How could Belle give up all that for a law degree? Perhaps she would reconsider. "She," I said, drawing a little five-pointed star on Halloween. "The baby is a girl."

"Oh, don't start . . ." complained Heather.

The phone rang, all the more startling because we'd been waiting for it. "Stone says it's like an archeological dig." Phil's voice sounded chilled, the temperature it gets when she's deeply troubled. "They're finding everything from bodies to bicycles. Under the brick patio in back of the house. There's an elaborate barbecue where he used to host a Boy Scout outing every summer. Remains of three underneath. So far. Unidentified as yet, of course. I'll bet he had to keep enlarging that patio. Ugh. I'll call again when they're through for today, okay?"

"Heather's here. Why don't you come over for lunch?"

"Thanks anyway. I'm cooking up comfort food like mad, although I don't suppose Stone'll be hungry. It's my way of keeping calm."

"I know what you mean. I've been grinding flea powder."

After we'd hung up, I repeated Phil's report to Heather.

"Inlaid flagstones probably kept the Dobes from digging up the corpses," she said thoughtfully. "Is it too early, do you think, for something stronger than coffee?"

That weekend, Tip's father went on a raging drunk, beat up a Swedish sailor in a bar, and was jailed for thirty days awaiting a hearing. Meanwhile, Deidre pulled some strings with Social Services so that Tip could stay with me until his family got sorted out. I searched my heart and believed I had not wished for this turn of events nor caused them to happen with any exercise of craft. But it seemed to me that the boy belonged here in my home. I meditated over Tip and said a spell of words for our relationship, that it would be resolved in a manner that most fulfilled the boy's needs, not mine.

By the ides of March, the police had excavated every inch of Q's property and found a total of thirteen children buried there.

Forensic scientists began to match bodies with identities. Real boys came to life and were murdered nightly on TV newscasts as reporters interviewed uncles, cousins, neighbors, and the occasional dazed parent willing to bleed on camera. Whenever possible, home movies or still photos of victims like our local Daryl Hendler surprised us with their grinned normality—as if they should have known the horrible fate in store for them and smiled less.

But these boys were only "the tip of the iceberg," as the TV reporters were fond of saying—local children. Q was also suspected of a number of other unsolved murders all up and down the New England coastline—boys whose bodies were found tied to trees in dense woodland areas or buried in shallow graves.

All this made Tip even dearer to me. Joe and Tip and I seemed like a real family. Our simple round of school and meals and chores and walks on the beach with Scruffy seemed inexpressibly satisfying. Since Tip had never been able to afford the luxury of after-school activities and friends hanging around, because of the responsibilities he'd assumed while he lived with an alcoholic father, he was used to a solitary life like mine and fell in readily with my quiet routine. The love I felt for Tip reminded me of the early years with my own children.

Which made all the more cruel the misty April day Tip ran to me after school, glowing with joy so that he seemed surrounded by light as he raced up the walk to where Scruffy and I were surveying winter damage to the perennial herb garden.

"Maw's here! She's come to get me!" he exclaimed with a great, shining grin. "We're all going to live together in Maine with our new stepfather, Jake. And it's not just for Easter vacation. Timmy and me and Maw are going to stay together forever. Timmy's my little brother."

"You must be very happy," I said carefully, slowly. I felt as if someone had carved an icy cave inside me where my heart should be. I leaned on a garden wall, feeling the edge of it cutting into my palms. "So . . . how did this all come about?"

"Just luck, I guess. 'Cause Maw saw my picture on the TV. She called right away, she said, but there was no one at the house to answer. So then she talked to the neighbors and got all the news. You know, about Paw awaiting his hearing and our not bothering to contact Social Services about me. She was mighty worried about there being no social worker watching out for me, and me just living as a handyman and all," he said proudly. "Okay if I pack up my stuff I left here?"

Not waiting for more answer than a nod, he bounded up the back stairs to the porch, Scruffy following eagerly, knowing there was something exciting going on, maybe a new game with the big paper bag the boy was carrying.

"I'll write you," he said when he'd thrown his things into the bag and was coming back down the stairs at a run. "Maw works in a drugstore where they have lots of postcards. I'll send you a postcard of Maine."

"That would be nice," I said automatically, frozen in the center of the kitchen. "Where's your mother now? I'd like to speak to her for a minute. Would you introduce us before you leave?"

"She and Jake dropped me off up on Route 3. They're going downtown with Timmy to get some stuff to eat on the road, and I'm supposed to be waiting right where they left me, with my stuff packed, when they come back this way. I think they're in a real hurry, you know, so maybe they don't have time to visit. They might have to leave without me if I'm not ready on time. Oh . . . I took the Walkman. Was that okay?"

"Of course. It's yours. I gave it to you."

"Tell Joe I said good-bye. And thanks for everything he taught me. You know, about carpentry and all."

"I will. You take care of yourself, now. And call me collect if you need anything. In fact, call me anyway and give me a phone number where I can reach you, okay? You know how to call collect, don't you?"

"Sure. Don't worry, Miz Shipton. Everything is going to be great."

"Remember that we all love you, Tip," I tried to say without any catch in my voice, but not quite managing it. He ran back and hugged me hard around the waist. "Me, too," he said. Then he knelt down to hug Scruffy, hiding his face in the dog's fur so that his voice was muffled. "I sure will miss you guys," he said. "Sorry you can't go with me, fella."

A moment later Tip was gone, the slap of the storm door echoing throughout the house.

Something's wrong with the boy. Scruffy whined, running from window to window to watch his friend hurry up the driveway to the main road. *I don't like what's going on here. What about the game we were going to have with the paper bag?*

After a while, I sat in the kitchen rocker and rocked, holding my arms across my chest, hugging my feelings inside. "I'm going to send him that clarinet I always wanted him to have, Scruffy," I said firmly, as if expecting the dog to attempt to talk me out of it. "Maybe they'll end up having to hock it, but at least he'll have it for a while." Then I cried.

Scruffy gave up his window watch and came to lie down on my feet, his nose between his paws. *I hate it when you cry, Toots. It's bad news, all right—the boy running off like that. You can't fool a dog, you know.*

There was no explaining Tip's continued absence to Scruffy. Joe and I took him everywhere in the Jeep to jolly him out of his listless depression, but he didn't even bother to drool on the open windows. Joe even threw the slimy orange ball across the yard as Tip used to do, but Scruffy simply raised his eyebrows and trotted up onto the porch for a nap. Finally, I appealed to Heather, who brought over a female greyhound who, while she wasn't exactly in heat, had not yet been spayed. Immediately, the old Scruffy reappeared, prancing and posturing for the nervous, anemic old lady with even more verve and bravado than ever.

Phillipa tried to talk sense to me. "Listen, Cass—raising children is over for you. Now you must let go of that part of your life and get on with the next phase, whatever it turns out to be. And besides, with Becky about to be married, you'll probably soon be a grandmother."

"Oh, thanks," I said. "You're a real comfort, Phil."

"And Tip will write to you, won't he?" She handed me a glass of exceptional sherry and frowned at me when I downed it like vodka.

"So he said. But boys never do write letters. It's not in their genetic code."

Next it was Joe. With an irrepressible gleam of anticipation in his eyes, he packed his duffel bag just before Ostara, the spring equinox, to join the crew of the *Moby Dick*. Greenpeace planned to anchor off Cherbourg in hopes of blocking a shipment of plutonium reprocessed in France and now bound for Japan. Neither the citizens nor the other governments along the proposed route knew about this deadly cargo. Joe told me that a person standing near an unshielded block of glassified plutonium would receive a fatal dose of radiation in just a minute's time. Greenpeace intended to alert the world to this dangerous prospect, since the Nuclear Non-Proliferation Treaty negotiations at the U.N. had failed to do so.

"You people at Greenpeace are crazy," I said. "Idealistic and wonderful, of course—but stark, raving mad. I suppose *this* plutonium must be well shielded, or the French would have to be prepared for a staggering crew turnover. How will the French government react to your presence, do you suppose? Didn't they blow up the first *Rainbow Warrior?*"

"I'll be fine," Joe reassured me, putting his warm, strong arms around me, always a surefire way to distract me from reasoning. "When this mission is over, I'll take a few weeks' leave, I promise. Now that I have you, I'm not going to work the same nonstop schedule as I have been. I do have you, don't I?" His arms tightened. What a shame that we would miss being together at Ostara, which was the high holiday much recommended in the old texts for sex magic.

"Yes, you have me. And my dog. And my odd friends." I reasoned with myself sensibly that Joe was a man of action—that was part of his sexy charm. Living with me somehow had demoted him to the role of assistant householder—except for those glorious moments when he had catapulted through the farmhouse window to save me and Tip. And Joe loved Greenpeace. Good causes, reckless companions, high adventure. On the other hand, life with me had not lacked excitement. I felt a thrill of satisfaction to hear him say that he would worry about me while he was gone and that he begged me not to have any more visions. But when I put him on a bus for Logan Airport, the world lost a dimension of color and depth, and the delicate yellows of spring faded back into dark winter shadows.

I miss that big, hairy man almost as much as the boy. What did you do with him?

"I miss Joe, too, but I promise he'll be back—if there's anything at all to love potions and related enchantments . . . and we know there is," I comforted us both.

Meeting at Heather's for the Ostara Sabbat, we remembered the last time we'd gathered there for a high holiday—the deep snows of Yule, the crimson warmth of her garlanded Victorian parlor, the alarming sound of a shot suddenly shattering the bay window. We laughed about the mischance of Fiona's answering pistol, and how, marvelously, the evil Q had brought kind, quizzical Stone into our world, especially into Phillipa's life. Imagine, a detective with a gourmet's appreciation of fine cuisine—just what the love spell ordered! We thought of the distance we had traveled since then, how dangerous and long it had seemed with Q threatening us at every turn. And we found much reason for rejoicing at this spring equinox.

It had been Fiona's turn to host a gathering, but that was impossible, of course, with Belle, energized by her pregnancy, scouring and scowling. My house would have been empty enough, devoid of kith and kin except for Scruffy, but we were saving its proximity to Jenkins's woods for Beltane, the May Day festival.

So Heather retired her canine companions early that evening in March to their kennel beds in the triple garage that once had housed English limousines and Italian sports cars. She'd given Ashbery a holiday to visit her sister in Vermont, so that we need not worry about any intrusion by the frowning, tight-lipped housekeeper.

Not the parlor this time—we celebrated Ostara in the conservatory, usually a romping room strewn with plastic bones and chew toys. Now it was cleaned and gleaming, decorated with ferns, coleus, ivy, and Japanese vases filled with forced forsythia. An altar at one end of the long, glass-windowed room was massed with clay pots of hyacinth and daffodils around a bronze statue of Ceridwen with her cauldron. Heather's triptych of Hecate, rescued from Carver, had been placed slightly off-center on the altar, with a cluster of candles in candleholders of different heights facing opposite. The goddess of the crossroads and crime scenes was looking a little worse for wear, having been nailed to a tree out in the wind and rain for months.

"Looks like a proper relic now, doesn't she?" Heather defended the bleeding wooden replica. "I give this Hecate full marks for protecting you when you were on your quixotic mission to rescue Tip."

"Dear Heather, though I may believe deeply in protective magic, the farmhouse where we nearly died before Q was captured was not within sight of this triptych."

"When I took her down, I sighted from Hecate's gaze directly through the crossroads to the farmhouse." With her bronze hair unbound from its usual neat, thick braid, Heather appeared as richly bronzed and gold as Ceridwen herself. "Remember, Hecate was looking three ways. It's a triptych, after all."

"How much chance did you think you had of surviving, Cass?" Dee asked.

"If I'd had time to think about it, one in ten thousand or so." I felt awed to remember the cold touch of the pistol against my breast.

"But you did survive. Miraculously, you will admit," Heather said, minutely adjusting the replica with a smile of satisfaction. Well, who knew? I blew Hecate a kiss.

Focusing on the four directions, Deidre, our mistress of arts and crafts, arranged a small shrine for each with thoughtful precision in matching corners of the room. Incense and Glacier narcissus in the East, a cauldron fire and Red Emperor tulips at the South, a bowl of water and a burst of Dutch blue crocus for the West, a pot of earth with sprays of pussy willow at the North. The last to arrive, Fiona came in flustered and bedraggled just as Dee finished her arrangements and was assessing them with shrewd blue eyes. We were ready.

Heather cast the circle with her athame, defining a new space and a new time "between the worlds," where alternate realities reveal themselves and the past and future open their doors. Dee followed, sprinkling each of us with sea water, for this was to be a purification ceremony to wash away the negative vibrations associated with Q, as well as a celebration of renewal. As the power of nature was invoked, I felt that other, deeper consciousness resonate within me. Nothing was fixed—everything was fluid. The universe was a dance of energies, constantly changing yet always one. With my sisters, I was lifted into the light, the stream of endless life.

We continued with the less traditional, more personal ritual that we had evolved for ourselves during this year of experimentation, which might have seemed like an exchange of gifts but was more a sharing of spirit. Deidre had made braided crowns of flowers and leaves. Phillipa turned over a Tarot card for each of us, with a mini-reading for the circle. "Five souls on the brink of surprise," she said, touching the center card, The Fool.

"Then we'll need to anoint ourselves, for protection and refreshment," I said, distributing tiny cobalt bottles of body oils—rose and jasmine.

Heather's largesse was low earthware bowls of St. Brigid anemone, budded and about to blossom. Deidre touched the folded pink bud wonderingly. "So spring is really coming, then. I hope I can resist getting pregnant."

I felt a pang of envy. All the world was about to flower while I was coming to the end of blooming reproduction—but certainly not ready yet to adopt the mantle of wise old crone. It was ironic to still feel so sexual without being fertile.

I came out of this depressing reverie to note that everyone was looking at Fiona expectantly. "Oh, very well," she said, "since I came here empty-handed . . . Oy, what a day I've had with that niece of mine attacking the woodwork with bleachy stuff, even behind furniture where it doesn't show, and needing help to move heavy bookcases . . . well! So for my spring thing, I will teach you all, as I have promised, how to assume a glamour."

"Finally," Phil said. "Although I might prefer that secret recipe for cream scones."

"Oh, great," said Dee, shaking her blond curls like a delighted child while Heather and I simply applauded.

Fiona rose awkwardly from the cushion she used for floor-sitting and walked through the double doors that led to the main house, a short, plump, frowsy woman in a raveled coat sweater, her crown of flowers askew on her wispy chignon. She stood there a moment, her back to us; then she turned around, smiled, and made her entrance into the room. At first I thought she was walking on tiptoe, but no, she simply appeared taller, poised and elegant, drawing all of us into her marvelous smile, her deep gray eyes. The circlet of leaves and flowers on her hair shimmered as if they were made of gold. The sweater swung around her hips like a short cape as she walked forward and said in a deep, husky voice, "Would someone get me a chair, please?"

Phillipa scrambled to her feet and hurriedly brought a cane

chair with an ornate, circular back. When Fiona arranged herself in the beautiful chair, I had the momentary illusion that we were being visited by Esther, the spirit of spring.

"Yes," said Fiona, "I am a goddess, and so are all of you, somewhere within your being, and you can summon that eternal woman at your will. If you trust in me, I will teach you of my timeless brilliance." And she proceeded to do that, instructing us in how to breathe for shape-shifting, to visualize ourselves as magical beings, to assume a commanding aura, to become whoever we wished in the eyes of the beholder. *"Believing is seeing. They will see it when you believe it,"* said Fiona. "And remember this . . . I am bloody tired of sitting on the floor. From now on, I expect to be offered a chair."

The laughter to follow dispelled some of the illusion, and we were soon back to ourselves. But we had learned a little more about this magical talent and would continue to adapt it to our needs.

No rite of spring could be complete without a dance, and dance we did—the fine Italian tiles cool under our bare feet, the candle flames flickering, and the ferns swaying with our dizzying motion around the circle, the walls resounding with our boisterous chant . . .

> *Like a wave of the sea or a leaf on the tree,*
> *Like all bright things that live and be,*
> *We come from the goddess, the great and the small,*
> *And dance through her seasons, the mother of all.*

For a sneak preview of
Dolores Stewart Riccio's next novel,
CHARMED CIRCLE
coming from Kensington in November 2003,
just turn the page . . .

Esbat of the Seed Moon

An enchanting afternoon in April, windows wide open to the scent of lilac and ocean breeze freshening the house—my spirit should have been lifting and soaring like a gull over the waves, but here was Deidre sipping tea and dispensing gloomy suspicions at my kitchen table.

"An entire family doesn't simply disappear into the blue!" I declared while I gently packed my blended herbal chakra oils. My friend Deidre Ryan would sell them at the shop she managed, Nature's Bounty, at the Massasoit Mall. "Perhaps the Donahues went on vacation. They could be at Disney World this very moment."

"Do you think the Donahues took Candy out of second grade in the middle of the term without informing Miss Hassel? Besides, Candy would have said something to my Jenny—they're best friends. They share every intimate detail of our family lives with one another, and you can just imagine how annoying *that* is. Last month on Parents' Night, while we were both waiting to see Miss Hassel, Denise Donahue asked me if I'd left the Church, just because Jenny told Candy a few little tidbits about our circle. I had a word with Jenny, told her how such gossip might affect her friendship with Candy. But I doubt I got through. You know how girls are." Deidre shook her short, blond curls in parental ex-asperation.

"There's no hiding what we do since Q's trial last year, Deidre. That dumb headline—*Local Witches Hex Sex Killer.* Maybe a rela-tive of the Donahues died suddenly, and the family was too dis-traught to tell anyone they were going to the funeral." Tenderly, I tucked shredded paper around the richly colored bottles, each tint representing a different chakra.

"Their Irish setter Patsy has been found wandering around the neighborhood, hungry and abandoned." The kettle began to whistle. Deidre put another tea bag into the pot and poured in more boiling water. The pleasant odor of ginger wafted out of the spout.

"A pox on them, then. It ought to be a felony to neglect a pet. Where's Patsy now?"

"Watch those casual curses, dear. Where do you think Patsy is? Heather took the poor, matted thing to Animal Lovers until we find out what's what." A sister member of our Wiccan circle, Heather Morgan, was practically supporting the animal rescue shelter with her lavish trust income. "She's ready to murder the Donahues. Unless, of course, they're already murdered."

"Who would do such a thing? And why?" I taped up the box of oils, ready to stash in Deidre's Plymouth Voyager. My home-based business—Cassandra Shipton's Earthlore Herbal Preparations and Cruelty-Free Cosmetics—was flourishing, thanks to Dei-dre's marketing skills and the success of my *Herbal Delights and Potions* catalog. A nice, steady little income to keep me and my dog companion Scruffy comfortable in the pleasant seaside home I'd inherited from my grandmother.

"Actually, I was relying on you to do one of your vision things to explain all that," Deidre said, her childlike, round blue eyes looking at once hopeful and apprehensive. Since her own area of expertise was in making poppets and amulets, Deidre was in awe of my clairvoyance.

"I don't *do* visions. They happen all on their own. And I have no control over when or about what." Sipping my fragrant tea thoughtfully, I wondered what it would be like to get a handle on those weird experiences, turn them on and off at will. Too much responsibility, I decided. Deidre and others would only plague me the more. What no one understood was the shock and pain of clairvoyance—except other clairvoyants, perhaps. It was like Alice falling down the rabbit hole, trapped in the weirdness of Wonderland. Visions never seemed to be about anything agreeable—winning the lottery or finding the man of one's dreams. More likely, they would be grim snapshots of where the bodies were buried, or worse, how they got there.

Deidre must have pushed the right buttons in my psyche, however, because later that afternoon, just as I was leaning over to settle the box of oils in the back of her Voyager, I got the first insight.

"Oh, sweet mercy!" The shutter of my inner eye blinked opened for a fraction of a moment, then shut tight. What I saw was a pink sneaker sticking out of the earth. A nauseating vision I wished I hadn't had. This was all Deidre's fault.

"What? What? Tell me what," Deidre kept saying insistently.

"I think you're right—the Donahues are in deep trouble," was all I could bring myself to say.

It was almost time for Beltane, May 1, a joyous High Sabbat of creativity and fertility. So naturally I was feeling somewhat depressed that my lover, Joe Ulysses, was in jail again, this time in British Columbia. I'd fantasized about making love outdoors at night. If the weather is warm, and you're not buzzed by little flying insects, and no one catches you at it, a woodland tryst is truly magical, an ideal way to celebrate the return of spring.

A ship's engineer, Joe worked for Greenpeace, an organization that frequently ran afoul of the law during one of its quixotic crusades. This time Greenpeace activists had attempted to block an access road on King Island in British Columbia. The Canadian government had awarded a logging contract to Interfor, allowing the company to clear-cut an ancient temperate rain forest also claimed by the Nuxalk natives of Canada. After confronting the Royal Canadian Mounted Police, the young activists had been rounded up, jailed, and were now awaiting trial. Joe, who should have stayed aboard ship, apparently couldn't resist jumping into danger himself. I suppose I admired that quality. In fact, I found Joe himself a gamble that couldn't be resisted. *Ah, well . . .*

And now, that unsettling anxiety of Deidre's about the disappearing Donahues definitely was not contributing to what should have been a bouyant springtime mood.

After Deidre departed in the late afternoon to make one of her microwave specials for the Ryan clan, three small children and her fireman husband Will, I continued to have misgivings. "Oh, I don't want to get involved in this," I told my dog Scruffy. For those who live alone, there's a great deal of comfort in talking to a dog, a cat, or even an iguana, if only to hear one's own voice saying what one truly feels. Most times, a pet listens in sympathetic silence, but Scruffy had a personable knack for making his own opinions known—at least, it seemed to me that I heard him clearly.

Hey, Toots, let's go out for a walk and forget all these hassles! Cavorting near the kitchen door, Scruffy nosed his leash invitingly. He's a bit too big and clumsy to be cute, a cross between a French Briard and the randy, sandy-colored mutt who fancied her. Some so-called friends have commented that my hair is the same color as Scruffy's, and about as neat.

"Oh, all right. Maybe the Atlantic will clear my brain of that pink sneaker. Ugh." I put on my old green lumber jacket that hung on the same hook as Scruffy's leash, and we set off down the rickety, rotting stairs that led from our neat little saltbox home to the rocky beach below, where Plymouth Harbor seemed not to have got the news that spring was here, that females like me were dreaming of lovemaking in the moonlight. An east wind roiled the waves to white froth. It would be mid-July before this water warmed up enough for the hardy to swim.

The dog and I took a good, long tramp along the beach. The sun lowering behind our house gilded the sails of a few brave boats. A school of bluefish began to agitate the water, and a host of screaming gulls gathered in a feeding frenzy. I let Scruffy off-leash to play Fetch the Stick as we walked. As the solitude bore down on me, the pink sneaker refused to fade in my mind's eye.

It's dinnertime, dinnertime! Scruffy looked at me meaningfully and turned back toward the stairs. Dogs always know to the minute the time at which they should be fed, and they push it ahead by a quarter of an hour any chance they get.

I love messing about with herbs, oils, and creams; it's a kind of enriching, aromatic, creative playtime I suppose that's how Phillipa, my friend who writes cookbooks, feels about cooking. Tactile joys. For her, it's the squish of hand-mixing meatballs, the scent of baking bread filling the kitchen, the satisfaction of whacking a winter squash with a sturdy cleaver. That Saturday afternoon before our April Esbat, I'd decided to concoct a Wise Woman Herbal Tea Blend, a mixture of sage, nettle, lemon balm, chaste tree berries, and dried orange zest. Perhaps I would add a little motherwort or elder flowers. My hand was drifting between the two jars, waiting for inspiration to illuminate the recipe, when there was a knock at the front door.

Scruffy leaped up from his midmorning nap under the kitchen table and began to bark in the frantic manner he assumes when he's been caught sleeping on the job. *Stranger! Danger! Let me out, out, out, and I'll chase it away.*

"Quiet, you mutt. It's probably a neighbor," I said. "Go around to the back door," I shouted. For generations, the cranberry-painted, broad-planked front door of this old house had been opened only to take out bodies feet first, and it was strangely reluctant to be employed for any less solemn purpose. If one tried to open it on some lesser occasion, the door creaked, groaned, stuck, and warped to express its displeasure. I tended to leave well enough alone. Closing the two jars of herbs, I dusted off my hands and went to unlatch the kitchen door, which is on the sea-side, along with an architecturally incorrect porch.

"Hi. Are you Mrs. Shipton?" The teenaged girl standing in the doorway could have been something left over from Halloween, with short spiked black hair, dark brown lipstick, starkly pale skin, and so many layers of sooty eye liner, they were turning the whites of her eyes red. Amber-colored eyes, a rare shade, I noticed. She wore a half dozen thin gold rings on one ear; a penta-gram hung from the other.

"Yes, I'm Cassandra Shipton." Scruffy had stopped barking and was sniffing the girl's imitation alligator boots with great in-terest. Her thighs were a chilly blue in that leather miniskirt, and there didn't seem to be too much warmth in the ratty, spotty fur jacket either. Maybe it was April, but the blast off the Atlantic was back in the middle of March. "Would you like to step inside? That wind is fierce today."

"Sure. Thanks." She shook Scruffy off her boots and patted his head absently.

She smells good, like hamburgers and fries. The dog's nose twitched appreciatively.

"I'm Freddie. Winifred McGarity." Freddie's amber gaze was busily scanning my kitchen as if looking for clues to a mystery. I was suddenly conscious that the countertops were cluttered with the tea blend in progress. "I'm here about the witch business."

"Witch business?" I wondered what the word was around Plymouth these days concerning our circle. It was hardly a secret anymore, as I'd pointed out to Deidre. Although we weren't being denounced from pulpits, this wasn't Salem where witches were needed to draw the tourist trade to the Gallows Tree and other local attractions. We were tolerated but not welcomed, like a flock of grackles who'd descended on bird feeders meant for finches and chickadees.

"Please don't screw with me, Mrs. Shipton. I'm a sincere per-son, you know what I mean?"

"I'm sure you are, Freddie, but as it happens, I'm in the herb business, not the witch business."

"Everyone says there's a coven right here in Plymouth, and you and your friends are it. So I'd like to apply for membership, you know what I'm saying? Do you have an application I could fill out or something like that?"

"Why don't you sit down, Freddie, and I'll make us a nice cup of tea."

"Hey, what's in that stuff?" Freddie asked suspiciously as I spooned in teaspoons of the new mix into my sturdy brown teapot, then added boiling water from the kettle on the stove.

"It's a new blend I'm creating. It's supposed to make you healthy, wealthy, and wise. Or at least wise." I filled a plate with ginger cookies. The girl looked borderline anorexic. Scruffy's nose followed my every move with rapt attention.

"Yeah. Well, you first."

"It has to steep a minute or two. Soooo . . . tell me, Freddie . . . *why* do you want to be a witch?"

"I already am. But I think I need, like, some training in the fine points. Sometimes things go wrong, you know what I mean?"

"What makes you think you're a witch? In fact, do you know what a witch is?" She was silent for a few moments, glancing through the kitchen door to the rooms beyond—looking for what? Satanic effects? I poured the tea, noting that it had a pleasing fragrance. Adding a spoonful of honey, I passed the syrup pourer to my guest, who was now feeding a ginger cookie to Scruffy under the table. He lay down on the fake alligator boots in total devotion.

"I can bend spoons."

I laughed with relief. This was just a romantic teenager who needed a stiff dose of reality. But my gaze couldn't help going to the two stainless steel spoons I'd laid haphazardly on the table. And Freddie saw me looking. She sighed and studied the spoon nearest her cup. Then she raised her hands over the table, not touching anything on it, and I noticed that each of her fingernails was painted a different dark shade, from deep plum to black.

After a few moments, her spoon appeared to shudder or shimmy. Then, as if the table had tilted fractionally, ever so slowly the spoon slid toward her. When it had reached a stopping place at her saucer, she picked up the spoon and rubbed it gently as if to warm the metal. I was transfixed and silenced by what was going on in front of me, and so lost track of how long in actual time Freddie spent stroking the spoon. But our tea had not yet cooled before the spoon folded over like a piece of foil. Not the thin neck of it, which is easy to do. The thick bowl of the spoon was bent double.

"There, like I told you, I'm a witch," she said and handed me the crumpled spoon. It was hot, as if it had been standing in boiling water.